The Black Madonna

PETER MILLAR is a British journalist, critic and author, named Foreign Correspondent of the Year 1989 for his reporting of the later days of the Cold War and the fall of the Berlin Wall for *The Sunday Times*. He is the author of *All Gone to Look for America*, *1989 The Berlin Wall: My Part in Its Downfall*, and the translator of several German-language books into English including the best-selling *White Masai* by Corinne Hofmann, and *Deal With the Devil* by Martin Suter.

The Black Madonna

PETER MILLAR

ARCADIA BOOKS

Arcadia Books Ltd
15–16 Nassau Street
London W1W 7AB

www.arcadiabooks.com

First published in the United Kingdom by Arcadia Books 2010

A catalogue record for this book is available from the British Library.

ISBN 978-1-906413-68-2

Typeset in Minion by MacGuru Ltd
Printed and bound in the UK by CPI Mackays, Chatham ME5 8TD

Arcadia Books gratefully acknowledges the financial support of Arts Council England.

Arcadia Books supports PEN, the fellowship of writers who work together to promote literature and its understanding. English PEN upholds writers' freedoms in Britain and around the world, challenging political and cultural limits on free expression. To find out more, visit www.englishpen.org or contact English PEN, 6–8 Amwell Street, London EC1R 1UQ

Arcadia Books distributors are as follows:

in the UK and elsewhere in Europe:
Turnaround Publishers Services
Unit 3, Olympia Trading Estate
Coburg Road
London N22 6TZ

in the US and Canada:
Dufour Editions
PO Box 7
Chester Springs
PA, 19425

in Australia:
The Scribo Group Pty Ltd
18 Rodborough Road
Frenchs Forest 2086
Australia

in New Zealand:
Addenda
PO Box 78224
Grey Lynn
Auckland

in South Africa:
Jacana Media (Pty) Ltd
PO Box 291784,
Melville 2109
Johannesburg

Arcadia Books is the *Sunday Times* Small Publisher of the Year

Foreword

This is a novel, a work of fiction involving adventure and intrigue. However, all the historical events, people and places referred to are accurate and verifiable. The juxtapositions are my own, and the conclusions are those of my characters. I invite readers to draw their own.

Peter Millar,
Munich and London 2010

'Ich habe das Glück, ganz in der Nähe von Altötting geboren zu sein... Der stärkste Eindruck war natürlich die Gnadenkapelle, Ihr geheimnisvolles Dunkel, die kostbar gekleidete schwarze Madonna, umgeben von Weihegeschenken.'

Papst Benedikt XVI

'I was lucky to have been born near Altötting...
The greatest influence on me was the Chapel of Grace
with its darkness full of secrets and the black Madonna
robed in her costly finery, surrounded by offerings.'

Pope Benedict XVI

*Ganz voll Vertrauen kommen wir in der Gefahren Mitte,
zu Dir, Maria, rufen wir zu Dir, Maria, bewahre unsre Schritte
O Mutter Gottes, wir sind dein, laß uns nicht unterliegen,
wenn wir am letzten Ende sin, verlassen sind und ganz allein,
O Mutter Gottes, wir sind dein*

Altöttinger Wahlfahrtslied

In the midst of danger we come to you, Mary, full of trust
we call out to you, Mary, guide our steps.
Oh Mother of God abandon us not, for we belong to you,
Alone at the end when all others have left us,
We belong to you.

Altötting Pilgrims' Hymn

*Ave Maria, gratia plena, Mater Dei, ora pro nobis,
Ora pro nobis peccatoribus nunc et in hora mortis*

Hail Mary, full of Grace, Mother of God, pray for us,
Pray for us sinners now and at the hour of our death

Prologue

Mesopotamia AD363

The ancient Greeks called it the 'land between two rivers', now it was hell on earth. In the baking heat of the summer sun, the soldiers in the first rank peered with scorched, reddened eyes into the hazy distance searching for their unseen assailants. None of them knew when the next attack would come, nor how many it would kill.

They had been told the natives would be grateful for their deliverance. The soldiers of the superpower had come to free them from despotism, to bring the Western values of law, order and civilisation to a land run by a cruel tyrant. They had advanced quickly, almost easily, pushing the enemy back across the desert to the capital, the great sprawling city on the banks of the Tigris, so unlike anything back home.

But the dream of subduing a region that plagued their leader's vision of a new world order now looked like his greatest mistake, a military blunder that could end his dream of a glorious place in history. These were not men used to retreating but now they were getting out, and getting out in a hurry; tens of thousands of them trailed in a line that was not as military in formation as their officers might have liked, across barren, hostile country.

It was a sentry on the right flank at the rear of the column who noticed the telltale signs first: shifting shapes among the rocks, indication that the cowardly enemy hiding unseen in the desert was closing in, preparing to strike. Most frequently the attack, when it came, hit the rearguard, like a viper sinking its fangs into a sandaled heel.

Then the wind rose, and they came out of it in a cloud of dust and deafening noise. Where there had been silence and shimmering heat haze there was suddenly a whirlwind of death and devastation, as from nowhere the ungrateful enemy opened fire on the unloved invader. Men in the marching ranks were cut down before they even knew they were under attack.

The officers tried to rally their troops but as the casualties mounted a sense of panic spread. Then in an act of supreme courage the general himself, knowing the effect his presence would have on his forces, appeared among them – bravely bare-headed so as to be immediately recognisable – urging them not to yield to mindless panic. They were, he yelled, knowing deep down they believed it themselves, the best trained army on earth, the crack troops of a global superpower, and were not about to be frightened by a bunch of cowardly curs who were little more than hit-and-run terrorists and lacked the nerve to fight them head-on.

The effect was immediate. The officers marshalled their men and what had been a rout became an advance. An enemy that preferred sniping from a distance now turned rather than engage these professional battle-hardened troops at close quarters. In the ranks a few men exchanged grim smiles: they would teach this desert scum another lesson, one that this time they would not forget so quickly. If their commander could face up to the enemy unprotected then they could go after that enemy and hunt them down like the desert dogs they were.

'Advance!' came the order. There would be no stopping them now.

As at last the merciless sun began to set over the barren horizon the sands were littered with bloody corpses. Only with the fall of night, however, did the last of the enemy disperse disappearing back into their own unremittingly hostile landscape. It had been a victory, of sorts, for the good guys, or so the weary soldiers told themselves as the lucky ones settled down for the night while the less fortunate drew lots for sentry duty.

Only then did most of them hear the bad news, the news the veterans had been dreading but which even to them seemed unbelievable now that it had happened. The general had been hit, badly. Fearless to the last he had refused to withdraw to relative safety and been wounded in the chest. Mortally, it was feared. Within the hour the dire news was announced. The missile that had pierced his ribcage had done irreparable harm. The general was dead.

Throughout the makeshift camp the news spread like wildfire. A catastrophe had befallen them. An army in a hostile land had lost its commanding general. But the consequences would be far greater, they knew, than their own immediate plight.

The general was more than just any general – the men who had followed him halfway around the world, from the banks of the Rhine to the shores of the Tigris, had long ago acclaimed him as more than that – he was *imperator*, the emperor. The entire Western world had lost its leader.

Late into the night, as the sentries stared into the alien darkness, groups of men sat around fire and muttered darkly to themselves as they heard the news. And one, sitting sombrely amidst a group that had lost their weapons in the battle, fell quietly to his knees and made the sign of the cross.

As all Christians knew, the death of one man could change the history of the world for ever after.

Part One

AVE MARIA, GRATIA PLENA …
Hail Mary, full of Grace …

1

Gaza City, present day

The dust hung in the air like a dirty gauze veil across the face of the city, drawn not out of modesty but to hide its ugliness. No matter how much Nazreem Hashrawi loved her work, and of late she had come to love it very much indeed, the business of getting there was never a joy.

She picked her way through the honking horns and concrete rubble of a city that was both Mediterranean and Middle Eastern, part ancient metropolis and part jerry-built refugee camp, negotiated the street vendors with their piles of oranges, lemons, tomatoes and cheap cotton T-shirts, made in China. A residual tang of sea salt, rotting citrus and powdered concrete lingered in the hot heavy air. The streets were always like this nowadays. There was scarcely a building that did not seem to be in the process of construction or demolition. Bombsites and building sites resembled each other.

On the corner of Omar El-Mokhtar Street a clattering khaki truck laden with scaffolding, breeze blocks and leather-faced labourers with Arafat-style keffiyehs and stony eyes nearly sent her sprawling into the gutter, and prompted a shrill blast on the whistle and a sharp rebuke from a hassled-looking traffic policeman. The driver and the workers ignored him, clattering on their way. The people laughed at their own police, the bitter laughter of those who could not take their puppet state seriously, yet knew it was all they had. And perhaps all they were likely to get.

For over 2,000 years Gaza had been one of the most important cities on the Mediterranean, while from the landwards side it was the key to Egypt, a city prized by the Pharaohs before it was captured by the Philistines, ancestors of her own people. The Hebrews' legends said their hero Samson had broken down its gates, but ended up blind in its jails when his hair was cut and his magical strength failed.

Alexander had laid siege for three months to wrest it from the Persian empire. In Greek and Roman times it was famed as the end of the incense road, from where ships set sail for Athens and Rome. Napoleon had called it the Forward Garrison of Africa and the Gate to Asia.

Yet for all that history, there was precious little to see. The twentieth century had not been kind to Gaza. Her own little museum was a token: a monument to the past in a millennia-old city that was not only unexcavated but where each day new rubble was piled upon old. It had remarkably little to boast, and much of that was borrowed. Or had been until now.

The events of the past week had changed everything. Which was why Nazreem was heading in to work now, on a Friday evening of all times, when the museum was closed. That meant it would be quiet, as quiet as anywhere ever was in overcrowded Gaza, and she would be undisturbed. She had a dossier to prepare, a dossier that could change her entire career and she intended to work through the night if need be.

As she took her keys from her purse and opened the side door into the museum she could hear the last call to evening prayer echoing from the minaret of the Al-Omari mosque, which had once been a crusader church, itself built on the site of an ancient pagan temple. What goes around, comes around, she smiled to herself as she climbed the stairs to the little room that served as a staff kitchen. She was going to need a pot of strong coffee.

Outside, the small dusty square was settling into its familiar sundown routine – the men gathering to smoke and argue over sweet mint tea at the dilapidated corner café, the women retiring indoors to get on with the cooking, the daytime stench of diesel exhaust gradually yielding to odours of grilling lamb and strong tobacco. Then the universe imploded.

She heard the scream first. The unmistakable high-pitched keening of a kerosene-fuelled missile. Then she felt the shock, the earth tremor of impact, a millisecond before the thunderous detonation, the roar of collapsing masonry. And then the human screaming started. A thick plume of dirty, grey-black smoke rose from a side street barely a hundred metres away. In the distance sirens howled against the familiar futile staccato of men firing automatic weapons into the empty sky. And in the midst of it, the building around her erupted, as if in sympathy, into a wail of its own.

Nazreem leapt to her feet in horror. For a second she had stared in shock at the unfolding drama, terrible but almost too familiar to be frightening. Now she was genuinely scared. But not for herself. She pulled open the office door and sprinted the few metres of corridor that led to the stairs. She knew what had happened: the alarms had gone off. The museum was being broken into.

Or rather she fervently hoped it wasn't: that the shock wave generated by the nearby explosion and collapse of a building had set off the sensors. It was a coincidence, that was all. A coincidence rather than a genuine attempt to break into her museum on the first night in its still brief history that it held a find of significant importance. A find of such potential that they had tried to keep it secret, at least until it could be verified. But rumours spread. And you never knew.

You never knew what was round the next corner, she told herself as she ran into the main gallery. A pulsing red glow from the activated motion detectors played surreally on decapitated heads and fragments of torsos, salvaged stones from Greek and Roman statuary. Her city was as old as civilisation, but had next to nothing to show for it. Until now.

Then she stiffened. A shadow, or a movement in the shadows. In the flickering crimson light it was impossible to tell. The howl from the alarms was deafening, but so was the clamour outside. The police should have been here by now. The police had other things to do; there would be Hamas fighters in the street baying for Israeli blood. The shadow moved again. This time she was sure of it.

Beyond the sarcophagus. The museum's sole relic of Egyptian mummification – on loan from Cairo – was a marble slab with a few faded hieroglyphs that proclaimed it the last resting place of an official who may or may not once have been the province's governor. She was almost certain she had seen something move beyond it; between her and the object she wanted more than anything else to protect. She looked about her for a weapon, rejected a priceless ancient Pharaonic flail and settled on a small handheld fire extinguisher. Her sole hope was that whoever had forced entry had no idea there was anyone else in the building. She advanced cautiously, her footsteps masked by the sirens. The gallery beyond was the special exhibition space.

The sarcophagus was just a few feet away. To her left, standing upright against the wall, was the cedar mummy case it had once contained. She shot it a passing glance and saw the shadow emerge from it. Her own scream was lost in the collective cacophony. A man's hand clamped over her mouth and nose.

The fire extinguisher clattered from her hand, discharging its spume of chemical foam uselessly across the floor. She tried to bite fingers that were smooth but brutal, smelled of stale cigarette smoke and threatened to squeeze the life out of her, while the other hand twisted her long dark hair up into a thick knot. She cursed herself for not wearing her headscarf.

Stumbling forward, gasping for air, she could feel her captor's breath, hot, warm and sickly sweet on the back of her naked neck. Her arms flailed helplessly against the powerful body pressed against her, earning only a painful blow from a knee to the base of her spine. She felt herself fall forward and sent sprawling onto the chemical-covered floor. She tried to scramble to her feet, her knees even, but her sandals floundered in the slippery white goo spreading across the parquet.

Instinctively she turned her head to try to see her assailant, pushing herself up into a crawl. She saw no more than a glimpse of a tall dark shape before a ferocious kick to the backside sent her sprawling again in agony. Frantic now, she willed her fingers to drag her away. And then he fell on her. A great crushing weight, pinning her to the floor. There was a rip, a sound of cloth tearing, cloth from her own long cotton skirt. The hand that had wound itself back into her hair jerked her head roughly from the floor and a folded strip of cloth covered her eyes, pulled so tightly it hurt her eyeballs, and she felt the knot being tied in with her hair behind her head.

Then, all of a sudden, he was off her. For a moment she almost lost control of herself completely. Was that it? Or was she milliseconds away from the bullet in the back of the head. She was not afraid of death; she had faced death before. But not now, not like this. She shuffled forwards on her knees. A metre, maybe two, maybe more. She would be in the exhibition room by now. Beyond that, no more than half a dozen metres away, was the door to her own office. If she reached that, then maybe … no, it was impossible.

A blow to the small of the back knocked her flat and he was on her again. Not lying this, time, but squatting on her legs. Another rip, and her arms were jerked behind her back, the wrists bound, painfully tight. Another rip and this time she felt her bare thighs exposed, and then she felt what they were exposed to, and realised why he had released her for a second; to open his flies.

Her teeth gritted, her eyes weeping painful tears into the fabric of her own torn clothing. Still uncertain if it would end with a bullet in the head. She felt the same smooth brutal fingers rip away her underwear and force themselves into her. He was on top of her now, the free hand feeling for her breasts, the hot, sweaty weight of his belly on her buttocks and the hard penis pushing, thrusting, penetrating. Penetrating. And then she realised what was happening. Rape was not bad enough. The bastard was sodomising her. Nazreem Hashrawi did the one thing left to her: she screamed with all her might into the unlistening noise-filled night.

And as she did, the blindfold on her eyes slackened almost imperceptibly, just enough for her to glimpse, on the pedestal in the centre of the exhibition room, an ancient serene expression of endless compassion. Christians called her *Mater Misericordiae*, Mother of Mercy, the Immaculate Virgin. Nazreem's scream became a howl of bitter rage.

2

Oxford, England

It was a late spring morning and pale sunbeams filtered through the golden stone Gothic window frames of the Senior Common Room along with the subtle scent of new mown grass from a quintessential English lawn. One of the older Fellows rose from his armchair muttering something about a draught and closed the window.

Marcus Frey shook his head in wry resignation: that was All Souls for you. The place was an anomaly, an eccentric anachronism. Officially named the College of All Souls of the Faithful Departed, in commemoration of those who died in the Hundred Years War with France, it was a 500-year-old college that remained substantially true to its origins. Above all, it had never been tempted into the modern folly of lecturing to the young.

All Souls had no students, only a body of worthy academics – some of who bore the title 'Professor' while others did not – elected to be Fellows, and whom the ancient founders' munificence continued to allow to pursue their undistracted studies. Or not, as the case might be, he reflected, watching Dunkin, the elderly Fellow who had closed the window, sink back into his preprandial slumber.

Now approaching his thirty-sixth summer, Frey was one of the younger inmates of this unusual institution. He had arrived at Oxford from his native South Africa as a postgraduate Rhodes Scholar with a bit of a reputation. His doctoral thesis, inspired by growing up under apartheid and then through the dramatic transition to today's much-hyped 'Rainbow Nation' had been a study of how history had been rewritten over those decades, martyrs and terrorists redefined. He had experienced, and described, how the past – because records and memories of it existed only in the present – was actually perpetually in flux. The flux was called history, a shifting science of the subjective. It was controversial but hardly new. Marcus's favourite quote came from the nineteenth-century satirist Samuel Butler who had written, 'The only reason God tolerates historians is because they can do the one thing He cannot: alter the past.' The study of those alterations was called Comparative Historiography, and it was people like Marcus who were making it fashionable.

The thesis had been a success, not just academically, but repackaged for a more populist audience in book form as *Nelson Mandela, Saint or Sinner* and it had gone on to be a bestseller. He had won his fellowship on the strength of it. As a follow-up he had chosen another of the world's most intractable subjects and the new book, *Promised Land or Stolen Land: Palestine versus Israel*, had done almost as well.

That was why he so unexpectedly disturbed the somnolent peace of the All Souls Common Room when he picked up his copy of *The Times*, turned to the foreign pages and almost immediately spilt his tea. The loud clink of bone china cup against saucer and muted cry of pain as the hot liquid splashed onto his trouser leg earned sharply disapproving glances from the grey heads that surfaced momentarily from the leather armchairs. But he paid them no attention. He could not take his eyes from the page in front of him.

The headline on the news story running along the bottom of the page, in a space normally reserved for more light-hearted or offbeat items read, rather archly: 'Maybe Mary Goes Missing.' It was not the report, however, but the photograph next to it that had seized Marcus's attention: standing amidst rubble on the sun-drenched steps of some Mediterranean building, wearing a yellow headscarf which almost but not quite covered her raven-dark hair, was a striking young woman whom Marcus Frey knew for a fact was not called Mary.

The caption beneath read: 'Nazreem Hashrawi, curator of the Museum of Palestine in Gaza tells reporters of the theft of a recently discovered, possibly priceless and historically important early Christian artefact.'

But Marcus could not concentrate on the words. His gaze continually drifted back to the photograph of Nazreem. It had been more than five years since he had last seen her and her familiar big dark eyes seemed unusually hard and focused. He was strangely unsurprised to find she had gone back to her childhood home, to Gaza City, even though it was one of the most dangerous places on earth. She had no real alternative. Except of course for the one he might have given her. Nor was he particularly surprised that she had risen to become curator of her own museum, a remarkable achievement for a woman in the male-dominated Muslim world. Nazreem Hashrawi was a formidable young woman.

She had impressed him the first time he saw her, sitting at a café on the edge of Cairo's bustling Khan el-Khalili market. Marcus had been immersed in on-the-ground research for his book about the Israeli-Palestianian conflict, and had been introduced to her by a professor at the Faculty of Economics and Political Science at Cairo University whom he had asked for assistance. He needed to learn more about what Arabs thought today about the history of the conflict, particularly the 1967 Six-Day War which had been so disastrous for their attempt to eliminate Isreal. But what he also wanted was someone who could act both as a guide and interpreter, preferably with some knowledge of the Palestinian territories. He could not ask for anybody better, the professor had assured him, than Nazreem Pascale Hashrawi. To be sure, she was not studying politics – Marcus reflected that that was not necessarily a bad thing in the circumstances – but a graduate student in the Department of Archaeology. She was bright, multilingual – half-French, though her mother had died in childbirth – with a good command of English, and had been brought up in Gaza City itself. Marcus could not have asked for more.

The work had thrown them together, literally in the end: during an overflight of Sinai their Soviet-made Egyptian Army helicopter had gone out of control and crash-landed. The pilot and co-pilot had died and Hamzi, a photographer along for the ride, had been trapped in the wreckage and had to have a leg amputated. Nazreem and Marcus had been thrown clear but even so he had metal fragments embedded in his leg and was forced to spend several weeks in Cairo's Ahmed Maher hospital. Nazreem had visited him daily and their relationship developed beyond work so that when he was released he had moved into her apartment, and a few days later, almost to his own surprise, into her bed.

The fact that they had become lovers did not impinge on their working relationship; she continued to be his guide when his research took him to Gaza, Jerusalem and the West Bank, proving not only remarkably knowledgeable but also singularly open-minded about the evolution of a conflict in which the two sides often

14

seemed implacably opposed. He had discussed offering her co-authorship but she had declined, refusing even a dedication, telling him the book would do better under his name alone – she was offering nothing more than context and background, the interpretation was all his – and in any case, she had a career of her own to make.

When he left, as eventually he had to, there were regrets on both sides, promises – sincere but unspecific – to keep in touch. But no tears. Yet to see her now, standing in a Middle Eastern street that even in a still photograph suggested noise, colour, vibrancy, danger, Marcus realised how far their worlds had drifted apart.

Frey lifted his eyes for a moment from the photograph and looked around him at the worn leather armchairs, the stone gargoyles visible through the great Gothic windows, and the human gargoyles dozing beneath their newspapers. Somehow this had become the setting for his career, his world, while she had made her own, just as she had promised she would, in her own, very different world. Marcus had never heard of the Museum of Palestine – it seemed more like an aspiration than an institution given the irredeemably fraught situation in that part of the world – but that only made him think all the more of her.

She had achieved success on her own terms, in her community. Except that now, it seemed, fate had struck her a terrible blow. Marcus knew the world of museum curators: losing an exhibit was a disaster. Losing a major exhibit, and a new find at that, was a catastrophe.

There was no photograph of the find. Marcus wondered if that was because there was none available or because some sub-editor had preferred a photograph of a pretty young woman. Nazreem was undoubtedly as striking as she had ever been even though it was not a particularly flattering picture: there was a hard set to her jaw and her eyes appeared to lack their usual spark. It could have been just the angle, but it gave the impression she had taken the theft badly, personally almost.

According to *The Times* reporter, the circumstances of the stolen artefact's discovery indicated it as being of 'no later than the first century AD': it had only recently been unearthed, hidden in the foundations of an ancient Christian church, itself only recently discovered after the demolition following an air raid of later buildings erected on the site. It seemed to Marcus as if the reporter was deliberately hedging around the subject of exactly what it was that had been stolen and why it might be so important. It was only towards the end when he reached the line that stated 'Dr Hashrawi refused to confirm or deny the persistent rumours that have caused such extreme controversy in local religious and archeological circles' that he let a long, low whistle escape from between his teeth. Ignoring the frowns that greeted it, Marcus drained the remains of his now cold tea and stood up: what the report clearly implied was that Nazreem had found – and lost – one of the most important, semi-legendary items in Christian lore: the only depiction of the Virgin Mary created in her own lifetime.

3

Rafah, southern end of the Gaza Strip

The room was dark, hot, stifling. Unless the door was opened, which it rarely was, no air entered, with the result that after a while it became hard to breathe. Not that that mattered much; no one who had spent much time there had ever left the room alive.

Then the light came on. A harsh white artificial light that flickered a second or two before exploding into sharp white merciless and all-revealing fluorescence. The man by the door, with his hand still on the pull cord that triggered the light, spat on the floor. What air there was in the room was thick, heavy with the smell of bleach and cheap antiseptic which did little to mask the stench of sweat, blood and urine.

The room was lined with concrete breeze blocks and empty save for a metal locker in one corner, an enamel sink with a bucket in it and a small metal table with a plate of surgical instruments. The only other furniture was a single chair, set not next to the table, but about a metre and a half out from the far wall, facing away from it. When occupied, it was normally straddled, backwards, to allow close-up examination of the poor soul suspended, spreadeagled and naked from the manacles fixed to the wall.

The figure had flinched when the light came on, but more out of instinct than awareness. Mercifully he was aware of almost nothing any more. He would in any case not have rejoiced at the company. The man who had entered the room crossed to the bucket, took a wet sponge from it and moistened the face and lips of the prisoner. He did not do so out of kindness, merely to keep the man alive. For the moment. The moisture on the sponge was vinegar. His captors had thought it wryly appropriate.

The figure hanging from the wall grunted and rolled his head away, the vinegar stinging his cracked, torn lips. He would dearly have loved to spit in the face of his tormentor, but even with the acid liquid rubbed across his mouth he had insufficient saliva. His bruised eyelids opened just wide enough for him to perceive the blurred image of a single figure in front of him. Just the routine tormentor. So it was not yet the end. Then, dimly, he made out the sound of a second voice. And changed his mind.

The man with the sponge moved away. Through his injured eyes and a mist of dull persistent pain the prisoner could only make out a blurred figure, dressed head to foot in black, but the voice alone told him the identity of the newcomer: Death himself.

His carer, jailer and torturer – for the man with the sponge performed all three functions as required – could see perfectly well and it did not stop him from being every bit as intimidated by the other presence in the room. He stood back respectfully as the tall, bearded man in his sombre attire came over to inspect the prisoner.

The tall man looked up and down the battered body hanging on the wall, at the array of purple bruises on his arms and legs, where bones had been broken, at the traces of blood that ran down his chest from the razor cuts on his nipples. The sight evoked no pity, only disgust.

The man holding the vinegar sponge said, 'You have more questions for this dog?' in a tone that he hoped implied total readiness to do whatever was asked of him. But the tall man shook his head:

'No. He has told us everything we wanted to know. And more. Far more.'

'Then it is time to put him out of his misery? I can finish him?'

The tall man turned and regarded his underling with a look that made the man tremble, fearing he had shown even a hint of compassion. That would not have gone down well. He reached for the pistol on the table to show willing.

The tall man raised a hand and hesitated a second, which to the other two living beings in the room seemed like an eternity, and then said simply, 'Yes.'

The figure hanging from the wall slumped visibly, but in reality it was more out of relief than despair. He knew his body had taken all it could endure.

He was wrong.

'But not like that,' the tall man said softly, his hand reaching back to the open box on the table. From it he took a blood-streaked surgical scalpel and handing it to his accomplice, pointed and said: 'There.'

4

Frey was almost running across the quadrangle, even though he knew it would provoke not only stern looks from his fellow dons but possibly even a rebuke from the Warden. Even so he mounted the stairs two at a time, shooting past the descending portly figure of Nicholas Butterworth, an individual whose only day-to-day relationship with rapid motion involved the operability of quantum mechanics at near-light speed.

Once inside his comfortable if spartanly furnished set of rooms, Frey switched on the small flat-panel television which despite their acquaintance with cutting-edge scientific theory most of his colleagues regarded with little short of wonder, and flicked through the Freeview channels to BBC *News 24*. It was only when he read the last few words of *The Times* story that it had occurred to him it might have made the television news at well, if only as a tail piece. But it was not so much the facts that interested Marcus, as the possibility of seeing more of Nazreem.

The featured item when he turned on was a long dreary report on yet another funding crisis in the National Health Service, but using the red interactive button on his remote, Marcus found there was indeed an item on the theft from the Gaza museum. His suspicion that it might have been given the 'light news' treatment was confirmed when he hit the button and heard the anchorman's opening words:

'And finally, controversy raging amongst clergymen and archaeologists today amid reports that what is believed to be the oldest known image of the Virgin Mary has been found in Gaza City, and then stolen all within the space of a few days.'

The report gave details of how the find was made when contractors clearing debris had come upon remains of an ancient, previously unrecorded Christian church and called in local archaeologists.

And then, all of a sudden, there she was, standing on the steps of a nondescript concrete building amid all the noise and chaos of

a typical Middle Eastern street. For a moment Marcus sat spell-
bound, staring at the face and listening to the voice of the woman
that had once meant more to him than anything else: that familiar soft but slightly husky accent that bore indecipherable traces
of both French and Arabic, as she told a gaggle of reporters that
although the missing artefact had yet to be authenticated its loss was
a devastating blow, not just to a new museum struggling to restore
a sense of identity to the people of Palestine, but to the whole world
of archaeology. Passionate, proud, just the same as ever. But no, not
the same. Different: the figure on the television screen was simultaneously harder and more vulnerable than the Nazreem he knew. As
if there was somehow unfathomable hurt and repressed fury lurking
beneath her tone. And then she was gone again.

Marcus was almost tempted to jiggle with the red button to go
back to the beginning of the piece, but he found himself instead listening to a Roman Catholic archbishop described as a 'senior antiq-
uities expert': 'The discovery of an image of Our Lady created in
her own lifetime would of course have been a huge blessing for the
faithful, presuming of course that it was proved to be authentic,' this
last phrase with a slightly sceptical upward curl of the lips.

'It has long been believed by many that the first image was created
by St Luke himself, painting on the Holy Virgin's own kitchen table.
However, we have unfortunately had no information yet as to the
precise nature of this archaeological discovery, which it would seem
has almost immediately been tragically lost. Needless to say we must
pray for the miracle of its recovery.'

Marcus wasn't sure but somehow the expression on the face of the
man in purple did not exactly suggest a belief in miracles.

5

Nazreem Hashrawi felt like shit. She felt sullied, violated, as if all of a sudden the foundations of her life had collapsed under her, and there was nothing or nobody she could rely on.

Amidst the chaos of the air raid, it had taken six hours from the time the alarms at the museum had started ringing before anyone else had even thought to investigate. By then Nazreem herself was no longer there. When she had come to, bloody and defiled, she had felt sick to her core. She knew what had happened and took what little comfort she could in the knowledge that it could have been worse, much worse. Apart from anything else, she was still alive. She had made her way home, grateful for once for the darkness, and had showered as well as she could with the meagre water supply in her tiny flat.

She knew that in cleansing herself she was removing evidence, but it was not evidence that would ever be used to support a prosecution. The Palestinian police had not the resources for DNA sampling. Even if they had what good would it have done? An arrest for rape was as likely as an agreement over Jerusalem. If the Palestinian Authority was ever to become a government in any real sense of the word, one day their police would have to be respected as such, not just by the Israelis who treated them as potential enemies, but by their own people.

What had happened to her personally was not something she would admit, even to herself, though she knew she would never forget. She would not submit to the innuendo that would be ever after in their eyes if she told them. As so often, a lie would serve better than the truth.

She had let the idiot policeman who rang her at home tell her of the break-in as though she were hearing it for the first time. She feigned to appear shocked, distressed when she rushed to the museum, and then made the announcement to the press, that a great discovery had been snatched by petty criminals who almost certainly had no idea that it was of insignificant monetary value.

It was not what she believed. The statement was a sham. Sometimes it seemed to Nazreem that she lived in a perpetual sham, a state that was not a state, neither at peace nor all-out war, with politicians forever following 'road maps' they knew led to dead ends.

The police had other things to deal with of course. Even now police and emergency workers were still sorting through the rubble of the building around the corner, targeted by the Israeli air force allegedly because the head of a 'terror squad' had been using it as a hideout. Nazreem had no idea; she had only ever seen it used by old men for prayer meetings. She knew that that meant nothing. But the air-to-ground missile was a singularly blunt instrument for political assassination.

The Israelis called it retaliation. An eye for an eye, a tooth for a tooth. Tit for tat. To Nazreem it had become a bloody and wearisome game without respite or hope of conclusion. But it was not that nor her own brutal violation that preyed most on her mind; it was the coincidence between the timing of the air strike and the theft.

At any other time the chances of a successful break-in would have been far lower. But in the confusion and chaos that accompanied the air strike, with ambulances, police, screaming citizens and hotheads firing Kalashnikovs into the sky in the insane hope of bringing down an F-16 already fifty miles away, the flashing light and clanging alarm bells on a museum building had not even been a distraction. They had simply been ignored. By everyone, including the bastard who had violated her personally as well as professionally.

At any other time, there would have been next to nothing worth stealing. Whoever had broken in had chosen his moment. In advance. This was not an opportunistic break-in. He had seized only one object. The clear implication was that the thief had not only known about the discovery, he had known the timing of the air strike. Down to the minute. And that pointed the finger of guilt in only one direction as far as Nazreem was concerned.

She unlocked the side door to the museum, as she had done the day before, and let herself in. The place smelled fusty, desiccated compared with the odours of the street. She was surprised to find Ahmed, the janitor, shuffling along the corridor towards her, his face more lined and drawn than usual. But then he did not have much to laugh about. He had lost three children in the intifada. One son had been shot by an Israeli sniper for throwing stones at the cars of settlers. In response his daughter had become a suicide bomber, killing three Jewish children at a school bus stop.

His youngest son had died in his cradle, crushed by the tank sent to demolish their home in retaliation. He lived in a refugee camp with his sole remaining child, a four-year-old, whom he feared in turn would become a suicide bomber, now that they had nothing left to lose. Ahmed could not understand those who in response had become fanatical Islamists: Allah the all-powerful, the all-merciful, had done nothing for him. He had stopped even saying his prayers any more. Nonetheless, he greeted Nazreem with the traditional 'Salaam aleikum.' Peace be with you. 'And with you,' she replied.

She had to steel herself to walk through the main gallery, shuddering as she passed the open mummy case and the marble sarcophagus which now exuded a chill that vestiges of the ancient dead had never before evoked in her. Beyond, in the exhibition room, the central plinth was vacant. Absent-mindedly she ran a hand over the spot where she had last seen the face of the Madonna looking down on her.

She glanced around the rest of the room, at the various objects already assembled for the exhibition that would now have to be cancelled, an exhibition that was to have told one of the great stories of human religion. The story was not over yet, but the telling would have to be postponed.

Nothing else had been taken, nothing at all, not even the little clay cuneiform tablet, one of the famed Tell El-Amarna letters to the pharaoh, this one originally written by a provincial governor, possibly even the one who had been buried in the sarcophagus, from the imperial outpost of Uru-Salim warning of an invasion across the River Jordan by a tribe known as the Habiru. It did not take a great leap of the imagination to see that as the earliest verified historical reference to the Hebrews' arrival in Jerusalem, and the conflict that continued today.

She opened the door to her office. Thin shafts of sunlight filtered in through the closed shutters. She turned on the light and a slow rotating ceiling fan started the illuminated dust motes dancing. The office was sparsely furnished. The walls were lined with cheap shelving supporting a small fortune's worth of research and reference books in three languages: English, French and Arabic. Nazreem had a natural ear for languages. She had even a basic working knowledge of Hebrew, and found the guttural sounds of another Semitic language uncomfortably familiar.

There was a filing cabinet below the window and an elderly rubber plant with brown-edged leaves that suggested it needed watering. There was a bare functional desk with lockable drawers and a dusty computer with an old cathode-ray display. The desk was covered with papers, the product of weeks of research since the find. The thing that had preyed on her mind, even at the worst moment as the bastard thrust himself into her, was that he might ransack her office too. But the burglar had been single-minded. She herself had been his sole distraction. He had spotted his target and been gone from the building within minutes.

Nazreem turned the key in the lock behind her, then crossed to her desk and sat down. She looked at the mound of papers on her desk, shuffled a few of them and then set them down again, before using another key to open the deep lower drawer in the frame of the desk, opened it and biting her bottom lip, reached inside. At that precise moment a sudden shrill screech sent an electric spasm through every muscle in her body.

She slammed the drawer shut, then slumped back in her chair, shocked but ashamed by her own stupidity, and let the telephone ring twice more before answering. When she heard the voice on the other end, she was thankful that the adrenaline charge had given her the strength to reply.

6

The television was switched off and Marcus Frey's eyes were drifting over the perpendicular splendour of Nicholas Hawksmoor's Gothic towers outside the windows but his thoughts were a thousand miles and more away. His fingers drummed on the stained green surface of the ingrained leather on his Victorian oak desk, listening to the unfamiliar single tone ring on the other end of the telephone line.

It had been relatively simple to locate the telephone number for the new Museum of Palestine – a search on Google had pointed him to the web pages of the Palestine Authority's embryonic Culture Ministry. The bigger question was who, if anyone, would answer.

He had hesitated before ringing, wondering how he ought to ask for her, by name or as the curator; by name probably given the negligible state of his Arabic and the likely limited English of whoever might be charged with answering the museum's telephones.

He need not have worried; on the third ring the phone was answered by a voice that he recognised at once, an unusually quiet, almost breathless, '*Marhaba*.'

'*Marhabytn*,' he replied. Hello back. 'Nazreem, it's Marcus.'

For a moment it seemed as if he had been cut off, a sudden total silence, and then: 'Marcus. How did you …? Why? Now of all times. This is …'

He interrupted her, as he always did, as she always hated him doing: 'Congratulations, Nazreem – on the job, I mean. I had no idea. I knew you were capable of it.'

'Marcus, I …' he could hear the warning tones in her voice. Of course, she was hardly in a mood for congratulations. 'It's been so long.'

'I know, I know. I'm sorry. I didn't have a number. Or an email address. I didn't think to …'

'Nor did I. Never mind. It doesn't matter. Not right now.'

All of a sudden Marcus realised he had no clear idea of what he planned to say. Should he tell her he simply wanted to hear the sound of her voice again? It was the truth, wasn't it? There was a moment's awkward silence and then they both began talking at once. This time, however, it was he who gave way.

'Marcus, I'm glad to hear from you. I really am ...' Her voice tailed away. 'It's just that ... this is so unexpected, so many things have happened.'

'I know. I know. Terrible, it was in the papers.'

'It was? Where are you calling from?'

'England. Oxford. It was all in *The Times*. And on the BBC. Terrible, just terrible. Are we really talking about a portrait of ...?'

'Not on the phone. I'd like to talk to you, Marcus, I really would, but ...'

'Don't worry about the cost of the phone call. Anyway the college is paying. The book is finished, you know. I owe you.'

'You owe me nothing. But that's good. I'm glad.'

'But let's talk about you. How are you, apart from the theft, I mean. The report in the paper was very mysterious, suggested it might even be ...'

'NO! Marcus, no! Not now! I will tell you about it, but please not now, not on the phone.'

'Hey, easy does it. You archaeologists aren't tapping each other's phones these days, are you?'

Her reply, when it came, was suffused with the strain of tired exasperation: 'You don't understand, Marcus.'

'No, I don't.' He was confused. On the one hand, she seemed genuinely pleased he'd called. On the other he could almost feel the tension that he had seen in her face and heard in her voice on the television. In the circumstances, he said the first thing that came into his head: 'It would be great to see you again, one of these days.'

There was a silence on the end of the line, a silence that made Marcus swallow hard. He had forgotten that in the world Nazreem inhabited people scorned throwaway lines. Lives were sometimes cheap but words always had meaning.

'It would?' He knew the question was real, but so was his answer:

'You know it would.'

That silence again.

But only because he could not hear Nazreem Hashrawi's heart pounding on the other end of the line as her eyes flickered around her room, to the slammed desk drawer, to the pile of papers on top, to alight on one card, wedged under a scarab beetle paperweight. She snatched it, scanned it, then threw it down and reached in her right-hand desk drawer to pull out a dog-eared timetable that the cover announced was two years out of date but she hoped would still be valid. They said the past never escaped the present, and they were right, but sometimes the past, even the very recent past, could ride to the rescue of the present. Even in the improbable shape of an old flame that did not need rekindling.

In distant Oxford, Marcus Frey was struggling with his own particular demon: embarrassment. Awkward silences had always defeated him. He was about to give up and say something he knew would sound stupid like, 'Well, see you around then', when all of a sudden Nazreem's voice returned, clear as a bell and sharp as a sergeant-major.

'Then turn up at Heathrow Airport on Monday to meet flight MS777 from Cairo. I think it gets in around three p.m.'

'What? You're coming to England? Is there something …?'

There was a breathless urgency in her reply: 'Marcus, can you simply, just this once, do as I say? Yes or no?'

'Is something the matter?'

A pause. 'Marcus! Can you just be there?'

'Yes. Yes, of course.'

'Good. I'm counting on you.'

The line went dead.

A sudden rattling noise caused Marcus to look up. The golden stone of Hawksmoor's towers had turned to grey under the leaden shadow of an oppressive black cloud and fat summer raindrops were bouncing off the windowpane. In the distance there was a peal of thunder. It's a good thing, he thought to himself, that I'm not superstitious.

7

Rafah

There was a thin, faintly antiseptic smell in the still, clammy air, an indication that the minions had done their job well, washing down and swilling away into the grating in the corner every last trace of the blood and urine. The man in the long robes wrinkled his nose slightly. At least some things got done properly.

He was angry, although you would not have known it. He made a point of repressing outward signs of emotion, except when they were needed for particular effect. They were to be used sparingly, to be appreciated all the more because of the rarity of their appearance. He refused to express emotion when he was on his own. Just as he refused to tolerate weakness, incompetence or treachery in others.

But then tolerance was not something those who knew him well would ever have accused him of. There were many, many, willing to lay down their lives for him, many more who regarded him as a holy man. That was not a claim he made for himself. He considered himself devout, in his own way, but more than anything else he was a pragmatist, a believer in the power of the possible: that anything was possible, if you wanted it badly enough. And would let nothing stand in your way.

He had never let anything stand in his way. Not since he had been a child in the dust of Saddam Hussein's Iraq, growing up to loath the man who had murdered his parents, and rejoicing when the hated dictator went to the gallows. But he had also quickly come to despise those who had deposed Saddam, then ground the ruins of his country to dust to satisfy their oil lust and impose their so-called democracy.

He had grown up in Samarra, the city of the two shrines of the tenth and eleventh imams, second city in the province of Salah ad-Din. The name was that of the great twelfth-century warrior who had expelled the crusaders from Palestine but it also meant 'rightness of religion'. The heathen Saddam had tried to usurp that name for himself. How much more fitting that instead he had inherited it amongst his followers, a name that he hoped would one day yet again echo in history.

All things were achieved only by God's blessing, but also by the will of man, doing His work. That was what would be remembered in history. Yet sometimes artefacts from history could also make an impact on the present: artefacts such as the one that lay on the table in front of him in the place of the box of bloodstained surgical instruments.

The man they called Saladin sneered at the supposedly sacred image in front of him. He was familiar with the dolls and baubles of the idolatrous but still could not suppress an instinctive revulsion in their presence. He paced slowly around it, examining the quality of the workmanship, which was competent if unremarkable; this was not an object whose value relied on its artistic merits. Nor was it made of valuable material, or richly adorned. It was precious for what people believed it to be, it was an idol pure and simple. A fetish. A work of the devil.

There was no God but God – even the Christians claimed to believe this, they were like the Jews had once been, people of the Book, children of Ibrahim. Yet they had committed the ultimate blasphemy, the one which Mohammed himself (peace be upon him) had foreseen. He had forbidden the creation of any image or likeness of himself, whereas they had confused a prophet with the deity, and made images of his martyrdom to worship. Images of their man/god hanging on a cross, rightful worship of the one God surrounded by pagan rituals. And then this most absurd of fantasies, to take Miriam, mother of their minor prophet, exalt her to the status of 'Mother of God', to make images of her and worship her too. And these – these idolatrous crusaders – dared to claim the high moral ground for themselves and deride the children of Islam as infidel barbarians.

He reached out his hand, reluctantly, and ran it across the figure on the table. It was a simple piece of wood that had once been coloured. There were little more than traces of the original pigment still adhering to the surface: a hint of palest blue here, presumably to indicate robes of some sort, white here – a trim perhaps, it was hard to be sure.

And black of course. On the face and hands. Black. That was the worst of it. For if half of what the man who had betrayed his faith and his fathers had said was true – before he died like the swine he had become – then this thing was not just a fetish of foolish unbelievers, an obscene idol that merited little more than disgust or destruction; it represented something far worse. A blasphemy beyond belief. Evidence of a crime against God Himself.

For all his attempts to control it, the emotion he felt now was real: a deep rolling anger that gnawed at his innards, an anger that was fused with a hatred that was both visceral and intellectual, and focused, clearly and coldly, on the object in the centre of the table.

He turned on his heel and went over to the metal locker in the corner, took a key from his pocket and opened it. Having found the implement he required, he closed the door again and turned to the table. Briefly he fingered the figure on the table, rubbing his finger and thumb roughly over what appeared to be the face, as if he might rub off some of the vestigial traces of pigment.

Then, with a sudden violence, his face contorted into an expression of pure and holy hatred, he lifted high above his head a meat cleaver and buried it with a resounding, wood-splitting crash into the face of the Virgin Mary.

8

Altötting, Bavaria

It should have been a day like any other in the sleepy little Bavarian town of Altötting: a day full of clerical routine, quiet mediation and the contemplation of miracles.

As she walked across the expanse of neatly mown green lawns between the great churches towards the tiny chapel in their middle, Sister Galina paused for a while, as was her habit on warm days, in the shade of the ancient grove of linden trees, and felt at peace with the world. Her place in the hierarchy of Mother Church was lowly, but the job was special. Her place of work was the oldest Christian building in Germany and one of the country's most sacred shrines.

Compared to the monumental religious buildings from the fifteenth, seventeenth and nineteenth centuries that surrounded it, the tiny Chapel of Grace that gave the vast square its name was almost comically out of scale. Architecturally it tended towards the absurd: the pointy roof sat on the little octagonal chapel like a witch's hat and the external canopy that ran all the way round looked more in keeping with a bus shelter or some arcade in which bad artists hawked their works to tourists.

Close up that impression was reinforced: all the way around, fixed to the walls and even inside the canopy roof, were paintings. Almost without exception they were works of no value at all from an artistic point of view, but that was not the point. These paintings were not for sale; they were offerings. Each and every one of them, from the ancient, weathered, oil-painted wooden panels to the childish crayon drawings on A4 paper in a supermarket frame, was a testimony to the miraculous power of prayer and divine intervention. And that in itself was more than enough to make them special.

Sister Galina felt in the pockets of her habit among the rosary beads and her hand-carved crucifix, for the key to the little chapel, and smiled as she opened the door. It was dark inside, for the tiny windows had mostly been blocked; the light of day was not encouraged to penetrate a place which held such ancient treasures.

The familiar smell of old incense and doused candles greeted her, rich, pungent and slightly acrid. The nave of the chapel, a later eighteenth-century addition, was, like the canopy outside, adorned with pictures donated by pilgrims. Beyond, behind a dark screen was the tiny octagonal chamber that was the oldest part of the church, first built for the baptism of heathen warlords in the first half of the eighth century, in the days when Charles Martel, grandfather of Charlemagne, the first Holy Roman Emperor, was battling the Saracens in Spain and Christendom was on the verge of collapse.

The original font had long gone, of course. What made Altötting special, what attracted the tens of thousands of pilgrims from all over Germany, the rest of Europe, even the world, in planes, trains, buses, coaches, cars and even on foot, was the presence of the Mother of God. Or rather, Sister Galina corrected herself with a smile for she had almost erred on the side of heresy, Her miraculous image. The little seventy-centimetre crude wooden carving of the Holy Virgin had been brought to Altötting, nobody knew from where, some time in the early fourteenth century, but its cult dated from 1489 when a three-year-old child believed drowned had miraculously come back to life when brought before it. Since then the legend of miracles attributed to the statue had spread like a bush fire to make Altötting the German-speaking world's prime pilgrimage site dedicated to the cult of Mary, visited annually by up to 300,000 believers. The Altötting cult had reached its climax not in the Middle Ages but on the 15th of August, Ascension Day, 2008, when Benedict XVI, the first German pope in nearly 1,000 years, and coincidentally a local lad by birth, returned to his homeland to bestow on Altötting a papal Golden Rose, one of the highest honours of the Catholic Church.

It was not Sister Galina's job to attend to the Blessed Virgin; she was too lowly to be allowed the job of dusting around Her, let alone cladding Her in any of the vast wardrobe of silver, gold and jewel-encrusted robes accumulated over the centuries.

She bowed her head in the direction of the holy image before turning to open the door on the right which led into the sacristy. This was the mundane part of the chapel, a little room furnished in relatively modern style, that is with the dull functionality of the late twentieth century. It contained a desk, two chairs, filing cabinets and, as Sister Galina demonstrated by clicking a switch, even had electric light. The only obvious ecclesiastical item in the room was a large silver chalice which stood on the desk next to several heavy, leather-clad books.

She sat down at the desk and opened the uppermost ledger at the bookmark she had placed within its pages yesterday. Then she opened the desk drawer and took out the expensive italic fountain pen kept specifically for the purpose of making entries in the ledger.

It was not exactly state-of-the-art, but even a nun younger than Sister Galina brought up on the cusp of the twenty-first century would still regret the day – possibly not far off, now that the order had its own website and email address – when even tasks such as this were computerised. It would not exactly be sacrilege but a break with the past, with centuries of tradition. Here above all else tradition mattered.

It was Sister Galina's task, although she thought of it more as an honour, to record the letters, prayers and offerings sent by grateful recipients of divine mercy. She would note down, as her colleagues and predecessors had done for hundreds of years, the names of those offering their thanks to the Madonna, the city, town, district or even foreign land they came from, what their prayer to her had been and in what way it had been answered.

Some pilgrims whose prayers had been answered, often months or years afterwards – and sometimes with the intervention of modern medicine rather than by instantaneous intercession, but deemed their cure miraculous nonetheless – came back to leave offerings. There were crutches no longer needed piled by the door. Others, following an ancient, if somewhat grotesque, tradition, sent replicas of their formerly afflicted organs. The custom had begun with mediaeval princes, some of whom had donated near life-size silver images of themselves. The greatest among them had obtained permission for their hearts, after death, to be encased in elaborate gold or silver urns and entombed in niches in the wall around the sacred statue. No fewer than twenty-two members of the Wittelsbach clan, Bavaria's ancient ruling family, had their hearts removed after death and enshrined in the Chapel of Grace, the most recent among them Antonia of Luxemburg, Crown Princess of Bavaria, who had died in 1954.

Their modern imitators were more often reduced to sending plastic models, almost invariably made in China: little hearts or arms or legs hung from the ancient timbers of the outside canopy like the carnage from some massacre of the puppets, until the elements faded the colour to a grimy pink as if drained of blood. Other grateful supplicants more prosaically sent cheques for the maintenance of the shrine and continuance of the brothers' work. They were appreciated none the less.

Over the centuries the gifts showered upon Altötting's shrine were such that a special treasury had been set up within the great fifteenth-century Foundation Church nearby to house the most valuable gifts of gold and silver. Only a very few of the most sacred or historically important remained in the inner sanctum with the Virgin Herself.

Sister Galina ran her eye with benign interest over the last few entries: 'From Uschi Bernstein, Halle, thanks to the Holy Mother for restoring my husband to health following a heart attack', donation: photograph of smiling pensioner in jogging suit. 'From Gabi Urkamp, Regensburg, grateful thanks to the Queen of Heaven for recovery from breast cancer.' 'From Sylvie Schabowski, Munich, super thanks for getting me through my school exams.' Sister Galina smiled; nothing was too insignificant for the attention of the Mother of God.

She was just wondering what today's post would bring when there was a knock on the door, a loud knock, the sort that suggested a more businesslike attitude than the usual hushed reverence demonstrated by the faithful. 'Enter,' she said in a voice that she hoped was both firm and gentle. She was not expecting the apparition which confronted her. Rather than being opened gently, as was usual, the door was flung open rudely and Sister Galina found herself staring in shock at a faceless figure in black. She pushed back her chair and stood up. Sisters in holy orders were not used to unannounced visitations from leather-clad motorcycle messengers in visored helmets.

'Delivery,' said the muffled voice, as the figure produced a weatherproof silver bag and dumped it unceremoniously on the desk next to the leather-bound ledger, nudging the ornate chalice aside. A Protestant, Sister Galina decided.

'Sign here.'

'Which company are you from?' asked Sister Galina, removing the top of her fountain pen for the first time that day and fastidiously inscribing her name on the grubby piece of paper proffered. 'Not DHL or Fedex? I don't recognise the uniform.'

'Private,' came the gruff reply from the already retreating back. The door closed behind him and within seconds the nun could hear the growl of a powerful motorbike starting up outside. Funny that she hadn't heard it arriving. She also realised that the paper she had signed had been taken away without her receiving a copy. Sloppy. A sign of the times.

She opened the desk drawer again and took out a long silver paper knife with the familiar Altötting heraldic depiction of the Madonna and Child in yellow and red enamel on the handle. The blade, however, was not sharp enough to open the thick weatherproof bag. A pair of scissors did the trick.

Sister Galina cut carefully along one corner. There was something about this that made her uneasy. Call it superstition, or intuition; the Queen of Heaven moved in mysterious ways. There was no indication to whom the parcel had been addressed. Possibly that had been on the receipt so rudely thrust under her nose and taken away again; if so, she had not noticed. She assumed, since it had been brought directly to the sacristy of the Chapel of Grace, that it was intended as a gift to the Madonna, although normally items dedicated to the shrine were not received directly at the sacristy, unless pilgrims themselves left them.

She wondered if she was wise to open it, if it might not be better left to someone else, but then quickly decided that under the circumstances she had little choice. It was always possible there was a covering note of explanation inside.

There was not. Instead, inside the bag was another, black, made of some thick rubbery material, heat-sealed. Whatever was inside was small, irregularly shaped. It felt somehow distantly familiar as if it was something she ought to recognise, bizarrely out of context.

Carefully she took the scissors again and cut along one side of the rubber bag, near the seal mark. Almost immediately her senses were assailed by a strange, sweet-sour smell, like something that had been left in the fridge too long. She looked inside the rubber bag and saw that whatever it contained was further wrapped in a normal transparent plastic bag. Gingerly she extracted it by one corner, wishing all of a sudden that the sacristy had a pair of the rubber gloves they used in the convent for washing-up.

The object in the plastic bag was fleshy, lobed, and she realised with an unmistakable creeping horror, bloody. But that horror was as nothing to that which exploded an instant later as she realised what she was holding in her hand. Immediately, convulsively, Sister Galina committed an act of wholly unintentional sacrilege: she threw up into the silver chalice.

Lying on the ancient ledgers of donations to the Mother of God, was a bleeding heart – not the idealised sacred image that glowed pink and perfect on images of Christ – but the authentic organ, assymetrical and caked in dried brown gore. Worse was what lay next to it, shrivelled, obscene and almost unidentifiable at first glance: the severed sexual organs of an adult human male.

9

Terminal 3, Heathrow airport, London

Marcus Frey stood in the arrivals hall scanning every face that emerged from the sliding doors with scarcely concealed anticipation. It had been more than three years since he had last seen Nazreem.

He knew from the newspaper that she had changed little physically, except perhaps for that hint of hardness in her eyes that may have been a trick of the light, although it could also have been the hard knocks of the world she lived in and chose not to leave. Nazreem had always had more self-confidence than most women who grew up in such a male-dominated world. But over time the process of attrition was bound to take its toll.

He had no idea how they would react to each other. Her manner on the telephone had been tense, and not just because of the theft from her museum. It was almost as if she was afraid of something. Marcus was worried. On the other hand, he told himself, maybe he was just imagining it. The truth was, he was nervous about seeing her again. Why she was coming to London, he had no idea. He was certainly not vain enough to imagine that it was to see him. There was another question: how was she managing to come to London at all; as far as Marcus knew the Rafah crossing into Egypt was currently closed, opened only sporadically to let through emergency supplies, usually in inadequate quantities. The Palestinian Authority's attempt to set up its own embryonic airline had been left literally in ruins by the bombing raids that had ripped up the runway of Gaza City's short-lived 'international airport'. The port was blockaded and the Israeli navy patrolled the coast. The occupying army might have gone, but Gaza remained little more than an open prison.

The information displayed on the arrivals board indicated that the EgyptAir flight from Cairo had landed some forty minutes ago and that the baggage had already been transferred to the arrivals hall. But Marcus was not surprised to be still waiting. In the current international political climate security checks were strict, particularly on passengers arriving from the Middle East. Even as he scanned the arrivals board, he could feel the ubiquitous surveillance camera panning across the crowd. It was all in the name of passenger safety, but sometimes he felt there was nowhere in Britain nowadays that didn't have a 'big brother' looking over your shoulder.

The doors slid open again and a new batch of arrivals emerged, pushing trolleys loaded with heavy bags, blinking at the waiting crowds, looking for family members, men wearing sunglasses indoors, holding message boards with Arabic names written in English, waiting chauffeurs or mini-cab drivers. As a rule Marcus hated airports. But Heathrow Terminal 3 exuded a whiff of spice and the tropics: Saudis and Gulf State Arabs in white djellebahs and checkered keffiyehs, Nigerians and Ghanaians with colourful floor-length robes and pill-box African headdresses, Iranian or Afghan women in body-covering black chadors or burkhas with tiny slits for their eyes, Americans and Australians in either sharp suits or bulging out of ill-advised tourist leisurewear, businesslike Japanese tour groups, Indian and Pakistani women in brightly-coloured saris, Sikhs in turbans – although many of them he noted actually belonged to the airport ground staff. As an old colonial boy, he never ceased to be amazed by how multicultural London had become.

And then he caught sight of her: a slight figure bustling in a businesslike manner through the ambling crowds of passengers. She looked more like a hassled Western backpacker than a museum curator, with a functional-looking green coat over trousers, a headscarf pushed well back so that it was more like a neckerchief; her only luggage a rucksack and a leather bag slung over one shoulder. She saw him immediately.

For the past forty-eight hours Marcus had been trying to imagine this moment, wondering how he would react, and only now realised that he still didn't know. He beamed, held out his arms and brought them back together and then with an awkwardness he could scarcely believe, held out his hand. Nazreem walked straight towards him and with a wry smile on her face, took it, then stood on tiptoes and pecked him on the cheek.

'Good to see you,' she said.

'You too.' For an instant their eyes met.

'Here, let me take that,' he said, reaching for the rucksack. 'You travel light. Looks like you're planning on camping.'

She pushed him back, firmly but still smiling. 'It's okay. Thanks, but I can manage. And it's practical. I don't like suitcases. You never know what people can put in them.'

'Right, of course. I hadn't thought of it like that.' He had almost forgotten where she had come from. 'How did you … I mean …?'

'How did I get out of Gaza? The great open jail?' She touched the side of her nose, gave him a cynical glance and mimed throwing a shovelful of earth over her shoulder.

'The tunnels? I thought they were all …'

'The Israelis tried to bomb them all. The Egyptians fill them in. We dig more. It is not hard to know someone who knows someone, and on the other side it is still Rafah, the same language more or less, the same people more or less … and from Cairo, I still have a French passport, you remember, the one gift from my mother.'

'Of course.' He could hardly have forgotten. Had Nazreem possessed nothing more than the so-called passport issued by the Palestinian Authority, travel would have been a nightmare, an everlasting series of queues for visas, and unwanted interrogations, and that from those countries that professed to look on it kindly.

'I have a car,' Marcus said.

'Good. Then let's get out of here.'

As they turned towards the exit doors from the terminal making their way to the car park, a dark-haired young man with dark glasses and a beard who had been holding a sign indicating he was a chauffeur sent to meet M. Joliet arriving from Tangier obviously decided his charge was no longer coming, and did likewise.

On a high stool at the Costa Coffee bar by the exit a young woman with blonde hair and more stylish sunglasses worn high on her forehead chatting girlishly on her iPhone watched him go. Only the most assiduous observer would have noticed the change in the tone of her conversation.

10

The traffic meant it took Marcus nearly forty-five minutes to get into central London from Heathrow, complicated by the fact that he was unfamiliar with driving in the metropolis and that he had no idea where they were headed.

'Just drive,' Nazreem had said, climbing into his battered baby-blue Peugeot 406 in the concrete maze of the Terminal 3 car park. She had insisted on throwing her rucksack onto the back seat on top of Marcus's piles of papers, sandwich wrappers and empty Lucozade bottles.

'Where to?'

'London. Where else?'

Almost anywhere else, Marcus had thought, dismayed by her brusque, almost unfriendly tone. He had imagined taking her back to Oxford, showing her round the 'city of dreaming spires', dinner at High Table in All Souls, the other dons taken aback by his beautiful exotic companion. But deep down he had known that was just wishful thinking. Nazreem was a woman with a purpose. He would just have to wait for her to share it with him. Or not.

He was not sure if she had ever been to London before. Probably not, he surmised, although she seemed to be paying undue attention to the queues of cars exiting the car park and on the crowded M4 motorway, even for a first-time tourist. London's traffic was bad but it was not unique.

'We need to find rooms,' she had said, beginning to lighten up as they came down off the Westway overpass into the busy Marylebone Road. Marcus noted the plural, but then he had not been making any assumptions. 'Something cheap, where I can pay cash.'

'There's no need ...' Marcus began. If she was going to be a first-time tourist in London he could at least afford to put them up somewhere decent, not the Savoy or the Dorchester perhaps but not one of the flop houses around Paddington.

'Somewhere close to the British Museum.'

Marcus nodded. Maybe that was it: this was a business trip, she had a meeting set up and he was just a useful incidental. He didn't know much about hotels in the area but was pretty sure there was a respectable establishment on Russell Square, a short walk from the museum.

The traffic crawled along the Marylebone Road and through the Euston underpass. A taxi driver leaned out of the window of his black cab and swore vociferously at Marcus when he pulled abruptly across the road to be in the right-turn lane that led down towards the British Museum.

He had come this way before and found it confusing: despite a mixture of names that suggested a series of broad open expanses – Upper Woburn Place, Tavistock Square, Woburn Place, Russell Square – and a volume of traffic that suggested a major thorough-fare, the reality was one continuous relatively narrow, clogged road, with the odd patch of green to the side, pedestrians darting continuously into the spaces between cars and double-decker buses relentlessly elbowing their way through.

The difference was that since the last time Marcus had driven down here the route – the very place names – had acquired a fresh veneer of horror. He could not look at the red double-deckers without thinking of the horrific image of one very similar on this very road, its top ripped off, the buildings around smeared with blood. Thirteen people had died on one bus in the most publicly visible attack on the bloody Thursday in July 2005, when Al Qa'eda had struck at the heart of London. He wondered if Nazreem was even aware of it when she suddenly grabbed his arm, saying: 'Stop here. This'll do.'

Marcus looked askance at her and then at the drab red-brick building she was pointing at. It was indeed a hotel, but one that looked as if it had seen better days, although possibly it never had. It was a six-storey, anonymous-looking pile except for a blue neon sign that said Country Hotel. He was about to protest, but Nazreem was already opening the door in the stationary traffic and hoisting her rucksack from the back seat.

Marcus found it surprisingly easy to find a free parking space with a meter until he read its extortionate rates per minute and the reminder that he would also have to pay the £8 daily central London congestion charge. He hurried into the hotel lobby, a dingy place with a smoky, down-at-heel atmosphere peopled by men in tweed jackets or anoraks and women in sturdy shoes. The concierge shot a shifty glance at him as he came up behind Nazreem.

'Two rooms was it then, miss? Adjoining okay? Shared facilities,' with an insinuating smile. Marcus decided the hotel clientele was probably used on an equal basis by out-of-town farming folk and adulterous couples looking for a cheap venue for illicit trysts.

'That'll be £40 each for the night then. Cash upfront will do nicely. Oh, and sign the register, would you. As you like.' It was obviously a pro forma rather than official request.

Marcus managed to edge Nazreem aside and get his wallet out – he was determined to pay if nothing else – and was bemused to see Nazreem fill in the registration forms in the names Marie Mathieu and John West. He said nothing and grabbed her rucksack with one hand, only to put it down again suddenly, surprised by the weight.

'I take back what I said about you travelling light. What's in here anyway?'

Nazreem spun round and shot him a dark look. 'Leave it alone. It's books. Important ones.'

'You've brought them with you.'

'Yes, for a friend. At the museum. I told you.'

He was about to say she hadn't but thought better of it. Nazreem hoisted the rucksack onto her back and gestured at him to follow her towards the lift.

'Is there a reason why you gave them false names?' he said as the lift groaned to a halt at the fourth floor. 'Protecting our modesty?'

Nazreem gave a long, weary sigh and turned to him with a ghost of a smile, the first he had seen on her face since that initial moment of meeting at the airport: 'Oh, I don't know. Maybe it's just a reaction to not having to produce identity documents every five minutes.

'Look, Marcus, you're right. There's lots we need to talk about. But just right now, I need to freshen up. A good long soak in the bath to wash the desert sand away.' She leaned forward and gave him the slightest of pecks on the cheek. 'Just let me wind down a bit. I'll knock on your door in …' she looked at her watch. It was just gone five p.m. '… two hours' time?'

Marcus smiled back and shrugged: 'Whatever you say. You're the boss.'

The room was even dingier than the lobby, with peeling wallpaper in one corner and a low, metal-framed cot with worn sheets. Marcus shook his head and wondered how he was going to pass the time. There was an ancient-looking fourteen-inch television but he couldn't find the remote control. He heard the lock turn on the other side of the door to the bathroom which the two rooms shared, then the sound of water running. He turned the television on manually and pushed buttons to see what was on. There was no cable or satellite, just the five terrestrial channels, and reception on the fifth was fuzzy, but BBC2 was showing highlights from the British Lions' rugby tour of South Africa. He sat back relatively contentedly to watch.

The room was stifling however and smelled of stale cigarette smoke. There was no air conditioning and after a few minutes, he got up, crossed to the window, pulled the flimsy net curtains aside and opened it. The sound of the street rose to meet him, a dull cacophony of traffic noise. The air was not much cooler, but at least it was relatively fresh, if you discounted the exhaust fumes. He leaned out to push the window wide and immediately caught his breath. There on the pavement below him, unmistakable with her mane of thick dark hair now completely uncovered and the preposterous red and green rucksack on her back, was Nazreem climbing into the back of a black taxi.

For a moment Marcus stared in sheer disbelief. He wanted to call down to her, not that he would have been heard, but he realised he had no idea what he would have said. He was literally speechless. The cab pulled out into the crawling traffic, moving at little more than walking pace at best. He could run down the stairs and be out in the street in less time than it would take the cab driver to reach the next corner, barely twenty yards away. But what would be the point? If she wanted to slip away without telling him, there was nothing he could do about it. And despite the rising lump in his throat, he didn't believe that. If she had not wanted to see him again, there had been no need even to mention that she was coming to the country, let alone ask him to meet her at the airport. No, she would be back and she would explain. If she wanted to.

It was then that he noticed the bearded man with dark glasses on the other side of the street folding up a copy of a newspaper and climbing into a black Mercedes with tinted windows. There was something that for a second seemed disconcertingly familiar. Not about the car; black Mercedes were common enough, particularly as chauffeured cars, the sort you routinely saw waiting to pick up guests at the airport or outside hotels. Not hotels like this, though.

11

Munich

Lieutenant Karl Weinert of the Bavarian Kriminalpolizei paced up and down in the corridor outside the forensic laboratory of the Landeskriminalamt in Munich's Maillinger Strasse. He had been there for twenty minutes already and he was not a man accustomed to being kept waiting, especially when he had been told the results were ready.

It was not as if he was expecting much. The odds on getting any sort of identification were slim, but under the circumstances they had not much else to go on. In all his years in the force he had seen more than his share of gruesome sights: girls imported by people traffickers and kept as prostitutes in conditions that would have had animal rights campaigners up in arms, horrific facial scars and physical mutilations inflicted on victims in Turkish gang wars, and more recently the cynically brutal, almost wanton slayings that were the mark of encroachment by Russian Mafiosi. But he had never seen anything quite as grotesque as this.

The bumpkin provincial officers in the little town of Altötting, used to little more than crowd control and the occasional outbreak of pickpocketing during pilgrimages to the local shrine, had been overwhelmed. The town police chief had breathed a visible sigh of relief at being able to hand over to the big boys from the state criminal police.

Weinert and Richard Hulpe, his regular collaborator, however, had not been 100 per cent sure they weren't the victims of some sort of practical joke, until they had got there and seen the evidence themselves. He was still straining even to imagine what sort of warped and seriously sick mentality could conceive of having such a vile parcel delivered – by an apparently anonymous courier service (they were working on that) – to a nun in the chapel of one of the holiest shrines in the country. Unsurprisingly, the good sister was still in a state of shock.

They had found it difficult even to start an investigation on the spot; there seemed little point in conducting interviews at random amongst an extensive religious community or even the local lay people employed, but it would have to be done. Under the circumstances he found it more than incredible that the perpetrator could be local, but it was the first rule of police procedure that the murderer usually knew his (or her) victim.

The trouble in this case was establishing the identity of the victim. There were no reports of any missing persons in the Altötting area, and certainly not among the tightly knit religious community. He had hoped to keep the more salacious details out of the public domain. When searching for a killer, particularly a sadist which this one undoubtedly was, it was always better to keep something back. He had said as much to Sister Galina, but the nun, who was still in the order infirmary, had made it abundantly clear – with no more than a hand gesture – that she had not the slightest intention of revealing any more than the absolute minimum. And under the circumstances, Weinert had had no problem believing her.

But inevitably the word had got out. He did not know who had leaked it and there was next to no point in trying to find out. The tabloid press had a way of finding out the goriest details of murder cases, and in one like this there had never been any prospect of imposing a gagging order 'for the sake of the investigation'. It had been for his own sake too, he admitted privately. As it had turned out, however, the circumstances – the religious setting and the sense of deliberate desecration – had kept the worst elements of the force's inimitable black humour at bay. So far.

He had no doubts that when the investigation ran into the sand, as he had a horrible feeling this one was going to, he would still end up being labelled 'Inspector Dickhead'. At least they had kept the worst of it out of the press. Releasing the details about the heart was gruesome enough to feed the interest that might – just might – produce a lead; keeping back the more grotesque details about the genitalia would at least give a means to weed out any phoney confessions. God knows, releasing that sort of detail might have prompted a deluge of them. There had been that guy who volunteered to be eaten alive, penis first, by Germany's home-grown cannibal, and had his wish come true.

Weinert had little optimism about anything useful coming out of the forensics. Apart from Sister Galina, none of the other members of the religious community had touched the bag, unsurprisingly enough. The local police, who had been summoned immediately, had been so horrified at the thought of leaving evidence of murder within the confines of a sacred chapel – particularly evidence of this nature – that they had immediately removed it to the mortuary of the local hospital. Admittedly they had preferred to use tweezers to hold even the bag, but Weinert thought the chances of retrieving identifiable fingerprints slim. Identification of the victim was the first step and it did not look like being easy.

The lab boys back in Munich had not held out much hope. The chances of the victim's DNA being on a database were negligible. It was at times like these that policemen were tempted to wish that governments would introduce compulsory DNA registration for the entire population. In Wienert's opinion this was going to be a case that stayed open for years, or rather opened and shut in everything but name. Because the sister had failed to get even the probably phoney details of the supposed courier company, there was no way of being sure the package had been sent from within Germany.

Weinert was therefore irritated at having to wait outside the labs until some boffin in a white coat came out to tell him, as he was certain they would, that the case stopped here. It was at that moment that the lab door opened and Dr Heidi Wenger emerged and held out her hand with a grim but satisfied look on her face.

'Nasty business. Very nasty.'

Weinert nodded. He had no time for platitudes.

'Sorry to have kept you waiting. I don't know whether or not you'll thank me.'

Weinert smiled tightly. He knew: he wouldn't.

'Right, well as you can imagine, the most immediate conclusion was that the deceased was an adult male.'

Weiner grunted a suppressed laugh. That much had hardly taken a forensic scientist to deduce.

'That, however, hardly narrows down the field. Then we took a DNA sample.'

Yes, yes, that had been the whole point of the exercise.

'But unfortunately it didn't match anything on any of the Bavarian databases.'

God, these people could draw out statements of the bloody

obvious. Time to go back to his own office, fill in the paperwork, then do a few perfunctory interviews in Altötting before consigning the case to the 'dormant' files.

'We drew a blank on the national database too.' Yes, yes, surprise, surprise. 'However,' Wenger emphasised the word looking down her nose at him as if his scepticism was a bad attitude in a sulky schoolboy about to be given detention, 'as we already had to get in touch with the boys from the federal Kripo up at Wiesbaden, we asked them to run it through their international records too.'

Weinert frowned: he had never had direct dealings with Interpol himself, but he was well aware that international cooperation, even between the EU countries, was seldom as straightforward as might be hoped. There were always human rights hurdles to jump to get access to other forces' national DNA records.

'Oh, I know what you're thinking,' said Wenger. 'That sort of thing can take days if not weeks. Not in this case, however.'

'You're not going to tell me we've got an identity match? That we know who the victim is.' Weinert had noticed a suppressed smirk of satisfaction on the forensic scientist's lips. Now it broadened into almost a smile:

'Oh yes. In fact we've been able to ascertain more than you might have expected. A lot more.'

Weinert grunted. If he was about to be impressed by this long-winded self-important woman in a white coat, he was damned if he was going to let it show.

'To be precise, in theory we know exactly where and when he died.'

'You do?' Weinert could scarcely restrain a look of extreme scepticism. Even presented with an intact corpse, pathologists in his experience were seldom eager to volunteer a time of death to within less than a period of several hours. Forensics could usually be relied on to give some clues as to where a murder had been committed if the body were not found *in situ*: there were things like fibre samples, pollen, stuff like that. But self-confidence on this scale was something new to him. There again, he wondered what that 'in theory' bit meant.

'You look surprised,' Heidi Wenger said. 'You should be. Apparently he died at 00:18 hours yesterday.'

Weinert physically felt his jaw drop. It was not the unusual

– almost unheard of – precision of the timing that astonished him. It was the date. 'But … but … the … the "thing" was delivered twenty-four hours earlier.'

'Quite. Do you want to know where we believe he died?'

Weinert nodded: talk about a question of the fucking obvious. But there was no stopping her relishing her moment of glory.

'Would you believe a place called Erez?'

Weinert shrugged. He could believe almost anything. 'Never heard of it.'

'I'm not wholly surprised. It's an Israeli checkpoint at the northern end of the Gaza Strip.'

12

The man behind the wheel of the black Mercedes cursed under his breath. It was not in his nature to blame others but he was sorely tempted. If anything went wrong he would take the retribution alone. He was in charge and failure was not suffered gladly.

When his older colleague had pleaded the need to relieve himself, it didn't seem like much of a risk. He would only be a minute or two and would go into the seedy-looking hotel itself and make discreet enquiries at the same time: find out which room they were staying in. The girl and her big friend, whoever he was, had only just arrived. They would not be leaving immediately. They were probably rolling together in carnal lust already, the old man had spat, although the note in his voice was more of envy than disapproval. The girl was a looker all right, and obviously a hussy.

But barely seconds after the old man had gone into the hotel, the girl herself had emerged, looked briskly up and down the street and climbed into a taxi. He had had no choice but to set off immediately in pursuit; the risk of losing them in the London traffic was too great. He had taken the cab's number automatically, but the streets were full of them and if it gave him the slip, finding the same cab again would be not so much like hunting a needle in a haystack as searching for a particular straw.

At least the traffic was moving slowly. He tried his colleague's mobile and got a ringing tone but no answer. He wondered if the old fool even knew how to work it. The taxi edged forward and through the traffic lights ahead of him. Damn! If it turned right into the one-way system around Russell Square Gardens, he would have to guess which exit it might take. Where on earth could the woman be going?

She appeared to be carrying the same baggage – a ridiculous rucksack – that she had arrived with. Perhaps they had a lovers' tiff and she had walked out on him. He wished he knew who the man was, but he had no idea, had been given no warning that she would be met at the airport. He had filed away a mental description: tall, well-built, Anglo-Saxon in appearance, English probably or just possibly American although he seemed neither smartly nor sloppily enough dressed for that. Fair to mid-brown hair, and he walked with just the hint of a limp in his left leg. Not that he mattered now. The orders were to follow the girl.

For the moment the taxi was still visible in the traffic ahead. Then it turned the corner. The lights changed. He pressed the accelerator and took off after it. His mobile burst into life as he turned the corner; the old fool had obviously emerged from the Gents and found out how to work his phone. He ignored it.

The taxi was still ahead but turned left at the edge of the square, then took a left into Montague Street, the long road that ran down one side of the great neoclassical bulk of the British Museum. Of course, why hadn't he thought of it. She was an archaeologist. Where else would she be headed but the home of one of the greatest collections on earth? On impulse he grabbed his still ringing mobile from the seat next to him, hit answer and told his perplexed partner to grab a cab, cut around the back of the museum and get out at the main entrance. That way there would be two of them again, enough to tail the woman properly without both having obviously emerged from the same vehicle. Sometimes God indeed moved in mysterious ways.

Sure enough, he watched with satisfaction as the cab's indicator signalled right at the end of Montague Street. He slowed at the corner and turned right into Great Russell Street. The museum's monumental portico and colonnade ran the length of the block, the steps behind the railings crowded with summer tourists, but there was no sign of a taxi in front of him. It wasn't possible. There hadn't been time for her to stop and settle up. Unless she had cut and run. But why? And there would have been an outraged cab driver in the middle of the road.

Nor could they have shot on ahead of him: a little further on the road became one-way in the opposite direction. He edged forward and glanced down the narrow road on his left to see a black cab turning right at the end of it. The same one? He couldn't make out the number, but it had to be. He had been wrong about her destination. He accelerated to the end of the street and saw it again stopped in traffic edging towards the lights at the end of Bloomsbury Way.

It made no sense. In a moment they would be back at Southampton Row, which was where they would have ended up if they had not turned at Russell Square. Perhaps she had changed her mind. Could she have realised she was being followed? It was not impossible; he had been as discreet as he could under the circumstances but then the circumstances had been far from perfect.

The lights changed, the cab turned right again, down Kingsway, a big broad, split-carriageway road which was one of the few in London where traffic could really move. To make matters worse, there was a bus lane; the cab pulled into it and accelerated away. It was illegal for the Mercedes to follow suit, not that its driver gave a damn about the law or the possibility of a fine, but the last thing he wanted was to be pulled over by the police and in any case to have done so would have made certain she knew she was being followed. To catch up he would have to rely on the city's most dependable attributes: congestion and badly phased traffic lights.

They did not let him down. The lights at Aldwych turned red before the cab reached them, then green just in time to let him follow it to the left around the great one-way semi-circle. There were two options at the end of its curve: left along Fleet Street towards St Paul's and the financial district of the City, or sharp right towards Trafalgar Square and the West End. They turned right, but when the Mercedes did likewise, it was facing a wall of identical black cabs spread across the road.

Almost too late he spotted the one with the girl in it, pulled right over beyond the traffic islands into a left-hand lane that led not ahead but over the bridge. He braked too slowly to avoid being sucked along with the traffic flow down the Strand, and watched the cab turn the corner as the lights changed. Almost immediately the cab was out of sight; he revved the Mercedes hard and threw it at the line of raised kerbing marking the central lane division. There was an agonising scrape of metal on stone as the big car bumped over, and a flurry of blaring horns as he ploughed across the next lane and shot the red lights. He had no idea what damage he might have done to the undercarriage, or whether there would be a police car on his tail any minute. To his right as he shot out onto Waterloo Bridge the great Ferris wheel of the London Eye rotated majestically, transporting its pods of tourists ogling the Palace of Westminster beneath them and distant St Paul's, but he had eyes for one thing only: the black cab approaching the roundabout at the other end of the bridge.

Waterloo, he suddenly realised. Was she heading for Waterloo. A train out of town? Or to somewhere in the southern suburbs? The centre of the roundabout was taken up with the great cylinder of an Imax cinema, blocking the view and as he rounded it once again his field of vision filled with black taxis, but most of them were emerging onto the roundabout from the station pick-up area. The obvious thing was for her cab to have merged in with them on the station approach. It was off-limits to ordinary cars, but he would have to take the risk. And then at the last minute, glancing left to take account of oncoming traffic, he spotted the number plate he had memorised stopped on the right-hand side of the road just beyond the bus stop down Waterloo Road. Facing towards him. The driver had done a typical London cabbie's U-turn in the middle of the road. Someone was getting in! A pre-arranged meeting? And then there she was, on the pavement, her brightly coloured rucksack standing out from the crowd. For a moment he breathed a sigh of relief, before a wave of angry frustration overcame him as she disappeared into the Underground.

There was nothing to be done. Even if there had been two of them, it would have been a problem. There were four lines passing through Waterloo. She could have taken any of them. He muttered a few words into his headset in response to the babble of his panicking colleague, and then turned it off. He swung the Mercedes out into the traffic and back onto the roundabout, heading north and east, to Finsbury Park.

He would have to make his report. But first he would have to say his prayers. Oh yes, he would definitely have to say his prayers.

13

'Believe me,' Dr Heidi Wenger said, 'it's not exactly what we were expecting either. And before you ask: No, I've no way of explaining it. At least not one that makes any sort of sense.'

'Then how do you know …?'

'Take a look at this. Not that it's going to help with any of the questions you want an answer to,' and she handed the bemused Kriminalpolizei lieutenant a sheet of paper. It was a printout of an email message, though he noticed that the headers had been blocked out with a thick black indelible, and impenetrable, marker.

'It's a translation of the official Israeli report of the incident,' she said.

Weinert read: 'Report from 1st battalion, 3rd Coy, Gaza frontier unit, IDF (Israeli Defence Force, he understood), Major XXXXX (blacked out) commanding:

'The incident was logged as commencing at 00:10 hours when the duty sentries at the Israeli end of the Erez crossing point into Gaza became aware of some form of altercation at the Palestinian checkpoint some 150 metres distant. Heightened observation immediately after identified a vehicle heading for the main checkpoint fortification at approximately thirty kilometres per hour. As crossings without prior notification are heavily restricted, all checkpoint personnel were immediately put on full alert.

'As the vehicle continued to approach, floodlights were trained on it and the usual warning given in Arabic, Hebrew, English and Russian. The vehicle continued its progress and warning shots were fired into the air.

'With the aid of night vision binoculars, the forward watch ascertained that the vehicle in question was an early-model Honda CR-V with limited four-wheel drive capability and darkened executive windows. It was not possible to see inside the vehicle or know how many people it contained.

'As is customary in the current heightened security situation, the officer commanding gave the order to fire once more into the air above the vehicle and repeat the warning, this time in Arabic only, that failure to halt immediately carried potentially lethal consequences.

'Notwithstanding the vehicle continued. When it was approximately seventy metres distant, the commanding officer issued the general order to fire at the vehicle's tyres with the express purpose of halting its progress, with permission granted to aim at the radiator grill or other bodywork if necessary but not yet at the cabin pending further, imminent instruction.

'Hits were marked on the vehicle's front radiator grill and left-side front tyre, causing it to skew but not halt. At this stage the commanding officer considered due process to have been observed and ordered blistering fire at the windshield which disintegrated, affording a partial view of a single occupant in the driving position now hunched forward presumed hit.

'The vehicle however continued to advance in the face of withering fire to within ten metres of the checkpoint at which distance it was consumed by a powerful explosion presumably as the result of onboard devices detonated by the occupant. There were no other casualties. IDF forces secured the area with no Palestinian resistance. Representatives from the Palestinian Authority denied all responsibility for the incident, claiming their own security people were "distracted".'

'And you're trying to tell me the man inside the car was ...'

'Exactly, the same individual whose vital organs had arrived in Altötting nearly twenty-four hours earlier. From what the Israeli forensic team pieced together ...' Weinert winced at what he was not altogether sure was an unintentional pun, 'he was pretty high on the list of wanted terrorists. Just not their list.'

'I don't follow.'

'Oh, they wanted him okay, as did a lot of other people. They just hadn't expected him to turn up on their territory.'

'So how did they identify him?'

'By the DNA, there and then like here and now. He was on an internationally distributed database. They'd taken comprehensive samples when he was in jail in Spain.'

'Spain?'

'Yep. Their bits of body, just like our bits of body, belonged to ...'

she consulted another piece of paper, 'one Ahmed Abdul Rashid al-Zahwani. Moroccan by birth, last known place of residence: Algeciras, Spain. Served six months in 1999 for incitement to violence. Part-time Islamist, full-time hood, not so much martyr as materiel supplier with links to Chechen gangs and anybody else who can make holy war into a nice little money-spinner. He's been high on Interpol's wanted list since 2002, suspected of having sourced the explosives used in the Madrid bombings and possibly even involved in the attacks in London as well. Scotland Yard say he was suspected of being a courier between Islamist groups on the continent and in England.'

'Well that certainly deals with any sympathy I might have been feeling for the dear deceased.'

'Indeed, on the other hand, there's no suggestion here that he himself was a prospective martyr.'

'You mean?'

'I mean that according to Interpol, and the portfolio the Spanish and British police and security services had put together on him, his personality profile does not match that normally attributed to suicide bombers. He wasn't even one of those who goads others on to do his dirty work. He liked women – preferably not heavenly virgins – gambled heavily and drank alcohol. In short, al-Zahwani was a thug, a criminal who saw Islamic fundamentalism as nothing more than a nice little earner.'

'You're saying you don't believe he volunteered for this mission.'

'Let's just say he wouldn't have had the balls for it.'

14

The first indication Marcus had that Nazreem had not walked out of his life as abruptly as she had re-entered it was the sound of running water coming once again from the adjoining bathroom around six-fifty p.m. Ten minutes later, promptly, there was a knock on his door.

He opened it to find her there in jeans and a white T-shirt. Not a headscarf in sight, but not acres of bare midriff exposed either: she could have been French or Italian, a picture of understated Mediter-ranean sophistication. Marcus was impressed and he smiled to show it.

She smiled back, somehow indefinably more relaxed, as if she really had spent the better part of two hours in the bath. Curious as he was, Marcus had no intention of quizzing her. If she wanted to she would tell him in her own good time, though he could provide the opportunity:

'Did you get a good rest?' he asked, trying to sound as natural as possible.

'Yes,' the reply came without a second's hesitation. 'I fell asleep. I'm sorry, I hope you didn't want the bathroom.'

'It's okay, there's one along the corridor.' Her own good time might not be any time soon. 'So, where would you like to go for dinner? And then you can tell me all about it.' Or not, he thought. 'There are several Lebanese restaurants around.'

'Oh, I don't mind. Maybe something local would be nice though. But not something boiled. I have heard things about English food.'

'It's not as bad as it used to be. How about the national dish?'

Nazreem looked sceptical: 'Fish and chips, yes?'

Marcus laughed. 'Not any more, these days they reckon it's Chicken Tikka Masala. Indian food, sort of.'

She laughed back: 'Sounds excellent.'

'Good. I know just the place.'

It was raining when they got downstairs, one of those seasonal thunderstorms that alternated with hot spells, and had recently become part of what the newspapers had started calling the 'English monsoon season'. Marcus insisted Nazreem stay in the lobby while he went to fetch the Peugeot. He had thought of taking a cab, but the pouring rain meant there were few free and this was not the sort of hotel that had doormen in top hats who stepped out into the street to summon them. Also the Peugeot needed to be rescued from its exorbitant meter before full rates cut in again at eight a.m.

As they made their way eastwards through the dark and quickly emptying streets of the City, Marcus checked his rear-view mirror carefully. There was no obvious sign of an unusually attentive black Mercedes.

Perhaps he had been over-reacting, although he was not quite sure he believed that. He knew he should tell Nazreem what he had seen. If she was really being followed, she ought to know. But to tell her would expose her lie to him. It was difficult. The whole thing made him slightly uneasy.

Priji's in Brick Lane would cheer him up. It was his favourite curry restaurant in London. Maybe dinner would provide a chance for them to talk properly, for Nazreem to open up. He found a parking space in Fournier Street, by the side of Christ Church, Spitalfields, the newly restored eighteenth-century masterpiece that was one of his favourite London buildings. It had been designed by Nicholas Hawksmoor, the same architect who had given All Souls its Gothic spires. It was also in easy walking distance of Priji's.

The rain meant there were fewer than usual of the curry touts hassling passers-by. Priji's had been recommended to him by a South African friend of Asian extraction. The food, like most of the Brick Lane eateries, was not actually Indian but Bangladeshi, and the chef-owner, a second generation Londoner of Bengali extraction was not just a master in the kitchen but a host with a heart of gold. He noticed Nazreem looking disconcertedly at the sea of brown faces and at the street names written in both English and Bengali.

'This is ... like a ghetto?' she said.

'I suppose, but the word has too many negative connotations these days. I prefer to think of it as the historical equivalent of an airport arrivals lounge.'

'I don't understand.'

Marcus smiled. 'Well, it's called Brick Lane because back in the middle ages there were fields here where workmen dug the clay to make London bricks. They didn't build houses on any scale until after the Great Fire of 1666. Once they did, because the area was so close to the docks, it became a bedding-in zone for new immigrants.

'Back in the seventeenth and eighteenth centuries they were mostly Huguenot Protestants, expelled from Louis XIV's fervently Catholic France. In the late eighteenth and early nineteenth centuries it filled up with eastern European Jews, fleeing the pogroms. And from the early twentieth century onwards Bengali seamen off tea clippers from Calcutta began to settle here. Gradually the community grew until just after the Second World War they opened Britain's first "Indian" restaurants. It has been a magnet for others ever since so that now the dominant community is Muslim. The Brick Lane area is now home to the biggest community of Bangladeshi Muslims outside Southeast Asia. The locals call it Bangla Town. You see that building on the corner, the one with the sundial protruding from high up on the wall?'

Nazreem looked in the direction he was pointing and saw a big, old-looking building of stone and brick with what looked like Arabic on a board that was just too far for her to read. 'Yes?'

'The whole history of this part of the East End is summed up by that building. When it was built in 1743 it was a Huguenot church; by the end of the nineteenth century it had become a prominent synagogue. It's now a mosque. There are shops around here that started life as French butchers, became kosher and are now halal. I like it. It's the sort of place that makes you understand why history matters.'

Priji's was in the middle of a line of similar-looking restaurants, but first Marcus took Nazreem into a newsagent opposite that also advertised itself as an off-licence and bought two bottles of cold Cobra lager from the cooler. 'A lot of the restaurants around her don't sell alcohol to avoid offending their Muslim customers but they don't mind if you bring your own,' he explained. 'Drink?'

Nazreem nodded with just a hint of a self-conscious smile: 'I'd love a little white wine. Hamas have banned all alcohol in Gaza.' Marcus chose a half bottle of Petit Chablis and said, 'This do?' She nodded again, blushing like a guilty schoolgirl.

When they entered Priji's, Ali himself was sitting by the kitchen door and immediately came over to greet them. He was a plump cheerful man with an accent that mixed broad East End cockney with just a hint of the subcontinent: ''Ow are you, Professor Fry,' – he always overstated Marcus's academic status and missed the nuance in his surname – 'and 'ow's your luvvly lady friend? Table in the window, or perhaps the corner, a bit more private?'

'The corner would be fine, Ali,' said Marcus, and let them be shepherded to a small table near the rear of the restaurant. A waiter brought menus and took the wine and beer away to open the bottles.

Marcus ordered starters, the famous chicken tikka masala as well as a couple of more authentically Bengali dishes including balti lamb, shorisha king prawns in chilli and mustard sauce and a garlicky lentil tarka dall. He was hungry. The service was quick and attentive. He sipped at the cold beer, while Nazreem sipped her white wine with her eyes closed. He waited for her to begin the conversation, but the starters arrived almost immediately. Nazreem picked up a pappadum, dribbled some mint yoghurt on it, raised it to her lips and then put it down again without eating.

'Do you want to talk about it?' Marcus said at last.

'Hmm?'

'What's going on … in your mind. Is it what happened in Gaza. This find of yours, the theft. I just wondered if you wanted to talk about it.'

She looked up at him and gave him a thin resigned smile.

'Of course. More than anything else.' But she didn't.

'In the paper,' prompted Marcus. 'They hinted that this find … was something rather special. Particularly for Christians.'

She gave him the same thin-lipped smile of resignation, accompanied by a slight shrug of the shoulders.

'Who knows? Who knows what to believe?'

'How did it happen?' Marcus tried, then sensing from her frown that he had trodden on sensitive territory he retracked, 'the find, I mean? The paper seemed to imply that the context dated it to the first century.'

Nazreem took a long sip of her wine and leaned forward. 'That much is indisputable,' she said. All of a sudden, as if the memory itself had reinvigorated her, she began talking quietly, briskly as if reliving the moment itself:

'It was just to the north of Gaza City itself, a place the Israelis call Tel a-Shakef, a sensitive location. Not so long ago it was an Israeli army base before they pulled out of Gaza. About three weeks ago bulldozers went in, to clear away rubble. The road leads towards

Erez, the crossing point. They were pushing back the drifting sand when they came across old stones, paving, very obviously ancient not modern.'

Marcus was struck by how her mood had changed. Archaeology was her life blood.

'They stopped work immediately – it does not take much to make them stop work,' she added with a pertinent look. 'The foreman sent someone to the museum, to ask for advice. In the past, during the occupation, the Israeli archaeologists would have been all over it. We were lucky. If you can describe anything that happens in Gaza as luck.

'I went with some workers, a few volunteers. It did not take much to discover we had found an old Christian church, a *very* old church.'

'Not from the first century?' Marcus looked puzzled. The early Christians had met in private homes. Under the Roman persecution they had gathered in caves and cellars. Purpose-built churches didn't start to appear in any number until the Romans did a U-turn when the Emperor Constantine made it the state religion in the fourth century.

'No, of course not,' Nazreem said dismissively. 'The uppermost ruins included a beautiful mosaic floor – the sand dunes had protected it – that inscriptions made clear dated from the reign of the Emperor Justinian in the sixth century. They were all in Greek of course; that was effectively the official language of the eastern Roman Empire by that date. It appeared the church was dedicated to St Julian.'

Marcus made a face: 'I'm afraid I'm not very good on my saints.'

Nazreem shrugged. 'Obviously, nor am I, but my Egyptian colleague, a Coptic Christian, reckoned it had to be St Julian of Anazarbus, a Roman citizen of senatorial rank who was born in what is now Turkey and put to death around the end of the third century during the persecutions of the Emperor Diocletian. Sealed in a sack of vipers and thrown into the sea.'

'Nice.'

'But that church was built on top of one that was even older, and others beneath that. It had obviously been a holy place for many centuries.'

Marcus was impressed: 'The Coptic Christian church was allegedly founded by the apostle Mark shortly after the crucifixion. But I'm surprised you kept digging after making a find like that.'

Nazreem shrugged and sighed, 'It was an accident. You know sometimes how our workmen are. One of them was trying to move the bulldozer out of the way, when the ground beneath it suddenly dropped. The weight had obviously collapsed some subterranean chamber, possibly part of a crypt.'

Marcus winced. It was exactly the sort of thing archaeologists dreaded: their own interventions spoiling the evidence. Nazreem closed her eyes an instant in tacit acknowledgement of his understanding.

'Anyhow,' she said, 'part of the layer below was still a void, although we still haven't quite worked out its relationship to the church above. Initially we thought we'd hit a treasure trove – there were large numbers of coins.' She almost laughed: 'My biggest fear was that the workers would start to pocket them, when their main importance was to help the dating.'

'And they did?'

She nodded: 'Almost all from the reign of the Emperor Tiberius.'

'Suggesting the early part of the first century.'

She nodded. 'That was when we found the casket. I had to fight to stop the workmen dragging it out. I suppose they thought it had more treasure inside. That's when we noticed the inscription: not in Greek, but in Latin. Older therefore. Just two words: *Regina Coeli*.'

Marcus whistled under his breath: 'The Queen of Heaven.'

'We took it out carefully. You can imagine, didn't even open it on the spot. Some of the workers got restless, thought we were making off with treasure. I had to point out the writing, that it was a religious artefact, a Christian thing. I don't know if they believed me. It was only when we got back to the museum that we opened the casket.'

'And found …? Come on … don't keep me in suspense.'

'An image, a graven image. Female. The workmen sneered at it.' Marcus wasn't surprised: Islam forbade any depiction of human beings or animals, let alone the divine or semi-divine. Idolatry was a cardinal sin. 'The location would suggest that it could be a Madonna and the date would make it the earliest known. But obviously we wanted to date it definitely before revealing it to the world.'

'But you didn't get the chance. Somebody leaked.'

She shrugged, a bitter, half-hearted little shrug.

'Isn't it obvious?'

Marcus looked at her quizzically. All of a sudden there was that glazed hardness again in her eyes.

'I'm sorry,' he said. 'Maybe I'm missing something, but it's not obvious to me.'

'Mossad.'

'Mossad?'

'The Israeli secret service,' she spat out the words.

'I know who Mossad are, I just don't see why ...'

'Why? Because they want it for themselves, that's why! Because they will claim it was theirs all along, like everything else. Like the grains of sand on the beach, the air that we breathe, because they will leave us nothing of value, and if possible nothing at all, least of all our history, our decency or our self-respect! Do you think they want Gaza to become a shrine?'

'Wait a minute,' said Marcus, trying to calm her down and at the same time taking in the implication. 'You think this really could be a picture of the Virgin Mary done from life?' He found it hard to keep the incredulity out of his voice. Most Madonna figures were mediaeval, although he vaguely thought he had heard of one or two dating from the dark ages.

The waiter appeared to clear the pickles and bring the main courses. He looked disappointedly at Nazreem's half-nibbled pappadum but set out a tempting array of dishes on the plate warmers in front of them. Marcus helped himself though he could not help being annoyed that the arrival of the food had disrupted Nazreem's chain of thought. She had sunk back into herself, taken just a small portion of chicken and rice and was pushing it around on her plate. Then, just as he was trying to think of a way to bring her out of it again, she leaned forward and looked him straight in the eyes, asking in a quiet voice:

'Marcus, would you call yourself a religious person?'

He was taken aback. Religion was a topic they had never discussed, not on a personal level at least, only insofar as the subject permeated the politics of the Middle East, as a denominator of race and politics rather than a matter of conscience.

'No. Not really.'

'But you are Christian.' It wasn't a question.

'I suppose so, culturally at least.'

'And a Roman Catholic?'

'No, not at all, more a sort of lapsed Calvinist, really.'

'That is a schism, a sect, like the Shi'ites? You must forgive me, I am not very aware of these things. It is why I need advice. That means Protestant?'

'Yes, absolutely. Sort of the original Protestants, you might say: after John Calvin. In my case, it's a South African thing. A lot of the Boer settlers who went out there were Dutch Calvinists. Bigoted bastards, most of them.'

'These are your own people you are talking about.'

He gave a little laugh: 'In a way. Ancestors maybe, but things change – we evolve, you know, even white men. That's what I write about. Remember?'

'I'm sorry, I know. It's just that, out there – at home – things are different. It is not so easy sometimes, to criticise your own people, even when they do terrible things.'

She looked around her, but no one was paying them any attention. Marcus picked up her meaning. Britain's Muslim community had been shocked and damaged by the discovery that the four young men who had carried out the July 2005 suicide bombings that killed fifty-two Londoners were from second-generation immigrant families. But Nazreem knew only too well what it was like to have people you knew to be serious, kind, sensible human beings turn themselves into suicide bombers on the promise of martyrdom.

'Do Protestants believe in the Virgin Mary? The way the Catholics do, who call her the Mother of God?'

Marcus took a forkful of curry and a swig of cold lager to chase the heat: 'No,' he said. 'That is, I mean, yes, sort of. We – they – believe she existed all right and was the mother of Jesus.'

'But for you Jesus was not just a prophet, as the Muslims believe, he was also a god, I thought.'

'Well, yes, the son of God, anyway, although it's sort of supposed to be the same thing. Somehow.'

Nazreem looked at him questioningly:

'So Mary is the wife of God? Or the mother?'

Marcus took another sip of cold Cobra. He hadn't been expecting a theological debate: 'It's not quite like that. Well, I suppose it is and it isn't. It's all to do with the Holy Trinity, the three-in-one. God the Father and God the Son are the same. Only different. And then there's the Holy Ghost.'

'A ghost? Like a dead person?'

'No, quite the contrary, or sort of. It's also called the Holy Spirit, the third part of the Trinity.'

'But not the mother? Or the wife, or whatever?'

'Eh, no. I mean, it's complicated. Didn't you learn any of this at school, or from your mother at least?'

'No. The only thing we are taught about other religions in Muslim schools is that they are wrong. My mother, you must remember, died when I was very young. I was brought up by my father's family. In deference to her wishes, they gave me an education, but it was an Arab education: I know about Jesus – we call him Isa – who was a prophet, and his martyrdom. And the legend of his virgin birth, but not these Christian things: about who is related to whom. It all sounds like … do you say "incest"?'

Marcus spluttered into his beer: 'No. I don't and I don't advise you to either, but I know what you mean. Look, I'm not the person to explain any of this to you. You need a theologian: a Catholic one. Has this got something to do with the theft from the museum, the picture of the Madonna? Do you seriously think it might have been the original?'

'You mean there is an original?'

Marcus shrugged: 'There is a legend that the earliest image of the Virgin Mary, the first icon if you like, was painted by one of the apostles, St Luke, on her kitchen table.'

'This is true?'

'I doubt it, but that's the legend. There are pictures of him painting her, from the Middle Ages. There's a particularly famous one by some Dutch artist or other. In a gallery in Munich, I think. Anyway that's why St Luke is the patron saint of artists.'

'Strange. Sometimes I think Christianity is very strange.'

'Yes, well, some parts of it seem pretty strange to me too at times. But like they say, it takes all sorts.'

Nazreem gave him a look that implied she wasn't sure about that: 'Tell me, in this painting, what colour is she?'

'What colour? Mary, you mean? White of course. She probably looked exactly like a fifteenth-century Dutchwoman, most likely one of the artist's mistresses.'

'Not black?'

'No,' Marcus almost laughed. Marcus thought of the Afrikaner women of his childhood who wore big hats to protect their pale skins from the sun that even after four generations their genes had not adapted to accommodate. Dutch-descended women who would have been horrified that anyone might think they had even a drop of Negroid blood in their veins. And then something occurred to him:

'There is a famous black Mary in a church in Soweto, though, painted in the 1970s.'

Nazreem waved the comment away: 'But this is not something ancient, more a modern statement, I think, political correctness?'

Marcus visualised the fine mural on the church wall, and its poignant expression of universal humanity and suffering, seemingly timeless but also so obviously a product of its time and place, the features of the mother and child so obviously African.

'I suppose so,' he said.

'But there are other black Madonnas, aren't there? Real ones.'

'Well, you could say ...' he was about to question what she meant by 'real' in the context of religious iconography, but Nazreem was not listening.

'Old ones, worshipped for hundreds of years.'

'You're serious about this, aren't you?'

Nazreem nodded, her eyes big, dark and fiercely concentrated, with not a trace of a smile on her face. She was serious all right. More serious than he had ever seen her before.

'Yes, yes there are. Quite a few of them in fact. In Poland, Spain, places like that.'

'And people make pilgrimages to see them.'

'Yes, I suppose they do. The late Pope John Paul II had a lot to do with it of course. He was very keen on the cult of Mary. And then there was the black Madonna of Czestochowa ...'

'Jemster ... what?'

'Czestochowa,' he repeated, spelling it out. 'It's in Poland, pronounced "Chen-stok-ova". Lech Walesa, the leader of the free trades union Solidarity back in the eighties used to wear a lapel pin with her image. He believed – and probably the pope did too – that the virgin, in that particular incarnation, would save them from communism in the end.'

'And they think it worked?'

'Well maybe it did. Or maybe just the fact that people believed it did the trick.'

'Trick?'

'Trick, miracle, whatever you want to call it. Sometimes believing in something helps make it happen.'

'Sometimes. Maybe.' She looked thoughtful for a moment, then took a forkful of chicken curry and washed it down with a swig of the wine, and said: 'I need to see her.'

'What? A painting of the Madonna? Why?'

'One of the figures, one of the oldest ones, the very oldest. Why are they black, when the later pictures show her as white?'

Marcus was taken aback. 'I don't know. I think the reason most people accept is that they have spent centuries wreathed in holy smoke.'

Nazreem gave him a quizzical look as if to see if he was joking.

'Candles. Incense and stuff. Spend a couple of centuries in an airless room with tallow burning all around you and you'd be pretty black too.'

Her eyes narrowed.

'I'm not exactly white.'

Marcus sighed. The face across the table from him was an almost perfect golden café crème, the sort of complexion people not born with it might spend fortunes trying to achieve. The sort of face people looked at. The way the group of men who had just come in through the door were looking at her now. Except not like that at all.

And certainly not the way the waiter they were speaking to had begun to look at her as he made his way deliberately towards them, ignoring a diner at another table who tried to catch his attention. All of a sudden Marcus was aware that a second waiter had materialised just behind them and had put his hands on the back of Nazreem's chair.

'Are you all right?' she said, catching the sudden switch in his attention. Then she became aware of the man standing behind her. 'Is something wrong?'

Something was very wrong. The waiter was paying no attention to anyone but the men at the door, as if he was waiting for some sort of instruction. One of them, with a thin beard and dark sunglasses, was suddenly familiar. Marcus watched him put his hand inside his jacket; it didn't look as if he was reaching for his wallet.

He grabbed Nazreem by the elbow and pulled her to her feet, shouting 'Run!' as he pushed her past the waiter at his elbow towards the kitchen. The waiter thrust out an arm to stop her. Marcus pushed him hard on the shoulder sending him backward towards his colleague. The man behind him – and those behind him – lunged forward. Without thinking Marcus seized the cast-iron platter on the table, still hot but no longer sizzling, and hurled it with its cargo of steaming prawns in chilli and mustard into his face. The man howled and reeled backwards. Behind him there was pandemonium as his friends recoiled, tipping over tables, sending the other diners into screams of outrage that turned to terror at the sight of the gun in his hands.

Marcus pushed Nazreem through the swing door into the kitchen, into a scene of steam, burning gas rings and clattering pans. One of the cooks rushed forward to block their way. Marcus elbowed him in the face and pushed Nazreem past. Ali, the proprietor, was standing by a large saucepan with a ladle at his lips: 'Professor? Wot the …?'

His words were broken off by the commotion building in the restaurant. 'Trouble, mate. I'm sorry. Not our fault. The back door, where is it?' Marcus thrust two twenty-pound notes into his hand. The chef clutching his nose stared at them a split second then at the man with the beard and gun forcing his way into the kitchen.

In a second Ali had taken the money out of Marcus's hand, pushed over two twenty-kilo sacks of Basmati rice into the gunman's path and flung a ladle of sauce at him. Dragging Nazreem behind him, Marcus dashed for the open rear door, pulling pots and pans off the shelves to litter the floor behind him. As they gasped the damp night air they heard the voice of one of the waiters: 'Boss, no, they must not get away. The imam commands!'

Amid the bedlam Ali's reply was wholly unmistakable: 'Not in my fucking kitchen, he doesn't.'

15

'I can tell you one thing,' said Marcus as they ran down the alleyway behind the curry house, 'whoever that lot were, it wasn't Mossad, not unless they've started taking orders from a different set of clergy.'

Nazreem said nothing. She was panting, out of breath and clearly in shock. The night was cold after the heat of the day and the thunderstorm that followed, and she was shivering. From behind them the noise of clanging kitchen implements and shouting voices grew louder. It would only be a matter of minutes at most before there were people on their tail.

The curry house kitchen emptied into a warren of old artisan's yards, one darkened shed proclaimed itself a computer graphics workshop, another, lit from within, had adverts for Bollywood movies on the windows, another was semi-derelict with rusted meat hooks hanging from collapsing rafters. Outsize commercial wheelie bins overflowed with pungent kitchen waste and debris from cardboard packaging, most of it reduced to mush by the recent rainstorm. Marcus trod in something squishy and organic and tried to ignore it.

Angry shouts from the depths of the kitchen behind them were followed by an ear-splitting clatter and something that might or might not have been a gunshot. He grabbed Nazreem and pulled her after him, through the yard and out into the street, at right angles to Brick Lane, and then right again, away from the busy thoroughfare where more of the Beard's best friends might be waiting in front of the restaurant.

The streets were darker here, no garish shop fronts or pestering restaurant touts to get in the way. The little brick houses, most of them 300 or more years old, allowed brief glimpses through partly shuttered windows of Georgian interiors, some original and dilapidated, others expensively restored. There was a pub a few doors away but the doors were shut and there was little noise coming out. Then the bright lights of Brick Lane again, but if they were to get back to the car they would have to cross it.

'Wait,' he told Nazreem. 'I'll go first. The restaurant's farther up and they'll be looking for a couple. If nobody comes at me, wait until I've turned the corner and follow me.' With more than a little apprehension he strode out into the busy street, and crossed it without incident. A single man was an unpromising target for the curry touts; besides, most people's attention was diverted by the commotion. As he slipped around the corner into Fournier Street, he halted in horror. Almost immediately Nazreem was at his side.

Marcus motioned her back against the wall and gestured with his head. She followed his gaze and saw the car, as mercilessly illuminated as an ageing model on a catwalk. Banks of floodlights had been turned on to light up the soaring tower of Christ Church picking out its glistening white stone like some giant ivory dagger against the night sky, but also making it totally impossible to get to the car without being noticed. Then his heart sank further when he realised it would do them little good even if they could. The Peugeot was listing unnaturally and thanks to the brilliant illumination he could clearly see the reason: both of the offside tyres had been slashed.

He cursed himself for a fool. Obviously if they had traced them to Brick Lane, they must have somehow followed them in the car. And made certain they would not get away in it.

In the distance a police siren sounded, coming closer. From around the corner in the bright lights of Brick Lane came screaming in Bengali, then the one word repeated in English: 'Murder, Murder.'

Marcus pulled Nazreem towards him, out of the spill of light, instinctively flattening them into the high arched doorway of the building they were standing against, as if in the hope that it might open and offer them sanctuary. But the door was firmly locked. He looked up and realised where they were: outside the mosque that had once been a synagogue and before it a church. From the wall above his head an ancient sundial protruded, above it a two-word Latin inscription: '*Umbra sumus*'. We are shadows.

All of a sudden the spotlights were extinguished and the darkness swallowed them.

16

The difference between day and night is not what is used to be in the modern world. The sun's rays never entered the fifth-storey office in the grey granite slab on Millbank where Sebastian Delahaye was whiling away what for those outside were the hours of darkness. There were no windows from which to savour the view across the Thames to Lambeth Palace or along the Embankment to the Houses of Parliament. If there had been, Delahaye would not have noticed; he had his own windows on the world. Thousands of them open upon the streets of London alone.

There were eyes everywhere and he could look through any of them. As a senior field coordinator of the intelligence service – and a man with a classical education – Sebastian Delahaye liked to joke privately he had more eyes than Argus Panoptes, the hundred-eyed watchman of the Greek god Zeus. Argus was the name he had given to the multilayered computer program that could gain immediate access to any of them.

The powers it wielded had not come cheap. But the cost had been spread thinly. Surveillance cameras on motorway bridges had been paid for by the Highways Authority for the sake of safety, at ATMs by the banks to deter fraud, in shopping malls by the retailers to deter shoplifters and pickpockets, at pedestrian crossings and on street corners by local councils working with police to reduce accidents and street crime, in London by the socialist mayor keen to cut traffic levels with his congestion charge.

Britain's surveillance society had arguably grown from a single incident. In 1993 cameras at the Bootle Strand shopping centre outside Liverpool picked up crucial images of toddler Jamie Bulger being led away by the two ten-year-olds who were to murder him. That was followed by the 1994 Home Office paper entitled 'CCTV- Looking Out for You' and a mushrooming of cameras in every town and city, on every 'dangerous' bend on a country road or pedestrian crossing in a rural village. Civil liberties groups estimated that the number of surveillance cameras in the United Kingdom was in excess of six million, or one for every ten members of the population.

In the days that followed the London bombings of 7 July 2005, surveillance cameras had identified the four British Muslims – three of them born and bred in Yorkshire – who had fallen under the spell of Al Qaeda – and murdered fifty-two of their fellow citizens. They also tracked down another gang of intended suicide bombers two weeks later, but when it came to action on the ground, the police instead misidentified and killed an innocent Brazilian plumber.

The advocates of surveillance, who included Sebastian Delahaye, insisted that error was human but surveillance remained efficient. That efficiency was being put to the test right now. As first reports of a killing in London's volatile Bangladeshi community had come in, Delahaye had begun doing what he did best: sifting and collating.

For the better part of three months Delahaye's department had been keeping loose but strict tabs on the movement of a man known as Sidi Al Barani, an Algerian granted political asylum from his country's military regime after the rigged elections there in 2002, despite being known as a dedicated Islamic fundamentalist. Since his arrival in Britain Al Barani had taken pains to keep on the right side of the law, avoiding the outspoken Muslim clerics who attracted police and media attention with their virulent anti-Jewish sermons and praise for suicide bombers.

But those who worried the security services more were the ones who kept a deliberately low profile while maintaining links to more sinister figures abroad, the ones who flew below the radar. It was they who prepared the 'specials', the sleepers who laid in wait. They were the ones to watch. Sidi Al Barani was one of them.

Active monitoring of his movements had been stepped up after he was seen meeting with a young Iraqi, one of the rare few who came to Britain after the war that toppled Saddam but subsequently returned home. A young Iraqi reliably understood to be a courier for the shadowy figure who gloried in the cover name of Saladin, a man high on the West's wanted list, believed to consider even Osama bin Laden a spent force.

Signals had rippled up and down the intelligence community like an electric current when Al Barani had set off in his trademark black Mercedes and sunglasses for Heathrow only hours earlier. It was unlikely – given his status – that he was intending to leave the country, there being few others that would have welcomed him. The possibility, therefore, had to be that he was meeting someone else. And someone Al Barani wanted to meet was someone British intelligence wanted to get to know too.

His appearance at Terminal 3 posing as a chauffeur waiting for a M. Joliet from Tangier had caused mild amusement, but also a thorough scrutiny of all known databases for anyone whose real or cover name was Joliet with a record of travel to Morocco. The discovery of a middle-aged Marseille businessman of that name with a business importing merguez sausages was received for a few minutes with some excitement but quickly dismissed, especially when the young female agent deployed on the spot reported that despite the placard, Al Barani had not met M. Joliet nor anyone else; he had not even waited for the arrival of the flight from Tangier.

In fact, according to the MI5 agent who had been watching Al Barani at Heathrow, it appeared their target was engaged on a surveillance operation of his own. The object of his interest she reported was an arriving passenger, a pretty, dark-haired woman of Mediterranean appearance met by a Caucasian male in his mid-thirties. Neither had employed routine counter-surveillance techniques.

On the recorded images from the airport cameras Delahaye could make out his own agent at the coffee shop in the background paying no obvious attention to anyone or anything except prattling aimlessly into her mobile. A few metres in front of her was the unmistakable figure of Al Barani holding his placard for the spurious M. Joliet. And in front of him stood a good-looking, tousle-haired man with a furrowed brow and an apprehensive expression staring directly at Sebastian Delahaye, or rather at the terminal's arrivals board above which the camera was situated.

So that was 'Professor' Marcus Frey. Delahaye let the name roll over his tongue as he often did when he first learned the identity of whichever of the grains of sand on the digital beach had been chosen by fate to come to his attention. The name had been provided by the head waiter in the Brick Lane curry house where the killing had taken place. He had been an 'occasional regular', someone the late owner – 'Mister Ali' they all called him – had made a fuss over. The waiter said he was a professor from Oxford University, an important man. No, he did not know what his connection was to the gunmen.

But he thought for certain it had been 'the professor' they were after, and not Mister Ali.

It had not taken Delahaye long to ascertain that the man was telling the truth. There was indeed a Marcus Frey who held a position at Oxford. He was not actually a full professor but a Fellow of All Souls, a South African who had written a controversial book about the Middle East, which might or might not have been relevant. Until now he had made no appearance on Delahaye's radar at all, and yet here he was twice in one day, linked to a man about whom they thought they knew everything. For the man on the screen in front of him, standing in the arrivals hall at Heathrow, was unquestionably the same man as the South African-born historian in the passport photograph in a tabbed browser window on the screen to his left.

The identity of the woman, however, was for the moment a mystery. She was wearing a headscarf, not wrapped tight in the traditional Muslim way but sufficiently to obscure her face from the cameras mounted above, save for one brief, tantalising moment when she stood on her toes and looked up at the professor to give him a remarkably chaste peck on the cheek. Indeed the whole meeting was indescribably gauche. Delahaye had suspected – as he usually did in male-female encounters – that the pair were lovers. Watching their greeting to each other he decided that was a mistake.

He watched Al Barani's head swivel as she came through the sliding door. The swivel any man's head might make when a beautiful woman came into sight. But not quite. His interest was definitely more than sexual. Delahaye frowned.

Delahaye turned back to the screen on his right, clicked the tab button on the corner of his customised Argus browser to call up another image from the queued files that had been hurriedly patched together. This from the camera installed just below the roof-line of the newly restored Hawksmoor church in the East End, close to the scene of the shooting. Installed to deter graffiti artists from defacing the pristine white walls, it usefully also contained within its scan and pan field the main entrance of the one time church, now mosque, opposite.

The image on Delahaye's screen was timed at 21.58 the previous evening. It showed a remarkably clear view of the wall of the Hawksmoor church on one side and a row of terraced houses on the other ending in the staid bulk of the mosque. Pressed into its doorway, were two figures. Seconds later, in the zoomed, cropped and enhanced image, Delahaye could see the expressions on their faces: a panicky desperation on the clearly identifiable Frey and a pretty, dark-haired young woman with a look that was not so much of fear as of hard anger on her face. The headscarf was pushed back, her hair awry. Now that he could for the first time see her face clearly Delahaye felt there was something about her that was familiar, although for the life of him he could not say what or why.

The counter at the bottom of the image clicked over to 22.00 and the bright image disappeared into darkness. Delahaye cursed. That was bloody environmentalists for you: saving the planet by turning off a few floodlights. The camera quickly began to readjust to the diminished lighting, then became a blur as its sensors reacted to the rotating flasher on a police car roof. The couple in the doorway were gone.

He switched tabs again to the last image, which Argus's facial recognition software gave an eighty-five per cent probability (it worked better with two faces together) as being the same couple, in the entrance hall of Liverpool Street Underground station, some forty-five minutes after the incident in the restaurant.

He clicked back to the airport arrivals image from the morning and scrolled the camera timeline forward to the moment when Frey's passenger emerged to greet him. Rear view. Difficult at first. He switched to the view from the camera opposite, mounted on the currency exchange booth, but the pan was wrong, the angle too oblique. Back again, a few seconds further down the timeline, the image was better, a profile shot. He nodded his head appreciatively. Definitely the same girl in all three captures. Good-looking. Probably early thirties. Dark, shoulder-length hair, with a headscarf worn more like a Western-style fashion accessory than a token of Islamic orthodoxy.

A quick check of the Heathrow Terminal 3 online arrivals list for the relevant time window offered Osaka, Lagos and Mumbai as possible embarkation points for the woman, but also Cairo and Kuwait as well as a delayed flight from Istanbul – why did she seem familiar, and where, if anywhere, did she fit into the bigger picture? The trouble was, Delahaye mused, as he scrolled the video footage from the Heathrow camera forward, frame by frame, that he was no longer at all sure what the bigger picture was going to look like. It was as if he was collecting ever more pieces of a jigsaw puzzle, but had lost the photograph on the lid.

He turned his head back to the single screen in the room that was displaying data rather than images and scrolled once again through the information the system had collected on Frey: thirty-five years of age, South African by birth, Rhodes Scholar at Magdalen College, Oxford, currently research fellow in comparative historiography – whatever that was – at All Souls. Not a professor, but an academic of some standing nonetheless, with a couple of books to his name, notably the one on the Israeli-Palestinian conflict which had aroused anger in Jewish circles, although it had been praised as remarkably impartial by non-partisan reviewers.

Delahaye was not a huge fan of the ivory towers and their left-leaning inmates but Frey wasn't an obvious reason to be an assassination target for a bunch of mad mullahs. Something here didn't look right on the face of it. If, Delahaye wondered, glancing sidelong once more at the strangely familiar picture of the girl, he was looking at the right face. Given Al Barani's interest wasn't it more likely she had been the target, not him?

A glass chime announced the arrival of an incoming instant message. A small avatar of cartoon punk announced it was from the indefatigable Chloe, working late again – or was it early by now – the sort of information scientist who made her business seem like a black art: 'Still chasing more stuff on this guy, Frey,' she said, 'but a few things popped straight out of the hat. I took a quick skim, but decided you'd probably want to take a look yourself. We may have found the connection.'

17

The sun rose pale and watery in a flaccid sky dimly glimpsed through grimy net curtains. Marcus opened his eyes wide and saw Nazreem's dark hair spread across a candlewick coverlet. They were both fully clothed.

As pandemonium engulfed Brick Lane, they had abandoned the now useless car and ducked back into the side streets behind Spitalfields Market. There were three Tube stops within running distance. But the two closest, Aldgate and Aldgate East, were on lines with fewer trains; the last thing they wanted was to be trapped on an Underground platform. Marcus still had the sound of the gunshot ringing in his ears, followed by the scream of 'Murder'. Someone had died, and he was sure it had been intended to be one of them. Or both.

Dashing into the station, they had gone down to the Central line platform, deliberately ignoring the Metropolitan and Circles lines that also ran through Aldgate or Whitechapel. Nazreem had surprised him by producing a pre-paid London Transport Oyster card. He wondered where she had got it, but now wasn't the time to ask. They travelled three stops to Chancery Lane, a station that was bustling in daytime but relatively quiet out of business hours and got out onto the platform alone. Sure for once that this time they had not been followed, they climbed the stairs to the street. They were within walking distance of their hotel but one thing was clear to both of them.

It was Nazreem who said it first walking down Holborn in the late evening drizzle: 'We can't go back.'

Marcus nodded. That much was obvious. Marcus had used his credit card to pay upfront for their rooms and had left nothing in his room, not even a toothbrush, not having planned to spend the night away from Oxford. Nazreem, however, was different.

'What about your things?' he asked. 'Your clothes, the big bag, all those books?'

She simply shook her head: 'It's not a problem.'

'It's not?'

'While … while you were resting, at the hotel, I … I went out.'

Marcus let her talk. Maybe she was going to come clean with him at last. It was about time. Whatever was going on in her life it wasn't another man. Not unless he was extremely jealous.

'I took the books to the person they were intended for, at the British Museum. I meant to tell you. It's just, it didn't seem …'

'Important?' Marcus smiled. It made sense, sort of.

'Yes, it was just an errand. That's when I got the travel card.'

Marcus's smile faded. He had seen her get into a taxi. But then perhaps she had picked up the Oyster card on the way back. He let it ride. For the moment they had more pressing problems.

'What about everything else? Clothes, passport, money?'

She patted her shoulder bag. Everything I need is in here. The clothing is not important: just jeans, shirts. Remember, I live in Gaza. The dispossessed have few possessions.'

Marcus turned and grabbed her by the shoulders, gently but firmly, looking her straight in the eye.

'Nazreem, what's happening? Who were those people? Why are they after you?'

She sighed, deeply, a weary sigh that could have been fatigue or exasperation, and looked him direct in the eyes: 'I don't know. I really don't.'

'You realise they may have killed someone tonight.'

'The Israelis kill many … every day …'

'Nazreem, those were not Israelis. You heard them, for G …' he had been about to say 'for God's sake' but thought better of it. 'They had the waiters in the palm of their hands. One of them talked about an imam.'

She said nothing.

'We should go to the police.'

She said nothing.

'I mean it.'

'Do you? I am a Muslim, a Palestinian. How much time do you think the British police would give me?'

Marcus thought about it, and realised they would give her a lot more time than she imagined. Far more than she would want. Most of Britain's huge Muslim community were decent law-abiding folk who abhorred violence, but 9/11 and the Iraq war had polarised sections of society, even before the London bomb attacks sent a frisson of horror the length and breadth of the country threatening to destroy Britain's already fragile multi-ethnic consensus. The fact that most Islamic extremists cited the Palestinian situation as justification for terror would hardly help them.

'Come on, let's get out of here,' he said. 'We need to find somewhere to sleep. We can think about it in the morning.'

The guesthouses around Paddington were a step down even from the tawdry Country Hotel, but they asked no questions and were more than happy with cash. Nazreem looked askance at the double bed in the only room offered them, then lay down on it, curled into a foetal ball and within minutes was asleep. Marcus kicked off his shoes and lay next to her, flat on his back and stared at the ceiling for what seemed like hours until eventually sleep overtook him too.

Now, in the pallid light of morning he looked at the young woman still asleep next to him. He longed to put his arm around her, at least to stroke her hair, but he knew that to do so without invitation would be taking a liberty. Something had happened to her since he had last seen her, something worse than just this business with the missing icon or whatever it was. Something that had to explain why a gang of what appeared to be Muslim fundamentalists were trying to capture or kill her. And him if need be. And God knew who else.

He got up, splashed water on his face from the tap in the cracked porcelain sink, scribbled a quick note in case she awoke, slipped on his shoes and made his way quickly downstairs. A smell of sour coffee and bacon fat accosted him. He opened the front door and went out. From an Italian sandwich shop on the corner opposite he picked up two polystyrene cups of strong espresso and a couple of fresh buttered rolls. At the entrance to the Tube he found a copy of a special edition of *Metro*, a free commuter newspaper put together in the early hours. The splash headline grabbed his attention immediately: 'BRICK LANE SLAYING!'

The front-page picture showed a scene of urban chaos: red-striped police cars, flashing lights, people wildly gesticulating. Beneath was a photograph, several years out of date, of a face Marcus recognised: Ali, the restaurant owner. The report said he had been shot once, in the head. Three people had been arrested, two of them waiters at the restaurant, but it was not clear which, if any, was suspected of being the killer. The murder weapon had not been found. There were rumours of gang wars between rival groups of Bengalis and Pakistanis. Some eyewitnesses had spoken of a young woman involved, and a white man. Police were asking for others to come forward. They were continuing their inquiries.

Marcus cursed under his breath as he climbed the stairs back to their room. It was his fault Ali was dead. If he had not chosen that restaurant, if he had not over-reacted when the waiters began closing in on them ... No, that at least was not a mistake. Whatever they wanted with Nazreem, it was nothing good. They had not been carrying weapons for show; they had proved that.

When he opened the door, she was awake, sitting on the bed, staring at the carpet. She looked up when he came in and made an effort at a smile. He handed her the coffee and the roll. She set the roll aside but removed the plastic lid from the polystyrene cup and sipped at the hot, sweet coffee. He had ordered it with extra sugar, the way he knew she liked it. He was in two minds about showing her the paper; what had happened was no more her fault than his. He opened it at an inside page, folded it over and set it on the table. She lifted it anyway.

Marcus sat on the end of the bed, drank his coffee and ate his roll and waited for the exclamation. He did not have to wait long. Within seconds Nazreem gave a sharp intake of breath.

'It is not possible,' she exclaimed. 'This cannot have happened?'

Marcus sighed. What was he to tell her? That they had unwittingly caused an innocent man's death? That unless she came clean about whatever it was that his killers wanted from her – and he refused to believe she had no idea – then the same thing could happen again. He turned to face her, only to find that she was not looking at the front page of the paper at all, but at a story on the page to which he had casually folded it: a story on the foreign pages.

'Merchant of Death loses heart – literally!' the headline ran. 'In a bizarrely gruesome case, German police are investigating how the severed heart of an Islamist terrorist, wanted in connection with the Madrid and London bombings, turned up in a Bavarian monastery within hours of his death in an Israel suicide bombing.' He did a doubletake and read it again. It seemed bizarre all right, but he did not see how it affected them. The suicide bombing had taken place three days ago, he read, at Erez, the crossing point from Gaza into Israel.

'Horrible story, but Nazreem, I have to tell you, something as bad happened last night. A man was killed almost in front of our eyes. Killed by accident. It was you they were gunning for.'

She looked up at him with an expression of anguished resignation, and said quietly, 'I know, I know. But this. This is connected. I know it is. It is part of it.'

Marcus looked at her blankly. 'Part of what? You think this, this piece of butchery in Germany, is significant? I simply don't understand. Do you think this has something to do with the theft from the museum?'

'Yes. I don't just think it. I know it.'

'How? Why?'

'For a start it was because of the industrial area around Erez that they were working on the road.'

'I'm sorry, you're losing me. The road?'

'The road they were repairing when they came across the ruins of the church. The crossing is only a few miles at most from where we found the artefact,' said Nazreem. 'This is a signal, a message of some sort. We must go there.'

'Erez?' Marcus was confused.

'No, Germany. This place, this monastery: Altötting, in Bavaria. Now.'

'What? Why on earth …?'

But Nazreem was already on her feet, splashing water on her face and checking the contents of her shoulder bag. 'Don't you see,' she said impatiently. 'Read the rest of it.'

He did: 'Police said they had no idea what the link could be between the Middle East, and a little town known chiefly for its Roman Catholic shrine to the black Madonna.'

'You understand now?' said Nazreem.

Marcus shook his head. He didn't understand anything.

Nazreem reached out and took his hand with what was almost a look of pity.

'Now I know where this road is leading me, but you do not have to come with me.'

18

Sebastian Delahaye rubbed his eyes and looked at his watch. No wonder he was tired. It was gone seven a.m. It would be daylight out there. Real daylight, not just the images of it on the screens around the seventh-floor room, although, of course, strictly speaking those in real time were showing real daylight too.

There was a slow dull ache along his forehead. It was time he had the optician check him over again; he had already been warned about the dangers of constant screen work. The bulky cathode ray tubes had long since been banished, but having thin OLED screens only meant there was room for more of them. For the last four hours, however, he had sat glued to just one.

It had been fascinating work, though not as rewarding as he had hoped in the end. As he took another long look at the montage of images of Marcus Frey on the screen to his left, he realised he had acquired a grudging respect for the academic and analytical powers of the man. Even if he did not agree with his conclusions. Part of the problem of course, was working out exactly what the man's conclusions were. At least now he had a keen idea of what 'comparative historiography' meant. He should have realised just from the titles of Frey's books that this was a man few Islamic fundamentalists – and few Israelis either – would fail to have an opinion about. *Promised Land or Stolen Land: Israel versus Palestine* was not exactly a title that ducked controversy.

Frey had tried to take both sides, not in order to find a compromise, but to show how they had both ended up at the extremes. Delahaye could imagine there were hardline Zionists out there who accused Frey of 'moral equivalising', the sort of people who insisted the word 'Holocaust' could apply to one historical event only and that Palestine had been a 'land with no people'. Dr Frey was a man who liked going walkabout in political minefields, and not on tiptoes either.

Chloe, in her unfettered brilliance, had dug up all the published reviews including those from the *New Statesman*, the *Guardian*, *The Spectator* and *The Sunday Times*, as well as the *Rand Daily Mail*, *Jewish Chronicle* and several others. Most significantly she had also found a filleted copy of a brief done by the 'other lot', the boys and girls in their big green building on Vauxhall Bridge – popularly known as MI6. It was an analysis of Frey's work's impact on intellectual circles in the Middle East. Not great, was the conclusion, but not negligible either. For a young man he had made a bit of a splash. For Delahaye the question was whether it was big enough to drown him.

Chloe had also produced huge segments of the original text. Under an unpublicised agreement, all copies of new publications sent as required to the British Library were vetted by government advisers. Non-fiction with a political bent was scanned and made available online to a strictly limited government circulation. There was no point, as one of the techies commented when confronted with questions about copyright legislation, in waiting until it was all on Google.

Delahaye sat back in his chair and pursed his lips. The reviews were all generally positive of Frey's original approach, writing style, extensive research. It was in their interpretations that they differed. Or rather their interpretations of Frey's interpretations. The man had made his name by turning accepted viewpoints of recent history on their head, and then turning them back again to see if they still looked the same. For example, in his first book he had chosen to resurrect some now deeply unfashionable attitudes towards Nelson Mandela, recalling that the man universally regarded as a statesman and almost a saint had once been widely considered a terrorist. The problem that Frey concentrated on was that, although people now liked to say that it was only supporters of apartheid who thought like that, it was substantially accurate. Mandela had not only been an advocate of, but an active practitioner of what those who supported it called 'the armed struggle' but those on the other end called terrorism.

Frey showed how in the aftermath of apartheid the myths that both sides had not only believed, but cultivated had been first glossed over, then abandoned and finally rewritten. The result was a functioning consensus based largely on hypocrisy and self-deception. His less than wholly reassuring conclusion was that this was no bad thing, but just because it was a happy ending it should not form the basis of reputable historical study.

The second book, and this is where to Delahaye it got really interesting, dared to link 'South Africa's March to Freedom' with 'Israel's Right to Exist', both of which Frey controversially labelled 'slogans rather than facts'. Frey outlined in detail how the young Mandela's *Umkhonto we Sizwe* (Spear of the Nation) paramilitary wing of the African National Congress was modelled on Irgun, the Zionist action group labelled terrorists by the British in the 1940s, but that went on to provide mainstays of the Israeli army and government. Frey then 'squared the circle', as he called it, by comparing Mandela with Yasser Arafat and *Umkhonto we Sizwe* with the Palestine Liberation Organisation, making the harshly ironic point that at least an element of Palestinian tactics was based on those originally employed by Israeli Jews.

He went on to revise the familiar arguments about the right to exist of the Israeli state and how using history to decide land ownership depended on the choice of starting date. Israelis refuted Palestinian claims that they were land thieves by claiming it had been theirs in the first place, 2,000 years ago. But they rarely mentioned that their own holy book – the Christian Old Testament – was a story of the violent conquest of the indigenous Canaanites.

But Frey went too far, in Delahaye's mind, when he drew another parallel that he claimed lingered in many Muslim minds. He pointed out that the Spanish history of the 'Reconquista' – the reconquest of 'their' country and expulsion of the 'Moors' – was in Arab eyes the theft by barbarians of El-Andalus, the country they founded in the ruins of the Visigoth empire. Delahaye's head was spinning – he knew nothing about Visigoths and ancient Spanish history, but he knew this was not something that would go down well in Madrid in the wake of the 2004 Al Qaeda bombings that had killed 191 people and wounded 1,800 in the Spanish capital.

Might was usually right, Frey pointed out pithily, and control of the present equalled control of the past. The history most people learned in schools was not something that could be used to win an argument but more often a lie taught by those who had already won it. Delahaye breathed in, long and hard. Right now he could see why any number of people might think the world would be a better place if the likes of Dr Marcus Frey were removed from it.

He scrolled rapidly through the PDF file in which the book was displayed on his screen until he got to the author's 'acknowledgments' at the end, the list of people who had helped with his research. You never knew what links you might find. Immediately one name sprang out at him: Nazreem Hashrawi, described by Frey as 'providing invaluable research and insight into the Palestinian perspective'. The name set off a bell, a connection to something recent. On an impulse he opened a straightforward web browser and plugged the name into Google's image search. Within seconds he had the link he was looking for: there on the screen, resized in its original context on a news page from *The Times*, was the photograph of a young woman who, even with the headscarf pulled over her dark tresses, was unquestionably the same as the one captured by the surveillance cameras with Frey. Except she was not in London, she was in the Gaza Strip. Only days ago.

He linked through to the news story and shook his head. Whatever connection there might be between some missing religious artefact and this dangerous dabbling Oxford academic stirring up a hornet's nest of Islamic extremists in the East End of London he had no idea, but this woman was clearly his collaborator. Delahaye had questions he wanted answering. Fast. And Dr Frey was going to answer them. Sooner rather than later.

Within forty-five minutes details and pictures of both Marcus Frey and Nazreem Hashrawi were flashed to every police station in the capital – and every force in the country – with the clear instruction that the pair were wanted for questioning by the security services: detain with discretion, was the recommendation. The pair were not in themselves suspects and were not considered dangerous. Under no circumstances was force to be used. Unless absolutely necessary.

It was some two hours, however, before there was any sort of response. It came, once again, not from any human observation but from the 'isolate and identify' subroutine running on the Argus system. The identification was quite clear and confirmed from multiple cameras, all situated within the terminal building and departures lounge at Stansted Airport.

Part Two

… MATER DEI, ORA PRO NOBIS …
… Mother of God, pray for us …

19

Despite its ancient status as a place of pilgrimage the little Bavarian town of Altötting has remained curiously aloof from the automobile-centred infrastructure of modern Germany, in a rural backwater an hour and a half's drive east of Munich across the flat and relatively featureless floodplain of the River Inn.

'How come,' asked Marcus as he tried and failed to overtake yet another tractor on a blind bend in a two-lane road, 'that this place is about the only town in Germany that isn't on an autobahn?'

Nazreem made an attempt to smile, glanced at the map as if to make sure they were indeed going in the right direction, then turned back to gazing out at the flat, farmhouse-studded German country-side. They flashed by another of the little onion-domed churches which could almost have been Russian but it appeared were also a feature of old Bavarian architecture. Marcus considered mentioning the fact but thought better of it.

He had all but given up on trying small talk to break the apparently impenetrable outer crust that Nazreem had somehow thrown up around her. Their conversations were perfunctory, her attitude to him friendly, but, in some intangible way, cold. She shrank visibly from physical contact, even though he had made no attempt to re-establish any kind of intimacy.

It pained him, but at the same time he was more than aware that he had no real understanding of what pain he might once have caused her. At the time of their break-up it had seemed – to him – that they were both simply yielding to matters beyond their control: the different worlds they came from, the pull of their careers. And yet there had not been a moment in the years since when he had ever been one hundred per cent certain that he had made the right decision. 'What did it profit a man,' he had on maudlin occasions over a pint too many in the King's Arms in Oxford parodied the biblical saying, 'if he gained the whole world, but lost the woman who mattered more than anything else in it?'

Maybe he had made a mistake – maybe they both had – but it was not something that could be fixed at the flick of a switch, if it could be fixed at all. He had to make it clear to Nazreem that, no matter how precious or painful the past might be for either of them, the present did not have to depend on it. More than anything right now, he realised almost with a shock, he wanted her to think of him as a friend. A friend she could rely on.

She had come to him. She needed help; he was able to provide it. Or thought he had been. And now it had all gone horribly wrong. A man had died. They – or Nazreem at least – were being pursued by men who would not stop at murder. And he hadn't a clue why. All he knew was they were now in Germany, in a hire car heading for a place he had never heard of, for no other reason than it was home to an obscure religious relic and Nazreem was offering no explanation that went beyond an oblique and obstinate insistence that she was in search of answers to questions Marcus had not even begun to ask.

She had not insisted he come with her, but made clear she would welcome his company. A brief spell in an Internet café on the Euston Road found them surprisingly cheap flights to Munich on a no-frills airline from London Stansted. They had booked two for the same day for less each way than it cost on the train from Oxford to London. Marcus thanked the fact that growing up in South Africa meant he never went anywhere without his passport. And Nazreem was never separated from the French passport which was her most precious possession.

They had arrived in Munich in the middle of the afternoon and picked up a car, also booked in advance over the Internet. It occurred to Marcus that using his credit card opened an avenue for anyone trying to trace them. But it was Nazreem they were after, not him. He doubted if they even knew who he was.

The car was a Volkswagen Polo and surprisingly nippy for its size. They had got around the city quickly on the autobahn from the airport, only to find that it ran out barely thirty kilometres from the Munich ring road in the direction of Altötting. The only major city in the same direction was Passau on the Austrian border, and that was scarcely a metropolis; it appeared that a continuation of the autobahn was in planning, but not on anybody's priority list.

For the most part, the landscape they traversed was rich

agricultural land – borne witness by the infuriating number of trac-tors on the road – with red-roofed farmhouses and barns, and the occasional high-tech low-level factory thrown in. At one point thick forest closed in on them as if from nowhere, and then it opened out again. Two high, pointed spires in the distance finally indicated they were in sight of their destination. Just what they were going to do when they got there, however, was another matter.

Like most Bavarian towns Altötting's centre was largely pedes-trianised. Cafés filled with middle-aged women with big hair and traditional dresses eating slabs of cream cake with frothing cups of coffee competed with bakeries, bookshops and traditional Gasthofs where their menfolk supped half-litre glasses of *Helles* beer. A gang of noisy teenagers with nothing to do hung around on a street corner kicking skateboards about and making gauche sexual passes at one another. A couple of leather-clad bikers dawdled as if rapt in endless admiration of each other's big machine. It could have been any small town in Germany. Marcus pulled the car into a space at the end of a one-way street and they got out to find the tall spires they had seen from a distance towering above them.

It was easy to see the geographical, if not immediately the reli-gious, basis for Altötting's ancient rise to prominence. The heart of the town was a large plateau raised from the surrounding country-side, the sort of place that would have been a natural gathering place for centuries if not millennia. The streets leading up to and around the sides of the great square itself were lined with religious souvenir shops selling more kitsch than Marcus had seen since his first visit to the Arab bazaar in Bethlehem.

Images of saints in plastic, porcelain and pewter jostled with wooden carvings that were almost life-size. One image, of a bald, bearded monk in a Franciscan habit who appeared to be called Saint Konrad, a local monk canonised in the 1930s, vied for prominence on postcards with another local boy who was altogether more famil-iar: a sharp-eyed smiling man with iron-grey hair and intelligent eyes. Altötting's shopkeepers were keen to capitalise on the fact that Pope Benedict XVI had been born just down the road. It seemed the recent scandal over abuse in the Catholic Church had made little impact on the faithful of the Pope's home district.

Signs advertised the beginning of the Benediktweg, a tourist route around the sights of his boyhood, even Papstbier, the pope's beer – 'a heavenly brew'. Marcus found himself smiling despite his cynicism: what could be more natural in Bavaria, where the monks had been brewing for a millennium? He wondered if the pained look on Nazreem's face reflected her inner contradiction about adhering to a religion which forbade alcohol while she enjoyed the occasional glass of wine. Then he realised it was that other great taboo of Islam – the making of graven images – which was rather more obviously in her face.

Marcus felt obliged to apologise:

'Kitsch, isn't it? At least the Germans gave us a word for it.'

Nazreem looked at him questioningly.

'Bad taste, I mean. All this plastic.'

Nazreem shook her head, but not in disagreement. In the window in front of her a flock of cherubic angels with prayer books – for all the world like little gods of love who'd mislaid their bows and arrows, gone on the Atkins diet and taken up reading – dangled on strings above a football crowd of plastic Konrads. But it was not this grotesque scenario that had captured her attention. It was a large porcelain statue obviously supposed to represent the Holy Virgin. To Marcus it seemed a conventional enough image, a Madonna in a sky-blue robe with a complexion like ivory and a gentler rosy blush to her cheeks.

'It's just that …' Nazreem said, hesitantly, 'no woman from Palestine could ever have looked like that.'

Marcus smiled: 'No, I suppose not, but then nobody knows exactly what she looked like. Do they?'

She pointedly ignored the question. 'But they have always known where she came from, where she is supposed to have lived, what her origins were.'

'What would you have preferred?'

'It's … it's not a question of "preferring". It's just that I thought she might look, at least, a little bit … Semitic.'

Marcus raised his eyebrows: 'In Bavaria? I don't think so. I'll tell you something an old English teacher of mine back in Pretoria used to say when asked why our traditional image of God was always some genial English country squire or sturdy Afrikaner *Voortrekker*. He said, "What do you expect? We made him in our own image." I suppose that goes for his mother too.'

Nazreem gave him a scowl. 'That is why Muslims forbid images,' she said mock sternly. 'When I see things like this, I feel maybe we are right.'

'Maybe you are,' said Marcus. 'Let's go and see if we can take a look at the real thing. If you'll pardon the expression.'

The great square that spread out in front of them as they climbed the gentle cobbled hill seemed totally out of proportion for the little town it dominated. Here in bricks, mortar, soaring spires and gilded stonework stood the physical manifestation of centuries of ecclesiastical institutionalism, monastic seclusion and the temporal power of the spiritual establishment.

Yet like pilgrims down the centuries, Marcus and Nazreem found their attention drawn as if by psychic magnetism towards the tiny building that stood amidst a formally planted grove of linden trees in the middle of the vast open expanse, a strange octagonal chapel with a high, pointed witch's hat roof.

They drew near, the curious little building exerting on them the same power as it had on tens of thousands of others. Several dozen people were clustered around. Two of them, women in middle age, stood out from the crowd: each carried a large wooden cross over her shoulder and circled the building incessantly. Marcus and Nazreem stood in silence for a few minutes, watching this display of ritualised devotion.

'Just like Mecca,' muttered Nazreem at length.

Marcus looked at her.

'The pilgrims, during the Hajj, endlessly circling the Ka'aba.'

It was only when they came close to the canopied walkway that surrounded the chapel itself that they understood that what appeared to be a complex form of decoration was in fact hundreds of individual paintings.

'But this,' said Nazreem, 'this is strange.'

'Strange isn't the word,' said Marcus, under his breath. 'More like weird. It spooks me. This sort of thing always has.'

He wasn't sure what precisely made him so uncomfortable but it had something to do with the fusion of the sacred and absurd, the tragic and mundane. Here was a drawing by a child on a life-support machine, a terrible intimation of mortality suffused with innocent hope and faith; here a grittily realistic amateur oil of a soldier cowering by a tank tread, a token of thanks for safekeeping throughout the Second World War – but surely that had been the devil's war, hadn't it, and the soldier was on the wrong side? And here, from as recently as 1998, a painting of men in suits gesticulating at one another across a desk. Beneath it was a prayer of thanks to the Virgin for getting the artist through 'a very difficult investigation at work'. The Mother of God was a busy lady.

Each and every one depicted in the corner a dark-faced crowned figure with doll-like baby descending from the sky in glittering robes surrounded by a halo of power. Reduced to such naïve renderings they reminded Marcus of the American superhero comics of his youth: a stylised Wonder Woman to the rescue, with babe in arms – the modern miracle mother. He didn't know whether to laugh or cry.

Nazreem, on the other hand, was rapt, the expression on her face a mix of absorption and incredulity. To most Muslims, even Sunday-school pictures of Jesus appeared blasphemous. This 'painting by numbers' display of devotion to the 'Mother of God' must have seemed like pagan idolatry run rampant.

She shook her head. 'I don't understand it. I just don't understand it.'

'It's just a different tradition. We're used to pictures of Christ and Mary and the saints. That's why people couldn't understand all that fuss about the Danish cartoons of Mohammed. Why some people thought it was all played up by extremists.'

'It was.'

Marcus gave her a quizzical look. It was a subject he had been reluctant even to mention.

'The whole thing was distorted,' she said. 'People got annoyed – rightly – because the cartoons implied all Muslims were terrorists, but the extremists played up the fact that infidels had broken the ban on portraying images of the prophet because they knew images corrupt religion and they did not want infidels to corrupt Islam.'

'I'm not sure I follow …?'

'Mohammed' – and Marcus noted that although she didn't say it aloud, internally she had automatically repeated the mantra 'peace be upon him' – 'did not issue his ban on images of himself because he was vain! It was because he had looked around him and saw what was happening in Christianity at the time. This! He saw that the statues, the pictures had taken over from the idea, they had become idols, fetishes. In his lifetime people had begun to worship the objects, not what they represented. He banned pictures of himself, not because he was afraid of criticism, but because people might come to worship them. Isn't that what's happened here?'

Marcus looked around them, at the devout kissing crosses and genuflecting before entering the chapel. He reached out a hand to Nazreem, but she didn't notice. 'Want to go inside?' he said.

He watched her weigh it up for a few seconds, seeing that she had not fully realised she would be allowed – most of Islam's holiest places are off-limits to non-believers, and several others even to the most devout of the faithful, if they happen to be women. Then she nodded. He pushed open the door, and stood back to let her go in ahead of him.

She looked back at him, apprehensively, then, out of instinct covering her head with the scarf she had until then worn loosely around her neck, walked into the sacrosanct darkness. And Marcus realised, all of a sudden, that in more ways than one she was crossing a threshold.

20

Inside it was dark. The antechapel was windowless and the walls and ceiling were painted black, or perhaps had just been blackened over the centuries by the rows of thin, smoking devotional candles that provided the only illumination. There were more paintings like those outside the building, but older: dark, sombre antique depictions of miraculous deliverance.

Several people knelt at prayer in a row of little pews, one of them a nun in a black habit, another a monk in a brown cassock. Beyond the pews a small door led into the sanctum sanctorum, the original ancient octagonal chapel around which everything else had been constructed.

On the other side of it a few people stood with their heads bowed, silent or mumbling prayers under their breath as they fingered rosary beads.

'Go on in,' Marcus whispered in Nazreem's ear. 'It's okay. You don't have to do anything. We Christians are more tolerant than our reputation.'

But she shook her head and waited for him to lead the way.

For a moment Marcus hesitated. He was at a loss to know what was going through her mind, a secular Muslim suddenly confronted by an exhibition of Roman Catholicism at its most extravagant. He wondered if she had any idea until now how much impact her find beneath the sands of Gaza might have had on these people. She had made what might have been the discovery of a lifetime, then lost it before its true potential had even been evaluated. Like a child promised the best present on earth only to unwrap the parcel on Christmas morning to find an empty box.

He knew Nazreem had never been devout, but religion was part of the tissue of her society, as it was here, in this shrine to the religion of the French mother she had never known. Christianity and Islam had been enemies, but were also intertwined, as they both were with Judaism, the three 'peoples of the book'. Who had spent centuries tearing each other apart.

Had she really gazed upon the face of the woman hundreds of millions of people believed to have been the vessel chosen by the Creator to carry His incarnation in human flesh? Had she seen – and touched – the very first image of which all others, all these porcelain and plastic Madonnas were just phoney imitations conjured up by imperfect imaginations? Was that what some jealous madman had snatched away from her?

Or had she simply held in her hands an early example of the blasphemous idolatry which her own religion preached had corrupted the word of God as told to Abraham, Allah to Ibrahim? The intensity he read in her face was surely that of a woman who had for so long regarded religion as little more than a badge of ethnicity suddenly struck by a desire to seek the truth.

They entered the chamber together. Immediately Marcus was assaulted by the warmth, not just physical, from the proximity of other people and the vast number of candles but the suffusing aura of their radiant reflection in the riot of richly worked gold and silver that adorned every facet of the tiny octagonal space. Precious trinkets of noble metals encrusted with gemstones hung on every wall.

In front of them, almost overwhelming in its ostentation, stood the candle-decked altar itself set into an arched alcove formed completely of beaten gold, with inlaid silverwork, on either side of which an almost life-size figure cast in solid silver knelt, one of an old man with a beard in a cassock whom he assumed was Saint Konrad; the other an eighteenth-century nobleman in gaiters with a perruque. Above and around the altar in the form of a giant horseshoe were caskets of silver set in golden niches and shaped like human hearts.

And then, set back in an alcove of its own, recessed above the altar, all but rendered invisible by the opulent splendour of its surroundings and even more so by the extraordinary cloth-of-gold robe encrusted with pearls and diamonds and dwarfed by a giant bejewelled golden crown out of all proportion to the tiny head of the figure itself, was the black Madonna of Altötting: a small statue, barely sixty centimetres high, of a woman holding a child.

Involuntarily Nazreem caught her breath and held it, as her brain tried to strip away the layers of extravagant adornment in an attempt to visualise the simple dark statue they all but concealed.

For a moment – just a moment – she could hardly believe her eyes. And then she closed her eyes, opened them and looked again with a different perspective.

'It is so like, so very like,' she muttered under her breath so that Marcus could barely hear. 'And yet at the same time, so very different.'

21

It was cold. A cold night in a hot country. But he was used to that. The extremes did not bother him. He had forsaken the soft life deliberately, to live closer to nature, to God. In the mountains and the desert the spirit of God was closer to hand, you could feel His breath in the night air and the warmth of His love in the burning sands. No one had ever said God's love was easy to live with. Any easier than doing His will.

God's warrior had for so long lived by proxy, pulled strings and operated the puppets in a pantomime he wrote but never watched. The metaphor was blasphemous, Like all metaphor. But it was apt. We all fall short of perfection. Particularly the incompetents on whom he was forced to rely. Now the time was at hand when he would have to soil his own hands. Soil them in order to cleanse them, to cleanse the world of blasphemy.

The cruel irony, the test sent by Allah, was that it was at moments like these when his faith itself was most challenged. Those he had considered loyal servants turned out to be slaves to lucre, men he had thought ready and willing to be martyrs had proved unworthy of the supreme sacrifice. Worse: they were prepared to betray the sacred call of their religion for something so petty as earthly survival. God's chosen warrior was of different material. When the time came for him, he would be ready. But first he had to complete the work he had been put on earth to carry out; it was his duty to send others to their Maker, while delaying that glorious day for himself.

The thought of the man whose tortured screams had so recently sounded in his ears tormented his soul. Not the man's death nor the manner of it. That had been fitting: a suitable punishment for a coward, traitor and apostate. But the wretch had betrayed both his spiritual master and his religion. A man thought to be a loyal soldier of Islam, who had provided materiel for the martyrs of Madrid and London, had turned out to be a venal turncoat. Worse: he had turned his back on the true God for the sake of an infernal creed.

Strapping explosives to his blood-soaked corpse, putting him behind the wheel with a brick on the accelerator and pointing him at the Zionist butchers, had been a fate too good even for the carrion he had become. He had served in death better than in life. His severed body parts would have conveyed the most direct of messages to the abominable incarnation of idolatry.

And perhaps the vengeance he had wrought would perform a miracle on the heart of a lapsed daughter of Allah: that the punishment of the wicked would convince her that the ways of her fathers were the ways of righteousness, and Western learning the province of false gods. Perhaps she would see the foolishness of her ways. He did not really believe it, but he nurtured the hope. To take the life of a fellow Muslim was an evil, even when necessary.

He hoped with all his heart, therefore, that he would be relieved of the burden of beheading Nazreem Hashrawi.

22

Outside, in the bright afternoon sunlight which seemed such an antithesis to the darkness of the shrine, Nazreem stood blinking and dazed. In the end he had almost to drag her away from contemplation of the little wooden figure, so little of which was actually visible beneath the gilded ornamentation that smothered the thing.

Eventually she lifted her head to him and said: 'There is so much I don't understand. What are all the things around the altar, the things that looked like urns. In the shapes of hearts.'

'Ah, yes, those,' Marcus had replied, nodding in affirmation. '.That's what they are. Just what they look like. Urns. For hearts.'

'Human hearts?'

'Oh yes,' he replied. 'It's an old practice in certain parts of the Catholic world. Something to do with getting as close as possible to the sacred in death.'

In the distance dark clouds grumbled on the horizon; it looked like a summer storm was moving in from the Alps. For the first time since they had arrived in Germany, Marcus felt a bit of a chill. He pulled up the collar of his jacket.

'Austria's Habsburg emperors used to have most of their internal organs removed and placed in urns around their sarcophagi. When Zita, widow of the last emperor, died, she was buried in the family vault in Vienna but they took out her heart and placed it alongside that of her husband in a Benedictine monastery in Switzerland. I think that one had a "black Madonna" too, come to think of it.'

Nazreem was staring at him with an expression somewhere between mystification and disbelief. 'They were still doing this, here in Europe, just a few hundred years ago?'

'A bit more recently than that. Zita only died in 1989, if I remember rightly.'

Nazreem stared at him as if she thought he might be joking.

'I know. You find it bizarre,' said Marcus. 'So do I.'

She shook her head: 'It's not that, it's just ... it's uncanny ... do you think ... that there's a connection?'

'I know what you're thinking,' he said. 'I don't know. It seems a bit unlikely that whoever cut out some Islamic extremist's heart would have sent it here as a gift to the Virgin Mary.'

'For a Muslim it would be a terrible punishment. But then, maybe it was intended to be a terrible punishment.'

Marcus gave her a puzzled look. She was losing him again.

'I wouldn't have thought people in the Arab world would have known about things like this.'

But Nazreem was shaking her head. 'Today, no. It is blasphemy. But it was not always so in my part of the world. A long time ago ...' her voice trailed off. Then she looked up at him: 'The ancient Egyptians would have understood. They would have understood very well indeed.'

Marcus blinked, taken aback for a second and then all of a sudden an image came flooding back in his mind, from the treasures of the tomb of Tutankhamun in the Egyptian Museum in Cairo. 'Of course, the Canopic jars!'

Nazreem nodded: 'For the vital organs of the pharaohs. There were four, with different heads, one human, one monkey, one jackal and one crocodile – one each for the stomach, the liver, the spleen and the intestines.'

'But not the heart?'

'Not the heart. Only later they took that out, and more often than not they fed it to the pharaoh's cats. But then the Egyptians didn't understand the function of the heart. Or the brain. They thought the consciousness was located in the stomach.'

Marcus gave a little laugh: 'I have friends like that.'

But Nazreem wasn't in the mood for jokes. She was silent. The clouds were growing closer. A pair of big black rooks landed beneath the linden trees and began pecking at the remains of a hot dog. Around the chapel the two women with wooden crosses on their backs continued their separate silent circumambulations.

Nazreem turned to Marcus and said: 'We need to speak to the nun. The one who received the ... the package.'

'That may not be easy.'

'We have to try. Go on, you speak German better than I do.'

Marcus shrugged. To the left of the chapel's main entrance was a door marked *Sakristie*. On a table next to it was a pile of leaflets with a picture of an old man with a beard and a halo. Marcus lifted one and glanced at it: it was the brief life story in English, German, French and Italian, of the ubiquitous Saint Konrad. According to the text Konrad of Parzham had been beatified in 1930 by Pope Pius XI and elevated to the sainthood only four years later. But as far as Marcus could tell his claim to sanctity was little more than having been the porter here at the shrine in Altötting. Just working here apparently could be a passport to heaven. He went over to the door and knocked on it. A man's voice beckoned him in.

He opened the door to find a middle-aged man in a housecoat, presumably the successor to Saint Konrad, standing in the corner looking up at a small black and white screen that was a closed-circuit television link to the inside of the chapel. Marcus realised he had not noticed the camera.

'*Kann ich Ihnen helfen?*' the man asked. Can I help you?

Marcus summoned up his German, relieved to find it less rusty than he recalled from his South African schooldays, and told the man they were interested in speaking to one of the nuns. The man gave him a look as if he had already anticipated which one.

'Not a reporter, are you?' he asked.

Marcus shook his head, suddenly understanding that they were obviously not the first to try to speak to the woman.

'Poor old Sister Galina's had about enough, I can tell you. We've already had the police. The boys from Munich.'

Marcus nodded his head. 'Yes, I'm sure. A terrible business.'

'So I'm not wrong then,' said the man, with the smug self-assurance of someone who had known it all along: 'That's what you want to talk about. The incident.'

Marcus decided there was no point in avoiding the truth, especially if it was so obvious. 'Yes.'

The man shook his head. 'Well. I won't ask why but I doubt anyone will see you. You need to go over there,' he gestured towards the corner of the square. 'Down there, on the right,' he said. 'You can't miss it. St Joseph's, the little church. That's where you'll find the institute.'

'Institute?'

'Institut der Englischen Fräulein. That's who you're looking for if you want to speak to Sister Galina.'

'The "English misses"', Marcus repeated queryingly.

'That's what they're called. Over there in the corner. You'd best get a move on. Like as not they won't answer the door after dark.'

The building turned out to be an eighteenth-century church in a side street leading onto the main square.

'Who are these people then?' asked Nazreem. 'They are English? Do you know of them.'

Marcus gave her a blank look. 'Quite frankly, I've never heard of them, but I told you, I'm no expert on the Catholic Church.'

'But England is Protestant, no?'

'Yes, mostly anyway.'

'And they are Catholic.'

'Yes.'

'So?'

'So at least there must be a fair chance they speak English.'

Compared to most of the other ecclesiastical architecture in Altötting, the church of St Joseph was relatively modest. It was also empty. A plaque on a door to one side, however, identified it indeed as the Institut der Englischen Fräulein.

Marcus knocked on the door and eventually it was opened by a smiling, elderly woman in a grey skirt and cardigan who looked more like a grandmother than a nun.

'*Bitte schön?*' she said.

23

The caretaker in the sacristy was right. With dusk falling it took three presses on the old brass button in the wall which rang a bell somewhere deep inside St Joseph's before the door was answered. And even then it was edged open only a crack by a hatchet-faced old woman dressed in a plain grey shirt and skirt who looked more like a Fury than a Sister of Mercy and told them with a scowl that the Institute was '*geschlossen*'. Closed.

Marcus responded with his most deferential, polite German to say they had come all the way from England to spend just a few minutes talking to Sister Galina. The result was a firm attempt by the hatchet-faced old woman to close the door in their faces, eliciting a sharp cry of pain from Nazreem. Marcus looked down and realised she had her foot in it.

'The police have specifically requested that she give no interviews,' the woman at the door said, still talking to Marcus in German but now glancing at Nazreem and her foot still wedged in the doorway with a strange mixture of annoyance and curiosity.

Nazreem reached out towards the woman with both hands and said suddenly: 'In the name of the blessed virgin Maryam, mother of Isa, please do not turn us away!' Marcus was taken aback. He was not sure that referring to Mary in the Muslim tradition as the chaste mother of a minor prophet would hold much sway with a Roman Catholic nun. But the effect of her words on him was as nothing compared to that it had on the woman in the doorway. She stood stock still, eyes fixed on Nazreem, the door opened almost wide enough for Marcus to force his way in if he had thought that would do any good. The old woman fixed her eyes long and hard on Nazreem before asking, in a thickly accented English:

'Where are you from, my child?'

'From … the Holy Land,' and then, seeing the old woman squint at her as if trying to squeeze more information through her eyes, 'from Palestine, the ancient city of Gaza.'

The old woman closed her dark wrinkled lids for a moment, bowed her head and crossed herself, then stepped back to allow them into a hallway dominated by a floor to ceiling oil painting of the Virgin ascending into Heaven, a figure swathed in blue robes, hands outstretched rising through the opening clouds.

'Please be so good as to wait a few minutes,' she said, again to Nazreem, again in the same accented English. By Marcus's reckoning it was fully five minutes before she returned, head bowed, and said that if they would kindly follow her, Sister Galina would see them. Nazreem gave Marcus a nervous smile and followed the elderly woman up a dark stairwell with another picture of the Virgin ascending on the landing to a corridor with a series of doors on either side. She knocked on the second on the left, opened the door and ushered them in.

The room itself was also dark, with only the watery dregs of daylight penetrating through net curtains over a window opposite. On the wall Marcus could make out yet another picture of the Virgin, yet again shown ascending into heaven this time as if through a thunderstorm. It took a few seconds before his eyes adjusted to the dimness sufficiently for him to make out the little figure seated in an armchair in the farthest corner.

She was not at all what Marcus had been expecting. It was only now he had subconsciously imagined her as a frail, elderly woman in a nun's habit. Instead, the woman who stood up and introduced herself as Sister Galina was a short, somewhat portly woman, possibly in her early forties, with mousey hair cut in a loose bob and wearing a grey skirt and cardigan, rather similar to the apparel of the older woman who had opened the door to them. She reminded him disconcertingly of a biology teacher who had taught him in his first year at senior school back in Cape Town. She rose to meet them and held out her hand. 'Welcome to Altötting,' she said in English in a voice that was mellifluous, deep and with a light, pleasant, almost Mediterranean lilt.

'I'm sorry,' Marcus said. 'I ... we thought you were a nun, a sister in holy orders.'

The gentle tone evaporated: 'And what makes you think that is not the case,' she said staring at him sternly, exaggerating the feeling that he was talking to a stern schoolmistress.

'It's just ... you don't wear religious dress, and your organisation has an English name, but I've never heard of it in England.'

The dowdy little woman reseated herself in the armchair and tutted: 'Our order does not have an English name; it is German. It merely refers to England, the country that banished our founder from its shores. Our order began as an order of exile. Mary Ward was an English Catholic girl who fled from the Protestants taking over her country in the early seventeenth century and established a house for her co-religionists in northern France.

'We do not wear religious dress because there were times in our history when we were forced to conceal our faith. Even today there are those who think devotion to the Mother of God a blasphemy rather than a sacred duty, that only the male aspect of divinity is worthy of worship. There have always been men who believed communities of women should be closeted away behind locked doors. Sometimes they have called it a convent, sometimes a harem. And there have even been some,' it was said with an unexpected twinkle in her eye, 'who confused the two. It was an elector of Bavaria who eventually became our order's protector. That is why, although today we have branches in many countries, we still consider here, southern Germany, to be our spiritual home.'

'I'm sorry,' said Marcus, 'I stand corrected. It's very good of you to see us.'

'On the contrary,' she replied dismissing Marcus and turning towards Nazreem with a gaze filled with a suddenly childlike mixture of awe, envy, hope and longing. 'It is a miracle that you have come to us. You who were chosen.'

'Chosen?' said Nazreem self-consciously.

The little woman smiled as if nothing could be more evident. 'Of course. We are not so cloistered here that we do not read the newspapers, or watch the television. Sister Ursula is surely right in thinking you are the one who discovered the likeness of Our Lady? And these things do not happen by accident, you know. For this you were surely chosen. Tell me my child, is it true you have looked on the true image of the Mother of God?'

'Yes, that is, no. I don't know,' said Nazreem awkwardly, wrong-footed at the awestruck tone of the little nun's interrogation. 'I have seen the image we found underneath a church in Gaza.'

'An image that dated from the time of the Christian gospels?'

Nazreem bowed her head and shook it. 'There was no opportunity to carry out a definitive dating, but because of the location it seems almost certain that it dates back to at least the second century AD, and probably earlier …'

The nun looked at her sternly. 'But you have doubts?' she said. And then, 'I am sorry. Of course you have. You are a Muslim, that is correct? You do not believe in "graven images".'

'Yes. But I am a scholar first.'

'And this is why you have come here? Now?'

'Yes … no,' said Nazreem. 'I believe there is a link, between the theft of the image we found in Gaza and the …' she struggled for suitable words, 'what happened here. The package that was delivered to the chapel.'

The nun let her head drop suddenly, and Marcus feared they had sent her back into some state of shock from which she had only just recovered.

'Go on,' she said quietly.

'It was just a feeling, no, more than a feeling, an instinct, when we saw the report in an English paper. About the heart. So horrible, and yet now, here, in this place, the chapel, you keep hearts, hearts of dead people, like sacred relics.'

The nun was nodding, silently, her eyes uplifted now, studying the mass of contradictions playing itself out on Nazreem's face.

'There is a difference,' she said at last. 'A difference between a heart given freely, of love, after death, and a heart ripped from a living body. And not the heart alone.'

Nazreem recoiled automatically at the image conjured up by the nun's uncompromising language.

'What do you mean, not only the heart?'

The nun's face contorted as if even the memory was excruciating.

'We are nuns,' she said. 'We have taken vows of chastity. That does not say we do not know the bodies of men.'

Marcus's eyes opened wide and then he involuntarily retched as he realised the implication of the nun's statement. He glanced at Nazreem to see if she realised what was being said, but saw only a look of almost Mona Lisa-like inscrutability on her face, eyes open wide, with almost the ghostly trace of a smile about her lips. Although he was sure he was imagining that.

24

Otap Cevik looked up at the heavy cloud formations coming in from the west. It was going to rain, a heavy summer rain, the sort his father said they used to dream of in the parched summer of the Anatolian uplands. Otap didn't know about that. He had never been there. He had grown up in the Saarland, but he had never felt at home there and did so even less down here in Bavaria. His religion forbade him beer and down here local life seemed to revolve around it. Beer and coffee and cakes.

All around Altötting's great pilgrimage square, the little tourist shops that nestled at the feet of the great ecclesiastical monoliths were bringing their outdoor displays inside, pulling down shutters and closing the doors as the approaching thunderstorm brought an early dusk.

In the Wiener Kaffeehaus cake shop on the corner a large woman with a candyfloss hairdo was shovelling a final wedge of cream torte into her mouth when she spotted the swarthy-skinned man polishing his motorbike outside staring at her. She scowled and turned away. Otap spat on the ground to show his disdain, then put away the polishing cloth

He had no time for the fat bourgeoisie with their BMWs, their ridiculous religion and their grinning pagan pope. He had never been particularly devout as a child but as he had grown into an increasingly estranged adulthood, he had realised that Islam was a badge of his ethnicity, and he wore it with pride. All the more so now that he at last had been called to be of service.

It did not concern him that the higher purpose of what he did was not explained to him. It sufficed to know that it was indeed a higher purpose. It was not demanding work. It was more like a game, a game that gave him an adrenalin rush while putting him in no real danger. He had not even been required to break the law, except perhaps in the avoidance of motorcycle license plate regulations; he kept a plate in his pannier in case he was stopped when 'on business'; that way he could say it had simply fallen off. At worst he risked a fine. And what was that to a soldier of the Kurdish nation in exile? A soldier, the imam had hinted to him, in the tradition of the greatest Kurd of them all: Saladin, the scourge of the crusaders, the man who had turned the infidels back into the sea and recaptured Al-Quds, the city the Jews who had stolen it again called Jerusalem. The imam had spoken of a new Saladin, but of that Otap knew nothing. The name itself was enough to inspire him. In the name Saladin he saw a thread that led him back to the roots his parents had abandoned when they came to this miserable country for the sake of mere money.

Pretending to be a messenger for a courier company had been the easiest thing imaginable – it was a job he used to do, back in Neunkirchen. Why the imam had wished to deliver a special package to a Christian nun in the vile little temple of idolatry the people around here regarded as a shrine – as if it were the tomb of a prophet – he had no idea. It was not his business to ask. In the same way he had no idea why he had been told since to stake out the site, to report any unusual visitors, either to the shrine or the building where the nuns lived. He took it in turns with another soldier, who also had a bike – it made it more convincing, they had been told – if they occasionally were seen together. Bikers did that.

In particular he was to watch for one woman, an attractive woman; he had a photograph, a picture that had been sent electronically to the imam but printed out from the computer on the best quality Kodak photographic paper. He carried it in the inside pocket of his leather motorcycle jacket, so that he could take it out regularly to refresh his memory. It might almost have been a photograph of his girlfriend. In fact, he had been in a bar just the previous night – drinking hot sweet coffee – when one of the pig-like locals sweating profusely and exuding sickly beer fumes had leaned over his shoulder and ogled her: 'Who's that then, Ahmed? Your girlfriend?' They all said 'Ahmed' if they didn't know his name, as if it was some sort of generic title for Muslims.

He had pushed the man away and put the picture back in his pocket. One of the others, who had been leaning on the bar also drinking heavily, had put an arm out and grabbed him, but the man he had pushed restrained the other, saying: 'Leave it off, Dieter, bloke's got a pretty bird, fair enough, he doesn't want an old fart like me giving her the eye. That right, Ahmed? No offence, mate,' and he had raised his glass and given him a beery smile. 'Girl from back home, eh?'

Otap had wanted to hit him, to smack him in the face, to smash his glass and jam it in his eye, for flaunting his drunken camaraderie, for patronising him, for calling him 'Ahmed' and thinking he was a recent immigrant when he was a born German, with a German passport, except that he knew deep down, that that was a lie. His parents had hoped that he would live the lie. His parents had been fools.

But he had been told not to draw attention to himself so instead he raised his coffee cup, gave a terse smile and paid his tab and left. On the way out, standing in the doorway before he headed off for the cheap labourers' rooming house where he had booked in for the duration of his task, he took out the photograph again and looked at it from a new perspective. A girl from back home? Hardly. There was no way the woman in the picture was a Kurd – the cheekbones were wrong, for one thing – but up until then he had assumed that, despite her jet black hair and sallow complexion, she was a German, or at least a European, Italian maybe, or Greek. The possibility that she came from further East had not occurred to him, but he had to admit now that it was possible.

Now, all of a sudden, he was certain of it. He had never really expected that this woman would cross his path – the imam had said it was possible, but not likely – and yet at this moment he was almost sure she had done precisely that: climbed out of a Volkswagen Polo and walked straight past him, her eyes unseeing, focused on the infidels' temples, in the company of a man, this one almost certainly a German, he had thought until he heard them speak to one another, and recognised the language as English.

He looked again at the photograph, staring hard to memorise every detail of her bone structure, the colour of her eyes. He had been told that on no account was he to make a mistake. He had watched from a distance as she and the man had gone into the little chapel. He had timed them. They were in there for nearly half an hour, then had come out, spoken to someone and then walked straight across the square to the house of the nuns. That had been the decisive factor. Whoever this girl was, whatever the imam or his distant masters required of her, it had surely to do with the package he had delivered to the nun.

There was no doubt now in his mind what he had to do. He moved into the doorway of the Kaffeehaus which had now closed and turned out its interior lights, and pulled out his mobile phone. He would ask for his orders. And then he would obey them. It was what a good soldier did.

25

'I need to know more,' Nazreem was saying. 'There are other black Madonnas. There is one in Poland, I believe, Chennsto … what was it?' she glanced at Marcus but it was the nun who finished the difficult word for her.

'Czestochowa. Yes, but it is different. It is two-dimensional, an icon, more in the Eastern manner.'

'But isn't that the legend?' Marcus could not help himself. He was not going to be ignored. He had an input to make too; after all that was why Nazreem had come to him in the first place, wasn't it? 'That St Luke painted the Virgin's portrait on her kitchen table.'

'That is the legend indeed,' the nun actually turned towards him. 'But there are many legends. And that is only one of many. There are paintings, in the Polish style, and indeed these are often attributed to St Luke, though not even the most pious in faith can believe he managed them all, in so many different styles. God works in mysterious ways, Dr Frey. As this young lady's presence here proves.'

'But the oldest images are not paintings?' Nazreem prompted.

The nun nodded, sagely, looking at her as if trying to read her mind. 'There are many of us who believe, particularly here in Altötting, that the oldest depictions of the Mother of God have always been figurines.'

Marcus blinked. It was the first time it had actually dawned on him that what Nazreem had found was not a painting but a sculpture. He wondered how he could have been so stupid: that was why they were here. Nazreem wanted to compare the figurine in the church across the road with the one she had found. How could he ever have thought anything else?

'There are many such figures,' the nun was saying. 'Many more than most people realise, and the majority of the ancient ones are black. They can be found all across Europe: in Bucharest, on Malta, in France, Belgium, Ireland, Italy. There is a particularly famed example in the monastery at Einsiedeln in Switzerland …'

'*That* was where they put the heart of the Austrian Empress Zita!' exclaimed Marcus, suddenly remembering the piece of information he had been searching for earlier.

The nun smiled at him as if indulging a child: 'You are well informed,' she said, before turning her intent gaze back to Nazreem to add: 'but the most important by far are the figure here and those on the Iberian peninsula. None of them, however, as far as we know can definitely be ascribed to a date older than the early Middle Ages. You believe the carving you found was substantially older, I believe.'

'Yes,' said Nazreem. 'It had to be. Much older. It had almost certainly lain undisturbed since at least 200 AD, and probably earlier. If the figure in Gaza was the original, then perhaps the others, some of them at least, might have been copies, made later but perhaps not much later, as a way of perpetuating the image, of allowing more people to see it.'

'We have long wondered the same,' the nun said. 'But only you know, my child. You and whatever evil or misguided people have snatched this treasure from the world.'

Sister Galina lifted both of Nazreem's hands in hers, raising them until they were almost in the classic gesture of Christian prayer, and then lowered them again to her lap. The two women were close together, looking into one another's eyes as if each could read the other's mind.

'But the figure here then,' the nun said eventually, her eyes focused on the face of the woman in front of her, as if everything she had ever believed on depended on the answer, 'is not the same?'

Nazreem was quiet a moment. Marcus wondered if she was worried what effect her words might have on a woman who had devoted her life to a wooden idol.

'No,' she said. 'It is not the same. It is similar, the same style. But not the same. To start with, I thought maybe it too was ancient, that maybe it was as old as …' Her voice trailed off. 'But now that I have seen it, close up. I am not so sure. It has many of the same qualities, the simplicity, but …'

She hesitated and Marcus had the impression she was trying once again, even here, to decide just how much of a description of her lost treasure she should share with others, even those she trusted implicitly. 'It is not the same, but I see now that maybe it makes sense. Maybe, if this was a copy of the copy, there could have been changes made.'

The nun was nodding, a wry smile on her face. 'The figure of the Madonna in the Chapel of Grace is ancient indeed,' she began, speaking slowly and distinctly. 'Although no one knows exactly how old. One legend says the reason it is black is because it was scorched when saved from a fire in the chapel in the early tenth century. But there are similar stories about the Einsiedeln Madonna – it is an easy way to explain away the dark colour which some find inconvenient.

'Art historians – the sort of people who claim to be able to determine such things – have said the figurine here is of Burgundian or Rhineland origin, no earlier than 1330 AD. The same people insist that the Swiss statue was made locally as late as the mid-fifteenth century. I have seen it and I can tell you that they are almost certainly correct.

'But in neither case does that rule out the possibility that the statues were copies, merely that the artist at the time preferred not to be slavish in his imitation. Or that the originals were indeed damaged by fire. I have no doubt that the figure here today is an early mediaeval copy of a Madonna brought to Altötting six hundred years earlier.'

'Six hundred,' Marcus intervened automatically. 'But that would take us back to the seventh century or earlier, before Christianity arrived in Germany.'

The nun raised her bushy eyebrows briefly but continued talking to Nazreem, scarcely acknowledging his presence.

'The legend has it that the statue was first referred to on the occasion of the baptism of Theodoric, or Dietrich as they call him in German. He is considered to be the first duke of Bavaria, but he was probably just a tribal leader. He became a Christian and insisted all his people do likewise. According to local tradition, the chapel was built for his baptism.'

'And was it?' Marcus couldn't help himself asking.

'People have been arguing for centuries,' the nun said, answering his question without looking at him, 'about the age of the chapel. I am no expert in architectural history. It is very ancient. That is enough. Suffice to say that this has been a holy place for as long as we have any sort of historical records.'

'But if all the oldest images of the Madonna have been lost, or destroyed and replaced with copies,' said Nazreem, 'there is no way of finding a sure link to the Gaza figure.'

'I did not say they have all been destroyed or replaced, merely that not everything is known. The three most ancient figures are all on the Iberian peninsula: one, our Lady of Nazaré, is in Portugal. The other two are in Spain, at Montserrat and Guadalupe.'

'Montserrat and Guadalupe?' said Marcus. 'I thought they were islands in the Caribbean?'

The nun looked at him for several seconds, the longest time she had let her eyes rest on him, and then said: 'Yes, you are right. But not just that. There are places bearing those names in many parts of the New World. The patron saint of Mexico is Our Lady of Guadalupe, named for a vision seen by a converted Aztec. But the origins of those names are in Europe, names taken with them by the conquistadors because of the power in men's minds of the images they left behind, at home in the barren hills of central Spain.'

'So why are the originals less well known?'

'Because they have remained as they always were: monastic retreats, not new settlements, and I assure you they are not less known to those who care about such things. Montserrat is in the high black mountains that rise beyond Barcelona, while Guadalupe lies in the Sierra that shares its name, to the east of Madrid.

'Both have had miracles attributed to them repeatedly over the centuries. The figure in Guadalupe in particular is of great age. It is said that it was brought to the shores of Europe by St Helena, the mother of the Emperor Constantine himself.'

'If that's so, that would date it to at least the latter part of the third century,' said Nazreem. Marcus could not fail to note a sense of almost excitement in her voice.

'If that is so,' echoed Sister Galina.

'There is some doubt?'

'My child, my child, there is always doubt. That is why there must always be faith. The Madonna of Guadalupe is the oldest known example – or was, until now.

'I do not wholly follow your reasoning. But then I do not understand so much in this world any more. The police said the man whose body parts were delivered to the chapel was a suicide bomber who died in Israel. Afterwards. It does not make sense. But then evil never does.'

Nazreem kept her eyes downcast. For a long moment she was silent, as if she was fighting a mental battle with herself. When at length she spoke, her words were quiet, almost muttered, and there was once more that black hardness in her eyes and in her voice as she began to speak, the words coming out as if she had composed them in advance:

'I don't believe in coincidence. I ... I believe there is a link between what happened here and what happened in Gaza. You will forgive me if I do not go into detail,' she glanced at Marcus briefly, 'but it has become clear that there is indeed evil involved. Evil and desperate men who would like to erase all memory of the existence of this figure.'

Sister Galina put a second hand on the one that already rested lightly on Nazreem's and said in a soft, quiet voice: 'Evil men who do evil things. But Our Lady is their implacable enemy. In our time of need she looks down on us, and will protect and comfort us.'

The atmosphere in the little sitting room was close. Sitting to one side, apart from the two women, Marcus felt almost excluded. With a lump in his throat, he watched as Nazreem lifted her eyes to the nun opposite and the hardness that he had noticed in them since she walked through the arrivals gates at Heathrow seem to melt for a moment. Then he realised that what he saw in her eyes was moisture. She was on the verge of tears.

Marcus went to put his hand on her shoulder, but she pushed him away, kindly but firmly, and pulled herself together.

'Are you staying long in Altötting?' the nun asked.

'We're in Munich actually,' Marcus intervened. 'At the Pension Blauer Bock,' he added, for the sake of something to say, the trivia of their accommodation an absurd yet welcome relief from the intensity of the two women's mind-melding empathy.

'I am grateful to you for coming to see me,' said the nun, turning again to Nazreem and taking her hands. 'I have spent my life in the service of Our Lady, and it was my deepest wish to look upon her countenance. But once again the likeness of the Mother of God has been snatched from us, maybe for ever.' Marcus noticed that the pitch of the nun's voice rose at the end of the sentence, as if she were hinting at a question.

'No,' said Nazreem all of a sudden with certainty in her voice. 'Not for ever.'

The nun reached forward again and took her hand, looking at her curiously.

'You seem very certain of this, my child?'

'I am,' said Nazreem with a resolution that surprised Marcus too. 'Absolutely certain.'

26

The black clouds had settled in overhead, fulfilling their promise of rain abundantly, with big heavy drops splattering on the windscreen as Marcus and Nazreem climbed into the car. Dusk was falling fast and the great square was deserted – even the pair of circling pilgrims had at last laid down their crosses and departed – save for the two bikers on the other side and even they were now pulling up rain hoods and revving up their engines preliminary to shattering the somnolent idyll of the rural Bavarian evening.

Marcus looked at his watch. 'It's nearly seven-thirty,' he said. 'I suggest we head back to Munich.' Nazreem merely nodded and looked ahead through the windscreen at the rivulets of rain. Then the wipers clicked in and swept them all away.

The road back was as tortuous as it had been on the way out save that there were fewer tractors. Only once on the edge of a little village of red-roofed houses with an onion-domed church that reminded Marcus incongruously of something out of *Doctor Zhivago* did a great bug-eyed behemoth with its giant headlights forcing a path through the constant rain pull out of a field laden with plastic-wrapped bales of summer grain.

Marcus braked hard to avoid getting too close to the heavy spray kicked up by the thick-treaded tyres. Only then did he notice the single headlight in his rear-view mirror hurtling towards him, then suddenly drop back as if the rider too had pulled hard on the brakes. He thought nothing of it until a second one appeared, the two drawing level, both beams side by side now, almost capable of being mistaken for a car. Then one grew larger until the motorbike and rider were clearly visible just a few metres behind them. In front the tractor still kept him crawling along at barely forty kilometres per hour. Now the bike drew level, the whine of its engine high-pitched against the dull purr of the Volkswagen and the grumble of the agricultural vehicle in front. He wondered if it was the two bikers who had been so evident in the square at Altötting and decided it had to be: two leather lads from the big city out for a summer's day spin, caught out by unexpected foul weather and hurrying home to put the bikes away and get out for a few beers.

But in that case why didn't they overtake? On these narrow roads, a tractor posed a serious obstacle to a car, but a bike could soar past. And yet they didn't. One remained a consistent distance behind him, as if deliberately matching his speed; the other was also matching his speed, almost parallel to him. Marcus squinted sideways and was almost certain he recognised the bike as the big black Kawasaki with the red stripe he had noticed earlier. Whatever game they were playing he was not happy about it. It seemed improbable that the same people who had been tailing Nazreem in London could have latched onto them so quickly here. Or did it? Not necessarily if her suppositions about the link between the Gaza statue and the one here were true. But if these were the people who had stolen the statue, surely they had what they wanted.

The tractor in front unexpectedly turned off into a farmyard and Marcus accelerated but there was more traffic in front: villagers in no particular hurry taking care in the bad weather. Traffic in both directions. The bike matched his speed, the rider playing with him, his colleague behind closing, just a few car lengths between them now. He braked sharply. The light in his rear-view mirror grew rapidly closer, then as quickly fell back. That'll teach you to keep your distance in the wet, thought Marcus. Any harder and whoever was on it would have been flying over the Polo's bonnet.

The biker beside them, however, caught out by the manoeuvre too, pulled into the space between them and the car in front. Marcus looked for a number plate but if there was one it was invisible, illegally unilluminated in the dark. Then the bike in front braked hard, playing Marcus's trick back on him, forcing him to slow down. He tried instead to pull out but was faced by a solid line of oncoming traffic. The bike behind had pulled level now and Marcus saw Nazreem gape in horror as the opaque black visor of the rider loomed large in her window, a faceless automaton. Jesus, he thought suddenly, what if he has a gun. He had never heard of drive-by shootings carried out by bikers, but that did not mean they didn't happen.

Then suddenly they were bathed in light, the road ahead cleared. They had hit the short stretch of autobahn that extended from the

Munich ring road. Marcus rammed his foot down, the revs screaming as the little car accelerated from thirty-five up to 130 kilometres per hour while he scrunched his way through the gears. For a gratifying few seconds the bike's headlights dwindled rapidly in the rear-view mirror. And then they grew again. Coming steadily closer. Marcus looked at the speedometer. There was no way the little VW Polo could outrace two performance bikes. If they wanted them, they would have them.

But it would not go unnoticed. The relative dark and anonymity of the country road was gone now. As they got closer to Munich the volume of traffic grew, the smart BMWs and Mercedes of affluent city dwellers replacing the small cars and trucks of the countryside. The motorway lights were bright. Number plates would be visible, a lack of them too. An incident would have witnesses. Not that he was reassured by the idea of 'witnesses after the event'. But the bikes showed no sign of closing, maintaining their distance some hundred metres behind. For a few seconds at a time Marcus was forced to stop watching them, heeding instead the traffic around him and the confusing signs as the autobahn split, weaving left and right, north towards the airport, Nürnberg and Regensburg, south to the Alps, Austria and Italy, then again, spurs tucking themselves into the city's series of concentric ring roads. When he looked again, they were gone.

Or rather they no longer stood out. In the long queue of vehicles behind them as they turned off the autobahn proper into a dual carriageway that seemed to lead towards the city centre, there was maybe one bike, maybe two. And then there was maybe none. Maybe.

'Are they gone?' Nazreem said to him, her voice betraying no trace of the anxiety he had felt.

'I think so,' he said, not knowing whether he really thought so. 'I think so.' Maybe the threat was in his head. Maybe they had been just two local cowboys, hotshots baiting strangers for kicks along country roads on a wet night. Maybe. But he didn't think so. There was only one obvious purpose to their pursuit and sudden disappearance: that they had succeeded in their aim. Identifying the woman in the passenger seat.

Whatever else was true or false in the labyrinth of conspiracy that Nazreem was clearly creating in her own mind, one thing was indisputable. She herself held the key.

27

The next morning the sun shone again as if the summer storm that had brought such a bleak end to the day before had never happened. Nazreem beamed over her breakfast orange juice as though she too had dismissed the dark forebodings that had clouded both their minds on the journey back into the city.

To Marcus the images of the dark riders on their black motorbikes speeding after them then disappearing into the night were still all too vivid. He could not escape the foolish fantasy that they were updated versions of Tolkien's 'ring wraiths': anonymous, faceless – even soulless – riders sent to stalk them by some unknown sinister power guiding their destinies. Common sense told him it was nonsense, but that didn't make the imagery any less pervasive or persistent.

'I think we should go back to Altötting, I would like to see Sister Galina again,' said Nazreem, pouring Marcus a cup of strong-looking black coffee as he sat down beside her. The breakfast room of the little hotel was bright, airy and decorated with fresh flowers, for all that its main occupants seemed to be tired-looking travelling salesmen and a few tourists.

The hotel had been as easy to find as the woman at the airport tourist office had promised, just a short walk from the city's central square, the Marienplatz. Marie, Mary, Maria. Miriam in Hebrew, Maryam in the Arabic Nazreem had quoted to such powerful effect in Altötting. In front of the square's great neo-Gothic city hall a statue of the virgin in her role as protectress of Munich stood high on a column: the Virgin Mary to Western European eyes: white and saintly with her halo and the Christ Child in her arms, one hand raised in a gesture of benediction. Almost a deity in her own right. Even so, Marcus felt he would never look at even the most banal representation of the Madonna in the same way again.

'But first,' Nazreem was saying, breaking into his thoughts: 'I would like to go to see the painting, the one you mentioned, by the Dutchman. It is here, in Munich, you said?'

Marcus blinked for a moment, his train of thought disjointed. Then he remembered: the painting of St Luke sketching the first portrait of the Madonna, by the fifteenth-century Flemish painter whose name still escaped him, the one he had mentioned to her over dinner in Brick Lane, before the chaos overtook them.

'Uh, yes, at least I think so. We need to check where though. Munich has a lot of art galleries.'

It turned out not to be as easy as Marcus had expected to find out exactly which of Munich's cornucopia of galleries was in possession of a particular painting, especially if you were unsure of both its title and the artist's name. But most of the major galleries were close together near the university buildings, a short U-bahn ride north of the city centre, and it seemed a safe guess that the great nineteenth-century gallery known as the Alte Pinakothek was the most likely place to house a painting by a Flemish master of the early Renaissance period.

Marcus found himself unable to stop searching the faces of people in the street and on the U-bahn, as if he suspected any of them – at least any of vaguely Middle Eastern appearance – to be part of some nefarious conspiracy that had designs on them, or at least on Nazreem. Several people matched the racial profile which he realised with some personal embarrassment he was applying, none of them appeared remotely interested in either Nazreem or himself. None of them obviously got on or off the U-bahn at the same stops they did. There were no clear-cut suspects, no menacing men on motorbikes lingering on street corners, at least not in the vicinity of the Pinakothek itself.

The gallery was a vast neoclassical stone building, with bomb damage from the Second World War patched in red brick like scars from ancient wounds. It held an enormous collection of European paintings from the fourteenth to the eighteenth centuries. Their task had been made somewhat easier: Marcus's brain had finally dredged up from his subconscious the name of the artist. The work they were looking for was by Rogier van der Weyden.

But even that did not make it as easy as it ought to have been. Van der Weyden was a significant figure for his day, important enough for him to have most of one room to himself on the first floor, but the painting of St Luke and the Madonna was not on display. Nor was it mentioned in the gallery's current catalogue. Yet Marcus was sure he had known it was here. Now he began to ask himself if he could have been mistaken. Was there another gallery in Munich with a similar collection? He found it hard to believe.

A tubby man nodding gently on a metal-framed chair in the doorway between the two rooms displayed a name badge which indicated he was gallery staff. Security probably, although he did not offer very much of that. At Nazreem's prompting, Marcus approached him. The man jolted and gave him a rude stare but his attitude changed when Marcus made clear he was from London and inquiring about a painting. But the best Marcus could glean from the man's almost impenetrable Bavarian dialect was that the painting was 'gone, taken away.'

Where? He asked, but got only a brusque shake of the head and an indifferent shrug. Only when Nazreem appeared at his shoulder with a beseeching look on her face and pressed a ten-euro note into the attendant's palm did his reaction alter, abruptly. Marcus waited for a shocked German reaction to her instinctive Middle East *baksheesh*, but the man palmed the note and grunted that they should wait here and disappeared into the next room.

A few minutes later he returned with a younger man sporting a short, spiky haircut and a leather jacket. For a moment Marcus thought he had fetched help to have them thrown out, but then the younger man, in perfect unaccented English, said: 'My name is Helmut Vischer. I am curator of the old Dutch paintings. This man tells me you are also academics and wish to see the Van der Weyden St Luke.'

The attendant at his side was smiling as if the role of expert facilitator was second nature to him. Marcus nodded and introduced himself as a don from All Souls in Oxford and Nazreem as his research assistant, which earned him a sharp look from her.

'Yes, we were surprised to find it not on display.'

Vischer raised his almost invisible blond eyebrows as if minimally surprised.

'But if it is at all possible,' said Nazreem.

He turned and gave her a brief cool smile, before turning back to Marcus.

'As it happens, you are very lucky I was available. I should be happy to show you the painting. It is hanging in my office.'

Marcus's eyes clearly suggested that this was something of an extravagance even for a gallery curator, but Vischer laid a hand on his arm almost conspiratorially: 'We are allowed our little indulgences, you know. I couldn't bear to let such a fine piece of work be confined to the cellars, simply because some group of pedants had declared it not to be the original.'

Nazreem shot Marcus a puzzled glance as they followed the man through a panelled door into an institutionally painted side corridor.

'Although personally speaking that doesn't detract from its worth, and in any case as you know these attributions are for ever changing,' Vischer was saying.

'You're telling us that the St Luke painting is a fake, a forgery?' Marcus could not conceal a note of incredulity in his voice.

'Oh no, good heavens, nothing of the kind. Just that it might not have been wholly painted by the master himself. Anyway, there you are.'

He opened a door on their left and ushered them into a small functionally furnished office which was completely dominated by the painting that hung opposite the desk.

'A fine thing,' said Vischer. 'I find it inspirational.'

Marcus was taken aback. The painting was bigger than he had imagined from pictures in books – over a metre across and maybe a third as much again in height. Also, it was painted not on canvas but on wood.

'Oak. Quite common at the time, especially for religious paintings,' said the curator, positioning himself alongside the painting as if admiring his own handiwork.

Marcus stood back to examine the work as a whole. The composition was exquisite, divided into three by the device of a window in the background with the graceful upright pillars. In the centre frame, beyond the window looking out over battlements at a winding river and a townscape that was wholly mediaeval down to the Dutch gables, stood a couple seemingly unrelated to the main subjects, yet giving perspective and a sense of unity.

In the foreground, inside the window on one side of the central aperture a man in russet robes with a skullcap half knelt with a quill pen hovering over a sketch pad in his hand. Opposite seated on the step of a wooden throne draped in cloth of gold was a woman offering her breast to a baby.

The appearance of the child itself was strangely stilted, with the fingers of the left hand arranged in a sign of blessing. The face had a strange, otherworldly smile and he seemed unnaturally disinterested in the proffered breast. The woman herself, however, could have been an archetypal Dutch beauty of the day, her eyes cast down towards the baby in her arms, demure, brunette and immaculately white of skin. Only the full heavy robe which draped her form was a rich velvet black.

'The real beauty lies in the balance of the composition, the subtle semi-symmetry and the sharply contrasting use of light and shade,' said Vischer.

Marcus nodded. 'It's quite remarkable,' he said. 'I'd come across illustrations before, in books, but never paid quite this much attention.' By his side Nazreem too appeared wholly riveted by the artwork in front of them.

'But what were you saying about it not being the original?' Marcus asked.

Vischer sighed. 'That is why it no longer hangs in the main gallery, despite the fact that for decades it hung there and was much admired.'

'I'm not sure I understand.'

'It is a question of authentication: our modern concern with brush strokes and pigments. The painting is not unique, you see. Few of this style, of this period are.'

Vischer was addressing himself to Marcus, but Nazreem had turned towards him with a strange gleam in her eye.

'There are others, also in fine collections you understand, one very like this indeed in the Groeninge Museum in Bruges, which for a long time was claimed to be the original because it is near where the artist lived, and another in the Museum of Fine Arts in Boston, Massachusetts, on a continent he did not even know existed. And another, this time on canvas, in the Hermitage in St Petersburg.

'People who know more about such technical things than I do say they reckon that the only one of the series that was wholly painted by van der Weyden himself is probably the one in America. I'm not convinced that detracts from the intrinsic value of ours ... or mine, as I sometime dare to think of it.'

'Why so many versions of the same painting?'

'Nowadays we regard works of art – old ones anyhow – as unique, masterpieces which must be allowed to stand alone and which must never be copied. But at the time these paintings were produced, they weren't seen like that. It was the image that mattered, not the artist – of course, people wanted things to be as well painted as possible, but it simply wasn't viable for one man to churn out endless copies.

'That's what they had assistants for – "schools" they called them then, but they weren't all to do with learning. "Workshops" might have been a better equivalent in modern terms. Just like the scribes producing all those illuminated manuscripts before the invention of printing. Just a primitive form of mass production really.'

'I hadn't looked at it like that before,' said Marcus.

'No,' said Vischer. 'Not many people do. But I believe that even from today's point of view it's the beauty of the object that counts, not the attribution.'

'It's a very different Madonna.'

'I'm sorry?'

'Hmm?' Marcus had been thinking aloud, rather than addressing the curator standing next to him. 'We've just been out to Altötting,' he added, suddenly aware that Nazreem beside him was throwing dagger looks in his direction. If Vischer noticed them he gave no indication. Instead, he appeared mildly puzzled by the comparison.

'Ah, Bavaria's famous black Madonna. No indeed, quite another thing. That's an older piece of work too, of course, although not as old as a lot of the pilgrims would like to believe. But you can't really compare a sculpture to a painting, can you, not unless you're trying to get some idea of what the actual person looked like. And that's hardly the case here, is it?' he laughed.

'No, indeed,' said Marcus dryly.

'So what did you think of our Altötting? You aren't pilgrims, in the religious sense?' Vischer asked with just a slightly nervous edge to his laugh. 'I thought all Englishmen were Protestants,' this with just the hint of a sideways glance at Nazreem.

'No. Not pilgrims,' answered Marcus, seeing no point in explaining. 'It's a fine place. Some remarkable architecture.'

'Oh yes, quite a collection of curios, Altötting, in every sense of the word. You know Pope Benedict was a local boy.'

'Hard to miss the fact.'

Vischer grinned. Somehow Marcus thought this was one Bavarian who was not a particular fan of His Apostolic Majesty. 'Did you see the Death?' he asked.

It was Marcus's turn to look puzzled.

'The Death of Eding? Oh I do hope you didn't miss it. It's sublime.'

'I think you've lost me again.'

'Oh what a pity. Perhaps you should go back. It really is – how does Michelin put it "worth a detour" – it's in the main church. A little statue, a figurine really on top of a very tall, quite fine, grandfather clock. It's a bit macabre really: a skeleton swinging a scythe. It swings back and forth every couple of seconds and superstitious people believe that every swing brings someone's death.'

'Charming.'

'Yes, it is, isn't it. Some people call it a *memento mori*, a reminder that this life is but transient, a pilgrimage to heaven. Others see the same thing and take the message *carpe diem*: enjoy yourself because this is all you've got.'

'I assume the Catholic Church prefers the former.'

'Oh absolutely, but then the Catholic Church is a relative newcomer in Altötting.'

Marcus looked at him askance: 'How do you mean? I rather got the impression that the whole place revolved around the Church, and the black Madonna in particular.'

'Yes, you would, and it's true nowadays and has been for centuries, but Altötting's history as a religious centre goes way back beyond any of that.'

Marcus nodded. 'Yes, one of the nuns at the institute hinted at something like that.'

Vischer smiled a knowing smile. 'Ah, you talked to them, did you? The *englische Fräulein*, the little English Virgins – there have to be some somewhere – you know they used to call them the "female Jesuits"?'

'No, I didn't.'

'Very self-assured, they are. Not without reason perhaps. They do a good job, teaching and so forth. By their own lights.'

'But you're suggesting there's more that they didn't tell us.'

'Oh, not at all, not at all. Not necessarily, but the Church rather prefers to play down the old pagan side of Altötting.'

'I didn't realise there was a pagan side.'

'It was considered sacred a long time before the arrival of Christianity? It has been the centre of religious cults for millennia probably. You noticed the trees?'

'The little grove, planted around the shrine.'

'Yes, except that there were trees there long before the shrine. Lime trees you sometimes call them in English, though I think you also use the German word – linden. They were sacred in old Teutonic cults from the dawn of time. Berlin's Unter den Linden ring a bell?'

'Yes, but surely that's not ...'

'I'm only joking, sort of – about Berlin – but I'm quite serious about the lindens in Altötting. Over the centuries they have been rearranged, replanted and made to look like a formal garden around the shrine. Originally they would have been a grove on their own, visible for miles around on that plateau, a place for worship. And for sacrifice.'

'You're saying ...'

'I'm not saying anything, other than telling you as one scholar to another that it's just another example of an ancient site the Church has appropriated to its own interpretations. They never dared cut down the lindens completely, you know. These things linger, in people's imagination – call it superstition or what you will – but there was an almighty fuss back in the seventeenth century when they cut down one of the trees that even then they knew to be at least 250 years old. They replaced it with an extra little shrine, a little metal chapel for candles, as if it was an exorcism.'

Marcus remembered noticing the little structure out in front of the old chapel, mimicking it obliquely in its metal shape. There had indeed been candles inside, and flowers. He had thought nothing more of it at the time. There had been candles everywhere.

'And then there's the Madonna herself, of course. You noticed what she was made of, the dark figure underneath all the gold and silver getup?'

'I took it for granted she was carved of wood.'

'Indeed, but not just any wood. Linden. The holy wood of the ancients.'

28

The sight of students in cut-off jeans and T-shirts lying on the grass in the warm summer sunshine or playing Frisbee on the lawns outside the gallery was a welcome reminder of the modern world at its everyday level. Marcus's head was spinning. He considered himself a master at reconciling conflicting versions of reality, but that was when he set his own agenda. Altötting had seemed a familiar if faintly absurd shrine to Christian tradition. Now all of a sudden he found himself forced to look at it as an alien, slightly sinister hangover from ancient Paganism. Which was true? Either, or neither?

Nazreem on the other hand had not seemed even mildly surprised. Her eyes shone as she studied the painting in minute detail, without taking part in the conversation between Marcus and Dr Vischer, yet she had clearly taken in every word. There was a disquieting quality to her silence as if she were in some state of hyper-awareness where everything assumed an added significance unnoticed by the uninitiated. Or maybe she was just daydreaming. Certainty was becoming a mirage.

'Does any of this alter anything?' asked Marcus as they walked between the university buildings in the rough direction of the city centre. 'I mean your idea that the first Altötting figure might have been a copy of the original life-portrait of Mary?'

To his surprise she almost laughed. 'Alter anything? No, not in the slightest. Unless of course you think these people were actually trying to depict the Virgin Mary?'

Marcus stopped abruptly, suddenly not sure what he was hearing. 'But I thought that was the whole point. That was why you wanted to see this painting. To see if it looked like her.'

Nazreem shook her head, as if in disbelief that he could have misunderstood. 'No, no. Quite the opposite. I knew that this was nothing like – you told me about the Dutch painters. I just wanted to see an early example, to get a better idea of how they did it?'

'How who did what? I'm not sure I understand.'

'Don't you see? This painting, this image of St Luke creating the Madonna's likeness, it's not real ...'

'Well, of course it's not real. It's just a painting, a late mediaeval artist's rendition of a famous scene.'

'But that's just it. It's not a famous scene. It's not a scene at all – it's a legend ...'

'That's what I mean.' Marcus was getting annoyed with her nitpicking.

'But you don't say what you mean, you're using a shorthand that implies that it really happened. Like a lot of people believe. But it's a legend okay, only not like in the fairy stories. More like in the spy stories. The legend is a cover story. A piece of propaganda. Black propaganda, if you want.'

'Now I really don't understand. What sort of propaganda? And for whom?'

'For the Christians, of course. To make the Virgin Mary look like one of them.'

'Hang on a minute, you're not trying to claim the Virgin Mary for Islam, are you?'

She looked at him with mock horror, and then laughed: 'Marcus, sometimes I wonder, for a university man, how little you know. The Virgin Mary is part of Islam. Just like Isa, Jesus, her son, who was one of the messengers from Allah, a prophet, one of the forerunners of Mohammed, as was Musa, the one you call Moses.

'In the Koran his mother, Maryam, *your* Virgin Mary is the only woman mentioned by name. Not even the daughters of the prophet himself are so honoured. The third chapter is named after her father, Imran, and his family, the nineteenth chapter after Mary, Maryam, herself, including the story of the visitation of the angel Jibril – whom you call Gabriel – and her virgin conception. Allah guided her to a palm tree with a little river running by it so she would have fresh water and a tree that showered dates upon her when she shook it, for food. And that is where she gave birth to Isa, Jesus.'

'That's not exactly the way we learned it in Sunday School.'

'No, of course not. But who was this Mary, some Dutch woman, or German or English – or African? I think that if she existed, according to the holy books of either religion, she was a woman whose world more closely resembled mine than that of some mediaeval European housewife.'

Marcus found himself nodding. She was giving him an object lesson in his own field of study: looking at the same story from a different perspective, the same supposed events told in a different way in a different culture. The difference between historiography and history, remembering that history is written by humans. It was the key point in all his lectures. Why should it not apply to religion too?

'It is one of the phrases from the Koran that is learned by heart by all Muslim girls, the words uttered by Jibril to the virgin.' She dropped her tone into a quiet hush and said something softly in Arabic, a recital learned by rote in childhood, then raised her voice again, as if the magic could not be conveyed in the English: '"Maryam, Allah has chosen you and purified you – chosen you above the women of all nations."'

'Now that is almost exactly the wording in the Bible.'

She shrugged. 'Why would it not be? But I do not know. In any case, once you have translated the Koran, it is no longer supposed to be the genuine word of Allah.'

Marcus looked suitably sceptical. 'I'm sure He's capable of more than one language.'

She smiled. 'I would like to think so, but it is a way of keeping the orthodoxy. Remember, for centuries the Christian Bible was only read in Latin, even though it had originally been written in Aramaic or Greek. These things serve human purposes. Like that painting in there. You have to agree that it is strange that Christianity, this religion which was born in Palestine and first flourished in Egypt and Syria, ended up an almost exclusively European religion.'

'It's a global religion today.'

'Only because it was spread by European colonialism.'

Marcus inclined his head. There was no arguing with that. Even the most ardent Christians admitted that the great European voyages of exploration had been the chief motors of Christian expansion. They tried to explain it as the will of God, even if some of the excesses of gold-hungry conquistadors looked distinctly un-Christian.

'I suppose,' he said instead, taking up the issue as seriously as he knew she intended, 'it goes back to the Emperor Constantine. If he hadn't made Christianity the state religion of the Roman empire in the early fourth century, it might never have attained more than cult status outside the Middle East.'

Nazreem was nodding now, as if pleased to see that he was open to the discussion and not just defending 'his' side against hers, Christians versus Muslims. That would have been an insult to both of their intelligences: 'And the emperor adopted it because he witnessed a miracle. Because God entered his heart and he saw the folly of his ways?'

Marcus smiled broadly. She was teasing him, goading him on. Well, he would give her what she was asking for. 'Not exactly. The legend is that he saw a vision before a crucial battle against one of his rivals for the throne – the Greek letters *chi* and *rho*, like a capital X and P in English, the first two in the word Christ – and so after he won the battle, he converted. Most of that is certainly legend. Even the early Christian historians admitted Constantine was a pragmatist who prayed to any god going for victory. He did end the persecution of Christians but didn't adopt the religion himself until his deathbed. Even then it was a close run thing. He was tempted by lots of others including some Persian cult I don't remember the name of right now, but it was more to do with pragmatism than religious conviction. But that was probably the Yorkshire in him.'

'What?'

Marcus chuckled. 'Yorkshiremen. It's just a little joke among British historians. He was staying at a military base at Eboracum – York – when his father died and he was proclaimed emperor. Yorkshiremen have a reputation for stubbornness, you know.'

'Sometimes I think the English are very strange.'

'Tell me about it. But it was because of Constantine that Europe, and as a result the modern 'Western' world, became Christian. Once the emperor had legalised Christianity and adopted it himself, though only on his deathbed, the religion was accepted as that of the state. The Romans liked the hierarchical structure, the chain of authority. It pretty much mirrored the empire. And eventually became it. The Pantheon in Rome is revered today as one of the oldest, finest Christian churches but it began life as a pagan temple. The roots of its very name – "pan" and "theos" – mean "all the gods".'

'Exactly.'

'What do you mean – exactly?'

'Christianity stole what it needed to establish itself as the imperial religion, to supplant all the others so that there would only be one system of belief.'

'They stole your black Madonna?'

She sighed in exasperation: 'Marcus, Marcus, it is not *my* black Madonna. It is not anybody's. It is certainly also not the Catholic Church's. At least not exclusively. That is what I mean by a legend, a black legend. That's why the oldest Madonnas are all dark. The white, European-looking ones only began to appear in the Middle Ages, when Christianity was running scared from Islam which had taken over the holy places and was threatening to invade Europe. They stripped the religion of almost all its true Middle Eastern roots.

'All these stories, these "other Marys", they're all attempts to explain away the images, their continued existence, the reverence people automatically felt for them. It's a way of usurping their status, their power if you like.

'But it's more than that. There's something else, older and somehow obvious but still hidden. Maybe it fits in with what the curator was saying about Altötting, about the linden trees, something that explains why no one in the Catholic Church wants to be precise about how long and why it's been a holy site. Sister Galina didn't understand but she knew all the same, that it goes way back, to before Christianity.'

'You're not just talking about the conflict between Islam and Christianity?'

She stopped and stared at him suddenly as if he was being inexplicably dense.

'Of course not. At their worst, the one's as good – or as bad – as the other. It's just that we let ourselves be blinded by what's in our faces. You don't think 3,000 years of culture disappeared overnight, do you. The Greeks, the Romans, the people who founded your culture, the Arabs who developed mine, all have roots in the sands of Ancient Egypt.' She smiled suddenly: 'Look around you.'

'Hmm?' Marcus looked puzzled and then realised where they were; their apparently random stroll back towards the hotel had taken them to the edge of Königsplatz, the great regal square laid out by Bavaria's nineteenth-century kings. On either side rose great stone neoclassical buildings, museums of ancient sculpture and archaeology, lined with classical columns, one Doric, the other Ionic.

Between the two, forming a third side to the square stood two Egyptian-style pylon gates. As chance had it, workmen were erecting a stage with gold and topaz sphinxes, for an open-air summer performance of Verdi's opera *Aïda*, a nineteenth-century Italian's hymn of praise to ancient Egypt, named for a Nubian princess.

Nazreem was looking at him smugly as if it was some sign of divine intervention. 'There are parallels between the story of Mary, Maryam, and the ancient Egyptian Isis, the goddess who was mother of Horus. When you first met me, I was studying Egyptology living in Cairo. I came to understand that ancient Egypt never went away; it was simply swallowed up, by your world and by mine.'

'You're not going to bring Leonardo da Vinci into this, are you?'

Nazreem smiled and shook her head: 'We're talking real history here, facts interpreted to make sense not nonsense.'

'So you're not going to tell me Jesus Christ was secretly married.'

'To be frank, Marcus, I neither know nor care about the man's sexual preferences, marital arrangements or lack of either. As far as I am concerned, he was probably some radical Jewish rabbi who attracted a following and ended up in trouble with the Romans. But you know there's not even any real historical record of that. Not that wasn't tinkered with later by the Christians to make it fit their supposed facts. Come on, Marcus, you're the expert in this field. You know how history can be rearranged to suit the present.'

'That's for sure,' he said wryly, looking around at the great square's imposingly monumental nineteenth-century pastiche of the ancient world's most grandiose architecture. 'You know what else this square is famous for.'

She eyed him obliquely, expecting a trap.

'In the 1930s it was paved over. To make it even more imposing, more of a synthesis of the ancient world and what they thought then was the new world order. That also made it more suited to military parades. They don't talk about it much in modern Munich but in the 1930s they called this city the "Hauptstadt der Bewegung", the "capital of the movement", the National Socialist movement.

'This square was the Nazi storm troopers' favourite marching ground. They carried out the infamous book-burning here, close to the university. So let's not think of it as a monument to ancient truth.'

'I'm talking about the power of religion. Wasn't Nazism a sort of religion?'

Marcus thought of the swastika, an ancient ayurvedic symbol stolen and abused, the mass parades, the ritual obeisance and the fanaticism, Dr Goebbels the little prophet and Adolf Hitler his

135

improbable Messiah. Oh yes, Nazism had been a religion all right.

These buildings, museums built in the style of ancient temples, had temporarily been appropriated to fit. Was religion like history, not a matter of eternal truth but just a question of which side you were on? Why the hell not? Hell was real enough. Hell on earth.

29

The shadows were shrinking to pencil points on the pavements as Marcus and Nazreem turned the corner onto the broad Ludwigstrasse, the great nineteenth-century Italianate boulevard that ended in the Theatiner Church, a hulking monumental symbol in pastel papal yellow of rampant Bavarian Catholicism.

'What you were saying, you know, about thinking of Jesus as just another prophet,' Marcus said, acutely aware that he himself would once – long ago now, mercifully – have risked being burned for even discussing such blasphemy in such a bastion of Christendom, 'it wasn't always just a Muslim view. It's not unlike the Arian heresy.'

'Aryan? Marcus, you are not really bringing the Nazis and their crazy race theories into this?'

'Hmm? Oh, God no! Not at all. I mean not like that. Not Aryan, with a 'y' – Arian in the sense of the heresy comes from Arius, a sort of mad monk.'

'Who?'

'Arius was a fourth-century monk from Libya or Egypt who disputed the idea of the Trinity, held that Christ might well have been the Son of God, but that meant logically that God existed first and that therefore they couldn't be one and the same. His followers were called Arians and they concentrated very much on Christ the man.'

'But they still believed Jesus was divine?'

'Yes, I think so, but sort of lesser. To be honest, nobody knows exactly what they believed because the cult was wiped out. Arius was condemned as a heretic and fled to Palestine, as it turns out. I've heard people say that some of what he preached had echoes in Islam.'

Nazreem looked at him sceptically: 'I've never heard of him.'

'Well, that might not be true. The reason his name survives is that some of his teaching caught on amongst the German tribes who invaded the early empire after Constantine. Even when the official church outlawed it, it remained the belief of the Visigoths in particular.'

'Which Goths? I never understood early European history.'

'I'm not surprised. There were two main branches of the German tribes that fell on the Roman Empire, the Visigoths in the West and the Ostrogoths in the East.'

'You mean like the Wessies and Ossies in modern Germany.'

Marcus laughed. 'Yes, I suppose so, the same root words anyhow. I've never thought of it like that. But the Visigoths ruled Spain for several hundred years, right up until the first Moorish invasions really. That was more or less the end of Arianism.'

'Spain? Where that other black Madonna is, the one Sister Galina mentioned. I wonder … could there be a connection?'

Marcus gave her a sceptical look: 'I doubt it. I don't think the Arians had any time for the cult of Mary as such.'

'I think they might have been wise. I think that there has been a lot of wool pulled over a lot of people's eyes for hundreds of years.'

'Are you trying to tell me, Nazreem, you as a good Muslim, that religion is not about the quest for the truth?'

She stopped for a second and caught his eye: 'You are teasing me. You know perfectly well that my religion is part of my culture but that over the centuries all religions, that of my culture as well as that of yours, have been used and abused by cynical men for their own ends.'

'If you say so.'

Nazreem frowned. 'Don't tease me here. I believe in God, like I think maybe you do, and I believe there are many ways to do so. But history and archaeology are supposed to be about facts. I do not believe for example like your Christian creationists that God just put dinosaur bones in the earth to test our faith. We must work from the evidence, not in spite of it.'

'There are plenty of mullahs who would say faith is supreme.'

'Marcus, you know only too well there are plenty of mullahs who say all sorts of silly things, just as there are Christians, and probably holy men of all sorts of religions who are more than a bit mad – that does not mean we should listen to all of them. The reason God gave us a critical faculty was so we could decide who is talking nonsense and who is not – that is the real test.'

'And you still want to go back to Altötting. To see the nun, even though you think everything she believes in is phoney.'

'I didn't say that.'

'It sounded like it to me.'

'She is a good woman, I think. I would never say anything to insult someone else's faith. But I need to ask her some more questions, subtly perhaps, I do not want to cause offence, but after what this man said, I need to know if there is anything else.'

Marcus let out a long breath. 'If you want to. But don't you think there's something else we have to do?'

'Like?'

'Like find out who the hell those characters on the motorbikes were last night. I've tried to pretend it was coincidence, that they weren't checking us out, but after London, and everything I heard yesterday and today, I don't believe it. You seem to be suggesting somebody may have taken revenge for … for what happened to you … and yet somebody, maybe the same somebody, seems after you. I mean, last night, if they had wanted to they could possibly have killed us. We know they're not afraid to use guns.'

Nazreem looked down, a cloud over her face.

'No, of course. You must believe me, I feel horribly guilty about what happened to that man, in the restaurant, in London. You are quite right – it is my fault. I am sorry.'

Marcus put his hand on her shoulder. 'No, no. It's not your fault. You weren't to know a gang of homicidal maniacs were after you. These things happen. But we have to stop something similar happening again. Maybe to you next time.'

'I know that. Believe me, I know that. In fact, right now it's the only thing I do know.'

'Look, Nazreem, what is it you're not telling me? You seem convinced there's a link of some sort between the theft of this statue, whether or not it really was an original of the Madonna, those nutcases in London and an atrocity dished up on the desk of some nun here in Germany. But to be honest with you, other than your presence I don't see it, and it was you who brought us here.'

She dropped her head but continued walking and said in a quiet voice: 'Marcus, you have to believe me on this. I just know. I'm really pleased you're with me, but you don't have to be. In fact, it might be better, better for you, if you were to go back to England.'

'That's not what I meant. Of course, I'm with you on this. It's just … it's just that we have to see things clearly. Look, if this has to do with the statue, it has to do with whoever stole it. You said you thought the Israelis were involved, but you have to admit those men who came after us in London gave a very different impression.'

'Yes,' she said, lifting her head and turning briefly towards him, finally admitting something difficult to herself.

'So who could have had a reason to steal it, and if they did, why are they still pursuing you? And how does that fit in with what happened with the nun.'

'I don't know, Marcus. I'm not pretending I have the answers. But …' She hesitated a moment.

'But what?

She shook her head.

'But nothing. I don't know. I just don't know.'

Marcus looked at her but she kept her head down, her eyes on the pavement at her feet. Not for the first time in the past few days, he felt that for a woman who claimed she was engaged on a search for the truth, she gave the impression of not always telling it.

30

The girl behind the hotel reception desk gave them a frosty smile as they entered the lobby. Marcus wondered if they had outstayed their departure time. Maybe it had been eleven a.m. instead of noon. He had initially only booked the rooms for one night. Even now he wasn't sure if it was worth booking for another or if they would be better advised looking for something in Altötting.

The reason for her attitude, however, was sitting on the other side of the lobby. Marcus hadn't noticed the two men in the bucket chairs next to the pot plants. But as he approached the reception desk to ask for their room keys, he was instantly aware of the pair standing either side of him. His initial reaction was verging on panic, when the one on his right, a man of about forty with a long thin moustache touched him on the arm and said politely in fluent, but heavily accented, English: 'If we could please have a minute, sir.'

Marcus turned abruptly, his nerves immediately on edge, wondering what he might use as a weapon if he needed one. He had just about decided that the heavy ashtray on the reception counter was his only option, when the man who had spoken to him produced an official-looking identity card and held it out to him.

'Detective Lieutenant Karl Weinert, Bavarian State Police,' he said formally, pronouncing his rank the American way – 'loo-tenant', a man who had obviously picked up a proportion of his English from TV cop shows – 'and this is my colleague, Detective Hulpe. We would like to talk to you and the young lady, please, just for some minutes.'

The girl behind the reception desk continued to display her frozen grin, but Marcus felt she was already double-checking his credit card details.

Nazreem looked visibly nervous as the second detective took her by the elbow, gently but nonetheless obviously, and led her after Marcus and his colleague towards a small seating area off the lobby.

'Is there some sort of problem, Lieutenant?' Marcus was already asking.

'No more than I think you already know about,' Weinert replied, motioning for them both to sit. Marcus and Nazreem found themselves side by side on a well-sprung leather sofa with Weinert in a chair opposite them on the other side of a small glass-topped coffee table. The second detective remained standing.

'May I see your passports, please?' the lieutenant asked.

Marcus was immediately taken aback. 'I'm sorry, you'll have to explain what this is about.'

'Of course, in a minute. But first if I might see your passports?'

Marcus reached inside his jacket pocket and produced his. Nazreem fished inside her shoulder bag and did the same, with the practised sullen resignation of someone used to producing documents on demand.

The policeman examined them. 'I see,' he said, 'you are South African, Professor ... Fray, is it?'

'Frey,' corrected Marcus, 'pronounced like the German "*frei*".'

'Ah yes, of course, Dr Frey,' Weinert repeated ponderously. 'And you, Miss Hash-ra-vee,' he struggled with the pronunciation, 'are French?' He eyed her suspiciously as if he did not quite believe it.

Nazreem saw no reason to lie. 'I am a French citizen,' she said, 'but I live in Palestine, in Gaza.' The policeman handed the passports to his colleague who sat down in the other armchair, took out a notebook and began to jot marks in it.

'Excuse me, but I think you need to tell us what's going on here. Have we been accused of something?' Marcus said.

'I believe you were at Altötting yesterday.' It was scarcely a question but the intonation invited an answer.

'Yes,' said Marcus, sensing that these were men's men who expected him rather than Nazreem to provide the answers.

'And spent some time talking to Sister Galina at the Institute.'

'Yes. Is there something wrong with that?'

The policeman looked as if he wished he could say yes. Instead he said: 'You are aware of the incident that occurred there earlier in the week?'

'Yes, but I don't see ...'

'Were you also aware that we had specifically requested that Sister Galina give no interviews?'

'No, I mean yes. But not at first. One of the other sisters did mention it, but this wasn't an interview, not like you mean. We're not reporters or anything like that.'

'I'm glad to hear it.' The policeman's eyes narrowed. 'I am taking you at your word, Dr Frey, because you gave the sister at the institute the name of this hotel and it is indeed where we have found you. Therefore I am giving you the benefit of the doubt.'

'What do you mean, the benefit of the ...?'

The policeman waved his objection away. 'It is an expression. Forgive me. Perhaps I use it wrongly.' But Marcus did not get the impression he had done.

'I have to ask you what the nature of your conversation with Sister Galina was and in what way you are involved?'

'We're not involved,' Nazreem interjected. 'I wanted simply to talk about the Madonna. I am a historian.'

The policeman looked at her trying to weigh up the value of her words. 'And you also live in Palestine. You are aware that it appears the man who was mutilated was apparently a Palestinian.'

Marcus could hardly keep from swallowing hard. He found himself watching Nazreem with as much anticipation as the two policemen. He had no idea how much she intended or wanted to tell them, but he suspected she had absolutely no desire to go into personal detail.

'As I understand it, he was a man of violence. We may have lived under occupation for many years, but not everyone believes that violence is the right way to achieve justice.'

The policeman nodded, as if she were a child who had given the right answer to a pre-prepared question in an oral examination, and moved on to the next one.

'Did you discuss any of this with Sister Galina?'

Nazreem gave him a look of genuine bemusement. 'No. As I told you, I am a historian. We were discussing the relationship between the relics in Altötting and a recent archaeological find in Palestine.'

Marcus breathed a sigh of relief. She was doing the right thing – telling them as much of the truth as they needed to know. Whatever the problem was here, it would not be solved by inventing some story. If there was any link between the two men on motorbikes who had behaved so threateningly the night before and the thugs who had pursued them in London, then sooner or later they were going to need police on their side.

'And this "historical discussion" was successful? You discussed everything you need to, satisfactorily?'

Odd question. Yet again Marcus wondered where all this was leading. Nazreem too seemed perturbed but did the sensible thing and gave an honest answer.

'Yes, very, but we would like to see her again,' Nazreem added.

The policeman was watching her intently. 'So would we,' he said.

'I'm not sure I understand,' Marcus said.

'Don't you? Shortly after seven-thirty last night, which I believe was not long after you left her, Sister Galina left the institute for the first time in a week. She told one of the other nuns she was going to pray. For you,' he said, looking directly at Nazreem. 'Do you know anything about that?'

After just a moment's hesitation, Nazreem returned his look and said simply: 'Yes. I hadn't asked her to, but she said she would. It was … a personal matter.'

'I see. The problem is,' said the policeman, 'that she hasn't been seen since.'

31

Nazreem slumped on the sofa like a marionette whose strings had been suddenly cut, her face ashen. Marcus put his hand on her shoulder and then turned towards the police lieutenant accusingly, but at the same time questioningly; he too could not believe what he had just heard. The senior policeman returned his attention, as if estimating to what extent the news he had broken was really a surprise.

The quality of disbelief on Marcus's face, however, would have been hard for even the most accomplished actor to feign: 'It's not possible,' he said simply. 'There has to be a mistake. We were with her until after seven p.m.'

'My point exactly,' the policeman said.

'I mean, she couldn't have … What happened? How on earth …?' Marcus let his voice trail off; the last question was the only one to which he had an inkling of the answer.

'We were hoping you could enlighten us. Sister Galina had not left the institute for several days. She had been unwell. Nervous tension, a state of shock, following … following the incident, of which I believe you are aware.'

Marcus nodded. Nazreem's eyes were downcast, focusing on nothing, or something deep in the recesses of her mind, to all intents and purposes cut off from the world around her. But at the reference to 'the incident' she twitched suddenly. Marcus was afraid she was about to faint. The second policeman, the one who had remained standing called something in German over to the receptionist who disappeared and then came back with a glass of water, hovering with an expression of concern and ill-concealed curiosity until she was politely but firmly waved away. But Nazreem ignored the proffered water, shaking her head and the policeman left it on the table in front of her.

'As I said,' the lieutenant continued, 'Sister Galina had not been out of the institute for more than five days. Then suddenly you arrive and immediately afterwards she disappears.'

'Disappears?'

'Just like that.'

'Nobody disappears just like that.'

'I quite agree. Perhaps you would like to tell us exactly what happened when you left.'

'What? Of course. Nothing happened. We … we said goodbye to her shortly after seven p.m. and then drove straight back to Munich.' Even as the words were leaving his mouth Marcus realised he was telling the truth but not the whole truth. But how could he even begin to explain about the 'black riders'? And what was there to tell? They had been hassled by a couple of bikers, that was all. Anything else was his imagination. That was how it would sound. But he could not get the sinister image out of his head. Had there just been the two of them on bikes? Had there been others, agents of whatever or whoever was pursuing Nazreem and her missing Madonna, lingering around the square, in the dark shadows of the great churches, watching and waiting? He had thought not, but maybe he had simply not been thinking.

'She showed you out?' the policeman asked.

'Yes. No, not exactly.' They had said goodbye at the doorway of the little sitting room. The nun had held Nazreem's hand and looked into her eyes and watched as they opened the door to the street. Marcus was almost certain he had seen her close the sitting-room door again as they left, and said so.

'But nobody else saw you leave alone? None of the other sisters.'

'I … no, I don't think so.' The hallway had been empty. The nun who had opened the door for them earlier was nowhere to be seen, and there had not seemed any point in looking for her.

'Sister Amelia, the nun who let you in, says she went back to the room where you held your conversation just after eight p.m. and found it empty. One of the younger sisters, a novice, said she saw Sister Galina go out about half an hour earlier, wearing only a light raincoat. The novice assumed she was going to the chapel, to pray. It was something she used to do in the evenings apparently. The young nun wasn't aware she hadn't been out since … the incident.'

Marcus thought back to the night before, the dark clouds and the heavy, almost viscous raindrops splattering on the windscreen as he gunned the car engine into life in the all but empty square. Empty save for the two men on motorbikes, the two who played tag with them on the country roads and then the autobahn, his sinister 'ring wraith' figures in black. He had a vision of that faceless opaque helmet turning to peer in through the passenger window, then pulling back and disappearing, as if frightened away by the bright lights of the oncoming city.

Could the faceless men on motorbikes have been merely a decoy, something to distract him and Nazreem from their real target? Had there been men hiding perhaps by the life-size crucifixes deposited under the awning surrounding the little chapel, malevolent figures concealed among the votive pictures he had found so disconcertingly sinister? Men with chloroform-soaked rags, a car with a waiting empty boot, ready to take the near-lifeless body of a middle-aged woman in holy orders who had already had the shock of a lifetime? But how could they have known she would go out alone? And why did she? Had she really felt so bound by her promise to pray for Nazreem that she had gone out almost immediately, on a wet, unseasonably wintry night, to fulfil it straight away? She could have prayed where she was, couldn't she?

But no, he realised, not after that conversation, dominated as it had been by the brooding presence of the dark figurine in its niche, surrounded by guttering candles and silver urns of human hearts. No, if she had wanted to pray for the quest she imagined Nazreem to be on, to recover a stolen image of the true Mother of God, and at the same time to exorcise the evil memory of the evidence of atrocity, she would have wanted to be in the presence of the Madonna. That was the true purpose that images like that served, he had long ago been told by a Catholic theologian, the excuse for the apparent idolatry, that figures of the saints, the Virgin, even Christ himself, were not objects of veneration in themselves but conduits, something on which to concentrate in the act of prayer, mental conversation with the Almighty.

He had thought it a lot of hypocritical hokum himself, but he had every reason to suppose that for most intelligent Catholics something like that made up part of their acceptance of the Church's customs. For the more simple-minded, no such construct was necessary; they would be content with the painted images. He could not be certain which camp Sister Galina fell into, but he felt wholly certain that if she had gone out to pray she would have gone to the little chapel in the middle of the great square.

He could see her walking out there, a dumpy little figure, a scarf pulled over her head, bowed against the rain, the thin raincoat pulled tight around her, heading for the witch's hat chapel in the middle of that great empty square. Empty except for sinister men on motorbikes.

'Maybe she was feeling better,' he said, thinking of the way she and Nazreem had seemed to strike up some sort of affinity. But he knew it wasn't an adequate answer. 'Time to return to her old routine,' but even in his own mind he could imagine no good coming from the woman going out to seek comfort from an ancient wooden statue that he could no longer think of in any terms other than as a black-magic talisman. Everywhere they went the symbol of a black Madonna exerted a baleful influence, even by proxy.

'Yes, I suppose that is possible,' the policeman was saying. 'Except that there is no evidence that she went there. The novice who saw her leave says it was shortly before eight p.m. – the chapel normally closes at eight, and the porter who locked up saw no sign of her or anyone else. In fact he says the rain had come on so hard the whole town centre was deserted. On his way back to his own accommodation in the lower town he says he saw only one person, a man in a black beret leaving the Gents' toilets. Do you mind if I ask where you and Ms Hashrawi were by that time?'

'Not at all,' Marcus did not like the suspicious tone to the man's voice: 'We were halfway back to Munich.'

'I see. And you came straight to this hotel?'

'Yes.'

The two policemen exchanged looks.

'Can I ask what your plans are for the next few days?' the lieutenant asked Marcus.

'Yes, that is, well, we had intended to go back to Altötting to have another chat with Sister Galina. But under the circumstances ...'

'Quite,' the policeman said. 'However, also under the circumstances I hope you understand I will have to ask you not to leave Munich without letting us know.'

'Of course,' said Marcus automatically before adding: 'But why? Surely you can't think we had anything to do with her disappearance? Is there some reason to fear something has happened to her?'

The policeman was shaking his head. 'I'm afraid that's something we don't know,' he said. 'So if you don't mind. It would be a courtesy.' His attitude said it was a courtesy he expected to be heeded. They shook hands formally and left.

The receptionist gave them another glacial smile as they turned from the door and then, almost reluctantly, reached below the desk and handed Nazreem a plain white envelope. It was sealed but only lightly and Marcus could see in the woman's eyes the temptation to have opened it in the presence of the policemen.

Almost absent-mindedly Nazreem ran a finger under the fold, took out and unfolded a single sheet with a small printed crest at the top. She glanced at it and then quickly at the woman behind the desk: 'How did you get this? And when?'

'It was delivered,' she said, clearly kicking herself now for not having yielded to the temptation. 'First thing this morning. By hand, a courier. Is there anything wrong? Is there anything I can do?' Her neck was craning forward in an attempt to make out anything of what was written on the paper, but Nazreem folded it away quickly and turned towards the corridor leading to the lifts. Marcus hurried after her, well aware of the mistrust and suspicion written on the receptionist's heavily powdered face.

'I hope there's no need for me to call back the police,' she said icily to his retreating back.

'I'm sure that won't be necessary,' called Marcus as he caught up with Nazreem at the foot of the stairs, just out of the receptionist's line of sight.

'What is it?' he said. 'What's the matter?'

She shook her head, staring past him at the wall, and handed him the unfolded letter. It bore the plain blue heading of the Institut der Englischen Fräulein, and beneath, written in ink with an old-fashioned fountain pen and a clear, steady hand:

'It's in Latin, just two lines and some numbers,' Marcus said: '*Nox luxque aeterna*. A poetic phrasing. Eternal night, eternal light.'

'It's the bit below that matters.'

'*Spero in matre dei, regina caeli*. I place my hope in the Mother of God, Queen of Heaven.'

'It's from Sister Galina,' said Nazreem with total certainty. 'It's her way of telling us she's in trouble.'

Beneath was the single word 'Guadalupe' and a cross followed by a series of eleven numbers, all but the last three grouped in pairs. It began +34 91 76 …'

'And this has to be a coded message of some sort.'

'I don't think it's a very complex code,' said Marcus. 'It looks to me like a telephone number.'

32

The two policemen sat in the unmarked Mercedes on Sendlinger Strasse, a few dozen metres from the hotel. There were noisy tourists pouring out of one of the big beer houses and glancing up at the dark clouds gathering above. Munich was in for another downpour. Lieutenant Weinert grunted as he turned the key in the ignition and with more than the usual cursory glance in his rear-view mirror pulled out into the light traffic.

'What did you think?' he said to the bulky shape of his colleague.

'Think?'

'Of our love birds?'

'For a start I didn't think they were that.'

'Really,' the police lieutenant raised an eyebrow.

'I don't know,' Hulpe continued. 'There was just something about them, about the woman in particular, as if she wasn't involved. Not just with him, with anything. Until you mentioned the nun. Then she looked as if she'd been hit by a train.'

'Maybe she'd been thinking of going into holy orders herself?'

'She's Palestinian, with a name like that, even if her passport is French.'

Weinert shrugged. 'Who knows? Some of them are Christian, I believe. And why else would she come all this way just to see a statue of the Virgin Mary? If that's really why they're here.'

'You think maybe it isn't? You think there's a connection? To the nun's disappearance? Or to the other thing?'

Weinert turned onto the inner ring road, accelerated into the underpass and through it before turning north over the Donnersberger Bridge that crossed the railway tracks, then taking a right and finally a left into Maillinger Strasse.

'Are you having me on?' said Hulpe as they pushed through the swing doors into the lobby of the Landeskriminalamt and strode towards the lifts. All the way back in the car he had been trying to make the connection but had so far failed.

'Don't you think it's a bit funny to say the least, the whole business? I mean the Palestinian connection. First some nun gets a plastic bag full of mutilated body parts dumped in front of her that turn out to belong to a wanted terrorist who apparently doesn't die until a day later, in a supposed suicide bombing in the Gaza Strip. Doesn't make sense for a start.

'Then within days up pops a Palestinian woman, from Gaza too as it happens, who just decides she wants to make a pilgrimage to a Roman Catholic shrine and happens to drop in for a cup of coffee with the nun in question, who subsequently vanishes off the face of the earth. Yes, I think there's a connection. In fact I think there's more than a connection. I think there's a whole bloody Gordian knot of connections.'

'A what?'

Weinert sighed. He had long since given up on his deputy's lack of a decent classical education. 'Never mind. It was a famous puzzle, a test. They said only the greatest of men could solve it.'

The lift opened, they got in and Weinert waited until his deputy pressed the button for the third floor.

'And did anyone?'

'Anyone what?'

'Solve it, untie the knot?'

'Oh, just one man, Alexander the Great.'

The lift door opened and they walked out into the big open-plan office that was the main work area for the rank-and-file of Munich CID.

'He cut through it with a sword.'

'Sounds a bit like cheating to me.'

'Yeah. Me too. Later, Monika, later,' he said to the dark-haired woman who had got up from her desk and was approaching him with several bundles of paper.

Seeing there was little hope of getting the lieutenant's immediate attention she dumped the lot in his in-tray, on top of an already substantial pile and was heading for the safety of her own cubicle when Hulpe caught her by the arm and said, in his best conspiratorial-cum-ingratiating manner: 'A couple of cups of strong coffee would be cool.'

'They certainly would be by the time you got them. What do you think I am, a secretary?'

'Sorry, sergeant,' grimaced Hulpe. He knew when he was being put in his place.

'Maybe we can all sit down over a nice cup of coffee when he gets his head around that lot.'

'Anything particularly pressing in it?'

'Maybe, maybe not. But that just came through on the Europol link,' she said, lifting one sheet from the pile and thrusting it into his hands. 'From London. Top priority, it says. And that tends to mean their spooks rather than Scotland Yard these days. I printed it out specially.'

Weinert looked up, wrinkled his nose and snatched the sheet of paper irritably: 'Fucking hell!' he said, ignoring Monika's stern frown. 'Fucking bloody hell!'

He had found a sword all right, a double-edged one. There were two photographs on the sheet of paper, beneath an urgent request for any information or sightings to be passed to the security services of the United Kingdom. They were unmistakably those of the South African man and Palestinian woman they had left less than twenty minutes ago.

'Come on,' he called to Hulpe, turning on his heel and heading straight for the staircase. 'Let's hope the birds haven't already flown.'

33

It was just gone five-fifteen p.m. on one of those English afternoons that could either turn into bright sunshine or squally showers when the phone on Sebastian Delahaye's downstairs desk in Thames House – the one that did have a window with a view – burst unexpectedly into life. The call being patched through to him, it was rapidly explained, was from a German police lieutenant in Munich who had information on the elusive Dr Marcus Frey and his companion.

The man's name was Weinert, he spoke reasonable if not perfect English, and he was somewhat embarrassed. He had come through on the direct line given on the urgent information request bulletin put out over Europol. Delahaye and his likes had scant regard for the Hague-based agency, which they regarded as more of a sop to EU political correctness than genuine cross-border crime fighting, but it had its uses as an information dissemination network.

He took the call politely; unlike some of his colleagues on the domestic intelligence front, Delahaye was of the opinion that being rude to foreigners wasn't necessarily a national obligation. Particularly as he already had more than a premonition of what the man was about to tell him.

To say he was embarrassed was something of an understatement, however. Delahaye could positively feel the man's cheeks glowing down the other end of the telephone line as he was forced to admit that he had interviewed the couple British intelligence wanted to question just a few hours earlier. He had sent men back to their hotel but they had already checked out. He was extremely apologetic and would give the British agent all the information he had on the couple.

It turned out to be a lot more than Delahaye had bargained for. He had only just been told from an intercept of Stansted passenger lists that Frey and his lady friend had flown to Munich without – that being the way with budget airlines these days – return tickets. Until now, however, he had had no idea why. Any link to the mutilation and death of a known Islamic terrorist only increased his interest in Marcus Frey a thousandfold. That they were also suspected of involvement in the disappearance of a middle-aged nun seemed bizarre to say the least.

'The one thing we are certain of is that she didn't leave the country with them,' said Weinert, relieved that he was giving his British colleague information he didn't have. It was still only compensation but he had kept the best bit for last. 'The reason I am calling personally is that you may still be able to pick them up when they land. The Bundesgrenzschutz – the border police – at Munich airport registered their departure on a flight forty minutes ago ...'

'... to Madrid.' Delahaye couldn't resist finishing the sentence.

'You knew already?' There was an unmistakable irritation in the German policeman's voice. He had clearly hoped he was delivering an important tipoff.

'Just an informed guess, lieutenant, but I would be more than grateful for the flight number.'

'Ah, quite, indeed,' said Weinert, and supplied it, clearly happy that there was something he could deliver. 'You will keep us in the loop if there are developments. In relation to the disappearance, and the mutilation incident.'

'Absolutely. And thank you once again.' Delahaye put the phone down and smiled to himself. The flight number was useful. He was more than happy to have pinned down Frey definitively and on consideration had no regrets at all that the German had not picked him up. Nor was he about to take the conscientious Munich lieutenant's suggestion that he have Spanish security detain them the minute they disembarked at Barajas airport. From the moment of the Brick Lane incident, Frey had been running somewhere or to someone. Delahaye wanted to know where. And why. As long as Frey had no suspicion he was under surveillance by a government agency, keeping tabs on him was the easiest thing in the world.

His 'guess' that the 'nutty professor' – as he had now mentally labelled him – was on his way to Madrid was not exactly wild. The minute he had been put on the internal security service's 'of interest' list, procedures had been set in motion, as a result of which the screen in front of him currently displayed a constantly updated list of all calls made from Dr Marcus Frey's mobile phone: the latest, timed at barely three hours ago, had been to a fixed landline in Madrid.

Delahaye had already had his people call it, from a shielded phone, intending to come across as a wrong number. But that had not been necessary. The voice on the other end had belonged to an answering machine. The curiosity was, however, that it had not spoken Spanish but some other, loosely-related, Romance language.

Part Three

… ORA PRO NOBIS PECCATORIBUS …
… Pray for us sinners …

34

Madrid

The heat was stifling. The taxi meandered its way down a warren of impossibly narrow streets also scraping walls with its wing mirrors before emerging into a small triangular plaza where it disgorged Marcus Frey and Nazreem Hashrawi at the side door of the great nineteenth-century pile that was the Hotel Victoria.

The clerk behind the great mahogany reception desk looked up inquisitively at the couple who stepped through the side door only to pull up short at the incongruous sight of a metal-detector arch. He dashed forward to usher them through, apologising in broken English: 'Most sorry *señor, señora*, but it has been necessary. *La seguridad*. You understand.' Marcus nodded. In March 2004, a team of Islamic fundamentalist bombers had killed more than 200 people in central Madrid. He understood only too well.

'We believe there is a reservation for us,' he said as the clerk returned to his side of the vast desk, looking around at the grandiose lobby. The Victoria obviously played up its old links with the world of bullfighting: there were antique posters and various *taurino* memorabilia dotted around the lobby. Marcus was still coming to terms with the fact that they were now, wholly unexpectedly, in Madrid.

Barely five minutes after the two German policemen had left them in the lobby of that very different hotel in Munich, Marcus, at Nazreem's insistence, was calling the number on the card they assumed had been sent by Sister Galina. +34 had turned out to be the international code for Spain, 91 the area code for Madrid. The voice on the other end of the line was male and it took Marcus a second or two to realise it was an answering machine, but somewhat longer to work out exactly what it was saying.

He had assumed it would be Spanish, but Nazreem, who had a little of the language assured him it was not. It wasn't Italian either

– Marcus had a smattering of that – and Catalan seemed unlikely in Madrid. It was then that he realised that he was listening to a message left on a twenty-first-century answering service in Church Latin, the mediaeval language used by Roman Catholic cardinals in conclave.

He had felt rather stupid but Nazreem insisted they left a message in English, announcing themselves as friends of Sister Galina of Altötting, nothing more, nothing less and giving the number of Marcus's mobile. Almost immediately, the call was returned by a man speaking a crisp, precise if somewhat stilted English. He announced himself only as a servant of the monastery of Guadalupe and when Marcus began to tell him what had happened hushed him, as if he feared their conversation was being listened to.

'Come to Madrid,' the man said simply, not so much in the tone of a man used to giving orders, but in that of one used to being listened to obediently. 'Straight away. Stay at the Hotel Victoria on the Plaza del Angel. I will make the booking.' With that he put the phone down. When they called the number again, there was only the answering machine.

Fired by Nazreem's newfound decisiveness, they had found themselves barely fifteen minutes later on the S-bahn headed for Munich's Franz Josef Strauss airport. It had not dawned on Marcus until they were actually in the air that they had promised to inform Lieutenant Weinert of any radical change in plans.

There were other things on Marcus's mind. Not least the fact the clerk confirmed there was indeed a booking for two single rooms in their names. What was disconcerting was that the hotel had their names at all despite the fact that the man they had spoken to on the telephone had neither asked, nor been given them. The clerk regretted he did not know who had made the booking.

'Oh,' he added, removing something beneath the room reservation form, 'there is also this,' and he handed Marcus a sealed envelope. Marcus ran his finger under the seal and opened it to discover two tickets for that evening, tickets to an event that, far from being something he was keen on, he actually believed ought to be banned.

The man in the cream Mercedes of the type that served as taxis in central Madrid sat with his 'for hire' sign turned off next to the newspaper kiosk in the Plaza del Angel with a cup of coffee and a well-thumbed copy of *Hola!* magazine. The little three-sided square which abutted the larger Plaza Santa Ana was a favourite place for cab drivers to pause for a break. If any of the four or five others parked there had bothered to be more observant, they might have noticed that he had been there substantially longer than the average coffee break.

They might also have remarked on the fact that the cab lacked the usual advertising that defaced most of the city taxis' doors. But being busy men who valued their few minutes of free time when they could briefly ignore the hassle of the crowded city streets, they paid him no attention. Most finished their coffee and cigarette and then took their place in the queue on the rank which in this bustling neighbourhood was one of the city's busiest, even at the relatively early hour of five-thirty, which most *Madrileños* regarded as mid-afternoon.

The driver of the cab parked next to the kiosk, however, had no intention of taking his place in the rank, now or ever. The only ranks in which he had ever taken his place were those of the soldiers of God. But his patience at last had its reward. Over the top of the magazine he watched the couple he had been waiting for leave the front entrance of the hotel and turn right heading down towards Puerta del Sol. He had no doubt that he had identified them correctly, the man tall, blond and typically Anglo-Saxon in appearance, walking with an ever so slight but just noticeable limp, the young woman shorter, dark-haired, olive-skinned, could almost have been a typical Latin beauty, from the south, Andalucia maybe, although he had been reliably informed she was not. Still, there was enough shared material in the gene pool.

He gave them five minutes, just to be sure there was little chance of them realising they had forgotten something and turning back, although it would have been a nice irony if they actually flagged him down. He would have given them a ride all right, even if it had not exactly been what was on the agenda. But they did not, and following them down the warren of narrow streets that led down to Sol was not an option. That was not a problem. He was fairly certain he knew where they were headed, and there was an easy way to make certain.

A few seconds later, the reception clerk who had welcomed Marcus and Nazreem to the Victoria and was still smarting from the fact that he had not been given a tip, saw an olive-skinned man who certainly did not look like the usual class of resident in a four star hotel dash through the door, in a state of some excitement.

'Taxi,' the man announced, explaining everything, 'for Señora Hashrawi,' looking at his watch, 'with apologies. I am a little late. The traffic.'

The receptionist nodded. Madrid traffic was a nightmare these days, especially in the narrow streets between Sol and Angel. The taxi driver spoke perfect Spanish albeit with just a slight accent which he couldn't place. He looked at his books and then up again with an expression of stage commiseration: 'Ah, the Middle Eastern lady. I am sorry. They have just left.'

The driver looked devastated. 'Another missed job. The boss will be furious.'

The receptionist looked at this disconsolate individual cluttering his lobby and felt obliged to offer at least a word of consolation: 'My fault, I'm afraid. I had no idea they had ordered a taxi. They didn't say. In fact, I advised them to take the metro. I wouldn't worry if I were you – tell your boss it would have been a bad fare. They were headed for Las Ventas, and if you thought the traffic around here was bad think what it'll be like up there in the middle of San Isidro.'

The taxi-driver smiled gratefully and nodded his agreement: 'Ah, that was it, no wonder they were in a hurry. They'll be faster on the metro right enough and I can make more in a couple of jobs out on the street than sitting up the Alcalá for an hour or more. Have a good evening then.'

'You too,' said the receptionist and watched with satisfaction as the swarthy customer left through the revolving doors. What was it about that accent?

Back behind the wheel of the cream Mercedes, it was indeed time for the taxi-driver to report to his boss. He already guessed what the orders were likely to be and was not surprised when, after a brief conversation, his expectations were confirmed. He started the engine and turned the cab into the Calle del Prado, a clogged narrow street of bars and small restaurants and squeezed past the parked cars that straddled the kerb to emerge past the Cortes and join the broad boulevards that were Madrid's main traffic arteries next to the great museum itself. He headed north for a few hundred metres then swung right around the great fountain onto the vast Calle de Alcalá.

The congestion was every bit as appalling as predicted, although still not as bad as the unorchestrated confusion that passed for traffic in the city where he had grown up. It was forty minutes later before he pulled up at the kerbside next to the great arena that rose like some mad Disneyland nightmare dominating the streets around. He pulled the cab onto the triangle of dusty ground next to the metro station and cab rank, lit up a cigarette and settled down to wait. His 'for hire' sign was still turned off. With luck he would be taking a passenger after all this evening, and not a paying fare.

35

Marcus felt as if he could hardly breathe. A blue-brown fug of exhaust fumes hung over the Calle de Alcalá from the parping, grumbling traffic piled up all the way back to Plaza de Roma. Marcus was glad they had taken the hotel concierge's advice and used the metro. But even the fact that the bullring had its own stop – Ventas – had not quite prepared him for the massive structure that loomed above them the instant they emerged from the relative cool of the underground into the still sweltering early evening and the milling crowds of aficionados.

The Plaza de Toros Monumental de Las Ventas was exactly what it said on the label: monumental in every sense, a latter-day Coliseum in a fusion of Gothic and Arabic brickwork. It might have been a million miles from Munich.

Marcus had been to a bullfight only once before, on a holiday to the Costa del Sol his first summer in Europe. He had left early with a sense, not of disgust but of mild distaste for the provincial matadors' somewhat messy dispatch of a handful of less than threatening bulls. It had taken place in an arena scarcely bigger than a big top circus ring. By contrast the building in front of them now was a vast ornate red-brick structure, decorated with crenellations and ceramic inlays that made it look like a cross between the old Wembley football stadium and a Moorish seraglio.

'Incredible,' Nazreem was saying. 'This belongs to the world of Islam. The curved arches, the decoration, it could be in a mosque in Morocco or a Turkish palace.'

'It's called Mudéjar,' Marcus replied, dredging up more of the obscure information that his brain was programmed to download to the dark recesses of its organic hard drive for potential future academic projects. Some of it had recently begun to turn out more useful in his daily life than he had ever imagined. 'After the end of the Caliphate, when the Moors who had ruled Spain for more than 600 years were finally driven out, a few Muslims who had converted

– under duress – to Christianity stayed on and maintained artistic traditions. But that was back in the fifteenth century. I never imagined it persisted as late as this.'

'How old is it?'

'Not very. At least, not as old as you might think. Look.' He pointed up to lettering done in black tiles on white above the main gate and an ornate balcony window that could have been inspired by the Taj Mahal. It read: *Año 1929*. The building was less than a century old.

'Where do we go?' Nazreem asked, staring in bewilderment at the teeming throng pressing towards ticket windows and towards the entrances. The fiesta of San Isidro was the highlight of the bullfighting year and tickets were notoriously hard to get, particularly for the sought-after places in the shade. Touts selling black market tickets at up to several times their face value attracted little knots of arguing prospective customers. Marcus heard the figure of 200 euros being discussed angrily and glanced again at the pair he held in his hand.

The two tickets were marked *Palco 6 Tendido 9 Sombra*. Tickets in a lodge, in the shade. They had no face value. Marcus suspected he could have asked whatever he wanted for them.

'Come on, let's see what's in store for us,' he said. Not only was an evening of gore in the midst of tens of thousands of bloodthirsty enthusiasts less than appealing, he was all too keenly aware that they had very little idea what they were letting themselves in for. One thing at least was reassuring: if they had any doubts as to the intentions of whoever it might be they were actually meeting, this was about as public a forum as possible. On the other hand, he thought, as they swept through the entrance to section 9 of the amphitheatre and the torrid heat gave way to clammy, sweaty corridors of people pushing past each other to get to the great staircases leading to the upper levels, in a crowd like this you could slip a stiletto between someone's ribs as easily as pick their pocket.

On presenting their tickets to the usher however, they were directed not to the teeming staircases but to an elevator. Within seconds they were stepping out into a passageway three floors higher, at the top of the vast arena. Nazreem leaned out through one of the exotic arched windows running her hands over the richly decorated enamel tiles, looking for all the world like a Moorish princess. Beyond, the great fume-belching metropolis of Madrid stretched into the distance, struggling back to life after the soporific heat of the day while the merciless sun tried to sweat the last drop of blood from the city before it set.

An attendant interrupted their reveries with a respectful, '*Señor, señora, por favor, su palco,*' ushering them into the equivalent of a private box at the opera. There were fifteen seats in three rows of five each. Several elderly men stood up and nodded politely as they entered. Marcus looked around, wondering where their mysterious host was and where they were supposed to sit, but the usher indicated that their places were in the empty row right at the front. Here, below them lay the dusty red sand of an arena the ancient Romans would have found familiar.

Somewhat hesitantly, unsure of both himself and their situation, Marcus and Nazreem descended the few steps to the front of the box and sat down. It was only then that he took in the full vista spread out before them. He felt like Nero taking his seat in the Coliseum. In front and below was a vast stadium packed with more than 20,000 people seated in steeply banked tiers around the arena itself, a sandy ring in which already the evening's performers in their glittering costumes were taking their bows. A curved line as sharp as a lunar eclipse cut across the arena and the capacity crowd, separating those in the expensive shaded seats from the hoi polloi sweltering in the sun.

A band struck up and Marcus and Nazreem followed the eyes of the assembled multitude towards one of the boxes in the same row as theirs, near the centre of the arena's shaded zone. The decoration surrounding the box at the very middle was a magnificent riot of Mudéjar exuberance, but it was to the one alongside that all eyes were turned, as a tall, self-important looking man who appeared to be the master of ceremonies draped a coloured handkerchief over the front of the box. Fanfares sounded, a roar went up from the vast crowd and they realised that not only were the matador and his two aides, all resplendent in pink satin with gold braid already twirling like ballet dancers in the centre of the ring, but that a huge black bull had thundered into the middle of it.

There was something almost playful to the great beast's attitude, Marcus thought ruefully as it snorted and bellowed, cantering around the ring before it caught sight of the ridiculously dressed human trio, in particular the man at the centre gesticulating with his cape, and threw itself at him. The man effortlessly swept out of its way as the animal in its confusion turned to first one, then the other of his colleagues, their flapping capes vying for its attention. Marcus looked around. Nazreem seemed almost as absorbed by the grotesquerie being performed before them as the old men in the seats behind, one or two of whom he noticed had purple showing beneath their dark jackets. Perhaps they had found themselves in a box reserved for the clergy. Nothing would surprise him in a country like this. No one, however, had yet appeared to announce themselves as their host.

He turned his attention back to the arena and found, despite himself, that he was impressed by the studied insouciance displayed so arrogantly by the svelte young men in their absurd finery as they danced and pirouetted around the ring while the matador himself flamboyantly manipulated his cape. Each of them was playing to the audience as much as the bull. The bull, however, now had more to worry about. The picadors, two men, each on horseback, had entered the ring armed with long lances decorated with gaudy strips of cloth, and begun to goad the animal.

The bull's response seemed provoked almost as much by the sight of the horse as by the human baiting. It was as if the animal had a natural antipathy towards its fellow four-legged beast, thrusting at it with its horns in a way that made Marcus think blood-sport opponents had more to worry about here than just the fate of the bull. The horses were blinkered and had thick protective padding on their sides but their main protection came from the men on their backs as they kept the bull at a distance by thrusting the points of their lances into the taut muscles of the animal's mighty neck.

A horn sounded. Now the *banderilleros* were in the ring, like circus athletes coming on after the dancing ponies as the horseback picadors trotted out. Two of them took turns running and jumping in front of the angry bull now beginning to drip rivulets of blood from its wounded shoulder blades. Then plucking two gaily decorated steel barbs from an aide behind the protective barriers, the first began to perform an almost ridiculous shilly-shallying dance in front of the wounded beast, waited until it lunged towards him then made as if to plunge them into the beast's neck only to retreat at the last second as its horns veered towards him and run, legs wheeling like a circus clown, for the cover of the wooden barricades from behind which his colleagues looked on.

Jeers, whistles and boos mingled with scornful laughter. From the far, sunbleached side of the ring a few heavy cushions were hurled into the sand of the ring. The coward was being given the bird. Even his colleague seemed to shake his head at him in wondering disapproval before emerging himself to twirl and leap in front of the bull before waiting until it moved towards him and then expertly planting his sharp and savage barbs into the muscles behind its head. A mild ripple of applause ran around the arena only to be replaced by boos again as the coward re-emerged.

To Marcus's disbelief it looked like a repeat performance was about to occur as the man ran towards the bull, then away from it and then did the same again, this time ending up on the far side of the arena. The bull had lumbered towards one side, snorting angrily. The *banderillero* was standing in front of the royal box, head hung down, as if embarrassed by his performance, but more to the point dangerously ignoring the angry animal pawing the ground before him.

And then, just as it seemed the animal was about to charge and Marcus all but closed his eyes so as not to see the inevitable goring, the man spun on one heel as if gifted with second sight. One moment he had been a sorry-looking clown, the next he was rushing headlong towards the animal as if he, not it, was the charging beast, facing directly at its lowered horns, only to spring at the last moment with the astonishing agility of a leaping gazelle, thrusting down with his barbs and planting them into the massive neck while he himself flew up and over its back in a somersault, landing upright on two feet with his empty hands thrust upwards towards the crowd like some twelve-year-old girl gymnast. The crowd erupted, roaring its approval. On the far side of the arena, from where the cushions had been thrown, a few flowers fluttered into the ring. In the seats just below their box there were squeals of delight and a flagon of wine tossed into the air. From the old gentlemen in the seats behind them came a ripple of mild applause.

Marcus looked round at them and made a deliberate grimace. He might have the best seat in the house courtesy of some unknown host who so far had not had the decency even to show himself, but this was not a spectacle he would have chosen to attend and he saw no reason to disguise his distaste. He was amazed Nazreem could continue to watch so impassively. Then without warning a voice in his ear said: 'You have a problem?'

36

Marcus turned in surprise to find one of the elderly gentlemen who had been seated in the rows behind them had softly relocated to the seat next to him, and was looking at him sideways without taking his eyes wholly from the bloody spectacle unfolding before them in the arena.

'Not to your taste, I see,' the old man said loudly in English. I have to say that last performance was a bit theatrical even for me. I am a traditionalist, myself.'

'I don't see why they have to torture it so,' Marcus said pointedly, wondering at the same time why he was bothering to reply.

'They are weakening it, making it possible for the matador to kill it,' the older man said as if it was the most natural thing in the world. 'That is his job, you see.' Then, after a slight pause: 'I think you do not speak much Spanish? The verb *matar* means to kill. Now he is watching, observing the movements. He must be skilful, you see. Nobody wants an ugly kill. It should be noble for both man and beast.'

Marcus shook his head. He had heard stuff like that before but it had never cut much ice. But he was intrigued by this stranger who had suddenly decided to join them without introducing himself. Could this be the man who had provided the tickets? Was he a representative of the bishop from Guadalupe? And if so, why had he not made himself known to them earlier? Nazreem too now had let herself be distracted from the gory spectacle in the arena and was studying the craggy face of the elderly man who had joined them.

'Let me ask you a question,' he said, talking to Marcus but returning Nazreem's attention. 'If you were given a choice of living to the age of twenty years with only male companions in little better than nursery accommodation, then knocked unconscious, strung up by your heels for your throat to be cut, or if you could live to be twice that age, free and well fed, and given the choice of the finest women before being put in an arena to die with a sword in your hand, which would you choose?'

'I don't know what you're talking about.'

'That is the difference between the life of an average English bull and a Spanish *toro bravo*.'

'That's ridiculous. It's a phoney comparison.'

'Is it? Perhaps. Perhaps not.' He looked at Nazreem and even Marcus, to his irritation, could see the trace of a faint smile playing on her lips. 'The *señora*, however, does not seem to share your opinion. You do not find the bloodshed of the *corrida* shocking?'

'No,' she replied, remarkably calmly. 'I am familiar with the halal slaughter of a goat, when its throat is cut while the animal is still conscious and the blood gushes forth. That is different, of course; it is a religious ritual.'

'Rather than a sport,' Marcus added, keen to regain the offensive, though why they were bothering to discuss bullfighting at all with this man whose name they didn't know was beyond him.

'You think this is a sport?' the man replied, still concentrating his attention on Nazreem. 'Perhaps because the English call it 'bullfighting' and say it is not fair because the fight is not equal. But for us it is not a sport. The Spanish word is *corrida*. It is a ritual. You will not find the descriptions of today's events here in the sports pages of our newspapers; you will find them listed as *espectaculos*. A spectacle perhaps, but such a literal translation is less than adequate. It is culture, I think. Not yours – maybe – but ours all the same.'

'You mean like the opera?' Marcus was finding the man's pious equivocation irritating. Most of these people were here for the blood, with the chance of a matador being gored an extra thrill, like the possibility of a fatal accident at a Formula 1 Grand Prix. And yet he was aware there was more to it too, something almost sexual. The strutting matador in his tight-fitting costume presenting his satin-clad buttocks to the horns of the bull with a display of calculated insouciance. The picadors with their phallic barbs. The final act of fatal penetration. He had noted how the bottle blonde three rows below their box clutched her partner's thigh every time the *banderilleros* planted one of their barbs.

'Or like your church,' Nazreem said, in a remark that to Marcus seemed unwarrantedly rude and wondered if she was aware of the fact, but there was no indication that the man had taken it so. On the contrary he smiled and said, '*Touché, madame, touché.*'

'Excuse me,' said Marcus, his irritation finally getting the better of him. 'I think you ought to tell us ...'

A horn sounded again and the man next to him raised his hand slightly, in a way that made clear he was used to people heeding his authority and gestured to the ring: '*La suerte suprema,*' he said.

The matador himself, alone now and strutting in his skin-tight silk and satin finery, the personification of Latin vanity. Nazreem took her eyes away from the spectacle for a second to shoot a glance at Marcus's sombre, uncomprehending face.

She could feel the old man's eyes flicker towards her and then away as he too drank in the sight of the young athlete in the ring ceremoniously doffing his black tricorn hat to the bull he was about to kill. At his side this time was no longer the great bicoloured cape he had waved at the opening. '*La muleta,*' their host indicated. The red rag to the bull.

The matador used the wooden stick to which his cape was attached to flick it to one side, a flash of brilliant crimson against the churned, stained sand, then lifted his sword until the tip caught the sunlight and brought the blade to his lips. Across from him the great black beast, wounded, shook its heavy head slowly from side to side. Then advanced.

The cape now along the length of the matador's left arm, the sword held downwards from his right hand behind it. He stood his ground as the bull advanced, then in a sudden rush lurched forward, its horned head bowed, the horns rearing upwards. But the man pulled back his body from the rag, and the beast, uncertain as to which posed the threat, followed the ruse.

Quickstepping backwards with the skill of a prima ballerina, the matador swept the *muleta* out and away from him so that the bull's horns at one stage passed within inches of his waist. Then he flicked it up and out of the animal's line of vision, retreating smartly, backwards. When the bull turned its head again he was almost half the arena away, posing for the crowd in profile, left knee bent, cape stretched out along the left arm, right hand held high holding the sword pointed forward and down, the classic position for the kill to come. He held his ground, then lowered his weapon and advanced on the bull, daring it forward.

It did as bidden. Lunged, horns finding nothing. Then again, and again, turning on itself in frustration, the *banderillas* planted in its neck swaying, the blood from the wounds they caused trickling down the dark hide. Exhausted, confused, it stopped and stood and shook its head. As the matador crossed the line from shadow into sunshine, the evening rays glistening on his satin suit. Behind him, the bull stood and swayed as if it were rallying its forces for one last lethal lunge. Slowly it lumbered forward and a hushed cry ran through the crowd, as the matador delayed for a heartbeat before he turned and once again displayed his crimson cape to the steadily advancing animal.

The matador circled, repositioning himself in the shade, out of danger of a blinding ray that might be fatal. The bull turned towards him and he advanced to meet it. The animal's head was down now, and Marcus suddenly realised the practical point of the wounds inflicted in its neck: unless its head was down there was no way the matador could even attempt to kill it with a single thrust.

The matador raised himself on his toes, the sword aimed downwards, and gripping the pummel suddenly plunged the blade straight between the damaged, but still mighty, shoulder blades. The animal sank immediately to his knees and rolled over. The audience rose to its feet with a roar of approval and all of a sudden the stadium was a flurry of white handkerchiefs.

From the presiding box too now a handkerchief was waved in return. Reluctantly Marcus gave the old man next to him a questioning look.

'*Una oreja*. He has awarded him an ear.' And then when Marcus's puzzlement obviously increased. 'For a noble kill. And a noble death. Sacrifice, and atonement. I had hoped you would understand.' He looked across at Nazreem, and Marcus could see there was moisture in her eyes.

'But perhaps your young lady does. And in the end maybe that is all that matters.'

37

A line of taxis stood at a rank on the edge of a dusty triangle, their drivers standing together smoking cigarettes and swapping gossip in the lengthening shadow cast by the great amphitheatre behind them. Occasionally a roar would go up accompanied by a chorus of klaxons from within the arena, a muffled ghost of the blood and passion in the ritual drama in the dust.

There was still one bull to kill when the old man led Marcus and Nazreem out of Las Ventas and across the road into a small side street lined with seedy bars. The second on the left was called, with a drab predictability, *El Torero Bravo*. A man in a long white apron was sitting on a metal chair at a small table outside, mopping his brow and savouring a small cigar. He nodded as they approached and gestured them with one hand into the air-conditioned interior.

The long bar was all but empty, just a couple of men drinking beer at the far end and two waiters watching a replay of a football game on a television fixed high on the wall by a bracket. Behind the curved glass of the counter were dishes laden with tapas: olives stuffed with garlic or almonds, chunks of chorizo sausage in rich red paprika sauce, darkly marbled slivers of Jabugo ham, little rounds of bread topped with tripe in tomato sauce, others with thin slices of red onion and marinated anchovies, or boiled egg festooned with fat orange globules of fish roe.

'This place will be full once the *corrida* is over,' the old man said, 'but for now, the next forty minutes or so, it is quiet. We can talk. But first, let us sit down, make ourselves comfortable and get something to drink, yes?'

There was a row of Formica-topped tables along the wall opposite the bar counter, each equipped with little metal containers that dispensed the thin disposable napkins people wiped their fingers on after the tapas before discarding them on the sawdust-strewn floor. It looked like they expected serious business. The display of food had made Marcus just slightly peckish, despite the blood and gore they had just witnessed, but he could see Nazreem's mind was on other things.

This elderly bullfighting fan introduced himself simply as Julio. He was 'a close associate' of the abbot of the monastery in Guadalupe.

'We need to speak to the abbot. We were recommended to him from Sister Galina, from Altötting, in Bavaria, Germany.'

The man was nodding gently. 'So I understand. So I understand. May I see it?'

Nazreem was nonplussed, as was Marcus. 'See what?' he asked.

'Your letter of recommendation. You have one, I suppose?'

Nazreem shook her head, uncertainly. 'No. She just … she just gave us the contact information. She said if we left a telephone message at that number someone would get in touch with us. We were led to believe,' she went on with just a trace of hesitation, 'that that was sufficient.'

The old man drew a finger across his dry lips and said: 'Of course, of course. And here I am; here you are. It is just that normally … normally either people bring with them a letter of introduction or some direct contact is made in advance. In these days of telephones and email, it is not so difficult. Even at the monastery they have computers now.'

Marcus and Nazreem exchanged glances. How much to tell someone they knew so little about? 'Sister Galina sent her best wishes, but she is … indisposed,' said Marcus cautiously. The last thing they wanted was to be seen to be concealing things from people who were supposed to be their allies, but maybe the full truth – or rather what little they knew of it – would be better kept for the abbot himself.

'Ah, indisposed?' the old man said. 'Really?' and he abruptly turned his head to a waiter who had arrived and was hovering next to the table, looking at his watch as if he expected people to start flowing in from the bullring any minute.

'What would you like?' the old man asked: 'Coffee, tea perhaps – I am afraid tea is not very good here – or perhaps a glass of red wine, *tinto*, a Rioja?'

'Coffee would be fine,' said Nazreem, in a hurry to get such irrelevant details out of the way. Marcus asked for two espressos. The man passed on their order in rapid fire Spanish to the waiter.

'I have never been to Altötting, but they have an interesting

Madonna, I believe,' he said suddenly, the question of their references apparently dropped for the moment.

'Not as interesting as that in Guadalupe, though,' said Marcus, with an intonation that invited the old man to elaborate. The sooner they got onto the subject they were here for, the better.

Instead, he said simply: 'Ah, no, perhaps not. Perhaps not, indeed.'

There was an awkward silence broken only by the arrival of the waiter with their drinks, setting two tiny coffee cups on the table alongside a generous glass of red wine. The man lifted it with both hands as if it were a communion goblet he was about to offer them. Marcus wondered if it might be a habit.

'You ... are a frequent visitor to Guadalupe?' Nazreem began, hesitantly, unsure how to treat this man who was an intermediary to an unknown quantity.

'No,' he replied, as if it were an odd question. 'I live there and have done for some twenty years. And I consider it an honour and a blessing. But it is a small place, quite remote and not very grand. Except of course for the monastery.'

'And you know the abbot?'

'You may rest assured I have the very best connections with everyone at the monastery.'

'Yes. Thank you. It's just that we were a bit puzzled. Why we met here, I mean. In Madrid. At a bullfight.'

'I often come to Madrid, on little errands, for the monastery too. And I must confess to being an aficionado of the *corrida*. It seemed convenient. I thought you might enjoy it but alas ...' he gestured towards Marcus, who shook his head to indicate it wasn't a problem.

'I also – you will not consider it rude – sometimes like to check out people who want an interview with the abbot in Guadalupe. Monastic life is busier than many people think and there are so many time-wasters ... I do not mean you of course ... but these days everyone seems to think they can go straight to the top.'

The café was beginning to fill up now with a few early leavers from the *corrida*. The last *suerte* was not always the climax of the evening and leaving early was a way to beat the traffic, although Marcus hoped some of those wandering in now were not intending to drive. One tall man with skin burned the colour of old leather, clearly a regular in the cheap seats, was swaying down the bar unsteadily eyeing the display of tapas. As he passed them he suddenly lurched backward to end up almost sitting on their table, flung out an arm to steady himself and connected with Marcus's coffee cup splashing the hot dark liquid over his cotton chinos.

'For Christ's sake,' Marcus erupted, jumping to his feet and shaking the material to stop it burning his leg. The drunk reeled back against the bar, hands raised to his face as if in anticipation of a blow and muttering, '*Perdone, Perdone.*'

'It's all right, it's okay. Never mind,' began Marcus, patting down the stain with a plentiful supply of paper napkins from the table dispenser, thankful that he had only ordered an espresso. 'There's no harm done. It's okay. Okay.'

'Aha, Eenglish,' the drunk said, reeling upright, suddenly beaming, then looking extremely sorry for himself. 'I love Eenglish, so sorry,' he said. But already Marcus's squirrel brain had retrieved the irrepressible image of Manuel the stupid Spanish waiter in the old television sitcom *Fawlty Towers* and he was trying hard to keep a stupid smile off his own face. The old man at the table was frowning in puzzlement while Nazreem sat there tutting to herself.

'Is okay, *señor*, please. Liverpool. Manchester United. Very good. Please, drink brandy. From me.' And he was already signalling to the waiter on the other side of the bar.

'No really,' insisted Marcus, thinking that maybe this was the time to tell the man he wasn't English anyhow, but he imagined in his present state he could probably dredge up a long-lost love for South Africa too. Already the man was turning back round from the bar with two glasses of brandy – thankfully not large ones – and pushing one into his hand.

'No, really. Thank you. It's okay.'

The bleary cheery apologetic smile was immediately replaced by a huge drop-lipped tragic face of a sad circus clown. 'Pleeeese, *señor*, I am sorry. Please, forgive. We drink. Okay?' And he chinked glasses with Marcus and stood there expectantly like a small boy waiting to be told he can go out to play after all. Marcus looked around him. The barman made a mock drinking motion and winked; it was clearly some sort of custom. The elderly Julio shook his head as if in mild despair. Nazreem said: 'Just drink with him and be done. Then sit down again. We need to talk.'

Marcus shrugged and knocked back the brandy in one. The spirit burned as it rushed down but it was surprisingly smooth. His drunk new friend had obviously not skimped. The man emptied his likewise and beamed, '*Carlos Tersero. El mejor. Muy bien.*' Marcus simply nodded, shook hands and said, '*Gracias, adiós,*' testing the limits of his Spanish and at the same time making sure that the interruption was at an end. '*Gracias.* Sorry. Okay?' the drunk said in reply.

'Okay,' said Marcus and sat down again at the table to a weary sigh from Nazreem. To his relief, the drunk stumbled off, probably in search of a refill or one of his drinking cronies among the handful of men coming through the door with bullfight programmes in their hands.

The old man from Guadalupe gestured with his hands. 'I am sorry too,' he said. 'These things happen.'

'Forget about it,' said Marcus.

'When can we meet with the abbot?' said Nazreem.

The old man sighed and closed his eyes a second. 'I think it will be possible. Yes, there should not be a problem.'

'So when? And how do we get there?'

In fact she had already consulted the map and worked out it was at most a couple of hours' drive although they would have to rent a car, public transport connections were not good.

He looked at his watch, then took a long draught of his wine, emptying the glass, and leaned forward steepling his fingers together on the table. Not for the first time, Marcus wondered if he might be a retired priest. Then, glancing at both of them in turn but letting his eyes rest on Nazreem, he said:

'Perhaps it is best if you come with me. I am driving back there in any case tomorrow.'

Nazreem turned briefly to Marcus with a genuine smile and he said: 'Yes, that would be absolutely excellent. Thank you very much.' She nodded her head enthusiastically in agreement.

'Well then, that settles it. I have business in the morning. So let us meet around noon. It is annoying to travel in the heat of the day but unless we do we will not be there until late in the evening. How well do you know Madrid?'

Nazreem and Marcus shook their heads. 'Very well,' he said. 'Let us say the Plaza de Cibeles, by the fountain in the middle. I can park not far away and it is easy to find. Also very beautiful to look at if I am delayed. But I trust I will not be. Agreed?'

'Agreed,' said Marcus.

'Well, then, if you will excuse me ...' The old man stood up and began fishing in his pocket for a few euro coins, but Marcus put a hand out. 'No, no, that's fine. Really. We'll settle up.'

He nodded graciously and turned to leave them. 'Until tomorrow then. *Hasta mañana.*'

'*Mañana*,' said Marcus, getting up with him and holding out his hand but the old man was already heading for the door, fighting against an increasing one-way flow of hungry and thirsty customers pushing in.

Nazreem looked up at him quizzically as he sat down again next to her. 'What's the matter?' she said. 'You've got a funny look on your face.'

'I was just thinking,' he said. 'That it's one of those Spanish expressions that has crossed into English. *Mañana*. But when we use it, it means something that's never going to happen.'

The sky behind the great arena of Las Ventas was blood red in the last gasp of the Madrid sun. People swarmed towards the bars or into the metro, while cabs hooted and parped on the Alcalá as the traffic once again built up to a standstill. All except for one cab. With one passenger. The cream Mercedes that had sat on its own on the edge of the dusty triangle away from the busy rank, its 'for hire' sign resolutely turned off. The passenger had emerged from the Torero Bravo only minutes ago and walked straight towards his waiting ride with an assured self-confidence, and none of the drunken swagger he had exhibited so recently. He climbed into the front passenger seat wordlessly and both he and the driver watched as the stooped elderly man who had left the bar just before him headed for the entrance to the metro.

The man in the passenger seat turned to the driver and said: 'Five minutes.'

Marcus thought he had not seen Nazreem look so relaxed since she walked through the arrivals door at Heathrow. Once again it seemed she was seeing something in people that he was missing. He hoped for her sake it was intuition and not over-optimism. There had been something in old Julio's manner that he had found less than 100 per cent convincing, quite apart from his enthusiasm for bullfighting.

He tried to signal to the waiter for the bill, but the bar was too full now to attract the man's attention easily. Apart from anything else he was feeling slightly groggy. He knew the brandy had been a mistake. He looked around the bar, at the backs of people knocking back spirits, small glasses of red wine, cold beers and wolfing down anchovies or slivers of the dark red ham, but could happily see no sign of the drunk. He had no desire to resume their conversation. He decided to pay a quick visit to the lavatory before leaving and catch the waiter's eye en route to ask for their bill.

Nazreem nodded her approval and watched him push his way through the throng, treading gingerly on a floor by now covered with discarded tapas papers, this being a traditional bar where the custom was to discard them on the floor for the waiters to sweep up when business quietened down a bit. She thought he looked slightly unsteady, but it was probably just an attempt to avoid standing on a greasy napkin or a piece of dropped tripe.

It was only a full ten minutes later, when she had paid the bill and he had still not returned that she began to get annoyed. It wasn't possible surely that he had bumped into the drunk again and been cajoled into another brandy at the bar. It seemed highly unlikely but she had never quite got a grip on Western men's drinking habits and she knew from experience that they could get out of hand. After another five minutes, however, she decided to see where on earth he had got to. The bar was already starting to thin out as the bullfight crowd filtered away, having slaked their thirst and sated their early evening hunger, deciding the traffic had abated enough to think about going home for dinner.

A couple of large men at the bar smiled ingratiatingly at her as she passed, appreciative of such a classic dark-eyed beauty. She ignored their attention as she squeezed between them and a table to the little corridor at the back of the bar marked 'Servicios'. There was a door at the end and two on the left, the second of which was labelled 'Caballeros' with a picture of a matador's tricorn hat. One of the men who had smiled at her at the bar excused himself as he passed her and pushed open the door. Nazreem called, 'Marcus,' as discreetly as she could under the circumstances, but there was no immediate reply.

She looked around her. Of the drunk from earlier there was no sign. In fact, by now there were barely a dozen or more customers in the bar, dedicated drinkers mostly, the vast array of tapas had been decimated. Behind the counter the barman was rearranging what was left and repositioning it behind the glass. The waiter who had served them had taken his broom and was sweeping the debris on the floor towards the street door. She tried calling Marcus again, twice and a little louder this time, as the door to the Gents' opened and the big man who had just gone in came out again. He smiled at her once more as he squeezed past but it was a strange, questioning smile and she noticed that as he resumed his place at the bar he nudged his companion and made a twisting motion with one finger pointed at his head: '*Loca*?' A crazy woman.

'Marcus!' she called again, rapping hard on the door this time. There was clearly something wrong. Maybe he was being sick. She regretted having encouraged him to drink that brandy. 'Are you all right? Talk to me.'

'*Señora*,' the barman called to her. She looked back briefly in irritation and began banging on the door again. The man who had just exited the lavatory got off his seat and came towards her, the smile on his face now replaced by a dark frown. Instinctively she backed away, but the man kept coming, holding out his hands on either side as if to block her escape.

'Marcus!' she cried, louder than before, hammering on the door and lifting her hand to defend herself against the Spaniard if he came closer. The man held his two hands up, but at the same time backed off and said something to her softly at first. Then when he saw he was not getting through he tried again, more loudly, this time in broken English:

'Lady. No there. Is no one there.'

It wasn't a question. Nazreem suddenly understood, and looked first at him, then at the door, then back at him in horror. She felt suddenly short of breath as she summoned up all her courage and did something that as a Muslim woman she could never have imagined herself doing: she pushed open the door to the men's lavatory and rushed in.

To her relief – and horror, all at once – there really was no one inside. Streams of flushing water gushed down the white porcelain of the single urinal in front of her. On her left the door to a single empty toilet stall gaped open. Marcus Frey had simply vanished.

38

Marcus opened his eyes and instantly wished he hadn't. His head ached and even the low light felt like hot needles puncturing his retinas. He closed them again and realised there was nothing awaiting him but nightmares, waking or asleep. And sleep was no longer an option.

Slowly, like a man surfacing after a shipwreck, afraid of seeing only an icy, corpse-littered ocean, he let the outside world seep into his consciousness. Gradually his brain started trying to put back the pieces even if his fractured memory was not yet capable of reassembling them in the right order: the spectacle in the ring, the celebration of slaughter, the old man's strange pseudo-philosophical ramblings, then the tapas bar, and his unanticipated offer to take them with him to the monastery. And what else?

The drunk of course, knocking into him. And buying him the brandy. Carlos III – *Carlos Tercero* – his brain remembered, obdurately, because the way the man had pronounced it – *Carlos Tersero* – something odd about that, his brain seemed to recall though he had no idea what. It must have been one hell of a brandy if it had got him that drunk. No, impossible. He remembered heading for the loo, swaying slightly as he moved through the crowds at the bar, and then staring at the porcelain, feeling distinctly ill, having to reach out and grab the top of the urinal to stop himself falling into it. And then? Then there had been men, other men, one on either side. Catching him as he fell. Helping hands?

Like hell! That was what had been wrong with *Carlos Tersero* – one of the few things he did know about Spanish was that classic Castilian had a lisp – *Carlos Terthero* was what they said in Madrid.

The last thing that he could recall was guttural accents, the feeling of being dragged into fresh air and then a car door slamming. Something had happened that his mind didn't want to acknowledge – he had been kidnapped. His eyes sprang open, all of his senses suddenly awake. Where the hell was he?

He tried to move his feet and was surprised to discover he could do so freely. His hands too. At least he was not tied up. Nor was the surface he was lying on hard dirt. He was on a bed of some sort, although not a particularly comfortable one. He tried to persuade himself he just had had some sort of fit and been taken back to the hotel? But he didn't believe it.

The room might have been a hotel, but he doubted it. The bed he was lying on was double, but with just a simple sheet. There was a small bedside table but with no lamp on it, and a drawer that he doubted very much contained a Gideon's bible. The room was dark with just a pale ray of grey light coming in through what appeared to be closed venetian blinds.

Uncontrollably he felt a tremor in his left knee, a nervous tic deep in his flesh between muscle, bone and the tiny shard of shrapnel that remained lodged there, and he knew he was afraid. Very afraid. If he was in the hands of Islamic extremists he had good reason.

He had seen the videos. The grainy, ill-focused, low-resolution internet images of dishevelled, terrified hostages kneeling on the floor, pleading for their lives to some distant politician whose hand-wringing moral refusal to 'negotiate with terrorists' was their death warrant. The men in masks and checked keffiyehs slung around their necks, standing beneath Arabic slogans – phrases from the Koran – with Kalashnikovs in their hands. Except for one. The one wielding the knife. The long curved blade brandished like a butcher's imple-ment with which he would lean forward and cut the hostage's throat, while the cameraman captured it all, the blood and the screams and the death rattle, to be broadcast on the World Wide Web, picked up by television channels mercifully too squeamish to screen it, and sickos in US trailer parks who would watch it over and over again in the small hours of the Midwestern night telling themselves it was their patriotic duty to stoke up hatred for the invisible enemy.

Marcus realised he was terrified. If the last thing he had done before passing out had not been to pee he would have wet himself. There were no good ways to die but the one he relished least was as a trussed sheep whose legacy would be as a low-grade piece of snuff-porn.

He lifted himself up on his elbows trying to make out more of his surroundings. His head ached and he was not yet sure if he was up to standing. There was a washbasin against one wall with a cracked mirror above it. And a door next to it. Locked. Or open? There was only one way to find out. Gingerly he put his feet on the floor and tried to put his weight on them.

'I'd be a bit careful about that if I were you.'

The voice came out of nowhere. Marcus swivelled round to see a small bucket armchair squeezed into the darkest corner of the room parallel to the bedhead, and squeezed into the armchair a swarthy-skinned man with dark hair and a full moustache, studiously cleaning a handgun. The man looked at him, tilted his head to one side, then stood up, setting the handgun carefully down on the table, well out of Marcus's reach, and said in heavily-accented English: 'Good morning.'

Morning? 'Who the hell are you? And what do you want?' Marcus said, raising his head and shoulders, supporting himself on his elbows and avoiding the acute temptation to look at his watch. It sounded more resilient than he felt. For a fraction of a second he was glad Nazreem had chosen not to tell him more about her precious missing Madonna and then realised how willingly he would have given away anything he knew. It could have been the one chance to save his life. Where was Nazreem anyhow? He had left her seated at the bar, and had no memory of seeing her since. Had they got her too?

His jailer looked at him for a long moment as if trying to decide how to reply. The man looked back towards the side table and crossed to it and lifted his gun. Marcus swallowed hard. Then, tucking it into his waistband, he walked over to the sink against the wall, lifted a toothglass from a metal holder next to the cracked mirror and half-filled it from a small bottle of mineral water on the shelf below it.

'Here, for you,' he said. 'Water.'

Marcus took the glass gingerly weighing the wisdom of throwing it at an armed man's head, before the realisation that it was plastic mercifully dispensed with that idea. The man's eyes were hard, unblinking and there was a glint in them that suggested he was not troubled by slow reactions.

'Where the hell am I? What's going on?' He wanted to add, 'Where's Nazreem?' but stopped himself; if they already had her, he would find out soon enough and there was no point otherwise in jogging their memories.

The man narrowed his eyes and nodded as if he had been given an explanation rather than an angry question, then raised his finger to his lips.

'One minute,' he said. Then to Marcus's surprise he turned around and walked out the door.

Throwing the plastic water glass to one side – he was thirsty as hell but he wasn't going to drink anything he hadn't sourced himself – Marcus did his best to hurl himself from the bed. It wasn't as easy as it might have been, his head reeled and he almost lost his balance the minute he tried to stand. He patted himself down, discovered to his surprise – but not reassurance – that he seemed still to have his wallet; muggers would have been infinitely preferable. For a moment his hopes soared, but a hand thrust into the inside zip pocket of his jacket shattered them all too predictably: they had taken one item, his mobile phone.

Tentatively, he tried the door handle, easing the round knob as softly as he could – the last thing he wanted was to bring the thug with the gun hurtling back in to deal out a pistol lashing, or worse – and was scarcely surprised to find it was locked. He tweaked the slats on the venetian blind, only to find himself looking out on a sea of red-tiled roofs, concrete, stonework and television aerials with a forty-foot drop. He was on the fourth or fifth floor of an apartment block, probably somewhere in the endless Madrid suburbs.

It was in a flat like this, he remembered dimly, with a chill like iced water running down his spine, that police had cornered the Al Qaeda-linked Islamic fundamentalist bombers a month after the Madrid bombings. They had refused to surrender, battening down for a siege that ended only when they had deliberately set off a bomb inside the apartment, blowing themselves up at the very moment the police were about to storm the building. Cold comfort indeed. What was it he had read in the *Metro* that had sent them on the madcap journey to Altötting? That the heart dumped on Sister Galina's desk had been proved by DNA to be that of someone suspected of involvement in the Madrid attacks? He conjured up the image of some fanatic plunging a curved knife into his breast to extract his still beating heart, and bitter bile rose in his throat.

Then the door opened and the swarthy young man with the gun came back into the room, grinning broadly when he saw Marcus standing up. 'You are better,' he said. 'This is good.' And he turned to the large figure who suddenly filled the door frame behind him.

The imposing man who strode into the room with the rolling gait of a Worldwide Wrestling Federation champion entering the ring looked less like an Islamic fundamentalist than anyone Marcus Frey had ever seen in his life.

He had a head of close-cropped blond hair tending to grey that sat atop the vast body of a weightlifter run to fat, enormous rippling muscles decaying slowly to rolls of lard sweating profusely under a too tight T-shirt.

'That's the best news you'll get today, José,' he boomed. The voice could have been that of a retired Sergeant of Marines, as did the accent, an unmistakable Texan drawl. The logo on the T-shirt proclaimed 'Jesus Wants You for a Sunbeam'.

39

'I'm afraid we owe you something of an apology,' the Marine Sergeant voice boomed as Marcus sat down on the edge of the bed in stunned silence. He had been expecting a black-robed Iraqi executioner; instead he was facing George Bush's overweight cousin.

It was almost comic. Almost. But not quite.

The man facing him spoke his language and was superficially the same racial type, but you didn't grow up in South Africa without knowing that was nothing to go on. There was a glint in his eye that Marcus immediately recognised; he identified it with fanaticism. Or insanity.

'The hired hands can be a little bit overenthusiastic sometimes,' the large man continued, coming forward and reaching out a hand the size of a baseball mitt with two gold signet rings.

'Martin Jones, pleased to meet you, Professor Frey. And this here's my good friend and colleague, the Rev. Henry S. Parker.'

Until then Marcus had barely even noticed the wiry, grey-haired man with aquiline features and rimless spectacles who now emerged from behind his larger accomplice. He was wearing a dog collar underneath a lightweight grey suit and a thin smile that he obviously reserved for special occasions.

'At your service, sir,' he said politely, nodding.

It was more than Marcus could take: 'At my …? I don't think so. You kidnap me and lock me in a room with an armed thug and you have the nerve to … what the hell did you do to me? Drug me or something? Who the hell are you and what on earth are you playing at?'

'Like I said, we do owe you something of an apology,' the man who called himself Jones said, 'and now you've had that. As for what was slipped in your drink? Rohypnol, I'm afraid. It's best known as "the date rape drug", but you can rest assured, professor, we have no intention of anything like that, do we, reverend?' Jones said, bellowing at his own sense of humour.

The man in the dog collar gave him a stern glare. 'No indeed, sir. I should think not. We leave the devil's perversions to the devil's spawn.'

'José, why don't you go and get Freddie to brew us all up a nice hot pot of coffee. That'll do the professor here the world of good and I sure could use a cup too. How about you, reverend?'

The reverend nodded.

'You have to excuse the guys. Mexicans,' Jones added as the swarthy gunman left the room. 'Wetbacks. Still got Rio Grande mud in their toes, like most of the population of south Texas these days, but they mean well. A few friends in the right places to find them gainful employment and they've even seen the light of the true faith and given up the ways of idolatry for the word of the Good Book, by which I mean of course the King James' Authorised Version, isn't that right, reverend?'

'Amen to that,' said the man in the dog collar without the slightest hint of irony.

'We need them over here, on account of the lingo,' the big man said, tapping a finger to his nose as if confiding a business tip.

Marcus nodded, as if he understood anything at all. 'I'd like to leave now,' he said.

'Sit down, professor,' the big man said with a smile but in a tone of voice that made clear he didn't consider there to be an alternative. 'Make yourself at home. We've got a bit to talk about here.'

'I don't consider I've got anything to say to you or you to me, except to explain why your men abducted me and what's happened to the woman I was with. If you've touched her ...' Even as the words were leaving his mouth Marcus realised how hollow his bravado might sound. If he thought these people would be reasonable just because they were American Christians rather than Islamic fundamentalists, he might be seriously deluding himself.

The big man's eyebrows raised as if he would be entertained as to what the second half of Marcus's threat might entail. But all he said was: 'Ah, the Arab lady. Rest assured, sir, we did not touch one hair of her head. As far as we know she could still be sitting over a cup of coffee waiting for you to come back from the john, but I would imagine she'll be back at your hotel by now.'

'Then give me back my phone and let me call her.'

The minister looked sheepish but Jones shook his head. 'All in good time, professor, all in good time. We wanted what you might call a little "quality time" with your good self. You are, after all, one of us.'

'One of you?'

'Yes sir, a white man, for a start, if I can use that term these days in a non-derogatory sense. And a Christian. Brought up in the Dutch Reformed Church, I believe, a very honest, God-fearing branch of the true faith.'

Marcus said nothing. So they were as much guilty of swallowing the stereotype as he nearly had been. He remembered the self-righteous middle-class white women his mother used to associate with at the golf club going off to church on Sunday to pray for their fellow man and 'all God's children' before coming home and treating the black 'houseboy' like dirt. The man facing him was the type they would have expected to join the police, 'to keep the kaffirs in order'. Yes, he would have got on just fine in the Dutch Reformed Church.

Jones chose to interpret his silence his own way. Like most people did. 'You see,' he was saying, 'we would hate you to do something you would mightily regret, and think you ought to know the full facts about what you're dealing with here.'

Marcus snorted involuntarily. On that at least, he was in full agreement. But as yet he had no idea where these people were coming from, why they had abducted him and what they expected of him, though he had a keen idea that none of it would be a world's remove from his relationship to Nazreem and the cursed black figure she had dug up from the sands of Gaza.

'What do you know about *"la leyenda negra"*?' the big man said, leaning back against the washbasin with a smirk on his face, as if he had uttered some magic talisman.

Marcus looked at him in utter mystification for a moment, then sat down on the bed while once again, to his own surprise, his brain involuntarily delved into its cavernous treasure trove to bring up a few nuggets. In fact, the 'black legend' was one of those issues he had squirreled away with a marker: another example of history turning schizophrenic, two sides to every story. He could imagine which side Jones had heard.

'A propaganda exercise on behalf of English protestant monarchs from the time of the Spanish Armada onwards, trying to depict all Spaniards as cruel and Spain as a pawn of the devil.'

Jones turned to the minister who now perched like an underfed bird of prey on the edge of the little armchair and said, 'What did I tell you, reverend, the professor here's a smart guy.'

'I said it was a propaganda exercise. It fitted in with English foreign policy. Philip II had a claim on the English throne and Spain had a rich American empire. By demonising the Spanish the English legitimised the piracy of people like Francis Drake and Walter Raleigh.'

The American frowned for a minute then broke into a chortle. 'That's good, professor, it really is. They always said the sign of a good academic was a man who could turn history on its head for the hell of it. But I think you know as well as I do that the black legend had more to it than that. That's why you're here.'

Marcus played dumb.

'Come on, professor, the sooner we level with each other here, the sooner we can be best friends. You see we know why you're here.'

Marcus said nothing, but he was not surprised. He was beginning to see Nazreem's mysterious missing Mary as the source of all trouble. The Texan gave a sigh of mild exasperation as if Marcus was a sulky child: 'You're on your way to Guadalupe. That's why you met up with the gentleman you were with last night. And you're going there because of the so-called "black Madonna".'

Marcus shrugged. There was no point in denying the obvious. He needed to know what these men knew, and what they thought they stood to get out of him.

'It's not a coincidence you know, the black legend and the black Madonna.'

The door opened again and this time Marcus recognised the drunk from the Torero Bravo, the one who had so loved the 'Eeng-lish', poured coffee all over him and insisted on buying him a brandy, the brandy he now realised had been spiked with Rohypnol.

'Ah, caw-ffee,' Jones boomed. 'Thank you, Freddie.'

Marcus looked sceptical at the name. 'Alfredo,' said the big Marine, 'but he prefers to use a proper American name now, don't you, Freddie?' The man gave him a thin smile and said, 'Si señor Jones,' leaving Marcus less than convinced. Not that he cared what they called him. He couldn't imagine any chance he would get to pay the man back but if it came up he didn't want to miss it. Alfredo, aka Freddie, set down the obviously heavy coffee pot, laid out small blue porcelain cups and looked at his large lord and master questioningly as to whether or not he should pour.

'For you, professor?' asked Jones.

'No, thank you,' said Marcus firmly. 'I've had experience with the sort of drinks he serves.'

Jones shrugged, as if the sarcasm was wasted on him: 'Suit yourself. A lot of people, particularly in the United States today, will say – with some justification, mind you – that the black legend actually refers to a genuine Hispanic sickness of the mind, that Hispanics have a genetic predisposition to this sort of pagan idolatry, just like the black man has towards jazz,' he laughed.

Marcus watched the Mexican pour coffee for the two Americans.

'But I'm here to tell you it ain't true,' Jones went on. 'There's a grain of truth there, all right, just like there is in all those stereotypes, but these two boys have found that Jesus is about a lot more than bells and smells and black Barbie dolls, isn't that right, Freddie?'

'*Si señor*, I love Lord Jesus,' said the re-christened Alfredo, flashing gleaming white teeth at Marcus who came close to flinging his coffee cup into them.

But instead, on an impulse he reached for the cafetière and filled the third cup with coffee. If the other two had drunk from the same pot he had to assume there was nothing wrong with it. Maybe the caffeine would clear his head, which was still fuggy from the drug. In any case they seemed to want him awake and listening. But he still did his best to respond with a scowl to the smug smile Alfredo flashed him again before leaving the room.

The Texan leaned towards him conspiratorially making Marcus instinctively draw back.

'I'm going to tell you something, sir,' he said. 'You may have taken against those Mexican boys – and I can understand that, in the circumstances – their only order was to bring you here on your own, without causing any harm to your lady friend, and maybe they went a bit too far. If so, maybe that's my fault. But you have to understand what they were rescued from.'

'Rescued?'

'Rescued, sir. Rescued from the most insidious pagan plot known to man.'

Jones took another swig of coffee and refilled his cup. Marcus could see beads of sweat gathering on the man's nose. He bet he was a reformed drinker. They were always the worst evangelists. 'You may know – in fact, I'm sure you do – that the little statue your lady

friend is so keen to visit is not the only black Madonna of Guadalupe, in fact not even the best known.'

Marcus nodded. 'There's one somewhere in the Americas.'

'There certainly is. In Mexico City.'

'And what does the Mexican statue have to do with the one here?'

Jones smiled, like a precocious schoolboy asked to recite his
favourite lesson.

'Everything and nothing,' he announced. 'It's not a statue, you see.
In fact, it's not even black – that's just what they call it – but that
don't stop it being sinister. In fact, that's part of the plot.'

Marcus gave him just enough of a curious look to encourage him
to continue. Not that he needed any encouragement.

'As always, the legend here involves a simple peasant. Everybody
loves a simple peasant. This guy was allegedly an Aztec, although
interestingly enough he appears to have been called Juan Diego – I'll
come back to that. Now one day back in 1531 he was walking up a
hill near the old Aztec capital of Tenochtitlan – today's Mexico City,
more or less – when he saw a vision. Don't they all? A shining lady,
no less, who asked him, as they invariably do, to tell his bishop to
build a chapel to her on that spot.

'Our peasant did what he was told, but the bishop – allegedly –
was a sceptical guy and he told the peasant to get his lady friend to
produce a bunch of roses. You with me, so far? The point being, of
course, that this was not the season for roses. But hey presto, just
like a rabbit from a hat, the lady produces the roses and the peasant
wraps them in his cloak, a traditional Aztec garment called a *tilma*,
to take them to the bishop. And when he gets there – this is the good
bit – not only are the roses fine, but there's also a full-length picture
of the good lady herself on the cloak.'

Pleasing Jones was the last thing Marcus wanted to do, but he still
couldn't avoid a whimsical look of scepticism that clearly delighted
the big man.

'Exactly. Exactly. And that picture, still there today in the basilica
built on the spot is sure as hell one piece of holy hokum, a nice old
painting on a bit of cloth and proof of the conspiracy.'

'What conspiracy?'

'Here's the rub: that hill that old peasant walked up was known
to the Aztecs as Tepeyac and on it, before the Spaniards arrived,
was a temple to Tonantzin, the Aztec earth goddess – Tonantzin

even means 'our venerable mother' in Nahuatl, which happened to be the language the so-called Virgin Mary spoke to Juan the man. Tonantzin's symbol is the crescent moon, and guess what the so-called Madonna is standing on in the picture? Yep, a crescent moon.

'Now we come to the name. According to the story this fine lady, speaking Nahuatl remember, used the expression *coatlaxopeuh*.' He spelled it out for Marcus. 'Write it down in English letters and it looks like nonsense – but what the Spaniards heard was something that sounded like 'kwa-tla-hup-ehj' which they decided was an attempt by the natives to say Guadalupe, which just happened to be where a lot of the conquistadors came from. There ya go: proof positive that the Virgin Mary had travelled with them – or proof perfect that people hear what they want to!'

Marcus furrowed his brow. Reluctantly he admitted to himself that it was uncanny, the parallels between the Mexican story and Nazreem's idea that many of the 'black Madonnas' were derivative of the Egyptian Isis, and the argument she had put forward in the gallery in Munich about the 'legend' created to cover up the transition.

'What are you suggesting?' he found himself almost reluctantly thinking aloud. 'That the Spanish made a mistake, or …' he hesitated an instant, 'that they deliberately adopted the Aztec goddess and turned her into the Virgin Mary?'

Jones turned to the man in the dog collar: 'See, reverend, I knew the professor here would understand.

'But it goes deeper than that. At first the Spanish tried to give the Aztec goddess a makeover, see, make her look more white.' Marcus thought of the Dutch matron in the van der Weyden painting. 'But they let a trace of the olive-skinned native Indian features remain and as copies spread they became closer and closer to the native image.'

'But the real Mary would have had Middle Eastern features,' countered Marcus, resorting to Nazreem's argument.

'Professor,' said Jones, leaning back and slapping his knee. 'They didn't give a damn what the idols looked like as long as they kept them Indians loyal to Spain, old religion, new religion – it was all about politics, power and empire, not one iota to do with the teachings of the Lord Jesus on the Sea of Galilee.'

'But this is ancient history. The age of empire-building, colonialism is long over,' said Marcus.

'You think so, eh? Well, maybe you can think that over here in Europe. The way I hear it people over here are half-heathen nowadays anyway. But you're missing the point. This isn't old history at all. It's bang up to date.'

'Excuse me. You'll have to explain.' Whether he wanted to or not, Marcus had got caught up in the man's tale. And he had a feeling he was getting close to their connection to Nazreem's missing statue.

'You haven't been to Mexico, professor, have you?'

Marcus shook his head.

'I thought not. You go anywhere in that country, and indeed in most of Latin America and that pagan image is everywhere. I mean everywhere, on tin trays, in plastic shrines, on the dashboards in taxis, even behind the counter in saloon bars. They make 'em out of plastic, marble, wood, cake, candy, even tissue paper, and decorate them with beads, baubles, even sugar icing. And they have the nerve to call it Christianity.'

Marcus could hardly resist the ghost of a smile at the Texan's furious evocation of all the things that in his mind made Latin American culture so vibrant.

'You haven't heard the worst of it. Now you can check this out yourself, but most serious scholars don't believe old Juan Diego – or whatever his Aztec name might have been – ever existed at all. He was part of the conquistadors' myth-making.'

Marcus shrugged. He was hardly surprised.

'But some pretty important folks have done their damnedest – and I mean damnedest – to convince the world otherwise.'

'Meaning?'

'Meaning his so-called holiness, the late Pope John Paul II himself. In 2002 – and that's just a few years ago, not a few centuries ago – this Polish pope, who himself, you'll remember, was one of the foremost adherents of the cult of the black Madonna – went to Mexico City, one of the last big foreign trips he ever made, and declared this Aztec peasant, who in all probability never existed but was made up for propaganda purposes – to be a saint.'

'A saint?'

'You heard me all right. That was bad enough. Is bad enough. The last thing we need in this world right now is any more nonsense about black Madonnas. Do you see where I am leading, sir?'

Marcus thought that for the first time he was beginning to see clearly enough. These were people who had no interest in seeing the discovery of a new and supposedly holier still Marian relic.

'The basilica in Mexico City is the largest site of pilgrimage for the Marian cult in the whole world. Each year millions of people flock there to kneel and pray before a daubed Aztec shawl. The whole Latin American world worships this so-called image of the Virgin Mary as if this goddamn painted idol were the Lord Jesus Himself.' Marcus could sense almost an imploring tone in the man's voice, the voice of a self-convinced preacher in the wilderness.

'The worst of it is, sir, that these two young Mexicans in our employ are the exception to the rule. With every year that passes the Latino population of the southern United States is growing rapidly. There are whole swathes of Florida, Texas and southern California where the first language is Spanish. And they bring their perverse idolatry with them. I don't have to remind you, sir, that the United States – the original thirteen colonies and the nation that has grown out of them – has its origin in true Protestant Christianity, right back to the days of the Pilgrim Fathers themselves. Now, do you see the danger we're facing?

'We are fighting, sir, for the Christian soul of America itself!'

40

It was a calm night; the waters of the Gulf of Cadiz stretched out like a flat dark blanket beneath a moonless sky. To the south the lights of the old fortress city twinkled like fallen stars, to the north he could make out the protruding harbour wall and the busy little marina of the small town that they called Puerto de Santa Maria, the port of Saint Mary. The irony did not escape him that this should be the nearest place to the spot where he would at last set foot on the profaned soil of crusader-occupied Al-Andaluz.

The Son of Saladin was anxious for the moment, anxious to arrive, to begin the next stage of the task God had set for him. It was dangerous for him to be here. But he could no longer take the risk of leaving the matter in hand to bunglers or traitors. In the end it was a matter of trust, and he trusted no one that far: not to the end.

Death did not terrify him – surely there were delights enough ahead in Paradise as the reward for his labours – but ignominy did: the idea of being subject to the infidels' so-called justice, of being paraded like the monkey they had made of even their greatest ally in the war against the true religion, the evil Saddam – a thousand curses on his blasphemous memory. No, *that* he could not abide, not even the thought of being imprisoned in their stinking jails full of unbelievers, prey to the scorn of even the scum of their society, a subject of contempt instead of adulation, to be abused rather than obeyed. That alone was genuinely to be feared.

The journey had been a long one, particularly for a man whose movements made him vulnerable. Yet in many ways the greatest risk would soon be behind him. He had been in no particular fear of apprehension in an Arab country: those who wanted him had no international outrage to point to, no atrocity they could lay at his feet to demand his arrest. Even so, he preferred whenever possible to avoid drawing the attention of any government agency. He had used a false Egyptian passport for the flight from Cairo to Casablanca which had proved to be merely an endurance test as was the long drive in a truck full of citrus fruit up the coast to the grimy port of Tangier.

Yet now he was venturing into the lion's maw, into the world of people who scoured the planet from satellites, fed biometric details into machines capable of performing retinal scans, analysing DNA, the so-called building blocks of life. Such was their scorn for the wisdom of God, that they took unto themselves powers to tinker with creation. Because these would-be masters of the universe failed to see – even when their instruments were turned against them – that those whom their hegemony forced to crawl in the gutters could also destroy them.

In their idolatrous art they depicted crusaders on white horses trampling on the snake of Islam. The snake was a creature that in the sound of the Arabic language, the language of the Holy Koran, represented life. And a snake could cross the earth unnoticed and bite the unsuspecting.

So while the Spanish customs and excise patrolled the busy port of Algeciras and cruised the Straits of Gibraltar on the watch for drug smugglers in fast speedboats stashed with heroin, or tramp steamers docking at dead of night to unload cargos of dozens of illegal immigrants, no one paid any attention to a small fishing ketch returning to a nondescript little coastal resort up the Atlantic coast, or the fact that it had – out on the seas in the hours of darkness – briefly made contact with a similar vessel from Morocco, and taken on a solitary passenger.

The ketch bumped ashore on the long spit of sand. A few metres away, dunes topped with reedy grass separated the beach from the empty road that ran between it and what passed for local industry: the long lines of plastic tunnels covering tomato crops grown for northern European supermarkets, and the salt pans in which the locals, like their ancestors going back to the days of the Caliphate, extracted the precious mineral from the sea.

Stepping onto the shore, he restrained himself from bowing down to kiss the soil of a stolen land. On the roadway a vehicle turned on its sidelights. He walked slowly towards it as the ketch slipped back into the waves. In less than an hour they would be in Seville; he would have them drive through the heart of the city to afford a glance, no more, at the great Mosque of the Almohads, it too now defiled with the name of the Whore of Babylon. By morning he would be in Madrid, where his soldiers would be waiting for him.

41

'Let me get this straight,' Marcus said, watching uneasily as the big Texan got to his feet with a dangerous glint in his eye. 'You are suggesting that the United States is in danger of being taken over by Marian-led Catholicism inspired by immigrants from Latin America and that the late pope was party to the plot?'

The Texan looked down at him, with what Marcus imagined was intended as a blend of pity and compassion, as far as either could be realistically imagined as emotions readily felt by an ex-Marine with a neck like a butcher's block.

'I'm gonna have to give a B-minus there, professor. It seems you've only heard what you wanted to hear. This is not some conspiracy theory. There's no master plan out there. It's just what's happening. The other side is slowly winning.'

'The other side?'

'All those people that reject Christ's simple message, that reject the Bible, that reject the idea of One God, Father and Creator.'

Marcus nodded quietly. It seemed the only safe thing to do.

'Let me ask you something else, do you remember an old movie called *The Robe*?'

Marcus shook his head. The name rang a vague bell, but he couldn't place it.

'I'm not that surprised, I guess. It dates back to the 1950s and kind of got overlooked when *Ben Hur* came out a few years later. But at the time it was one of the highest-grossing movies of all time, second only to *Gone With the Wind*.'

Frankly, my dear, I don't give a damn, thought Marcus, wondering what the hell this madman was on about.

'One of the great Christian movies of all time, sir. Before Hollywood succumbed to Satan. Won a couple of Oscars. Starred that British actor, Richard Burton, and Jean Simmons. Fine actress.'

Marcus smiled weakly. Not just an ex-Marine Sunday-school teacher, but a film buff too.

The big man rewarded him with a none-too-gentle prod in the ribcage with an index finger like an iron poker.

'The point I'm coming to here is this: there's a moment in that film when one of the Roman centurions says to this Christian girl – they're in love, right – that all she has to do is accept that her God – this is the Lord God Almighty of Israel we're talkin' about here – is the same as the Roman Jupiter, or the Greek Zeus, that all she has to do is use a different name when she talks about him in public, and she won't be fed to the lions.

'What does she do, of course she tells him where to stick his Jupiter and his Zeus and all those other names of Satan, that she will not be fooled by the serpent, and she goes to meet her martyrdom, ripped apart by wild beasts in the arena. He thinks she's a fool who doesn't know how to play the game, but we know, we know that she has been saved, whereas he will rot in hell for all eternity.'

Marcus nodded again. You had to give Hollywood something, it impressed itself on people's minds. Jones was on a roll, the spirit of the Lord was with him:

'Let me tell you, the Catholic Church may think it took over some of the old ways and turned them to the ways of Jesus Christ, but they are the ones who lost their way, a long time ago. The Roman Church, sir, as it exists today, and particularly in this country, Spain, the country of the 'black legend', is riddled with apostasy and the remnants of pagan religions.

'Have you ever looked at some of those Spanish fiestas? Taken a close look, I mean, the way they carry on, at Easter in Seville with those white hoods, more like the goddamn Ku Klux Klan than true followers of Our Lord Jesus Christ.'

Marcus could imagine Martin Jones and his sinister minister getting on just fine and dandy with a local Texan chapter of the Klan, but he let it pass.

'Or those in Burgos or Santiago de Compostela, or Valencia or Elche, or just about any goddamn town where they need only the slightest excuse to get themselves up in these giant costumes, parade through the streets and get drunk as all hell.'

Marcus had seen several. He had always thought they looked rather fun. The children enjoyed the spectacle and the adults got pleasantly drunk and enjoyed the party.

'It's idolatry, pure and simple. Those saints, those giant images paraded around the town, you think they have anything to do with Christian holy men, with true followers of Jesus, the preachers and baptists who follow the Lord's word? My ass, they do – pardon my language, reverend.'

The reverend waved the minor lapse away.

'Those are pagan idols, that's what they are. Just like the images of the Virgin Mary that they carry around on trestles and then fall down on their knees to worship. Is that the way Our Lord taught us to pray? I think not.'

He opened a thick file of papers that Marcus had paid little attention to, seemed to pick one at random and read, with mock solemnity: '"With the singing of the *Regina Caeli* let us entrust to the Blessed Virgin all the needs of the Church and of humanity."' Do you know where that comes from?'

Marcus shook his head. He knew the words all right, the ones inscribed on Nazreem's buried casket.

'It comes from an address made in May 2005 by Pope Benedict XVI himself, the man who helped cover up decades of child abuse. And do you know what it is?'

Marcus shook his head again, though this time judging from the look on Jones's face he was not at all sure he had done the right thing. But it was the quiet little minister who suddenly interjected, his dull face erupting in a purple apoplexy of outrage:

'I'll tell you what it is – it's sacrilege, apostasy and an affront to the Lord God Himself. The words "Regina Caeli" are Latin, sir,' he said in a way that made even a rudimentary command of the language seem like a mortal sin. 'They mean "Queen of Heaven". And that, sir, is a pagan concept, a heathen idea not found in Scripture, not in the Old Testament, nor the New. It is a bastardisation of the true faith and an excuse for idolatry.'

'Calm down, reverend,' said the Texan. 'It is just one example, Professor Frey.' He gestured disdainfully at the pile of papers. 'I could find you hundreds. But the words to pay attention to there were "all the needs of the church and of humanity". Being entrusted, not to the Lord God, but to a statue of a woman.'

The reverend cleared his throat, and said in a more level voice than before: 'You will have heard some of those people refer to the Bishop of Rome as the Antichrist.' Marcus nodded. Whatever the man said, he felt sure he knew what was coming; he had a long-established mental image of the ogre-like figure of the Reverend Ian Paisley roaring diatribes against the pope as the 'Harlot of Rome'.

'You have to realise that not all of that is prejudice, particularly when it comes to the most recent incumbents of that office.'

He paused, for effect as much as for breath. 'Did you know that John Paul II was considering declaring the Virgin Mary "coredemptrix"?'

'No. I'm not even sure what that means, in a theological sense?'

'It means, sir, co-redeemer. Joint saviour, if you like! It means that he was about to put Mary on the same footing as Our Lord Jesus Christ Himself. It means putting a woman, however blessed, on a par with God. Do you know what that amounts to?'

What Marcus was hearing, he felt sure, was as upfront an admission of misogyny that he had heard in a long time, but at the same time, he had an inkling of what the man was trying to say in theological terms. Even so, he shook his head.

'It amounts to polytheism! Paganism by another name. Believing in more than one God!'

Maybe it was not the moment to mention the Holy Trinity.

'John Paul II is likely to be declared a saint.'

The Texan shook his head and the reverend snorted: 'Saint John Paul the Pole, Saint Juan Diego the Aztec, what's the difference? The saints, man, don't you see, are part and parcel of it. Nothing more than false little gods. When did you ever hear Jesus talk about saints?'

Marcus hadn't personally ever heard Jesus talk about anything and nor, he expected, had this large Texan ex-Marine, but he guessed this wasn't a time to start splitting theological hairs.

'Damn demigods able to intervene directly with the Almighty!' Jones fumed. 'There are holy men, saintly men even, but when we die we all await the resurrection the same and don't float around with angels. The saints, these big papier-mâché dummies they carry round at their fiestas, they're no different from pagan idols. This is a way in which the devil keeps alive the myths of the old gods, who we know to be nothing more than his demons.'

'And you're suggesting that there's some sort of secret society within the Catholic Church that is a party to this?' Marcus could hardly keep the scepticism out of his voice.

'We'll let you judge for yourself, professor. Let's just say that there is clear evidence of a faction within the church – not an open organisation like Opus Dei or the Jesuits, though the Lord knows those are weird enough distortions of his Holy Word. At times these people have been referred to as the Giuliani, in old Italian records, but the name is not important. What matters is what they have done: what started in the early church as a means of suppressing paganism by turning their feast days into Christian festivals ...'

'You mean like Christmas?'

'You see, professor, you're halfway there already. I mean exactly like Christmas, which has become perhaps the most pagan festival of them all, centred on a fat demigod in red rather than the miracle of divine incarnation. They took over the feast days, but the Giuliani – or whatever you want to call them – made sure that the ghosts of the old gods came with them.'

'Chief among them Mithras,' said the reverend gravely.

'Mithras?' echoed Marcus, whose squirrel mind once again retrieved at least a nutmeg of information. 'The Persian soldier god?'

'Not a god for real soldiers,' the Texan took up. 'No sir, not the God of Christian Soldiers marching as to war with the Cross of Jesus going on before. No sir! A pagan idol of the most pernicious sort, like you said: Persian. Iranian in other words.' As if that somehow made it worse.

'Do you know what the chief sacrament in the cult of Mithras was – I should say, is?'

For once Marcus's treasure-trove of the arcane looked like letting him down. He remembered only that the Mithras cult involved an initiation ceremony, in which the applicants were somehow supposed to be reborn. But the colonel was in any case not waiting for an answer:

'The central element in the legend of Mithras involves the ritual slaughter of a bull.'

Marcus blinked.

'Yes, indeed. A cruel pagan ritual that is very much alive and well in this country: one that you witnessed last night with your very own eyes.'

'Let me give you another example: you know about Pamplona, the bull-running fiesta of San Fermin? That there's a pagan rite which seduced even Ernest Hemingway, an honest American who fell foul of the demon drink and the sins of the flesh. What do you think that's all about?'

All that Marcus knew about the annual bull run in the mostly Basque city was what he had gleaned when it was shown on the television news because a few runaway steers had gored some lad in the narrow streets while his mates clung for grim life to drain-pipes on the walls above. Insofar as he had thought of it at all he had always considered it to be about testosterone-fuelled young Latino men showing off their *cojones* by publicly risking them in front of the girlfriend.

But Jones was not looking for a reply: 'They may not all know it, in fact I daresay most of them don't, in their ignorance, but what they are acting out is a pagan parable, the made-up story of Theseus and the Minotaur. The chase through the narrow streets is a very metaphor for the monster's labyrinth.

'The Minotaur, Mithras, the old gods dressed up as so-called saints. The "old religion", paganism in disguise. Call it what you want to. The so-called "black Madonna" is just another piece in their dev-ilish jigsaw. The piece that holds all the others together.'

The thin little minister by his side closed his eyes and raised his hands together like a schoolboy saying his prayers, then lowered them reverentially and, still with closed eyes, intoned gravely: 'For behold, the horned beast is among us.'

42

The sharp trilling ringtone of her mobile vibrating on the hard mahogany of the hotel bedroom desk was like a knife scraping on a blackboard. Nazreem snatched for it greedily, and held her breath when she saw Marcus's number indicated, her hunger for good news acidly laced with a frisson of fear. Just because it was his phone it did not mean he was using it.

It was not until she pressed 'answer' and heard his voice that she allowed the first wave of emotional relief to break over her. At least he was still alive.

'Marcus! What? Where …? Are you all right? What happened? Where did you go? I thought …'

The questions poured out of her uncontrollably, barely giving him time to answer.

But the voice on the other end of the connection sounded calm and composed. 'It's okay. It's okay. Don't worry.' Maybe too composed. Don't worry? How could he say something like that? Without explaining.

'Don't worry? What do you mean don't worry. Where have you been? What happened?'

A pause.

'It's a long story. But I'm all right. Everything's all right.'

'Where are you? What happened …?'

'It's okay. Trust me. The meeting. With the man from the monastery. Where were we supposed to meet him?'

'Plaza de Cibeles.' She spelt it out for him. 'It's a big square, with a fountain, not far from the hotel. Ten minutes' walk or so, but … where are you?'

'Later. I'll tell you everything later. The important thing now is to meet our man as we agreed.'

'Okay, but what about you? What happened last night?'

'I'll meet you there. Leave the hotel in about ten minutes' time. Tell them to put the bill on the credit card they took an imprint of when we checked in and pick up my things from next door. There's not much. Just trust me, Nazreem. Everything's fine. It'll be okay. It was just a misunderstanding. I'll see you soon. Just be there. Okay?'

'Okay,' she said, feeling anything but. Something in his voice was telling her he was not alone. What did he mean 'a misunderstanding'? She had hardly slept a wink all night, staring at her mobile, sitting in the hotel room, the connecting door to his open in case he should reappear unannounced, her head filled with visions of him chained to a radiator being tortured. She had fallen asleep around four a.m. and woken only when the cleaners opened the door to his room, saw the connecting door open, her sprawled half dressed across the bed, and had retreated rapidly out of misplaced tact.

That had been more than two anxious hours ago during which she had fussed and fretted and blamed herself for whatever might have happened to him, half praying for his safe return, half afraid that the only God she had ever worshipped, and that with perhaps less assiduousness than many of her co-religionists, might react perversely to a prayer uttered only in adversity. But wasn't adversity when most people prayed?

'I, the Lord your God am a jealous God', was part of Christianity's sacred ten commandments. And there were both Christians and Muslims – albeit a minority – who said it was the same God, deep down, more or less? If the eternal omnipotent could be either 'deep down' or 'more or less'. She didn't want to think about it.

Nazreem knew she prayed in the same way some people crossed their fingers, more out of habit and superstition than true faith. She was a historian not a theologian. Yet wasn't the situation she was in precisely the result of her historical tinkering with the basics of religion? She was challenging the gods. The gods, plural? Not the one God. Not Allah the Almighty but a perversion of the Christian version. Wasn't she? She was searching for the truth. How dangerous was that?

She had dragged her hand through her hair and not for the first time in her life wished she smoked to give her distraction a focus. The television news had been full of nothing, unknown politicians, talking heads, speaking in a language she didn't understand. Was this what it was like to live in a country where death and destruction were not part of the daily grind.

Then she remembered that the conflict that laid waste to her homeland had scarred this city too. She had gone to the window and looked out at the early morning Madrid skyline and wondered how far she was from the stations where the bombs had exploded, and if the people here hated all Muslims because of them.

And then the phone had rung. The shrill warble of the mobile she had almost forgotten to turn on. And here she was minutes later throwing their things into the lightweight travelling bags they had picked up, with the spare clothing, at Stansted. Picking up Marcus's spare socks, pants and shirt with all the domesticity of a woman clearing up after her man. Don't go there, she told herself. What's past is past. The relationship they had once had was a thing of another time, something to be remembered fondly but nothing to do with here or now. Yet, wasn't that why she had trembled so much when she finally heard his voice again? She splashed water over her face in the bathroom and dragged a comb through her hair. Pull yourself together, woman; men have no power over you. Not any more.

The hotel clerk gave her a second look when she declared she was checking out for both of them on Marcus's credit card even though he himself was not there. She turned down his offer of a taxi and she could feel his eyes on her back as she walked out the door, certain that it would not be long before he had conferred with the cleaning women and begun to conjure up stories she could scarcely imagine.

She consoled herself that the most likely conclusion to be drawn was of a lovers' tiff, of a woman abandoned after some passionate argument, nothing that required the attention of the authorities. Unless something caused someone to come looking. She still worried that they had left Munich peremptorily only hours after telling the German police they would do no such thing. If she had learned one thing from her upbringing it was that the best relationship to have with the civil powers in a country that regarded you as an alien was none at all.

Their two small carry bags, even taken together, were not heavy, but they were inconvenient and she switched them from shoulder to shoulder alternately as she strode at a brisk space down the narrow streets that gradually broadened out as she approached the grand boulevards of the museum district. She glanced at her watch. There was still just over half an hour before they were due to meet the man who was apparently the link between Sister Galina and the abbot of Guadalupe.

The thought sobered her. It was possible – probable? – that whoever had seized the nun within hours of their meeting was also responsible for Marcus's disappearing act the night before. But if so, why had they let him go? Or was she just imagining things? Could it just have been that in those minutes when she had taken him at his word that he was visiting the bathroom he had gone off on some agenda of his own? But what and why? Maybe it was all nonsense; maybe he had just met some girl, that was why he had been so odd on the phone, he had met some cheap floozie and gone off with her? Why not, he was a free agent, wasn't he? She could feel herself getting flustered and told herself it was because even the suggestion was preposterous.

But the only alternative that she could think of was that he had been kidnapped. And then released? As what, a warning? Why would they not have held him? Held him as they were holding the nun. As they had to be. Surely. Held him to ransom? As they were holding her? Yet ransom was impossible if the demand could not be delivered. Was that what had happened to Marcus? She needed to hear his story. But deep down, she knew also, she had to tell him the rest of hers.

43

Marcus handed his phone back to the big Texan who was watching him carefully. He resented the idea that this man who had kidnapped him 'for his own good', in the cause of some crackpot fundamentalist Christian conspiracy theory, was in even temporary control of his life. The man had refused point blank to let Marcus call Nazreem in private, in fact had insisted on hearing every word of both sides of the conversation. But then again both the Mexicans José and Alfredo, 'Joseph and Freddie', were very visibly carrying guns. They had said they were letting Marcus go. And he was not about to do anything to put them off the idea.

The Texan responded to his frown with a smile, unclipped his piggy-back listening device from Marcus's phone: 'Cibeles, eh? Your idea or his?'

'Sorry?'

'The meeting place – the fountain. Who suggested it? Your little "monkey" friend, I'm assuming? Geddit: monk – monkey.'

Marcus grimaced, but nodded in answer to the question.

'I thought so. Well, when you get there take a good look at it, my friend. And ask yourself if it's where a so-called man of God ought to choose for a rendezvous. Believe me, my friend, there's symbolism in everything they do in this country.'

Marcus let it ride. He hadn't a clue what the man was going on about, but he'd had enough theology, half-baked or otherwise, for one morning.

'Just bear it in mind, that's all I ask.'

Marcus nodded again. He had decided conversation with the Texan was easiest if kept to a minimum.

'Now, we're going to let you go, just like we said. No question about that. You can go and meet your little Arab girlfriend just like you told her you would. We're men of our word.' The remark did little to reassure Marcus. In his experience, even in the academic world, when people said there was no question about something it was usually a preamble to raising one. He was not disabused.

'There's just one thing,' the Texan added. 'You'll agree we haven't treated you bad? I know, I know, you may think we were well out of line going to the extremes we did to talk to you alone, and maybe you're right. Like I said, the Mexies here sometimes get a bit carried away, do things more like back home than our way. But in the end we've had a civilised chat and we've made a few points I hope you've taken on board.'

Marcus nodded. He wasn't about to say anything that would stop him getting out of there as soon as absolutely possible.

'Okay, good. And you understand that we want to get our hands on this evil idol for the best of reasons.'

'I understand you have reasons you deeply believe in.'

The Texan eyed him a moment.

'Okay, I guess that'll do. I have a strong feeling that you're gonna come around to our way of thinking pretty soon. But before we say goodbye right now, I'd like you to promise that you'll keep in touch. It only takes a quick ring on your phone here. Remember we could be there to help as much as anything else. You're involved in a complicated business here and you just might find there are more people interested in this so-called black Madonna than just us, people a whole lot nastier.'

Marcus wondered about that.

'Okay,' was all he said.

'Okay? Then if you don't mind I'd like you to swear it.'

Marcus shrugged. To get out of there right now he'd have sworn his own mother was the Virgin Mary. But before he could say anything the little reverend had produced a black, leather-clad volume with a gold cross on its cover.

'An oath ain't an oath unless it's sworn on the Good Book. Take it in your right hand.'

Marcus looked at it as if it were a prop in a play but did as he was told.

'Repeat after me: I, Marcus Frey, swear by the Holy Bible that I will keep Col Martin Jones aware of my whereabouts and reveal to him or the Reverend Henry Parker, here present, any information that may be of use in locating the statue discovered in Gaza and referred to as the black Madonna.'

It was absurd, surreal, yet the man absolutely meant it. The only people Marcus had ever seen swearing on a Bible were witnesses in a jury trial, and even then he found it hard to believe the ritual had any force or meaning for those who automatically performed it. Even so, as he repeated the formula with the book in his hand, the residual intimidatory power of religious ritual still sent a shiver down his spine. The Texan seemed satisfied.

'Okay, José, as they say in the movies. Let's take a ride downtown.'

The Mexicans appeared behind him and slipped a blindfold over his eyes held by elastic bands. Instinctively he brought his hands up to try to remove it, but found them held down by the Mexican in front of him, while a second blindfold, this time tied behind his head was placed over the first.

'Easy on, easy on, guy,' the Texan was saying. 'There's no issue here. It's just a precaution … until we get to know you better.' Marcus went silent. It wasn't an acquaintance that on the evidence so far he was keen to build on. 'That's British Airways Club Class shuteye you've got under there. Nice and comfy. The other one's just to keep it in place. Not too tight, Freddie.'

Minutes later, after a descent in a lift and a brief few steps in the open air – what sort of area was it, Marcus wondered to himself, where nobody noticed blindfolded men being led out? – he was eased into a cloth-upholstered back seat of a car that smelled of cheap pine air freshener. Marcus could imagine one of those horrid dangly things shaped like cardboard cut-out Christmas trees suspended from the rear-view mirror. He felt a heavy hand laid on his shoulder:

'Okay, fella, good luck now. Remember what I said. It's up to you what you do. But if you need any help, we won't be far.'

Marcus contented himself with another nod. It wasn't exactly the most reassuring thing he had ever heard. On the other hand, he had to admit that they hadn't hurt him badly; he had been scared, but it had not been the nightmare he had feared he was awakening to when the drug wore off. There were madmen and madmen. Maybe even not everything they had said was as mad as it sounded, was it? Maybe he would find out.

It seemed like an hour, but it was probably not more than twenty minutes later at most when the Mexican in the back seat next to him – 'Freddie' – untied the cloth blindfold and told him he could take off the other one. He pulled the satin up over his eyes – noting in passing the little BA logo that showed the Texan had been telling the truth about one thing anyhow – and let the already warm late morning sunlight wash over his field of vision.

They were on a main road, an inner-city dual carriageway, with heavy traffic all around. There was a pedestrian avenue lined with green trees in between the car-clogged roads. From what little he knew of Madrid's geography, Marcus guessed they were on the Paseo de la Castellana, the city's main north-south drag. Up ahead he could see an array of wedding cake buildings, one festooned with spiky antennae, which, as they drew closer, he realised formed four corners around a great central roundabout, in the centre of which was a statuary grouping spraying sparkling jets of water into the air.

'Cibeles,' said the driver, José, pronouncing it 'See-bellies' with the soft South American consonant that Marcus had noticed in the bar the night before. They came onto the roundabout and the car pulled in to the side of the road in front of the most fantastically turreted of the buildings around it. Alfredo opened the door and motioned for him to get out. Marcus stared up at the extraordinary building that towered above them. 'Palacio de Communicaciones,' said José who had obviously adopted the role of tour guide. The fountain is in the middle of the roundabout.'

'Nice,' said Marcus, flatly, getting out.

'*Adiós, amigo,*' said José.

'*Adiós* yourself,' said Marcus. 'And don't go drinking with your friend. He has bad taste in cocktails.'

José bared his white teeth and the car – a nondescript Seat clone of some Volkswagen model, the sort that could be seen in their hundreds in any Spanish traffic jam – growled off into the swarm circling the roundabout. Marcus thought for a moment he spotted a Barcelona number plate, but he couldn't be sure, any more than he could be sure about the two Madrid-licensed black Mercedes that seemed to sandwich it as it left the roundabout.

Marcus stared up at the 'communications palace'. It was a fantasy of Mediterranean neo-Gothic, a cross between a vampire's palace and a white marble wedding cake. The equally extraordinary pile that was the Prado museum was not far away. But it was the fountain in the midst of a vast ornate marble sculpture ensemble in the middle of the busy traffic roundabout that was the spot chosen for their meeting. An easy landmark to find, perhaps, as old Julio had suggested. Did it really have any more sinister symbolism? Marcus dismissed the thought as he was inclined to dismiss almost everything the Texan has said. Except for the threat.

His watch showed eleven-forty a.m. He waited for the lights to change to red and crossed to the centre of the roundabout. There was no sign of Nazreem yet, or of the man from the monastery, or, as far as he could tell, of religious fundamentalists, Christian or Islamic, lurking with him in their crosshairs, although of that he was by no means certain. Above him, however, loomed the statue he had been told to pay close attention to.

It was certainly hard to ignore and a significant enough piece of monumental sculpture to be a more than legitimate focus of a tourist's attention. He thought he remembered vaguely that it was the place from where all distances in Spain were measured, like Charing Cross, in London, or the imbedded cross on the Place du Parvis outside Notre Dame Cathedral in Paris.

Certainly it was an impressive affair: a well-built woman of noble bearing seated in a chariot, pulled by two huge stone lions that reminded him of Landseer's cast-iron beasts in London's Trafalgar Square, except that these were on the prowl. Behind the chariot two plump cherubic children played in its wake. The seated figure herself exuded an air of sedate majesty. Marcus wondered if it was meant to represent some historical figure and decided it was almost certainly mythical or allegorical.

He pulled out his phone and rang Nazreem's number. It rang twice before she answered, with a whoop so enthusiastic that it seemed he was hearing it in stereo. And then he realised he was. She was only a dozen metres or so away, on the other side of the traffic on the edge of the green sward of the Paseo del Prado. He put his phone back in his pocket and waved to her, with both arms, a good old-fashioned South African rugby supporter's wave. And then the traffic stopped for a red light and she was in his arms, all of a sudden, unexpectedly. And for a moment the whole world of religious fanatics, ancient statues and conspiracy theories seemed surreal and fantastical.

After a few seconds she pulled back and looked up at him in amazement as if scarcely believing he was still in one piece, unharmed and unmarked. A flood of questions spilled forth. 'What happened? Are you all right? Why didn't you …?

He could not tell if she was going to kiss him or hit him. Marcus put his finger to his lips.

'I was drugged. Kidnapped.'

'Wha …!?'

'I know, I know. You won't believe me. Nutters, but American nutters,' her jaw dropped open.

'But it's okay. Look they haven't hurt me.'

'Yes but …'

'I'll tell you everything later. But our man is going to get here any moment, and I need your help on something.'

She stood back and stared at him uncertainly: 'You do?'

He nodded. 'This fountain,' he said, gesturing with an arm to indicate the great structure that dominated the square. 'What do you know about it? And more specifically what do you know about the lady in the chariot? I had assumed it was supposed to be some sort of female personification of Spain, but now I'm not sure.'

Nazreem was staring at him as if he had lost control of his senses. 'Why? What does it matter?'

'The guide book, the green Michelin, the one we picked up at the airport. You have it? Quick.'

'Yes, but …'

She fumbled in her bag, and produced it. Marcus snatched it off her impatiently and flicked through to the section on Madrid and the reference to the fountain, paraphrasing rapidly aloud as he went: '… *dates from late eighteenth century… time of classical revival … the playing children a romantic affectation added later…* Here we go: … *seated sculpture of goddess of fertility and of the earth, known to the ancient Romans as Ceres, derivation of modern English "cereal",* yes, yes, yes … *also to ancient Greeks as Demeter, but in this incarnation taking the form of the Phrygian goddess Cibele and known popularly to Madrileños as Cibeles.*'

He tried pronouncing it both ways, 'See-bellies,' like the Mexican had said, or 'Thibelehs', as the locals did. Either way it meant nothing to him, except that the rednecks had been right about the old man choosing a pagan goddess as a rendezvous point. And where the hell was Phrygia anyhow, he wondered aloud.

'Wait a minute,' said Nazreem suddenly. 'Let me see that.' She grabbed the book from his hand, read the name again, and looked up at the great seated statue with a new recognition.

'Of course,' she said. 'That hat is wrong, but it is her okay. You were right, Marcus, it is all a matter of pronunciation. The problem is the Latin alphabet, the letter 'c'. To the ancient Greeks there was no such thing. It led to less confusion.'

'What?'

Nazreem was standing stock still staring up at the great piece of neoclassical statuary:

'Not "c", *kappa* – "k". Her real name is Kybele. I have been looking everywhere for her.'

He turned to her, dumbstruck: 'You have?'

44

If there was one thing that made Sebastian Delahaye uncomfortable, it was long-range operations. Not that he was an 'in your face' operator either: an up-front rough-and-tumble merchant. His strongest belief was that the secret world should stay, if not secret, then at least inconspicuous. He believed passionately that despite the concerns of the civil libertarians, technology was a weapon that improved security.

That was why he failed totally to understand why countries such as Spain and Germany lagged so far behind the United Kingdom in the implementation of closed circuit cameras in the public domain. He had had the discussion late at night in a Chelsea wine bar with a colleague from the BfV – Germany's Office for the Protection of the Constitution – the direct equivalent of Britain's domestic security service. A country that has known totalitarianism, the man had insisted, guarded even the littlest of its liberties all the more fiercely. Delahaye had refused to accept that a system such as Argus – although even to a German on the same level of security clearance he did not give it its name – infringed on the freedom of UK citizens.

'Ah,' the German had simply said, 'but in the wrong hands, it might.'

Delahaye had insisted that could never happen. The German had simply smiled and said, 'I hope you know your politicians!'

Delahaye knew that if he had the same conversation with a Spaniard it would probably have gone along the same lines. Even so, it was more than thirty years since the death of Franco and with the threat of Basque terrorism and the Madrid bombings he found it amazing that the Spanish security services had not increased their surveillance capabilities.

It was inconvenient, to say the least. He was fishing long and with a fine line. The London surveillance of Al Barani had been stepped up, with results. The past forty-eight hours had seen a remarkable alteration in his schedule. He had hardly moved. At first it was suspected he had become aware of the level of observation, then that he was ill. He had a steady stream of visitors, all of them logged and checked against the databases. Mobile phone traffic was limited, emails almost non-existent. The operation did not yet merit full-scale bugging, but it could if it escalated the way Delahaye was beginning to anticipate. The word 'Saladin' had been picked up more than once by long-range directional mikes. It was possible they were having a history lesson, but it was more likely that they were referring to the renegade Iraqi who had been on the fringes of the West's security radar for some time.

Madrid meanwhile concerned Delahaye more. He had a trace on Frey's mobile phone – enough at least to let him know within forty-five minutes that he had used it, what number he had called and roughly where from. But it was difficult keeping any closer tabs on him without calling in either Spanish internal security or going cap in hand to the James Bonds in the 'jolly green giant' across the river.

The building officially known as Vauxhall Cross was home to the Secret Intelligence Service, or MI6, as opposed to Delahaye's MI5 in the outdated parlance that still lingered from the Second World War. SIS, responsible for intelligence gathering abroad rather than on the domestic front, mostly referred to themselves as simply 'Box', a long antiquated reference to the anonymous 'Post Office Box 1300' to which their ordinary mail (when they got any) was even now addressed.

They were the James Bonds, at least in the popular imagination, the glamour boys and girls, the 'proper spies'. The fact that they were not the people at the cutting edge of protecting the British public from the increasing menace on their doorstep and in their midst had in the past been too often glossed over. The balance was changing but even so the 'other side' remained jealous of their territory and competition, although never as fierce as in the myths, was nonetheless real.

Which was why he had half anticipated the glowing button on his phonepad which indicated a secure internal connection to Vauxhall Cross and the silky smooth voice of Hilary Macken: 'Sebastian, good afternoon. How do I find you?' And then without further ado: 'It's about Madrid.'

Delahaye had already decided he was going to play this one

straight. He didn't want 'Box' screwing him over, but he knew this conversation – however it might turn out – was unavoidable.

'I think we have what you might call a bit of an awkward situation here, Sebastian, old man.'

'I see.'

'Do you? Good. That will make things so much easier all round.'

'It will?'

'Yes. You see it would appear we have something of an overlap.'

This was it: the reprimand, the strict instruction to hand over whatever he was dealing with and to keep his fingers out of foreign pies. Well, he would go down fighting.

'I can understand you want to take over, but I must insist this is a case of primarily domestic relevance. We are concerned with tracking an individual who we believe could be a threat to civil order in this country.'

There was a pause on the other end of the line.

'Sebastian, I quite agree. This is your pigeon, if you like, but you may not be ungrateful for our involvement. I'm talking about a real overlap – on the ground – and I'm about to provide a second string to your bow.'

'How do you mean?' Beware of Greeks bearing gifts. Or fellow spooks sharing their secrets.

'I mean we're already there, Seb. On the ground. And running.'

'How? Why?'

'Let's just say we've been going to Sunday School too.'

45

Marcus looked up at the statue and then back at Nazreem and put his hands on her shoulders. She had recognised something in the statue that escaped him, something that the Americans had wanted him to see? It was then that he noticed the man in black advancing towards them.

'*Buenos días,*' the elderly bullfighting fan said, nodding his grey head with a pleasant smile. 'I see you are enjoying the beautiful heart of Madrid.' Nazreem and Marcus pulled apart with more than a hint of embarrassment. His appearance had been ill-timed in every way.

'Please, do not mind me,' the old man said. 'It is just such a shame about the traffic. But there you have it, the modern world. There is no escape. At least not here. Guadalupe, you will find, is much quieter.'

'We were just admiring the fountain,' Marcus said, half-provocatively. 'A fine statue.'

'Yes,' was the non-committal reply although he could not help noticing that the old man was watching both of their faces with his head cocked on one side, like an inquisitive bird.

'Cibeles,' said Nazreem lisping in best *madrileño* fashion, and then: 'Kybele, the great mother goddess of the Phrygians.'

The old man narrowed his eyes appreciatively. 'You are a learned woman, particularly for a Muslim woman.'

'I am a historian,' she said simply. 'Historians are people who use science more than religion. I know something of the old pagan cults.'

'Interesting,' he said. 'There are those today who believe science should serve religion, particularly in the part of the world you come from.'

'Not all imams are fanatics,' she replied tartly. Marcus wondered if the man was deliberately trying to goad her.

'Oh, no, I am quite sure they are not,' was what he actually said. 'In fact, I was thinking of Christians. I am sure you know that the Catholic Church was once accused of refuting science – and justly so. I think it took us some six centuries before we apologised to Galileo. And that was probably a bit late for him.'

Involuntarily both Marcus and Nazreem caught themselves smiling. There was always something beguiling about someone who turned out to be unexpectedly self-deprecating.

'Even today,' he continued, 'there are Christians who are as blind as the most fundamental cleric of the Taliban.'

Marcus shot him a look. The conversation had gone off at an unexpected tangent. 'Today those who are more likely to have their heads in the sand are the Evangelical Protestants, mostly American curiously, fundamentalists in their own right: the sort of people who believe Darwin was wrong, and God put dinosaur bones in the earth to test our faith.'

Marcus looked at the man as if he were psychic. Not only did he remember having made much the same point to Nazreem over their ill-fated dinner in Brick Lane, but here was this supposedly duplicitous Catholic cleric of some sort, referring out of the blue to the same breed as those he had just become so intimately acquainted with. He had not asked the big Texan and his hot-under-the-dog-collar comrade what their views on so-called 'intelligent design' were, but he had a fairly solid hunch that for all their show of learning, they would have housed serious doubts about the work of Charles Darwin.

He deliberately let the smile fall from his face and put the question they had planted in his mind to the man direct:

'Why did you want us to meet here?'

The man gave a look of surprise that might and might not have been feigned. 'Because we are going to Guadalupe together. Isn't that what you wanted?'

As an answer it came close to the deliberately obtuse. Marcus hardened his tone. If he was being led up the garden path then he wanted to know who had opened the gate. And why.

'I mean here, specifically, by this statue? Of Cibeles, Kybele, whatever you call her.'

The old man made wide eyes as if he was genuinely astonished by the question, although to Marcus's bemusement he gave not the slightest indication of being annoyed by it:

'Because I thought it would be easy for you to find, of course, as strangers in Madrid. And because,' he gestured to the wide avenues of free-flowing traffic on either side, 'it is a good place to start from to get out of the city fast.'

'And that's it? There was no other reason?'

The old man was staring at him as if he had no idea what he was talking about. If it was a pretence, Marcus thought it was a good one. And yet …

'You're saying the statue has no special significance? That there aren't some people who have a particular veneration for it? That it has nothing to do with another sort of religion.'

The look of puzzlement on the old man's face slowly gave way to a smile and then the smile broadened and a twinkle appeared in his eye. 'I understand what you are getting at,' he said at last. 'You are teasing me. You have been doing your homework. I should not be surprised, given your background. You English,' he said, 'you are incorrigible.'

Marcus was immediately tempted to correct the man about his nationality, but on second thoughts it was worth waiting to see what he came out with first.

'I give in,' he said simply. 'You are right, of course …'

Marcus held his breath. This was not quite what he had been expecting. Had the Texan been telling the truth and was this man about to admit it? Was there really a hidden agenda within a strain of Spanish Catholicism? And yet there was something that did not seem quite right here. If that was really the case, the old man was making surprisingly light of discussing it in the middle of a busy traffic roundabout in the middle of Madrid. Then again, like the proverbial needle in the haystack or the pea under the princess's mattress, some things were invisible to those who did not know where to look or have the sensitivity to detect them.

'You are right,' he said again, with something of a sigh. 'This is also a gathering place for the followers of another sort of Spanish religion.'

Marcus and Nazreem exchanged a glance. Was it possible that he was going to reveal something neither of them had imagined, a cult object sitting openly in the heart of the Spanish capital, known secretly and venerated by thousands?

'They come here to celebrate on important occasions,' the priest was saying, still with that strange smile on his face. 'It can be a moving occasion, especially if you are one of them. As I once was, fervently, and still am, I suppose.'

Marcus was speechless. He had not expected to wring some sort of confession so easily.

'And they all wear white, of course. The most extreme call themselves *los fanaticos*. They wear all white and call this lady here the Queen of Madrid. They would, of course, the royal connection, you know. It is forbidden by the police to climb on the statue itself but there is always competition amongst the bravest – what would you expect? – and in winter they have even been known to cover their goddess's head with what they consider a more suitable hat.'

Marcus caught his breath. Wasn't that what Nazreem had said, just a few seconds before the old man had arrived: the hat on the statue was not quite correct: she should be wearing a Phrygian cap.

He could see the man in front of him struggling internally as if he was trying to work out what to say, how much to reveal: 'I am not certain of the correct word in English for this hat.' And then a sly smile crept across his face. 'Yes,' he said, 'I believe you call it a "beanie".'

'What!?' Marcus looked at Nazreem and then back at the priest still smiling at them with blithe inscrutability. A beanie? The idea of a religious cult adorning a statue of their goddess with a little woollen hat suddenly seemed too absurd for words. 'What is this cult you are talking about.'

There was an almost puckish look on the priest's face. '*Réal Madrid*. Football, of course. What are *you* talking about?'

46

The priest's battered old Seat Punto rattled with difficulty up the steep slopes of the great ridge of sierras rising to the west of Madrid. The clogged suburbs of the big city had given way, first to brash new settlements with American-style hoardings for Sandeman Sherry, the Carlos III brandy of evil memory and the Movistar mobile phone network, then gradually to dusty roads with speeding trucks and eventually, as they began to climb, to quieter vistas of small red-roofed villages nestling in valleys of evergreens and ochre escarpments of rock that jutted out perilously above the winding tarmac road.

The further they got from the hubbub of urban civilisation, the more the old man's mood seemed to lighten and his conversation expand. At the same time the Spanish landscape seemed to drop the centuries. They passed close to Toledo, near enough to see its great fortress the Alcázar.

'The castle. That is what Alcázar means. It is from the Arab,' the old man said, waving airily at the monolithic stone structure rising above the Tajo river.

'Sorry?' said Nazreem.

'It should not be so hard for you to understand. Alcázar is *Al-qazr*. The name is left over from the Moorish times. There are very many things in modern Spain that still recall El-Andalus. There are still those, are there not, who dream of restoring the Caliphate? It will never happen of course.'

For a devout Christian, the old man turned out to be a surprisingly erudite font of knowledge about the Caliphate, the centuries-long Islamic rule on the Iberian peninsula during which even the fact that it had once been a supposedly Christian country had, if not been forgotten, been largely overlooked.

'Christianity prior to the Islamic invasion was still very much in its infancy in Spain,' he confessed. 'Some people say that is why the Inquisition later was so extreme here: because the Church feared for its existence.

'To have been a Muslim here in the thirteenth century would have seemed no stranger than to have been on one or the other side of the Iron Curtain in the Europe of the 1960s or 70s. It would have seemed an order of things that was set in stone, and yet it was all to be swept away. Of course, it would have been the same to be a Christian in fifth-century Egypt, or a pagan in third-century Rome.

'Even in the place where we are going, which some call *la alma de España* – the soul of Spain, one of the most important Christian shrines in the country, maybe in all Europe, there is a memory of when it was part of the Islamic world.'

'There is?' Nazreem was genuinely surprised.

The old man smiled. 'Of course, the name.'

Nazreem was mystified. Guadalupe meant nothing to her, in any language.

'Like so much,' the priest said. 'It is a hybrid. Some of the names of settlements in Spain were only given late, or their names changed in between the transformation of the Caliphate into Castile. Like Alcázar, the name is a cross between a Latin word and an Arabic one: 'wadi' and 'lupum'. In English you would say, "Valley of the Wolf".'

Marcus eyed the thick pine woods on either side and thought it would be easy to imagine wolves prowling wild in them. 'But I always thought the Virgin of Guadalupe was in Mexico.' After the mad-sounding theories of the Texan and his Protestant priest, he thought it worth it to hear the version from the man they had warned him against.

'This country' – he gestured with one arm at the landscape all around them, causing Marcus a momentary panic attack as the car lurched towards the side of the narrow road – 'is Extremadura. It is the best part of Spain, but also the poorest. This was a land to leave behind, but also to carry with you. This is the land where the *conquistadores* grew up, this is the country whose legends, whose shrines they carried with them in their hearts. This is where those of them who came back returned to. The first native Indians from the New World were baptised in Guadalupe. That is why its name has conquered half the world, bestowed upon churches, islands, monasteries and thousands of little girls from Argentina to Peru. The original, meanwhile, like an old lady in her armchair, has fallen gracefully asleep. It was natural for the cult of the Madonna to be established there too.'

'But what about the other black Madonna?' said Marcus, still trying to get him to address the Texan's story about the Mexican 'holy virgin' being of pagan origin.

But the old man was off in another direction: 'Ah, you mean Montserrat. We must be careful to be polite to our Catalan cousins. You have been to Altötting in Germany. You have seen the Madonna there. It is old, so is the one in Montserrat.'

It took Nazreem to see what he was getting at. 'But not that old, is that it?'

Another shrug. 'How old does old have to be? Unless,' one eye in the rear-view mirror watching her reaction, 'we are talking about so-called originals.'

'Are we?' asked Marcus. 'What would an original be, in this context?'

'I think you know. There was a story in the newspapers, not so very long ago, about a find in the Holy Land.' Marcus could see the man's eyes flicker back to the rear-view mirror and suspected he was not just checking the empty road behind them. So he knew about Nazreem, or had he just surmised? No, he knew all right.

'There are people who have long believed in St Luke's painting of the Madonna, but there are others who believe that the oldest images of the Mother of God were carved. The Madonna in Montserrat, that in Altötting, and indeed that in Guadalupe are carved figures. The question is which is the oldest' – he paused for effect, or maybe just to concentrate on steering; beyond the edge of the narrow road a precipitous drop of scree and shrub fell away for maybe fifty metres – 'and whether another has been found that is older still.' There was a questioning note in his voice that was left unanswered.

'What are we talking about here in terms of age?' Marcus felt it was his job to keep the ball in the air.

'The statue in Montserrat,' Don Julio volunteered, 'used to be known as *la Jerosolimitana*, the woman of Jerusalem, because it was believed that was where it had come from, that it had been carved there by St Luke and that it was only removed because of the invading Saracens: the Muslims again.'

Again a glance in his rear-view mirror. Nazreem's face was studiously emotionless, but not blank, as if she was lost in thought, calculating correlations of which Marcus knew nothing. He glanced out over the steep-sided valley and wondered what this country had been like when it had been part of the Islamic world, and what it had been like when it was the battlefront in a clash of civilisations and religions that had occurred six centuries ago, but was now once again rearing its head, this time on a global scale.

'So how did it get to Montserrat?' asked Nazreem.

'No one knows, but according to one account it was there already by the year 718 AD.'

Nazreem leaned forward eagerly. That was much older than she had dared hope. But in that case why were they heading first to Guadalupe.

'And then?'

'Again no one knows how much of any of this is true, but there are no more references to it for over 150 years until it was allegedly rediscovered by some shepherds around the end of the ninth century.'

'The ninth century is pretty old,' said Marcus, turning to Nazreem. 'Maybe we should have been on our way to Barcelona instead.'

'I don't think so,' said their driver.

Marcus turned back to him, inviting him to continue.

'We mentioned the Madonna in Altötting.'

'Yes,' said Nazreem, 'but it was a copy, a mediaeval replica of an older original.' She left unsaid the words 'of a copy'.

The old man nodded. 'It is the same in Montserrat. It is a fine image, and very old, but not as old as the story. The scholars, the art historians are certain it is of Romanesque style, perhaps as late as the thirteenth century. Old but like I said, not as old as the story.'

'And the figure in Guadalupe, it is different?'

'Oh yes. Although in many ways it is very similar.'

'Has it performed a miracle?' asked Marcus with a straight face. Part of him wanted to know if he would find Guadalupe too adorned with plastic limbs and kitsch paintings.

'Oh yes, for years it too was lost, but then it miraculously reappeared. Just when it was needed.'

Nazreem leaned forward, her concern for the old man's well-being overcome yet again by her passion to know more: 'What do you mean, "when it was needed"?'

'It was the latter years of the *Reconquista*, the reconquest. The Moors of Extremadura were resisting all efforts, and threatening to strike back, even at Castile itself.

'One day up in this valley, the "valley of the wolf", a cowherd was searching for a sick cow that had gone missing. When he found the animal it was dead so he started to skin it, making a cut in the form of a cross; as he did the animal came back to life and the cowherd suddenly saw a bright light and heard a heavenly voice.'

Marcus smiled wryly at the way the man recounted the story as if it was a matter of fact.

'At that very moment a woman appeared to him and told him to take the cow back to his herd, go down and find the priests and bring them back to dig on the spot where he had found the stricken animal, and they would find a holy image for which they should erect a sanctuary.

'The cowherd rushed off to do as he was told, but when he got to the village found one of his sons had died. He immediately prayed to the Mother of God and the boy came back to life. They returned to the spot where they had been told to dig and uncovered the figure of the Madonna. News of the miracles preached from every pulpit in the country, the Christian troops were given heart and Extremadura was liberated. The rest is history.'

Marcus was tempted to burst out laughing. The whole story reeked of opportunism, fraud and superstition. But he did not want to cause offence.

'But the statue they found was much older than the others?'

'So it is believed. It had been sent to the early church in Spain as a gift from Pope Gregory to the Bishop of Seville.'

'This is the Gregory who gave us the Gregorian calendar? But I thought that was much later, the mid-sixteenth century.'

The old man was shaking his head, amused. 'No, no, no, not that Gregory. I am referring to Gregory the Great, although the later one is now better known.'

'And this Gregory was around when?'

'At the end of the sixth century. He became pope in the year 574 AD to be precise.'

Marcus could hear a sharp intake of breath from the back seat. 'And this dates from then?'

'Perhaps. It has not been carbon-dated. Such a thing would be unimaginable with such a holy relic. But it is certainly not of a style that fits with any recognisable later artistic style.'

'Then that means ...'

'What it means depends on the rest of the legend.'

'Which is?'

'That Pope Gregory had brought the statue to Rome in order to help cure the city of a plague, that before that it had been in Constantine's own city.'

'Constantinople.'

'Indeed, having been taken there because it was the imperial capital.'

'So where did it come from originally?'

The priest took his eyes off the road for just a second to glance directly at each of them in turn. 'From where? From Jerusalem of course.'

'Are you trying to say that …?'

'Oh yes, it is widely believed – and with some substantial justification – that the little statue which is known to the world as *Nuestra Señora de Guadalupe*, is the oldest known surviving image of the Mother of God. Or at least was, until now. That is why we are so fascinated – maybe even a little worried – by the idea that one has been discovered that may be older still.'

The old man smiled and turned his head to glance once again at Nazreem in the rear-view mirror, at the precise moment they turned a bend to find hurtling towards them, downhill, on a one-in-five incline, a huge tipper truck. The old man span the wheel and the little car lurched to the right, perilously close to the edge of the road. Its wheels churned brown dust as the clanking, clattering behemoth of what was obviously a construction vehicle scraped their wing mirror before thundering past them.

The car had stalled and jerked to a halt. The hulking truck continued rattling down the mountain track as if whoever was at the wheel had not even noticed their existence, much less the serious risk of running them catastrophically off the road. The old man sat there with one hand on his obviously palpitating heart. The other he used to mop strands of grey hair back from his brow. Nazreem was leaning forward solicitously with one hand on his shoulder. Marcus, however, had climbed out of the car and was staring futilely into the distance through the cloud of dust left by the lorry's wake.

'You must excuse me,' their elderly driver was saying. 'I sometimes do not pay attention enough.'

Marcus shook his head, climbing back into the car. 'No, it wasn't your fault.' He looked significantly at Nazreem. 'If I didn't know better I would say that was a deliberate attempt to run us off the road.'

But the old man dismissed it: 'There is a quarry up ahead. In the hills. It was an accident. Nearly.'

'Nearly is right,' said Marcus, unconvinced. Yet if anyone had really wanted to get rid of them, surely it wouldn't have been 'nearly'. He could imagine few things easier or more convincing than arranging an 'accident' with an elderly driver on a dangerous mountain road. On the other hand, 'nearly' was scary enough. And that might have been the intention.

'Are you okay to drive?' Nazreem was asking.

'Yes, yes, it is fine now,' he said, turning the key in the ignition. The engine made a grating noise for a second or two, but then sprang to life. The wheels spun up their own small dust cloud of grit before gaining purchase on the tarmac, and then they were off again, although they had twice to slow down while the old man adjusted the damaged wing mirror.

'Another miracle?' said Marcus.

47

The atmosphere in the little apartment high above the rooftops of Madrid's Almenara district all but crackled with adrenalin and repressed violence, the pheromones of fear mingling with the testosterone that automatic weapons induced.

While the Reverend Parker's wet trouser leg betrayed more of his inner emotion than the words of the 23rd Psalm, 'Yea, though I walk through the Valley of Death I shall fear no ill,' that his lips were silently forming, the former Marine Corps athlete held in a humiliating headlock next to him let his eyes exude an all but contemptuous hatred. The attitude of a man who at any moment expected the tables to be turned.

In front of him, the tall Muslim in the dark robes and white turban stood and examined his captives the way a slaughterman might size up a consignment of two-year-old bullocks. He seemed puzzled by the Texan's anger, a man more obviously used to silent submission. The silence of the lambs of God.

'Ah, it may be that you are waiting on your Hispanic friends. *Los Mexicanos*, eh?' he said, pronouncing it effortlessly, 'mehicanos', with an expression that ill disguised a sneer.

The little minister let his eyes stray to the Texan's face and saw the sickening realisation the Islamist's words had evoked etched across the big man's broad features.

'Oh ye of little faith,' the man in the turban said, a thin smile for the first time flitting across his sombre complexion. And then he barked something fast, in a guttural language that the Americans took to be Arabic. The Texan could feel for a second the blade at his throat disappear and almost thought of making a move except that the hold on his head simultaneously tightened.

Then the knife was back, and with a wet flop something soft and slimy landed on the floor in front of them. Instinctively he closed his eyes. The Reverend Parker, whose glasses were misting up and had been twisted out of their usual position, thought at first they had thrown some piece of shellfish in a plastic bag onto the carpet. It was only when he heard the outburst of fury from the Texan that he dared attempt a closer look. Only the iron grip around his head stopped him from throwing up as he recognised the object as a bloody human ear.

'I am most terribly sorry. It was necessary. He was very courageous, very protective of your privacy. We had been following the girl, you see. You stole a march on us taking the man. To each his own, I suppose,' he said with an almost nonchalant shrug. 'No matter, we have met up at last.'

He gestured to one of the two automatic-armed men who produced a mobile phone from his pocket, called a number and said something in what sounded like Arabic into it. A few minutes later the door to the apartment opened and two more black-clad figures entered, pushing in front of them, wrists tied behind their backs, the cowed and frightened figures of Alfredo and José, 'Freddie and Joseph', the former clutching a blood-soaked white cloth to the side of his head and snivelling uncontrollably. At a gesture from the mullah they were hustled into the bedroom. The Reverend Parker tried hard to control his sphincter as he heard the pitiful sobs coming from the former macho Mexican tough guy.

'What do you want with us?' the Texan snarled, his Adam's apple bobbing dangerously next to the sharp blade at his throat, seemingly oblivious to the irony that only a few hours before he had faced an angry and unwilling captive of his own.

The mullah stroked his beard for a second.

'I am an Arab, you are Americans. In the modern world, therefore, we are enemies.'

The Texan rewarded him with a low growl that confirmed the obvious truth of the statement.

'However,' the Arab said, 'as men of religion, we both know that the world is a fleeting thing. And sometimes there can be a communion of interests.'

'I don't know what you're talking about.'

The Arab closed his eyes a second as if dealing with a child.

'I think you do.'

He waited a moment, expecting the Texan to concede, but the man just glared at him. Eventually he said, 'I believe that you have no more love for idolatry than we do.'

Slowly the Texan blinked his eyes in place of the nod he could not risk without serious damage to his windpipe and then rolled them sideways to see the Reverend Parker was doing the same only more rapidly. For the first time it had begun to dawn on the self-important man of God that these preachers of an alien religion were not going to slit their throats for the crime of being 'infidels'. In fact, with a bit of luck they might not be going to slit their throats at all. Even if it was too soon to absolutely bank on that.

As if to prove him right, the mullah made a brief gesture and the two gunmen body-searched both of them, removing a small Derringer pistol from the reverend's socks, and then the razor-sharp knives were taken from their throats. The mullah gestured for them to rise, like the Mosque faithful after Friday evening prayers. The two men got up gratefully from their knees, each involuntarily rubbing the spot where the blade had been, as if to reassure themselves that their heads were still attached to their shoulders. The mullah barked something in Arabic and the masked men pushed forward two chairs, each positioning himself behind one. Irrespective of whose name was on the lease, for the moment the apartment clearly belonged to them, and the dark-robed figure in front of them.

'This is about the statue,' the Texan said, positioning himself on the edge of the seat. 'You want it too.'

'Want it?' The mullah raised his eyebrows.

'Of course,' the Texan almost managed a smile. 'You want it the same way we do ... only more ... you want it destroyed. What's the matter? Worried about a little extra competition on the mumbo-jumbo front.'

In an instant the blades were back at both their throats and a quickly muted whimpering suggested that the Reverend Parker was in danger of finally losing control of the rest of his bodily functions. The mullah's eyes flashed dark lightning, but again he gestured to his acolytes and the knives were removed.

'This is the famous American sense of humour. I warn you, in our world, religion is not a laughing matter.'

'Point taken, point taken,' the Texan said quickly. 'I meant no offence. You're right, of course. A dislike for graven images is one area on which our faiths agree. But why ...?'

'Why do we care about this image?' The mullah stroked his beard again and closed his eyes for a second. 'Let us just say that we also do not wish to see Gaza City, the first semi-independent Palestinian area for more than half a century, become dominated by a Christian shrine ...' He let the words hang in the air.

The Texan nodded slowly as if weighing up the argument, then said: 'I suppose I can see the logic of that. But what's the problem? The thing's gone missing.'

'The problem, as you know as well as we do, is how or where it might resurface. If we both share a common interest in its destruction, then we might increase our chance of succeeding in that ambition. I do not know what, if any, influence you may have had on the teacher. I suspect very little, but there is also the possibility that, as Americans, you have technological means of which we do not dispose.'

The Texan smiled broadly, taking this as due acknowledgement of the innate superiority of American civilisation, without even noticing the disparaging tone in which it was said.

'While we,' the mullah, 'have something that you do not.'

'And that might be?'

'Certain information.'

'What sort of certain information?' The Texan was trying to re-establish some sort of equilibrium here. If he was forced to collaborate with these Muslim fuckers, and 'collaborate' was the only word he could think of, particularly given what they'd done to one of the wetbacks' hearing equipment, he was not going to be continuously bullied.

'We know precisely who stole the statue. And why.'

48

Nazreem felt a crawling feeling on her skin and a nausea in the pit of her stomach which, put together, she imagined to be the physical manifestations of a sickness of the soul.

The contradictions buried within her unconscious were clawing their way to the surface, and she did not like it one bit. All her life she had been taught to regard 'graven images' as heathen conceits, toys of the infidel. Yet here she was approaching her first glimpse of the Virgin of Guadalupe with an almost religious feeling. Yet it made her want to throw up.

It was not as if she had undergone some cathartic conversion to Christianity in its Roman Catholic incarnation. Quite the opposite. It was as if the object of veneration, which for six centuries had been contained within this fortress-like sanctuary, and the small dark figure she had unearthed from the sands of Gaza were coalescing, leading her to an older, greater truth.

It was just that so far she still failed to see it as anything more than murky shadows, half-truths and shaky theories. And it was that which gave her goose pimples down her spine. Or the feeling of someone walking on her grave. The uncomfortable sensation that she was coming closer to something she had half-known all her life.

She had not been prepared for the scale of the place, or its physical appearance. She had expected to wind up through the sleepy streets of the little town they had driven into as the sun was beginning to cast long shadows, to find an ancient crumbling church surrounded by the low level dwellings of holy hermits, a neglected provincial relic of a religion in slow decline. Instead she had been confronted by a fortress.

Two giant square towers of stone, metres thick and bedecked with battlements, squeezed between them a religious façade reached only by ascending a steep flight of steps, dominated the tiny town square like an ogre sentinel at the entrance to a cave. All around, the monastery itself was concealed behind fortifications that could have seen off an army, as they had once been intended to.

'Begun by King Alfonso XI after the battle of Salado in 1340, the crucial conflict of arms which effectively marked the end of the Caliphate in Spain,' the old priest had informed them as the little car crept out of the afternoon sunshine into the sudden chill of the shadow cast by the immense edifice next to them. 'This fortress monastery was to house the wonder-working effigy that had inspired the Christians to victory.'

The little car pulled up outside a fine old white-walled building which ran parallel to the monastic battlements up a narrow cobbled street, and looked almost as ancient as the fortress itself. 'This is where you shall stay. It has already been booked.'

Marcus nodded his approval. The building looked as ancient as the monastery.

'It also dates from the fifteenth century. It is now a parador, a hotel run by the state, but it was once the hospital run by the knights of St John the Baptist,' said the priest. 'Many people came here, looking for a miracle. Many very rich people,' he added after a moment's hesitation. 'Today, however, it is not so expensive. You will be well looked after.'

'But,' Nazreem had begun immediately, her disappointment all too evident, 'I thought we were going to see the abbot. And the Madonna.'

'Tomorrow. The abbot too is no longer a young man. He will be pleased to see you in the morning. For now, please, enjoy your meal, a glass of wine. Relax. This is an old place. Neither it nor anything it contains will disappear overnight.'

Famous last words, thought Nazreem, but she smiled politely as he ushered them towards the hotel and climbed back into his little car. The events of the past weeks had taught her that things had a habit of disappearing just when you relied on them most.

They ate a delicious meal of roast kid with figs, beside a tinkling fountain in a courtyard that smelled of lemon leaves, and could have been a scene from the *Arabian Nights* rather than in the sacred heart of one of Europe's most devoutly Catholic countries.

Afterwards they drank hot sweet coffee on a balcony and listened to the cicadas in the pine trees. Never, thought Nazreem, had she imagined that there were such places where the Christian and

Islamic worlds overlapped as totally as here on this ancient fault line between them.

The next morning they breakfasted in the same elegant little courtyard and went to the front gate of the monastery where, on announcing themselves, they were ushered through a small courtyard into a great cloister.

The old man was not there to meet them. Instead a young monk, no more than thirty years old she guessed, had emerged from behind a great wooden door that separated the monastic environment proper from that part open to visitors.

It was the courtyard in which they now found themselves that astonished her most. Along one wall of the cool shady cloister loomed great paintings of scenes from Christianity's story: big dark works in oil by Renaissance masters.

Yet in the middle of this darkness all was light; hot bright sunshine on a formal garden of green plants arranged in geometric patterns around a tiny temple that was in itself a miniature masterpiece of almost totally Islamic architecture: a square, open-sided little building on a floor of marble mosaic around a circular pool. On each side opened a Gothic arch, each of which contained two smaller ones of Moorish style supported by columns of red, white or grey marble. Above it rose an ornately carved roof in the form of a triple-tiered octagonal crown.

Nazreem gasped at the sight of it: 'It's … beautiful. It could be in … Baghdad … or Damascus … or …' For a moment, just a moment, she had a glimpse of the mad dream of fanatics like Osama bin Laden, Islamic imperialists who dreamed of recapturing a lost world. And yet, this was not a monument from the days of the Caliphate, but created afterwards, before the Christian persecution set in; it was a relic of a period of fusion and tolerance. Maybe that was what made it so beautiful. And so rare.

The young monk gestured towards a doorway. 'Please,' he said, in heavily accented English, 'the abbot is waiting.'

They followed him out of the cloister with its stark contrasts between light and shade into a dark, curving corridor. Then he crossed himself and opened a door into a room that gleamed with gold and silver. They entered silently. The room was in the shape of a Greek cross with sunlight filtering in through the high dome at its centre on to an enormous pendulum chandelier that hung perilously from its apex. Every inch of every wall was covered either with gold leaf or frescos of the saints whose haloed statues stood in recessed niches. But the eye was immediately drawn to one.

Set above the altar was the smallest of all, yet the most radiantly attired, a tiny figure on a gold throne, with a halo like the rays of the sun, no bigger than a child's doll. Nazreem approached it with a mix of awe, scholarly interest and trepidation. Would it match the image she still held so vividly in her head?

But the closer she came, the greater her disappointment. The figure itself was almost impossible to make out, swamped, even more than in the case of Altötting, by the extravagance of its vestments: a great robe of crimson richly embroidered in gold, dotted with stars and crowned with a huge golden diadem that dwarfed the tiny, dark brown face that peered out from beneath it. That, a hand in which a gold sceptre had been placed, and an even tinier impression of a face poking from a hole in the robe and presumably supposed to be that of the baby Jesus, were all that could be seen of the figure itself. The form had been stylised, the ritual vestments concealing every element of the underlying sculpture except for the dark, almost primitive features.

A familiar voice behind them said, 'I hope you do not find her a disappointment.'

They turned and standing in the doorway where the young monk had been, arrayed in white abbatial robes, was their ageing bullfight fan.

'It is time I introduced myself properly,' he said. 'Don Julio Federico García, abbot of Guadalupe.'

49

'Please forgive me, for the little deception. It was, perhaps, unnecessary, but you will understand you came to me under disconcerting circumstances.'

'You mean the disappearance of Sister Galina?'

The elderly abbot nodded.

'Yes, I can understand that,' said Nazreem. Marcus said nothing, trying to evaluate the man now standing in front of them clad not in the grand purple or crimson of the upper echelons of Catholic Church hierarchy, but in sacking robes designed to resemble those of mediaeval paupers. Except that these had been subtly garnished and rendered in the finest of cloths for an ecclesiastical aristocracy. The Texan had told him to test the man's trustworthiness. Was this what he meant? Or was this still part of the act?

'What has occurred is certainly disquieting,' he said simply. 'We must talk about this in some detail, later. Right now, I believe we must satisfy your curiosity, and answer the question which, I confess, is in both our minds.'

Nazreem's eyes turned back to the great golden shrine in its ornately encrusted niche and to the little figure swamped in its folds of rich and ancient drapery and the royal paraphernalia that dwarfed it. For her, however, the regalia for all its splendour was an obstruction, a deliberate obfuscation. She closed her eyes and conjured up another image, a millennia-old sculpture pulled from the sands of her native city. She had to retrieve and retain that image, in order to compare, to try to match against what little here was visible beneath the trappings of centuries of veneration.

When the abbot spoke again she was surprised to hear his voice coming from in front of her. She opened her eyes to find him standing on the step of the shrine, looking down at her and felt – with an unexpected frisson of horror – that he might be about to bestow on her some Christian blessing as a penitent. Instinctively she made to recoil, but he merely lifted a finger to his lips and said words she had scarcely dared hope to hear:

'For you, my child, we are about to do something extremely rare. We shall disrobe the Virgin.'

Marcus stood back a step. The words had shocked him. Ridiculously. He knew that what the abbot – a man whose every word and gesture he now considered suspect – meant was that he was about to remove the ornate vestments that concealed almost all of the original sculpture, an act that in itself was an honour so rare that he suspected it was never carried out in public, but only by monks in private, exchanging one set of raiment for another. Yet even that, added to the words themselves, somehow conveyed an almost perverse sexual charge. For a moment the grotesque image that flitted through his mind was that of old men undressing Barbie dolls. There again, maybe in the cult of the Virgin there really was something left from more ancient, earthly rituals.

When the process was complete, and the costly regalia was laid to one side in trays of old Spanish oak lined with black velvet, and the abbot stood aside, the expression etched deep on the old man's face was one of conspiratorial embarrassment, like one who had indeed confessed to a guilty, shameful secret, and yet filled with fraught expectation in the hope that those to whom he had revealed his secret passion would share it rather than laugh at it.

Marcus had to bite his lip. His own reaction could not have been further from that he imagined the old man in his long skirts hoped for. The little dark wooden statue stripped of its golden robes was in such stark contrast to the grandiose baroque splendour of its shrine that it shocked him. Far more than he had expected. There was no logic to his reaction, but he realised, suddenly and with gut-wrenching disquiet, that he had been subconsciously expecting something much more remarkable in an anachronistically conventional way: a sculpture if not exactly on a par with the works of a Michelangelo or Donatello then at least in their tradition, a work of classical beauty, tender and lifelike on a par with portraiture. Was that not the whole magic of the promise inherent in the mystery: to actually see the face of Jesus Christ's mother?

Instead, the figure in front of him, in its unadorned simplicity, the bright robes replaced by a simply hewn, roughly coloured suggestion of clothing below that bland, straight-nosed face, was a naïve, primitive totem, the sort of thing he might have imagined being picked up in an African market offering naïve tribal carvings, more like a bush child's plaything, an inanimate expressionless wooden dolly with a stick-like baby. It was all he could do to keep from laughing. Baby Jesus reminded him inescapably of a fingerbob puppet he had bought as a child from a Soweto street trader. He had cradled it too on the way home in the car not dissimilarly to the way this supposed image of the Divinity perched on the knees of its wooden mother, and poked it through the crook of his elbow at the car window: Peek-a-boo, peek-a-boo.

With a smile on his face that he hoped suggested polite appreciation rather than concealed mirth, he put his hand on Nazreem's shoulder and made gently to turn her towards him to gauge her own reaction. But she resisted the slight pressure of his hand, as if she was not even aware of its presence. The abbot, far from registering Marcus's less than wholly respectful reaction to his unveiled Madonna, was paying him no attention whatsoever, his eyes fixed totally on Nazreem. Finally, after a silence that seemed to last a microcosm of eternity, he asked her in a quiet voice:

'It is the same?'

Another eternity, during which as far as Marcus could tell her eyes remained focused entirely on the crude little wooden statue, and then Nazreem said, in a voice that was surprisingly strong and yet subdued: 'No. Not exactly.'

And then she repeated the phrase, slowly, carefully, approaching and bending low over the little wooden doll.

'Not exactly.'

50

'How do you know? And what do you know?' The Texan all but shouted at the tall man in the white turban who towered above him. He reckoned he was a man who knew a con when he smelled one. He suspected one now, but deep down he had to admit he wasn't sure.

'We know because the thief was one of us. Or at least he pretended to be one of us.'

The Texan looked at him warily.

'The man who stole the statue from the museum in Gaza was recruited here. In Spain. You will appreciate already that the fact we are telling you something like this should in itself be proof of our good faith.'

The Texan nodded. The men standing behind their chairs with their goddamn scimitars or whatever they called those butchers' blades were equally eloquent, though the message was different.

'His name was Ahmed Abdul Rashid al-Zahwani, also known as Abu Ataa.'

The name obviously meant nothing to the Reverend Parker but Jones's eyes opened wide.

'Yes. He was known to your military intelligence. He was a man who had carried out many operations of jihad. But we will not go into that now,' he added just in time to counter an outburst from the Texan who had seen al-Zahwani's pictures on army wanted lists. He had also seen the report of his death.

'He was also a fool,' the mullah added.

'You had him steal the statue?'

'No. We do not steal from our own.' He waved a hand. 'Perhaps in this instance there might have been an excuse, but we did not know what it was he had stolen, were not aware of its true importance.'

Was the man saying he thought the statue was authentic?

'He used information acquired from us, about the timing of an Isareli air attack. To break into the museum amidst the chaos.'

The Texan made wide eyes again. The mullah waved them away.

'You think we do not know what the Zionists plan? What should we do? We cannot evacuate all of Gaza; there is nowhere to go. If they wish to stoke the hatred of our people then we cannot prevent them. Every attack creates another suicide bomber. This was no exception.'

'I thought I read in the papers that al-Zahwani died in a suicide operation. Driving full tilt at a checkpoint.'

'So it would appear. Perhaps the brick on the accelerator was too heavy.'

The realisation dawned. 'He was already dead. You killed him. But why, if he was "one of you"?'

'Because he was a liar, and a traitor to his religion. He tried to sneak out of Gaza with the spoils of his theft. But that is not so easy. The borders are controlled, by the Egyptians almost as strictly as by the Israelis. We have ways. But we also have watchers. He should have gone nowhere without our permission.

'A soldier does not desert his post. And he was not supposed to be taking with him something that belonged to the Palestinian people. Our people discovered it in his bags as he tried to enter the Rafah tunnels.'

'You're saying the guy was working for someone else?'

'The man was a mercenary, not a soldier of Allah but a piece of shit who on occasion happened to be useful – he would do things that a true Muslim would not, could not – but which could still, on occasion, be useful to us, but he was not trustworthy.'

'So who was he working for?'

The mullah looked at him with an expression of mild scorn mingled with exasperation.

'Who do you think he was working for? What body on this earth would have most interest in possessing what they supposed to be the original likeness of the Virgin Mary?'

The Texan almost cracked up at the obviousness of it, and the fact that filthy lucre had won over an apostle of Mohammed as surely as it had tainted the soul of Judas Iscariot to betray the Lord Jesus in the Garden of Gethsemane: 'The Vatican – the Roman Catholic Church itself.'

The mullah closed his eyes in what the Texan took for silent acquiescence.

'He told you this?'

'Let us say, he had to answer some questions which proved difficult for him.'

The Texan closed his eyes. He could imagine being interrogated by these guys in more detail than the unpleasantness they had inflicted on him since smashing down the apartment door.

'In the end, for the sake of his soul, and after some necessary persuasion, he told us everything, including what he had done to the woman. Under the circumstances,' he said, closing his eyes briefly as if envisaging the moment, 'even his bodily remains did not deserve the appearance of martyrdom.'

The Texan could see the muscles of the armed bodyguards tense. He wondered if any of them had witnessed – or carried out – the man's execution. He could imagine it proving a powerful incentive to loyalty.

But there was a problem with the mullah's story that only just dawned on him.

'Then that means ... you have the figure? Or at least it's still in Gaza. So why ...?'

The dark frown on the mullah's face deepened further like a thundercloud invading his soul.

'I told you the man was stupid,' he said. 'Had he reached his masters they would not have been pleased either. He took the wrong figure.'

'Wha ... at?'

The mullah flung his hand at the ground as if flicking away some piece of ordure that had stuck to it.

'The Christians have so many trinkets, so many idols. Even still, it was a stupid mistake. And not the only one he made. If he had come to us in the first place and told us what he had been ordered to steal ...'

'You killed him not just because he was working for the Vatican, or because you wanted the figure but because he was stealing from Gaza?'

'And also because he committed an atrocity in so doing. He violated one of our Muslim sisters. It was the first of the sins he confessed before going to meet his creator. That is no doubt why she is now working against us.'

'You mean ... the woman from the museum in Gaza, who found the thing? The professor's girlfriend.'

The mullah made a face.

'She has been offended, gravely. She wants her revenge. She wants it in the form of personal fame.

'She wants to know if this object really is what the world believes. She wants to know if it is rather what she believes it to be. She is a seeker after truth, but one who has abandoned the only real way to the truth, through her faith, through the Qu'ran. Because of what had happened to her, we did not prevent her from leaving Gaza. If he had confessed so quickly to the full nature of his betrayal that too would have been different.

'We let her leave because of the unclean thing he did to her – an act of compassion. As so often, it turned out to be our mistake.'

'You don't mean you think she …'

'We know. The museum in Gaza has been searched thoroughly. She left in a hurry, taking what appeared to be a single heavy bag. We believe it contained the real figure. It is the only reason she is still alive.'

51

The smell of roasted suckling pig and orange blossom filled the warm night air. In a corner of the great Gothic courtyard a duet of violin players wove strange bittersweet tapestries of sound that drifted up to the battlements and dissipated into a sky full of half-glimpsed constellations. Old sky gods turning still in their ancient accustomed rotations, imperfectly drawn echoes of man's eternally inadequate attempts to understand his place in the universe. The abbot of Guadalupe lifted one hand from his replete stomach to signal to the waiter for a second bottle of rich dark Rioja. Seated across from him Nazreem Hashrawi lifted her glass and touched the intoxicating liquor to her lips, savouring its powerful complex taste and the rare sensation of alcohol working its unfamiliar magic on her brain.

Marcus Frey sat alongside her, feeling very much the outsider at the feast. Far from soaking up the unexpectedly sensuous aesthetic offering of this remote little town with its hidden treasure and gastronomic delights, his mind whirred with complex, contradictory conspiracies and an ambiguity towards religious icons that had never before troubled him. He was not sure who to trust: the urbane, sophisticated and undoubtedly intelligent monk who indulged a passion for blood sports and, when it suited him, a convenient economy with the truth. Or a bunch of Bible-belt American rednecks who had kidnapped him and spouted bigoted anti-Catholic conspiracy theories worthy of seventeenth-century witch burners. The trouble was that the theories seemed less crazy with every passing hour.

Nazreem had been a different person since seeing the primitive little wooden statue that was the preposterous object at the heart of the cult of religious veneration that had spread from the Old World to the New.

At this moment she was leaning across the white tablecloth, wine glass held unsteadily in her outstretched hand. Marcus thought she had maybe consumed four glasses, but then that was probably more than on any other evening in her life. The abbot's eyes had drifted off as if he too were under the influence of the wine. There were fewer than a dozen other diners in the great Gothic courtyard: a family party of five adults and a couple of small children who kept clambering off their chairs and playing hide-and-seek with each other behind potted palms, a young couple who had only eyes for each other and may have come to Guadalupe, as many did, simply to obtain the Virgin's blessing on their union, a dumpy little man in a black beret alone at a table in the corner, his head bowed almost reverentially over a steaming plate of tripe in tomato sauce.

Over the course of dinner she had, possibly unadvisably in Marcus's opinion, related what had happened to them in London, Munich and Madrid, including Marcus's kidnapping and release.

'I am worried,' she said, 'about the fate of Sister Galina. You must be too. After what happened to Marcus I fear she may have been kidnapped by the same people. Or worse.' Marcus, who was fairly certain that the former at least was not the case, shook his head, but the abbot was speaking first.

'We should not assume that she has definitely been kidnapped.'

'I'm not so sure about that. If the German police have declared her missing and are concerned for her safety, then we should be too,' Marcus said. He was not yet about to reveal, for all that Nazreem seemed taken by the abbot, that he had been comprehensively warned against him and all he stood for, even if it was a warning from individuals of questionable sanity. Not yet. There was a benefit of the doubt to be given, but for the moment at least it had to be given both ways.

'Sister Galina is a remarkable woman,' the abbot said obtusely, 'one of great resources.'

'There is also the minor matter of the mutilated body parts dumped on her desk. I assume you know about that,' said Marcus.

'Ah yes,' said the abbot, and now he genuinely did look crestfallen, a dark shadow falling over his brows as he closed his eyes briefly, staring at the ground. A waiter appeared with the second bottle of Rioja, offered it to taste but the abbot gestured to him to serve it anyway.

'We must pray for her,' the abbot said at last, looking up again and giving each of them a grim little thin-lipped smile.

244

'You act as if you don't even care about her,' said Marcus. Nazreem looked shocked by his rudeness.

'That is not the case. Not at all. It is merely that for the moment at least the matter is not in our hands.'

'Look,' said Marcus suddenly, against his own best intentions losing his fragile cool: 'Whoever has been pursuing us, whoever has kidnapped her, the grotesque thing that happened in Altötting with the body parts, it's all somehow related to that little fetish statue with the gold braid frocks in there.'

Marcus had been deliberately goading the man, but rather than react with horror to such a sacrilegious description, the abbot simply leaned back in his chair and said quietly, 'Yes, of course, you're quite right. That is why the original must be dealt with properly.'

Nazreem had drained her glass of wine by now and done nothing to stop the waiter replenishing it. She was sitting back in her chair too, opposite the abbot like a sparring partner in a chess game, at which Marcus was no more than a spectator.

She looked him straight in the eye across the table and with a slight shake of her head that suggested she did not quite believe what she was going to say, said: 'You know, don't you.'

The abbot's eyes twinkled back.

'He knows what?' said Marcus starting to get angry at being treated like a schoolboy.

Her eyes still on the abbot who was holding her gaze, Nazreem said slowly, deliberately: 'He knows that the statue in this monastery, and the one we found in Gaza of which it is a very close copy, has got nothing to do with the Virgin Mary. Or at least has got nothing to do with any woman who might ever have lived in Palestine in the first century, whether or not she gave birth to some rabbi who claimed to be the son of God.'

To Marcus's astonishment, once again the abbot simply smiled and said: 'I told you before there are those of us within the Christian community who are not afraid of challenges to the orthodoxy. History is something we respect,' then, after a pause, 'even if, as you yourself know only too well, Dr Frey, there are often different interpretations.'

'That statue,' said Nazreem, pouring herself yet another glass of wine, and gesturing vaguely towards the great stone bulk of the monastery, 'is a sacred object all right. Even if it is just a copy.

Like the others. Sacred objects with a pedigree that stretches far back beyond the dawn of Christianity, just like the holy grove, the lindens, in Altötting, were sacred long before there were any Christians there.'

Nazreem was now quite clearly drunk. Marcus was beginning to get irritated with her. And with himself. This was not what he had intended at all. She was not used to wine, she was also understandably over-excited, but if she kept on like this she was in more danger than he was of insulting their host at his own table.

'The whole thing is a fraud,' she said, a little too loudly. In the far corner of the courtyard the violinists skipped a beat to glance in their direction. 'You know, don't you,' she spoke directly to the abbot, 'that it wasn't just Isis the church appropriated, it was every vestige of the old religions. The Mary cult didn't just swallow up Isis but Astarte too and the great earth mother, Kybele.

The smile had vanished from the abbot's face though his look was not so much angry as concerned, as if he too thought Nazreem had consumed too much wine.

Nazreem swigged back the last of the wine in her glass defiantly.

'You are a Muslim, even if not always a very devout one,' he said with only the slightest of glances at her empty wine glass. 'And I respect your faith. I really do. And for this reason I also understand that you have difficulty with the Catholic tradition of iconography – I mean of making what some would call "graven images", an impression which I think you, Dr Frey, coming from your own rather different Christian tradition also find somewhat difficult.'

'I like to think I can examine different faiths objectively,' said Marcus.

'Do you? Do you now? Deep down I think there is a part of you that believes we in the Roman Catholic Church particularly are in danger of becoming idolaters.'

Marcus looked at the man in some surprise. He had not expected to hear the question put quite so bluntly, though the reality was that he thought it a radical understatement, and his face said so even before he could formulate a reply.

'You are familiar with the old Latin expression *Ars longa, vita brevis.*' Marcus blinked, taken aback by an apparently complete *non sequitur*, realising as the thought flicked through his mind that there was even a Latin phrase to express a loss of the train of thought.

'Art lasts long but life is short,' he rendered in a recollection of schoolboy translation.

The abbot smiled. 'I thought so. You are also an admirer of art, I suspect, including much of the art that was created in the name of the church, even the Catholic Church.'

'Yes, of course, but ...'

The abbot held up one hand. 'Please, let me finish. Yet you live in a country which was responsible for one of the greatest acts of vandalism in history.'

Marcus gave him a quizzical look.

'During the English Reformation, tens of thousands of the most sublime works of art were destroyed, finely hewn wooden carvings – the works of the greatest masters – hurled onto bonfires, exquisitely wrought gold and silver plate melted down, stone statues of saints taken from their niches and smashed.'

He turned to Nazreem: 'The history of Islam is also not exactly free from similar barbarism.'

'We do not make images,' said Nazreem simply, but there was no fire in her voice, as if she knew what was coming.

'No,' said the abbot, 'and the decorative art of Islam is very beautiful as we can see even here in these rare examples where it has fused with the native art of Europe, but because art does not meet their religion's approval, should it be destroyed? As in Afghanistan, for example.'

She looked at him sideways, the taste of the wine souring in her mouth. She knew what he was about to say and said it for him:

'Bamiyan, the great Buddhas.'

'Indeed, the largest in the world, and nearly two thousand years old in the case of one of them. Blown to pieces by the Taliban. In the same way the gold and silver stripped from Catholic churches by English kings were used to buy powder and muskets, so the pieces of the great Buddhas of Bamiyan were hawked by the Taliban to buy AK47s. All, of course, in the name of God.'

'But the early Christians were just as bad, weren't they,' interrupted Marcus, 'taking over temples of the old gods and stripping them of their statues.' He suddenly stopped when he saw Nazreem staring at him and realised he had scarcely been listening to his own words; that was precisely the point – they had not got rid of all of them. Some they had made their own.

The abbot was holding his wine glass in his hand like a chalice and watching him over the top of it, his face pregnant with revelation. He leaned back in his chair and set the half-full wine glass on the white tablecloth in front of him, a chalice on an altar and said quietly, directly: 'Christianity is not one force, one religion, and never has been.'

'But I thought the Catholic Church ...'

'... the name means universal Church,' the abbot smiled. 'But it is universal perhaps only in its aspirations. It has never truly contained the body of faith of all Christians. Or indeed only Christians.'

'What do you mean?'

'Throughout the ages, there have been people who interpret things differently, those who would use religion to guide men and those who would use it to control them.'

On the other tables, waiters were beginning to clear away dishes noisily; the young couple had long gone, to an early bed; the family were getting ready to go home, the young children now hoisted onto shoulders, half-asleep; even the dumpy little tripe-eater had finished eating and seemed to be nodding off over a cup of coffee and a strong cigar. In the corner the musicians shuffled their sheet music before launching into a string nocturne that sounded like a lullaby.

'Some of us,' the abbot said, 'have always believed that religion and civilisation should go hand-in-hand rather than be opposed. That has, at times, made us enemies of fundamentalists, of whatever faith, men for the most part who reject culture and science almost equally, rather than embracing both and striving to see a unity.'

Marcus feared he was beginning to miss the point.

'I mean, for example, in the United States, primarily, those Christian fundamentalists who are ardent creationists, who insist on believing every word in the Bible so literally that they believe the earth to be only a few thousand years old.'

'I seem to recall that it's not so long ago that the Catholic Church persecuted people who said the earth was round.'

'I think you'll find it was longer ago than you think. I have never said we were always right or that there were never wrong-headed people, or that there are not now. But we have long since made our peace with Galileo. Some of us have no problem in seeing the Bible as a sacred text in literary form, containing truths to be interpreted and grasped at, not strictly meant to control our thoughts today. It is equally possible to take the wonderful literature of the Koran in the same way.'

'It is?' began Nazreem, and then stopped, remembering some of the verses her father had been fond of reciting, poetic yet almost impenetrable in meaning. And the apparent contradictions that could be found by those who tried to make the 'word of God' mean what they wanted it to mean.

Then she rounded on the old man: 'I'm right, aren't I? You know that the statue here is a pagan idol, or a copy of one that was confused – deliberately – with the Virgin Mary, with the Madonna. The figurine we found in Gaza, the statue we found, might just be the missing link, the "original" of Mary that is clearly older than the pagan goddess. Not Isis or Astarte but the one that's older than any of them – Kybele. In Madrid, at the fountain of Cibeles – Kybele – all that stuff about football, you were just playing with us?'

'Playing with you? I hardly think so. Besides everything I said was perfectly true – even about me having been a keen Réal Madrid fan. But in one respect you are not wrong: I was prompting you, not as a tease or a joke, but to see if our, if my suspicions, might be correct. I think the image that was unearthed in Gaza is indeed a figure of Kybele that at some stage was confounded with the Virgin Mary. And it may not be just any figure of Kybele.'

'What do you mean?'

'The Marian cult and the worship of Kybele have such strong links to Rome. The worship of Kybele – like the worship of the soldier god Mithras' – Marcus immediately heard in his head the words of the American Marine Colonel in the Madrid hotel room – 'became prevalent in Rome in the third century BC, but never more than when the city was in mortal danger.'

'Such as?'

'When the troops of Hannibal were at the gates, of course. Leading citizens demanded that the most holy of all images of Kybele, a black statue carved of stone, be fetched from Phrygia and brought into the city. One of the foremost *matronae* of Rome allegedly bore it from Ostia harbour into the city herself.

'When Rome was spared and Hannibal put to flight, the goddess was given the credit. Great temples were built to her all over Italy, the most famous on a hill outside Naples. The poet Virgil retired there. The ancient Romans called it Mons Sacer, the holy mountain, but in the seventh century it was christened – quite literally – Monte Vergine. A nice touch because some local folk confused it with the Virgil connection. It was dedicated to the Madonna, but the ruins of the original temple to Kybele are still there.'

Marcus and Nazreem exchanged glances. He could read in her face astonishment to hear so much of what she had obviously been trying to deduce confirmed from the mouth of a Roman Catholic abbot.

'The greatest temple,' the abbot continued, 'was built on the summit of the Esquiline Hill to house the black statue of Kybele and act as a home to her priesthood. It stood there for half a millennium.'

'What happened to it?'

'A church was built there in the middle of the fifth century AD, a church that was later greatly expanded to become the Basilica of Santa Maria Maggiore, the largest church in the world dedicated to the Virgin Mary.'

'And the statue?'

'The figure of the goddess disappeared. It is widely believed that it was taken to Constantinople, when the capital of the empire was moved, and simply lost en route. Or later disregarded as just another pagan idol. But some of us have always thought that that was most unlikely, given its importance. The other possibility is that it was hidden, deliberately. To protect her until a more civilised age when men would no longer destroy such sacred things. But it may be that such an age will never come.'

There was a cold fire in Nazreem's eyes as she listened to him and then with ringing scepticism in her voice she said: 'I'm not sure whether to be impressed with your intellect or horrified by your cynicism. You knew that your precious Madonna here might be a copy of a pagan idol?'

'That's not exactly what I said.'

'Not exactly, but pretty close and that still makes you a hypocrite,' Marcus joined in.

The abbot raised his eyebrows. 'Am I? I would have thought I was being anything but hypocritical.' Then abruptly he wiped his mouth with his napkin, discarded it on the table top, and said: 'Come. It is late. We can discuss all this in the morning.'

He signalled to the head waiter who bowed low indicating that he regarded payment as unnecessary. Immediately another waiter appeared behind the abbot's chair pulling it back to make it easier for him to rise, while a second did the same for Nazreem. Marcus, it was clear, would have to help himself. He took Nazreem's arm unable to help noticing she was unsteady on her feet. There was a glare behind the glazed film of her eyes as they watched the abbot's back retreating towards the Gothic arch that led into the monastery cloister.

'You can't leave it alone, can you,' Nazreem called after the old man. 'Any of you. That's why you tried to steal it.'

'He's right. It's time for bed,' said Marcus putting an arm around her. He could feel her slim frame shaking, but whether it was from the sudden chill of the night air or some repressed rage, he could not be sure. Her eyes remained fixed on the door in the far corner long after the abbot had closed it behind him. For not the first time since she had come back into his life, Marcus was worried about her. He was also worried by the final taunt she had flung at the elderly clergyman. '*Tried* to steal it'. Was she accusing the church? And if not, who? And what did she mean by 'tried'?

52

'Psst! Get up! We're getting out of here.' Marcus stirred in his sleep, then opened his eyes to a darkness that was total. Heavy wooden shutters on the windows were designed to keep out the noonday sun; they had no problem with moonlight. There was someone shaking his arm, then the next thing he knew the duvet cover was thrown back off him.

'What the …? Who the …?' he all but shouted aloud, reaching up and pulling the light cord that dangled above the bed. At once the room sprang into illumination to reveal Nazreem standing there above him, fully dressed and with her light travelling bag slung over her shoulder.

'Don't!' she said urgently. 'Someone will see.' And pulled the light cord again, plunging them back into darkness.

'Stop it, will you. This is getting ridiculous,' said Marcus, pulling the cord again and flooding the room with light. 'Who or what are you talking about. Besides, those shutters are completely lightproof.'

She glanced across at them and nodded uncertainly. 'Quick,' she said. 'Get up, get dressed. We have to go.'

'What is this? Why?' said Marcus sitting up and instinctively pulling the duvet back over the boxer shorts that were all he slept in. Nazreem threw it back again.

'There's no time,' she said. 'Come on.'

Reluctantly Marcus began to do as he was told, if only to humour her for the moment. 'Will you tell me what this is all about?' he said.

Nazreem shushed him. 'Not so loud. Everyone is asleep. Even on the reception. If we go now, we can sneak out before anyone notices.'

'And why on earth would we want to do that?'

She raised her eyebrows impatiently. 'You weren't listening to a thing, were you? He knows. That means he knew all along. If we leave it too long they won't let us leave.'

'What makes you think …?'

'It's obvious. We talked, back in Munich, about who would have reason to steal the statue. We dismissed the Catholic Church because if an independent museum had discovered the oldest image of the Virgin Mary, it would have been universally hailed as a miracle. Gaza would have become a point of pilgrimage for the whole Christian world. It would even have been a threat to the dominance of Islam in the area, that's why we decided that Muslim extremists might be after it too.'

'Yes, but … you're saying now that it's not Christian at all.'

'Precisely, don't you see. And they knew that. That's why they're so worried. Compare the statue from Gaza with the one here and you start to expose the whole Black Madonna cult for the sham it always has been: a cynical takeover of the old earth mother religions. The link between the Gaza statue and Kybele is clear. It would blow Marianism out of the water, and a good proportion of Catholic devotion would disintegrate.'

Marcus remembered the 'Texan Taliban' and their phobia about the spreading cult of the Mexican Madonna. If that were proved to have been all along just an old Aztec cult given a makeover …

'But that doesn't mean we're in any danger.'

'Doesn't it? I'm not waiting to find out.'

'But if the original is still missing,' Marcus said, climbing into his trousers and doing up the belt, 'what does it matter?'

She gave him a pointed look and said simply: 'Hurry up.'

'But … I know you said that if you found out what the statue really was you could …. Wait a minute!' The realisation came over him like a cold shower: 'You know where it is! You've known where it is all along. It wasn't really stolen, was it? It's still there, back in Gaza. Hidden. By you!'

'Come on, Marcus, let's get going. There'll be time enough for questions and answers later.'

53

Even the smallest Spanish towns go late to bed. In the bar on the corner of the square below the steps that led up to the great monastery's façade they were still stacking chairs inside while a few locals lingered over a last *pacharán* or *anis* with the late-night waiters. The dumpy little man Marcus had seen salivating over his tripe earlier in the restaurant was smoking a cigarette at the counter poring over horse-racing form in the local paper.

Marcus and Nazreem crept by like thieves in the night or illicit lovers doing a moonlight flit, but if anyone paid them any heed there was no sign of it. The reception at the Parador had been deserted and they had left their keys in their rooms. The desk clerk had again swiped Marcus's credit card on arrival so he did not have the excuse of worrying that they hadn't paid. Even so, he felt more foolish than clever creeping out of a plush hotel in the small hours of the morning, uncertain of where they were headed or why.

Beyond the square the dark streets were empty, the Gothic pinnacles and parapets of the monastic fortress a brooding presence over the little low dwellings. The main road out of town led past a post office, a few shops and a bus station, but a cursory examination of the timetable revealed the first bus passing through was the daily service to Cáceres, the provincial capital, at five-fifty a.m., in more than two hours' time. There was no sign of a taxi firm, and even if there was, Marcus wondered where they would go. It was a long drive back to Madrid. And then what? Whatever was in Nazreem's mind, she wasn't sharing.

On the far side of the road in an entry next to the small row of shops, an ambling figure who had obviously not long left the bar on the square was throwing a tarpaulin over the back of a pick-up truck, which the light of his cigarette revealed to be filled with large round dark objects Marcus took to be watermelons. In a second Nazreem had crossed the road and was doing her best to communicate in an elementary Spanish that she had somehow acquired with her customary facility. Not that it seemed to be doing her any good.

'*Mañana*,' the man was insisting, waving his cigarette airily at the darkness.

'*Ya es mañana,*' Nazreem tried back.

'*Si, si*,' the man said, hiccupping good-humoredly, obviously amused at being accosted by a pretty young woman in the early hours of the morning. '*Pero mañana en la mañana*,' he replied, smiling broadly but slightly wearily.

'*Donde?*' Nazreem was trying. Where was he going? Nowhere, thought Marcus, except to bed. At least if he'd any sense.

'*Donde? Cáceres. Mañana. En la mañana.*'

'*Hoy, ahora.* Now. *Por favor*.'

'*No, no es posible.*'

Then suddenly Marcus felt Nazreem reach for his wallet, and the next second she was holding two large green hundred-euro notes in her hand and the situation seemed to have subtly altered. The man was scratching his head and wavering, and then Nazreem was putting the money away again.

'*No, momento. Momento.*'

'*Ahora*,' she said again. '*Pero no Cáceres. Avila. Norte*.'

Marcus was doing his best to follow, reluctantly admiring her haggling skills in a language she barely knew, but then she had grown up in Cairo.

'*Avila?*' the man seemed more perplexed than ever and was shaking his head again, holding up his fingers, three of them. '*Tres. Tres horas*.' Three hours, the same time it had taken them to get from Madrid?

'*Tres*,' Nazreem responded, and pulled out a third green note. Marcus realised it hadn't been driving time the man was talking about.

'*Y media*,' the man said, smiling now, holding out his hand

'*No media, no más,*' Nazreem said, proferring the notes, but still holding them tight. '*Ahora?*'

'*Bueno*,' the man shrugged, threw his cigarette butt away shaking his head and holding out his hand. '*Vamos.* Let's go,' he said, suddenly discovering a bit of misplaced English as he shook Nazreem by the hand and pocketed Marcus's money, throwing open the door of the pickup cab.

'You do realise this is completely crazy,' said Marcus, deliberately scrabbling up into the middle seat. It was bad enough being driven

God knows where in the dead of the night by some drunk Spaniard without the man getting distracted and letting his hands wander over towards Nazreem. She piled in next, banging the door in after her. The man behind the wheel coughed, the engine spluttered into life and they were off, an improbable threesome in an old Toyota with a loosely wrapped cargo of watermelons bouncing behind them. The moon disappeared behind a cloud and Marcus wished he knew a prayer worth saying.

For the first few kilometres their driver made a brave attempt at conversation, a torture Marcus was prepared to suffer if only to keep the man awake. But the limited amount of their common language gratefully restricted any actual exchange of information to a few brief semi-understood comments on watermelons, monasteries (both *bueno*) and what Marcus took to be a last-ditch attempt to persuade them to change their minds and go to Cáceres because it was nearer. This mostly consisted of Nazreem and the driver swapping the names of their preferred destinations, a bit of disconcerting hand gesturing during which the steering lurched alarmingly, and only ended definitively when they came to a main road and the driver one final time made a plea for left and Cáceres, only to be told a firm no and Avila. A resigned '*Por qué Avila?*' brought the limited explanation. 'Train? *Ah, treno, bueno.*' And that was that.

As far as the driver was concerned anyhow. For the first time Marcus realised that Nazreem's intention went beyond simply getting away from Guadalupe and the black Madonna she had been so keen to see in the first place. He had been loath to ply her with too many questions in the cab of the pickup, both of them taking it in turns to grab a few minutes' sleep while the other made sure the driver stayed on the road. But as they rattled over the last sierra down onto a long straight road that had obviously been laid out when the main traffic was the rhythmic slap of Roman legionaries' sandals, he forced his reluctant brain back into gear.

'We're catching the train from Avila. Where to? And why?'

'There was no point in going back to Madrid,' she said. 'Besides that's what anyone would expect. I checked the timetables in the hotel. From Avila there's a good connection to Valladolid, where we can pick up the international line north.'

'North?'

'Yes, of course north. To Paris, and then London. For you: home.'

Part Four

… NUNC, ET IN HORA MORTIS!
… Now, and at the hour of our death!

54

'I don't like it and I'm not going to pretend I like it.'

The big Marine hushed the man next to him: 'Operational necessity, reverend. You can't always choose your short-term allies. Let me tell you: I've been there. Out in Saudi Arabia in the First Gulf War those goddamn ragheads wouldn't even let us praise the Lord in our own camps, or give our boys a Christian funeral. Not even when our boys had died defending their goddamn country.'

The reverend closed his eyes as if doing so would prevent him from hearing such infamy.

'That's right. It wasn't nice, but we gritted our teeth, because that's what we had orders to do. Now we have to work alongside some other shits, but we're still under orders, orders from the Lord, ain't that right, reverend?'

The reverend nodded, acknowledging the trials that faith required of the godly. 'It would indeed appear that that is the truth.'

'Then we'll see those orders are carried out. And then we'll see what we do. Okay by you?'

The reverend nodded again. It was okay by him. It was not as if he had a choice. The two men were sitting at a table in the Madrid apartment with a jug of coffee and a plate of half-eaten takeaway enchiladas which both of them had agreed were nothing like the stuff they got back home. The food had been fetched from a nearby restaurant by José, strictly accompanied by two of the Arabs, as both Americans referred to them. He had tried to persuade Freddie to eat some, and protested angrily that the injured man urgently needed a doctor. The protest, however, had been ignored; Freddie had been given a high dose of painkillers, the remains of his mutilated ear treated with proprietary antiseptics, bandaged up and he was now sleeping deeply on the same bed on which he had twenty-four hours earlier thrown the drugged Marcus. José sat slumped in the armchair next to him, alternately dozing and channel-surfing with the TV remote.

The Islamists, their dark hoods now removed to reveal the typical sallow complexions of southern Mediterranean-Middle Easterners – based on a few overheard words of what he thought was French, the reverend was coming round to the opinion that they might actually be Algerians – stood outside in the hallway, their weapons prominently on display, more like armed jailers than allies. Their spiritual and military leader had disappeared, although the Americans doubted he was far distant. He had given them strict instructions – it was hard to interpret the terms of their relationship otherwise – that their role in their common enterprise was, for the moment at least, primarily technological.

And although the Reverend Parker was less than happy with the colonel's seeming rationalisation of their situation, he was the military man, and if he was content to bide his time then that was what they would do.

The colonel pushed the half-finished enchiladas to one side, pulled out his iPhone, and touched the GPS icon.

'Well now, look what we got here.'

On the screen appeared a map of central Madrid. The app worked in conjunction with Google Maps which allowed him to zoom in to a relatively high degree of accuracy. He reckoned it was probably possible even to work out exactly which building the phone was in. But thanks to the SIM card-sized transmitter he had slipped inside Marcus Frey's phone, it also told him with the same degree of accuracy where the 'professor' was. It was, he liked to think, a reliable and, provided the other party was unaware of it, infinitely kinder way of keeping someone on a tight leash.

The Reverend Parker did as he was told, watching the map of Madrid disappear as if seen from a soaring rocket ship, then the screen refocus on a flashing red spot to the southwest of the capital amid the dark greens of the Spanish Mesa pine forests and the russet browns where they gave way to barren rock.

'That's Guadalupe?' he asked, uncertain of the degree of detail or magnification on an unfamiliar landscape.

'No,' the colonel said, 'and slid thumb and forefinger apart across the touchscreen to magnify the image of the landscape until it was almost filled with an irregular sandstone-coloured geometric shape. 'That's Guadalupe. The monastery itself, in fact. Big, isn't it?'

The minister nodded. 'But the point is,' the colonel said, 'our friends are no longer there. They're on the move. Look.'

He pulled thumb and forefinger together and the landscape grew again until now a red dot appeared in the centre of the screen, and almost immediately moved a few millimetres up it. 'They're heading north by northeast and from what I can make out,' he performed a few more manipulations, running his finger across screen, 'they're in a vehicle of some sort, heading along this road.' The map on the screen tilted and turned as if he were playing some sort of helicopter simulation, bringing the landscape itself into an approximation of relief contours, while road numbers flashed up and place names appeared: 'They could be heading for Cáceres, although I doubt it, because there's a more direct route from Guadalupe, or they could be making for Avila. Neither makes a whole heap of sense just at the moment. What I'd really like to know is: why? Have they cut some sort of deal with the abbot? Is he driving them? I wish to hell I had one of these little GPS bugs on that bastard too. Or have they cut and run?'

'What do we do?'

The Texan leaned back, his eyes resting on the little dot as it moved northwards, towards the edge of the laptop screen. He ran a finger over the trackpad and repositioned it in the centre. 'Right now, we do nothing. I believe in giving a man a lot of rope, especially if I anticipate eventually having to hang him with it.'

55

The turreted walls of Avila stood sentry round the heart of the ancient city like a fantasy made from children's sandcastles upended out of plastic buckets. As they had done for the better part of a thousand years.

Despite his training as a historian, the colonial boy in Marcus Frey found certain parts of Europe's flagrant flaunting of its incalculable heritage just a little too in-your-face. These crenellated walls, stretched in a perfect ring around a mediaeval city centre to create an ensemble as impressive as the great monastery they had just left in Guadalupe. The landscape in most of Europe had nothing on the South African Veldt, but the architecture sang of history. Maybe the abbot was right; the fusion of history and art was a religion in itself. If that's what he had been saying. Marcus was still far from sure.

Deep down there was something about a place like this that tugged at his soul. And no matter how uncomfortable he felt with it, the only word he could come up with was 'Christendom'.

'How long have we got to spend here?'

'A couple of hours at most,' said Nazreem. 'Then we catch the train to Valladolid with a connection to Hendaye, on the French frontier, where we can pick up a train direct to Paris.'

'I still think it would have been quicker and easier via Madrid.'

'It would, but how sure are you that we would have got away with it? I mean at least here we're away from the whole "Mary" thing.'

'Are we?'

'Aren't we?'

'It depends what you mean. I just had this feeling, as we drove into town, about how religion pervades our culture. And if the religion is corrupted ...'

'What is the problem with Avila?'

'Its saint. The way the abbot talked about pagan deities and Christian saints. It's been on my mind. Do you remember Saint Konrad, from Altötting, the one who had been sanctified despite not having done much more than been a doorman at the shrine all his life?'

'Yes,' said Nazreem, with a sudden smile. She had found it hard not to laugh out loud when Marcus had told her what he found out about the man's claim to sanctity.

'Well, what if it was not so much the man as the job he was elevating to the "pantheon" of saints.'

'A god of doormen?'

'A parallel for Janus – the Roman god of entries and exits, beginnings and endings. Where we get the word "January" from.'

'You really think so?'

Marcus shrugged. 'How would I know. My field is history not religion, though the lines are blurring fast here. It's just that there was a sign back there welcoming us to Avila, city of Saint Teresa.'

'There is a special saint for this town?' Nazreem was no longer surprised by anything.

'A patron saint. That's the thing about Catholicism. It agglutinates.'

'It what?'

'It builds upon itself. Like a cancer.'

'So who is the saint of Avila?'

'I'd forgotten,' he said. 'Until now: Saint Teresa. Or at least that's what they call her. But you could argue Aphrodite would be a better name.'

'Explain.'

'There's not much to explain. She was a local girl who ran away from home, had a mystical experience, came back and reformed the Carmelite order of nuns. But the reason for her fame is a statue. A quite extraordinary statue. Not here, though. It's in Rome.'

'Maybe there's a postcard.'

There was. In fact picture postcards of the statue followed only views of the city walls, its cathedral and little yellow egg-yolk sweets named for St Teresa as the most popular image. He picked one up from a revolving stand outside a tourist shop on the street and handed it to her.

'It's by Bernini. Around 1600, I think. Not long after she had died.'

Marcus could not suppress the smile playing on his lips as he waited for her reaction.

'This,' she said at length, 'is a saint!'

'Yep.'

'I don't believe it,' she was laughing and blushing at the same time. It was, Marcus suddenly remembered, one of her most endearing characteristics.

He looked over her shoulder at the picture, just to remind himself not just of the image, but of his own scarcely believing amazement the first – and only – time he had seen it 'in the flesh', in the radiant chapel of Santa Maria della Vittoria

There was no doubt it was Bernini's masterpiece, so vivid and achingly lifelike that it seemed the stone had indeed the quality of flesh, a moment frozen in time, its essence captured forever in the expressions on the faces of the two figures. And what expressions!

'It's pure pornography!' Nazreem said at last. And it was. The critics and art historians had argued otherwise, preached the sculptor's skill in summoning up the spirit of divine spiritual ecstasy unknown to ordinary mortals, but to the casual observer far from being exotic and unknowable it was all too familiar, ecstatic for sure but far from purely spiritual. The angel standing erect above the supine woman was more of a satyr, the smile on his face a smirk of unconcealed lechery while the saint at his feet was writhing beneath her flowing robes, her expression one of the purest, satisfied, carnal lust.

'It is, isn't it,' agreed Marcus. 'Either the angel of the Lord touched Saint Teresa in a way that took her seriously by surprise or she'd accidentally discovered masturbation, aided and abetted by a very vivid imagination.' He took the card from her hand and turned it over to find, as he had hoped, the relevant quotation from the saint's own autobiography. 'Here's the bit that inspired Bernini,' he said, handing it back to Nazreem.

The verse was printed in Spanish with translations into English and Italian. Nazreem started to read it aloud, but soon let her voice fade away in amazement: '"I saw in his hand a long spear of gold, and at the iron's point there seemed to be a little fire. He appeared to me to be thrusting it at times into my heart, and to pierce my very entrails; when he drew it out, he seemed to draw them out also, and to leave me all on fire with a great love of God. The pain was so great, that it made me moan; and yet so surpassing was the sweetness of this excessive pain, that I could not wish to be rid of it."'

'It's quite incredible,' she said at the end.

'Yes. That's the trouble. It starts to seem like the whole Roman

Catholic …' he struggled for a word, and then, when the only one that seemed applicable came to mind, could not avoid an ironic twist of the lips, 'pantheon …'

'Is what?'

'Just that, quite literally, a pantheon. Not saints at all, not human beings who have come close to God, but a collection of pagan gods in disguise.

'You know, Nazreem, before all of this I was an agnostic, but a happy agnostic. Happy to treat Christianity as just something we lived with, dogma you could ignore happily as long as you sub-scribed to what we loosely called "Christian values", and believed the world would be a better place if we imposed them on everyone.'

'Yes,' she said. 'I know what you mean. I think. But so often the values and the men of religion don't seem to go hand in hand. Like in Palestine, Iraq, the whole of what your people call the Middle East.'

'The thing is,' said Marcus, 'that maybe we were wrong all along. Those values, maybe they were never Christian. I mean, if you asked someone to list Western Christian values today, top of the list would probably be democracy. But that wasn't Christian at all: it had been invented in Athens, more than three hundred years before Jesus Christ was born. The same goes for Platonic love. And the ancient Greeks, including all their great humanist philosophers, got along fine with pagan gods. Christianity conquered the world via the Roman Empire, a dictatorship which had come into its own by over-throwing a republic.'

'So if the pagan gods somehow survived. In Christian clothing. What does it mean?'

'It means it's time for us to get the hell out of here!'

56

Hendaye was for half the twentieth century one of the final frontier towns in western Europe. It may no longer have the frisson of risk and romance that adhered to its backstreet bars and waterfront cafés when it was the gathering point for the idealist communist 'red brigade' volunteers about to risk their lives in the fight against Franco in the dark days of the late 1930s, or even in the seventies and eighties when it was a heavily policed haven for militant Basque separatists and arms smugglers.

But in a Europe of fallen frontiers and banished borders, the Bidassoa river still marks a tangible boundary. The minute the train rattled over the iron bridge from the lively little Spanish Basque town of Irún and rolled through the sleepy suburbs of Hendaye, Marcus and Nazreem were aware they were in France: it was only just gone ten p.m. but most of the lights were out as if everyone had already gone to bed.

'It's eerie,' said Nazreem as they stepped out onto the platform to change trains. There were few other passengers waiting for the overnight service to Paris, a couple locked in each other's arms in a corner of a waiting room, a few weary looking backpackers whom Marcus had picked out as British students, and a podgy little man in a beret basque engrossed in his newspaper.

'So obviously another country, and yet no barbed wire, no fences, not even passport controls. Nothing. I almost would prefer if they still had frontier posts and border policemen.'

'Would you? Really?'

To Marcus's surprise she actually seemed to consider the question for a moment before an almost wistful smile broke slowly across her face: 'No, of course not,' she said quietly. 'It would be nice if someone looked at my French passport and said "welcome home", but that's never what frontier officials do. People talk about security but for those of us who have lived most of our lives behind closed borders, staring at men with guns, there is nothing to surpass the taste of freedom. It ... just takes a while to get used to it.'

'Let's just hope it lasts. There are enough people ready to take it away.'

Nazreem nodded silently. She knew what he meant.

They took their seats in the compartment. At the same time the train began to pick up speed, the dark houses of the Hendaye suburbs flashing by and quickly giving way to pine forests on one side and tufted sand dunes on the other as the train rushed along the Atlantic coast towards Biarritz and Bayonne before it would twist inland to rush through the depths of rural France via Dax and Orléans to the Gare d'Austerlitz in Paris.

They were due to arrive just before eight-thirty in the morning. The train was quiet. Marcus had deliberately avoided the smart Madrid-Paris Elipsos 'Trenhotel' service. The NZ4052, which started in Hendaye, was one of the few long distance European routes not always operated by a high-speed line. Reservations were required, but could normally be picked up at the station. In any case there were only two of them in the four-berth compartment, although that could not be guaranteed.

Nazreem settled down on the hard leather-cloth seat near the window and stared out into the darkness. Marcus stood in the corridor for a moment then came into the compartment, noticing the quaint photographs of rural French scenes designed to tempt tourists with a future stop-off: the still elegant nineteenth-century splendour of Biarritz's promenade, the golden stone mediaeval clock in Bordeaux, the already dated-looking Futuroscope theme park in Poitiers. A conductor stuck his head in and said he assumed they didn't need help with the couchettes as there were only the two of them booked into the compartment and the upper berths were already made.

'Ça va, ça va,' said Marcus, struggling, and then wondered why he bothered, given that French was Nazreem's second language. But she was paying no attention, still gazing out into the fleeting night as the train hurtled with remarkable quiet stillness deeper into the dark. He realised all of a sudden that this was possibly the first time she had ever been in the country whose citizenship she held and where her mother had grown up. And he wondered what, if anything, that meant to her.

He reached out and was just about to put his hand on her shoulder when his mobile rang. He pulled it irritably from his trouser pocket and flipped it open. The number was withheld and it occurred to him for a moment that it would have been a better idea to reject the call. A feeling that was reinforced when he put it to his ear and heard the voice that spread a chill across him like a daytime recurrence of a bad dream:

'Hey, professor, how're ya doin'? Just thought we'd see how you were getting along, if maybe you need a hand, or two.' Marcus couldn't fail to recognise the voice. The Texan's tones were unmistakable.

Nazreem had turned her head towards him in curiosity, her attention at last drawn away from the nothingness outside the window, but Marcus only shook his back at her reassuringly, although the sentiment was anything but that which he was feeling.

'Hi there,' he said back, with a mock conviviality that was intended to reassure Nazreem as much as to give an impression of cordial cooperation to the man on the other end of the phone, whom he supposed and seriously hoped to be still in the suburbs of Madrid.

'Just checking, you see, that you were still in Guadalupe,' the Texan drawled, 'cos we were thinking of driving up there from the big city, to see how you were getting on, what the little lady's verdict had been, you might say, on the black Barbie.' There was a familiar unpleasant suppressed chuckle on the line but Marcus breathed a sigh of relief that the Americans had so far at least taken him at his word. What disquieted him most, however, though he had scarcely dared admit it even to himself, was how much their descriptions of the abbot's state of mind had coincided with the attitude they had found the man himself expressing. But that was no longer the point: he was more concerned about Nazreem, about what she was keeping from him, about the real reason for her fascination with the Madonna. He was beginning to suspect that she knew far more than she had revealed about what had really happened to the missing figure.

'Yes,' he said, 'sure thing. We're still here.' Nazreem shot him another glance and again he waved her away. He wasn't sure what he wanted her to believe or why he was maybe dissimulating, but then he still wasn't sure how to handle any of this. There was something about her, about the way she had been acting that wasn't the Nazreem he remembered, something that wasn't born out of just her quest to find out the truth about the black Madonna.

'It seems you were right,' he said after a pause, not because he meant it, or because he even knew what it meant, but because under the circumstances it seemed a neutral thing to say. It was seldom a phrase people didn't like hearing.

'That's what I like to hear,' said the voice on the other end. 'So it's time to discuss where we go from here. I take it you'd be happy to see us then?'

'Sure,' said Marcus. 'Sure thing.' It was the only thing he could say. He sincerely hoped that by the time the Texan and his friends got to Guadalupe and discovered they had done a flit, they would be hundreds of miles away. They were already across one, albeit non-existent border, by then they might be back in Britain, across another, one that for better or worse was still defended with a degree of xenophobia.

'That would be good, whenever you like,' he added, still standing up and watching Nazreem who had once more turned her eyes to the blackness outside, a blackness in which he could glimpse only an endless flicker of rushing vertical narrow tree trunks, barely visible beyond the reflection caused by the low wattage yellow light bulbs in the compartment ceiling, a reflection in which he saw himself in silhouette, his own tall unkempt shape with his arm bent at an awkward angle to hold the mobile phone to his ear. And another dark figure behind him.

The corridor door opened. He spun around. And found himself gazing into the muzzle of a handgun pointed at his head. And the smiling bulldog face of ex-US Marine Colonel Martin Jones.

'Well, well, well,' the Texan drawl said. 'You'll be real glad we're right here then.'

57

Marcus backed into the compartment at gunpoint, his hands, still with his mobile phone in his right, held high. Behind him Nazreem, a scream stifled in her lungs had leapt to her feet and reached for the red emergency stop lever above the window.

'I wouldn't do that if I were you, honey,' said the man with the gun. 'Not just yet. Unless you want your boyfriend here's brains splattered all over the nice clean bedlinen on those little bunk beds up there.'

Instinctively she glanced up at the couchettes and then, feeling at the same time ridiculous and despairing, brought her hand down by her side.

'There's a good girl,' said the man in what she recognised only loosely as an accent from somewhere in the southern United States. Texan, it had to be. This was the man Marcus had told her about. The ones who had drugged him and let him go. The Christian fundamentalists. 'As mad as the mullahs,' he had called them, 'the Texan Taliban.' Behind the big man now a second appeared, younger, thinner, darker complexioned, one of the Mexican thugs she supposed. He stood in the doorway, eyes darting up and down the corridor and then at her, looking her up and down in a way that for the first time in her life made her almost understand those of her co-religionists who chose to conceal their entire bodies beneath a burkha.

'It's a misunderstanding,' said Marcus. 'I was going to call you, but we left in a hurry. We need to talk about this.'

'Sure thing, professor,' said the colonel, though he had signally failed to lower his gun. 'After all, that's what we're here for. Sit down, why don't you. You too, miss. And then maybe the professor here can explain why he lied, why he broke his word to us, and not just his word, but an oath sworn on the Holy Bible. Not exactly the mark of a good Christian now, is it?'

'I can explain.'

The Texan looked at him sceptically. 'Actually, it doesn't really matter. Turns out, as it happens, the goalposts have moved. We need to talk to both of you, both you and the little Muslim lady here, and right here and now seems as good a time as any.'

Right here and now, thought Marcus, would be an ideal time for the conductor to come by and ask for their tickets. But he had a feeling that somehow that wasn't going to happen.

'I don't understand. How did you …?'

'This train originates in Madrid. Maybe you hadn't noticed that? Bit of a coincidence though, you and us happening to be on it at the same time.'

'How did you … You've been following us …?'

'Never you mind, professor. What say we just put it down to divine providence, say we all had the same idea at the same time, to head up north and see the lights of "gay Paree". That's what they say, isn't it? See Paris and die? Let's hope it doesn't come to that.

'The fact is, professor, since last time we met things have changed, and it hasn't helped you not being completely honest with us about your whereabouts. You see, we now have reason to believe you – or rather your lady friend here – is going to be able to lead us to this pagan abomination. And as you know we wouldn't like it to fall into the wrong hands, which might just be any hands but ours.'

'What on earth makes you so self-righteous?' Once again Marcus could see the fire burn in Nazreem's eyes, the fire that burned cold and black when the Madonna was mentioned.

The colonel smiled, a supercilious smile that was at once over-bearingly patronising and had all the self-confidence of a man backed up by a loaded weapon.

'Maybe nothing on earth, lady. Let's just say we're on a mission from God, and in case you get any funny ideas, it seems that for once your God and ours have the same idea.'

'What are you talking about?'

'Never you mind. You'll find out soon enough. You can make your confession on your own terms, or whatever you people call it. What we want from you now is to tell us where the pagan idol is.'

'Why should I – even if I knew – and why are you so desperate to find it? What is it to you?'

'What is it? Lady, I called the thing a pagan idol and believe me, it's not just any pagan idol. We are talking about a figure of a so-called goddess that was centre of one of the most depraved cults in ancient Rome, and that's saying something.'

'What do you mean "depraved"?'

'You don't know, do you, you really have no idea what you're dealing with here, for all your bookish learning, do you? You're refusing to see it in context, as if just because something is old, it deserves protection. The black bitch – Astarte, Hecate, the witch, you can call her what you will but Kybele was by far the most poisonous variation. She had a priesthood that were the sickest bunch of weirdos the ancient world could imagine. They honoured the female all right, but rather than let women be their priests they tried to turn themselves into them.'

'What?'

'That's right: the Gallae, they called themselves, dressed up in women's clothing and perfume, shaved their bodies, the whole thing and I mean the whole thing: they cut their balls off. Oh yes, you can stare: self-castration. More than a few of them died in the process, you can imagine. The rest danced and fornicated in the streets, with either sex. They were so debauched that the Emperor Augustus locked them up in their temple and only allowed them out on one day a year. That's the sort of adoration your so-called Mother Goddess inspired. And you wonder we want to destroy her. Perverts and sickos, transsexuals and transvestites, all that's at the heart of the moral turpitude of the modern world. You want to see that held up as divine? It makes me want to puke.'

There were flecks of spittle flying from the corners of the man's mouth. Even the most recondite corners of Marcus's mental squirrel store held nothing about a sect called the Gallae but he was only too well aware that a Texan Christian fundamentalist former Colonel of Marines was not someone likely to have a particularly liberal attitude to gay rights.

'And if you find the statue what will you do with it?'

'Just exactly what we said. Destroy it. The world will not weep for one less pagan idol, let alone one most people never knew existed.'

'Even if most of them might have thought it represented the Virgin Mary?'

'Yes, sir. It is still an abomination. Roman Catholicism has become a perversion of Jesus Christ's teaching that besmirches the true story of the birth and sacrifice of Our Lord.'

'You mean that that way you can keep the bits of the story you prefer.'

The colonel's eyes narrowed sharply and his arm lashed out to press the gun against Marcus's temple. 'You know, for a man brought up in a decent church, professor, you've sure let book learning tarnish your soul. Maybe too much time with the wrong books – guess you should have been reading the Good Book. Well, it's too late now.' His finger softly squeezed the trigger.

'No!' screamed Nazreem, 'No! You are right. It is only a statue. I will do what I can to help you.'

The colonel cast a quick glance sideways at her, not lessening the pressure of his finger on the trigger. 'You'd give away your precious idol, your claim to fame, just for lover boy here?'

'He is not my lover. But I will not see anyone, much less a friend, die to prevent you getting your hands on what you rightly call an "idol". In my faith too we abhor graven images. You may do with it as you will. I will tell you where it is.'

Slowly the colonel let his eyes run up and down her in the same way the Mexican had done, eyeing her up, wondering what she would be like in bed. The thought repulsed her. Were all men like this underneath? Was it the feeling of power that prompted their lust? And encouraged violence.

But Marcus felt the barrel of the gun removed from his temple.

'Well, well, well,' the colonel said abruptly, glancing at his wrist-watch. 'Under the circumstances, you'll forgive us if we don't take you at your word, Miss Hashrawi. But we'll let you lead us to it. Now get to your feet, both of you, and let's get going.'

'Going? Where to?'

'That's for you to tell us; we'll be one big happy family party together. We have alternative transport arranged, which you might find more comfortable. Or you might not. It doesn't really matter, because that's what we're doing.' He glanced at his watch. 'Get up. We've got five minutes, and then I'll let you have your play with that emergency stop switch after all. Now won't that be fun ...'

Marcus and Nazreem did as they were told, edging slowly towards the compartment door. In the corridor, the colonel gestured to the Mexican to go in front, with Nazreem just behind him. He followed, the gun wedged in the small of Marcus's back.

'And don't be tempted to do anything silly. I'm keeping this little friend of mine so close to your professor that any wrong move and the slug'll pass through him so fast it'll probably catch you too with what's left of his guts on it. But as long as everybody does as they're told, there's absolutely no reason for anybody to get harmed.'

Nazreem was sorely tempted to hammer on the doors of any compartment that was likely to have people inside. But she had no doubt that the colonel would not hesitate to put a bullet in Marcus, even if he might let her live as the sole means of achieving his end. This was one instance she hadn't considered when she decided that keeping Marcus in blissful ignorance was a means of protecting him. It was as if she was sleepwalking, as if the whole thing was a nightmare in which she was conscious she would soon awake.

There were five compartments to pass before the end of the carriage. There were lights in none of them, suggesting either they were unoccupied or the passengers inside had already turned in for the night. Two of them at least looked empty, their sliding doors partly or wholly open, the interior in darkness.

They had passed the second when Marcus heard a muffled thunk, like a fridge door being slammed next to his ear. Simultaneously the muzzle of the gun held against his back canonned into him. He waited for the searing pain of hot lead ripping into his abdomen. Instead he felt the huge weight of the colonel's body slump against him and caught a sudden stench of cordite. The dark glass of the corridor window blossomed into a messy flower of sticky red blood.

'Run, now. Get off. Before it's too late.'

'What!' That accent. The voice. Somehow familiar. Marcus staggered under the weight of the collapsed body, turned and saw the American colonel with a neat round hole in his head, black, smoking and big enough to put a finger into, oozing blood like tomato ketchup. He gagged.

The Mexican was gawping in stark terror into the silenced barrel of a gun in the hand of a small plump man in dark clothes and a beret. It was the little man who had been so engrossed in his newspaper on the platform, the same little man, Marcus now realised – staring at the red blood oozing from the hole in the Texan's skull – that he had first noticed filling his face with tripe in tomato sauce in the monastery restaurant in Guadalupe. Now there was something about him that seemed more familiar still. Something in the voice, the accent? The fridge door closed again and a smoking black hole opened up in the forehead of the mouthing Mexican. Nazreem's scream blended with the piercing howl of an electronic alarm as the train jerked and squealed under the impact of emergency brakes. Their saviour, the unknown assassin had pulled the emergency stop switch, just as the Texan had planned to. The voice behind him, the same brusque yet soft accent, uncannily out of context said: 'Go. Quick.'

The little fat man was waving his hand in front of his face with the pistol still in it. From further down the suddenly stopped train, Marcus could hear the commotion of confused, frightened passengers, and approaching feet and voices. He grabbed Nazreem by the arm and dragged her to the end of the corridor, pulled down the window to open the door from the outside and jumped with her almost in his arms onto the rough pebbles of the railway bed. With sore knees and aching limbs but fired by adrenalin they struggled to their feet into the dense forest of silver birch. Fleetingly he glanced back at the yellow light spilling from the open carriage door. But of the strange little assassin on the train there was no sign.

A clamour of voices rose behind them at the discovery of the bodies and the open door. A torch beam played haphazardly among the trees, a flickering strobe among the pencil-straight birch trunks. If they were not careful they would be the subject of a manhunt. Ahead beyond the edge of the forest, there was the susurrus of car tyres on wet tarmac. They could not be far from a road. Beside him Nazreem was panting, out of breath. And then they came upon a long straight empty strip of black flat-lining into the distance: the road that followed the train tracks through the great swathe of flat reclaimed land all the way up the Bay of Biscay coast.

'What happened?' asked Nazreem, her voice shaking. 'Who was that?'

And all of a sudden Marcus stood stock still by the roadside, gazing back into the barcode forest of pale thin tree trunks and dark spaces in between, as a realisation he had been fighting crystallised in his head:

'I'm not sure,' he said, half to himself, 'I'm really not sure.' And then, his voice fading away as the hot-wired synapses in his brain made links that didn't make sense. 'Maybe it was your fairy godmother.'

58

In the black Renault Espace in the depths of the forest, the Reverend Henry Parker was saying his prayers under his breath. His companions were not fond of him uttering them aloud in their presence. For them as much as him, this was an unholy alliance of necessity. But the man in the front seat gave the orders, and his orders were unquestioningly obeyed.

In fact, Parker had noted, he rarely ever gave orders as such, rather inspired his followers into anticipating them. It was an attribute he was literally in awe of and yet understood; there had been times over the past thirty-six hours when he had almost longed himself for the merest flicker of the bastard's approbation. It was an awe, he decided, inspired mostly by silences.

The silence now had been a long one, amplified by the location, deep in this endless wood. They had driven throughout the day while the colonel and José had waited to catch the train from Madrid. The sulking Freddie, his ear bandaged, was wedged in the centre seat between the two Algerians.

The reverend sat in the rear holding the colonel's iPhone and fervently wished that he understood the damn thing better. As far as he was concerned, the fact that he could see where a particular human being was on the face of the planet was itself an act little short of blasphemy, no matter how useful. Only God had the right to an all-seeing eye. But the US military had long ago successfully challenged his monopoly. And now the technology was in the public domain. He wondered why the little red dot on the screen had stopped moving. Especially as the man it represented should, if everything had gone according to plan, be in their presence by now. Albeit almost certainly reluctantly.

The bark from the man in the front seat startled him out of his reverie. It was answered, in the usual tone of military precision laced with deep deference, by the driver. The Arabic sounded harsh and guttural and wholly incomprehensible. When they talked among themselves they made little allowance for his complete and utter lack of understanding of the language of the prophet. But this time they made an exception.

'They are late,' the man in front said. The reverend had heard the others seem to address him as Saladin – which he thought about as absurd as the colonel styling himself Richard the Lionheart – but, given the position he was in, he was not about to show the man anything other than a grudging respect. 'What does the device show? Where are they?'

'Hmm? Oh,' it was only then that it dawned on him that he had been right to be concerned about the red dot's lack of movement. He was not very good at zooming in on it, getting his fingers to magnify the screen. He was terrified of doing anything that would lose the signal. In a minute the colonel would be back. By then the tracking device would have successfully served its purpose.

Except that the colonel was late. And the colonel was never late. One of the Algerians had got him to call the colonel on his mobile phone a while ago. He was reluctant to take the iPhone off the GPS programme, even to make a call. The colonel had said everything was on track, that the targets had, as expected, boarded the train at Hendaye. The rendezvous point had been set. Since then there had been silence.

The man in the front seat barked again and the people-carrier reversed out of the small clearing and onto the main road that ran in a tedious straight line parallel to the railway tracks through the forest-planted, reclaimed swamp that the French called Les Landes.

The headlights revealed nothing but an endless strip of black tarmac through the grid of vertical silver birch trunks on both sides. He used the Algerian's mobile to call his own again. It rang and rang, and then suddenly almost to his own surprise, a voice answered. But it was not the deep Texan drawl he knew so well. In fact, it was not even English.

'You have reached him?' barked the man in front.

'I ... I don't know. It's ... I think it's in French.'

A fist thrust back from the seat immediately in front and ordered: 'Give me.'

Parker looked apprehensive but the man they called Saladin made up his mind for him: 'Give it to him. He speaks French.'

'*Qui êtes vous*?' the Algerian snapped into the phone. '*Où est l'Américain?*' He listened for a long moment, asked a question and was obviously asked one in return for he thrust the phone at the little minister in the seat behind him, before rattling off a few sentences in what even to someone who understood nothing of the language was clearly angry Arabic. Then there was another silence, this time interrupted by the Reverend Parker, no longer willing to be treated like a piece of awkward baggage.

'What is it, for God's sake?' he could not help himself saying, 'Has something happened?'

'Yes,' came the monosyllabic answer from the front seat.

'What? What's happened to the colonel? Who was that?'

'Be quiet. There is a problem.'

It was not the answer Parker wanted to hear. He had not been happy in the first place seeing the colonel go off and leave him with the hard men and the injured, resentful Freddie still barely restraining the simmering rage that had boiled within him since his mutilation in Madrid.

Ahead of them on either side the headlights played like a stroboscope off the interstices between the trees on a road to nowhere. And then from the edge of the forest two figures emerged, and lurched, almost drunkenly into the road, gesticulating at them to stop.

For the first time the reverend heard what could only be described as a throaty chuckle from the sombre, sinister man in the front seat, as the car slowed on his command and the headlights picked out the two faces staring blindly into the glare like anxious rabbits.

'*Allahu-akhbar,*' he said in a low, deep voice.

For once the reverend could share his sentiment. Indeed, God was indeed great. Maybe any minute now the colonel would show up and everything would be all right after all.

59

Marcus had the distinctly nauseating feeling of having awoken from a nightmare only to find it was really happening. At first sight the approaching headlights had seemed like a blessing, the chance of a lift to the nearest town – Biarritz, he supposed – above all to get away from the stalled train. He supposed the police would be called if the bodies were discovered. But that too was an 'if'. As they had jumped from the train, he saw their strange unidentified rescuer pushing the bulk of the dead US colonel out of the compartment. Who had saved them, and why he had almost certainly been on their tail since Guadalupe, he had no idea. But this was not time to be challenging the existence of guardian angels. What mattered now was getting out of there, to somewhere safe, where they could catch their breath.

Hitching a lift seemed the only option. He had prepared their story: they were stranded after a day picnicking in the forest – the French, he assumed, would not query too deeply a young couple's quest for solitude on a summer afternoon – with a broken-down car and no mobile phone to summon help. All they needed was a lift to somewhere they could get a bed for the night. That much at least was true. He felt both mentally and physically exhausted.

So it was not so much a surge of adrenalin, but a tidal wave of horrific despondency when from behind the glare of the stopped car's headlights he saw two hooded figures armed with automatic weapons emerge, and then a tall, bearded man in a long black cloak stepped out of the front passenger seat, and spat out an order to them in no uncertain terms, in a language Marcus had little difficulty in recognising as Arabic. In case he was in any doubt, the man repeated it, in a harsh guttural English: 'Get in!'

But it was Nazreem who answered him, taking a step forward and staring up at him with an unbowed, cynical look in her eyes. The tall man looked her up and down in return, scowling at her uncovered head and her figure-hugging jeans with an expression of withering disdain. He wished he had more Arabic than a smattering of phrases, or at least the skill to recognise dialects to know which part of the Arab world this man called home.

'You know what we want, child,' Nazreem heard him say. 'We want that which you, if you were a true daughter of your faith should have automatically surrendered to us, even if you were ignorant of its true nature, which I doubt. You have betrayed your faith and your nation.'

Marcus shot her a glance. He had no idea what had just been said but right now Nazreem's face conveyed pure hatred for the man in front of her. Any moment, he realised, she was going to leap forward and scratch the man's eyes out, an action which would lead inevitably and immediately to the two of them kneeling down on the sandy soil beneath their feet to receive a bullet in the back of the head and an unmarked shallow grave in the forest of Les Landes.

'Whatever you want, deal with me,' Marcus shouted, not so much out of bravado as to defuse the situation, 'she is only a woman. I'm the one you want.'

'I don't think so,' came a voice from the inside of the people-carrier, and Marcus wheeled around to see the unwelcome if slightly ridiculous picture of the Reverend Henry Parker climbing out awkwardly across the centre seats. The two armed men moved fractionally forward, but their leader motioned them back.

'Let the American speak to him,' he said.

Marcus felt his jaw drop open in shock at the sight of the bespectacled Protestant cleric: 'You. You're working with these people? After all you said about Islam? I thought you wanted it wiped out.'

The tall man shot a glance at the clergyman which clearly disquieted him, but he made a show of dismissal

'I don't know how you avoided the colonel, but when he gets here, we'll deal with this properly.' Marcus noted the flicker of a glance exchanged between one of the armed men and their imperious leader. Somehow they knew what the Reverend Parker did not: that the colonel was not going to get here any time soon. But the American was gloating: 'You were a means to an end, professor, nothing more, but you may still be yet, if putting a few bullets into the fleshier parts of your anatomy is the only way of persuading your little friend here to reveal where she has hidden her pagan idol.'

Marcus looked at Nazreem whose face was blank. Somehow everyone but him seemed to believe the supposedly stolen figurine was actually in her possession.

'Why on earth do you think she has it when she was the one who alerted the world to the fact it had been stolen?' he said.

'So much for no secrets between lovers,' sneered the little reverend. 'You mean she really didn't tell you? What was stolen was the wrong figure – ask our Arab friends here, one of their men was responsible – that's why our little archaeologist did a sudden runner, not because she was scared for herself but to get her precious idol out of harm's way. She came running to you, not for your ineffectual help, but to find somewhere to stash the loot. Isn't that so?'

Marcus glanced back at Nazreem expecting a look of disbelieving astonishment but saw instead an expression of foiled fury. In an instant he took on board what he simultaneously realised he had subconsciously always suspected:

'Your bag ... the books for the museum!'

Nazreem shot him a lethal look. Instantly Marcus realised what he had done. But Parker was laughing:

'Don't worry, professor, you haven't given anything away that we didn't already know. Mr Saladin here has been on the ball.'

But the man to whom the name apparently referred was talking Arabic again, looking down on Nazreem like some stern Victorian headmaster on a naughty pupil to whom it was his reluctant but earnest duty to deliver a thrashing.

The man whom she now realised must be the one they whispered of in the backstreets of Gaza as the Son of Saladin opened his mouth for a second wordlessly, then said to her, in a voice more quiet and measured than she had expected:

'From the moment you first landed in London one of my men was watching you. But you knew, didn't you, he was clumsy. He followed you as you headed for the museum, and realised that might be your destination, but you spotted him and told your taxi instead to leave you at an Underground station. You were clever; he was stupid. He will not be so again.

'His colleague, however, was also stupid, but lucky. He was told to go to the museum and wait for the other to arrive. When he lost you, his colleague also forgot about him. So the man continued to wait, and was there when you arrived, carrying your precious bag. If he had known more this might all have ended there – a handbag snatch at a tourist site, it happens all the time. Allah works in mysterious ways. Yet his purpose is revealed in the end.'

'You would do all this, just to destroy a Christian statue?'

Saladin smiled, if you could call it a smile. 'Perhaps. But we are not just talking about an archaeological relic, are we? We are talking about a weapon. A weapon that can ignite a global conflict, which only the will of God will resolve, and which, therefore we will win.'

'You're not making sense.'

'Child,' he said scowling at her. For a minute Nazreem was uncertain whether he was going to smash the side of his hand across her face or caress her cheek. 'Only Allah makes sense in the end,' he said, lowering his hand. 'And now it is time for us to achieve that end. Get in.'

Marcus had not understood a word; his mind was still taking in the deception he had almost wilfully failed to recognise. But the threatening gestures of the two men with the automatic weapons made abundantly clear what was expected right now. Only the Reverend Parker seemed nonplussed.

'What about the colonel. And José, I mean Joseph? Freddie and I can't go on without … wait a minute, where's Freddie?'

On the other side of the people-carrier the door had been slid open and a cool breeze was now blowing right through the vehicle from the dark wall of the pine trees beyond. Freddie had done a runner. Marcus could see drops of what looked like blood on the rear seat, where he assumed the Mexican had been sitting. He had no idea what might have happened to Freddie – and he was not inclined to feel much sympathy – but it was clear he was a lot less trusting than the reverend of the intentions of their present company.

The armed men scanned the dark woodlands around them for a few seconds, before their leader waved them towards the car. Whatever had happened to the Americans' makeweight Mexican help, he did not seem to be unduly worried. Marcus was bundled into the rear seat of the vehicle, one of the gunmen next to him. For the second time within an hour he had a gun stuck in his ribs. The other thug threw Nazreem into the front passenger seat and then climbed in beside Marcus holding his gun to the back of her head. At least Freddie's disappearance would make the seating less of a squash: they would have trouble enough squeezing the reverend in.

Then the silent forest night exploded. Violently. In a staccato thunderburst. Marcus felt the sour taste of bile rise suddenly in his throat. Then, with the reek of cordite and a fine blue smoky vapour still rising from his muzzle in the warm glow of the cabin light that came on when he opened the door, the man they called Saladin climbed into the driver's seat and Marcus realised it was not going to be crowded at all. He had despised the little clergyman, but a bloody glimpse of the wreckage of his body, literally cut in half by the burst from an AK-47 made his stomach turn over.

He pressed his arm hard across his abdomen to suppress the urge to be physically sick, and looked unseeingly in the darkness towards Nazreem, huddled in the corner, immersed in thoughts of her own. Nazreem who had deceived him, dragged him with her on a wild goose chase that could cost both of them their lives without even telling him the truth.

The engine kicked into life and the tyres spun on sand as they lurched off onto the forest track, leaving the bloody remains of the Reverend Henry Parker, gone to meet his Great White Maker, on the dirt of the forest floor.

Insanely, Marcus found an old and melancholy melody running through his head and gritted his teeth: 'I'm being followed by a moonshadow, moonshadow, moonshadow.' Cat Stevens. It was with bitter irony that he recalled the singer nowadays preferred the name Yusuf Islam.

60

Sebastian Delahaye snatched at the phone the instant the green light indicating the secure link to Vauxhall Cross came on. He hated being dependent like this on the security service's self-styled 'big brother' – in this case 'big sister' – across the river, but if it brought in a result then reluctantly he would be the last to complain.

Hilary's tones were as dulcet as ever but he could sense, beneath the ebullient gloss, a hint that she might really have something positive to tell him. She had: 'It looks like good news, Seb. Well, goodish anyhow. I'll go into details later – perhaps we might do lunch in that little place in Chelsea,' – yes, yes, just get on with it, woman, Delahaye thought. 'We just got a quick message. Had to be sent unencrypted so it's a bit oblique but I think the gist is quite clear. Shall I read it to you? Bit of style really, just like the old days.'

'Yes, please.' Delahaye fumed silently. Why couldn't the bloody woman simply tell him what she knew?

'It says, "Salad all packed and ready for delivery, but burgers are off and the grocery boy has gone home early." What do you think?'

'What?!' It was all Delahaye could do not to scream down the phone. Bloody James Bond antics. It was as if they put wit, sarcasm and downright bloody obscurantism at the top of the list on their recruitment criteria.

'Well obviously we're hoping for fuller contact and a thorough brief as soon as possible, but I would have thought that was quite clear: it means our Mr Saladin has met up with your academic friends and is heading this way. Unfortunately our man has had to withdraw from the scene, at least temporarily. It's not too clear why, but no doubt we'll find out soon enough. At least the off-the-wall American threat has been eliminated.'

Delahaye breathed a silent sigh of relief. He had been worried about the US involvement. Part of the success story he envisaged for himself involved evoking a substantial amount of kudos among his transatlantic peer group. The sooner the 'Box' element was closed, the happier he would be. In fact, the sooner the whole operation was back on British soil the better. There were still problems enough to be resolved.

'So what do you say, Seb. How about one-thirty at Deloglio's? I'll get Terence to make a booking.'

Delahaye sighed inwardly. Anything you say, Hilary, anything you say.

61

Dr Edward Mansfield lifted his Rosetta Stone-emblazoned mug of tea from the pile of books on his desk where it had been precariously balanced and took a sip only to put it down in disgust. It was cold. Slowly, arthritically, he got to his feet and paced to the window. Outside the traffic crawled as ever along Great Russell Street, an endless caterpillar of carbon monoxide belching cabs, cars and buses, wholly undiminished by the mayor's congestion charge.

Nor were there any fewer tourists camped on the steps as if the world's greatest repository of cultural artefacts was nothing more than a neoclassical picnic venue, gawpers who ticked off the treasures by rote – Rosetta Stone, done that; Elgin Marbles, done them; Lewis chessmen? Most had never heard of them. As for the Assyrian friezes? He doubted any of them even knew where Assyria was. All they knew of Babylon was a song by Boney M.

Reintroduce entrance charges, that was the answer. Entrance charges to put off the freeloaders, reduce the crowds and make them put a proper worth on the experience. And do something towards topping up a staff pension fund that was on the slippery slope to bankruptcy. If bloody Madame Tussaud's could charge a small fortune and still get crowds queuing up outside to see its stupid charade of wax dummies that were no more lifelike than the Thunderbirds puppets of his youth, then why could not the British Museum charge at least half as much to get up close and personal with the whole of human history?

Because history was bunk. That was why. Henry Ford, inventor of the production line, had said so, and today's production line population went along with him. And so did the bloody government who in any case thought history began with the election before last and ended with the one after next. Mansfield was in a sour mood. As he was so often these days. He was bored, bored with his job, bored with life and bored with the museum. He would have done anything for a little excitement.

Only a few days earlier he had almost thought himself in luck, although, if he sat down and thought about it – which he had done since – he knew all along it was only a pipe dream. But the unexpected appearance in his office of Nazreem Hashrawi, the pretty and intelligent Palestinian woman he had met at a conference in Cairo two years ago, had been the first ray of sunshine to enter his fusty little world in ages. He should have known she was only there to ask a favour.

Time and again over the past few days his eyes had wandered to the heavy canvas bag in the corner, and wondered when she would be back to collect it. And if he dared ask her out for dinner when she did. In the meantime it simply sat there, teasing him. It was not that he begrudged it the floor space. There was enough junk on the floor, on the desk, in the cupboards, pretty much anywhere you cared to look in the grubby little glorified broom cupboard that the trustees of the British Museum dignified with the name of academic's office.

If it had not been for the little padlock on the zip he would have been sorely tempted to take a peek inside the bag, although more out of boredom than genuine curiosity. Books, she had said. Books that were one of her fledgling museum in Gaza's few disposable assets, assets that now indeed had to be disposed of, if it was to weather the crisis of confidence and currency that threatened its survival. It would all have been different, she had told him, very different, if only they had not suffered the catastrophic theft. He had sympathised, as one does, though privately he doubted that the figure she had so fervently hoped might bring her little museum international renown was anything like as rare or important as she had hoped.

As for who had stolen it, probably some nutcase Catholic collector who was daft enough to believe the old wives' tales about St Luke the apostle-cum-painter-cum-sculptor. Whatever. People would always have their dreams. He wondered if there was any chance she really would accept that invitation to dinner.

62

When he was a child, growing up in Cape Town, Marcus Frey had had a mental image of the White Cliffs of Dover. He had heard the sentimental old Second World War song played on the sort of nostalgia radio programmes his mother and her friends were fond of. He had imagined them as a towering, glacial, ivory wall surmounted by giant cartoon bluebirds.

Only now, as he watched the cliffs, in reality a medium-height green-flecked truncated chalk ridge much like the one on the French coast facing, did it strike him as odd that for all his years as an adult in England he had never actually seen them before.

Air travel and the Channel Tunnel had done away with much of the need for the old-fashioned ferry business. Yet it still survived, in fact did a roaring trade, not least in day-trippers who flocked to France and Belgium to buy cheap booze and cigarettes. It was also by far the softer option for anyone anxious to avoid the most rigorous immigration controls.

The big sign in white on blue declared UK BORDER but it seemed to Marcus the woman in the glass box paid little heed to the documents handed over through the window of the Espace as they rolled off the P&O Calais to Dover ferry. She passed them before some sort of scanner, but clearly no alarm bells had been set ringing. 'Remember to drive on the left – *tenez la gauche*,' was her only comment, the latter half in execrable French, as she waved them on their way.

Yes, Marcus felt like shouting at her, and have a nice day yourself, you've just let one of the world's most wanted terrorists into the country. He didn't, of course. He couldn't. Because they had only handed over one passport, his, plus apparently plausible-looking – who knew, maybe even legitimate – French identity cards for his two companions. No longer masked and in black, but wearing freshly pressed jeans and checked shirts they did a fair impression of itinerant jobbing waiters from Marseille of distant Algerian origin. For all Marcus knew, maybe that was even what they were.

Their leader, the one Nazreem now also referred to as 'al-Saladin' was travelling separately with her. On a bus, as it turned out. On another ferry. From another port. On God only knew what passport. What he had been promised, grimly, and had no reason to disbelieve, was that if either of them gave so much as a signal to the immigration or customs officials that they were travelling under duress or that their companions were anything other than bosom buddies, then the other would not reach London alive.

What would have happened if they had been stopped by immigration or customs, if their ID cards had been queried, Marcus did not dare to think. As far as he knew they had not risked bringing firearms into the country, but they had made it perfectly clear to Marcus that each carried a set of knives that no customs official could object to as tools of the trade for French chefs working in London: Sabatier cooks' knives, sharp enough to easily sever a head.

It seemed their captors had done their homework and calculated the risk accurately. Watching the queues of vehicles as two ferries docked within minutes of each other, Marcus had the impression that scarcely one car in a hundred was stopped and it was invariably that of a Brit, suspected of smuggling cigarettes.

As the vehicle swung out of the Western Harbour area and onto the main road, his two companions smiled for the first time in Marcus's short and brutal acquaintance with them, and hit their palms in the air in a wholly un-Islamic 'high five'. In so doing the car veered almost automatically onto the right side of the road and for a moment it looked as if the driver was going to leave it there, until an abrupt blast on a whistle from a policeman on points duty at the harbour exit corrected them. The constable held out his arm, but then merely pointed them back onto the left with a shake of his head and a steely frown.

The driver let out a sudden sigh of relief and then, as the vehicle began the long climb up the hill away from the coast, caught Marcus's eye in his rear-view mirror.

'Smile,' he said. 'Be happy.'

And then, as if an afterthought: 'Now maybe you live.'

Great, thought Marcus. He really didn't like the 'maybe'.

63

Edward Mansfield was not impressed. In his experience men who said they represented 'government security forces' were little more than armed villains. Men who were ready to die for their flag and country were usually willing to trample all over anybody else's.

He understood that there had always been warrior cultures; he just happened to prefer those that belonged to the distant past rather than the present. He had seen what the US army in the name of peace, democracy and civilisation had done for the treasures of Iraq, seen the tank treads scored into the ancient pavements of Babylon, watched on television as armed men trashed the remnants of the world's oldest civilisation, in the name of the modern variation. He was decidedly not impressed.

'I'm afraid,' said Sebastian Delahaye, seated in front of him in his little office in the back corridors of the museum, 'that it's imperative, a genuine matter of national security.'

'I don't see what the fuss is about. Dr Hashrawi merely entrusted me with some personal items, academic material, while she was travelling. I don't see any reason why she should not simply come in here and pick it up. It has been entrusted to my care, and I don't care to abuse that trust.'

Delahaye smiled, his biggest 'believe me, it's all for the best' smile. God, these old buggers could be difficult.

'We have reason to believe that Ms ... that Dr Hashrawi is in some personal difficulty. How shall I put it – that she may be being blackmailed?'

'Blackmailed? Over what? I don't understand.'

Delahaye sighed, a practised, well-meaning sigh.

'I understand, Dr Mansfield. It's just that this is somewhat delicate. We're not asking a great deal of you. Merely that when she calls in advance to arrange to pick up this bag she left with you, that you ask her to come in at a specific time, in the evening, after most of the museum has closed. You can explain that you are out – at a conference or something – the rest of the day, but that you will be happy to see her for a coffee. At the bar in the Great Court.'

'But that's ridiculous. Why wouldn't she come straight here, to my office, like she usually does? I don't want to sit out there, like some bloody tourist.'

'Believe me, I think Dr Hashrawi will prefer it. To be honest I think she may even insist that you meet somewhere more open, rather than in a, if you'll pardon my saying so, rather enclosed space like this.' He looked around him at the cramped, book-lined office.

'You make it all sound so terribly cloak-and-dagger. If it's so important to national security why are you leaving it here at all,' he pointed to the brightly-coloured padlock-zipped nylon bag lying next to the wastepaper basket in the corner. 'It seems there's no way for me to prevent you doing anything you want to.'

Delahaye swung his head round. He had not actually asked to see the object in question and found it almost bizarrely amusing that this cheap nylon 'made in China' bag contained something so sought after. He was sorely tempted to open it, but it would be difficult to do so without obviously tampering with the padlock. And after all, if it was really only some historical relic, he had very little interest. His sole interest in the thing was using it as bait.

'Because,' he resumed, 'she is expecting – the people with her are expecting – it to be with you.'

Mansfield looked at him askance.

'This isn't dangerous, is it? You're not asking me to stick my neck out to catch some criminals, mafia-types or something.'

'I can assure you,' Delahaye told him, 'that we will do everything possible to make sure that there are no problems. All you have to do is meet with Dr Hashrawi and hand over the bag as arranged. It should take no more than a couple of minutes and you can disappear back to your office as soon as you like.'

Mansfield harrumphed. 'Well, I don't know, I suppose so. She hasn't done anything wrong, has she? I mean, you're not going to arrest her or anything, just because she's Palestinian?'

Delahaye pulled out another from his repertoire of smiles for appeasing civilians, this time his very best 'wouldn't even think of it, don't you worry about a thing' smile: 'As far as we are concerned, Dr Mansfield, your colleague has done nothing wrong whatsoever. Believe me, we are simply trying to help her out.'

'So when is this all going to happen? She's due to call me, you said.'

'We believe so. It could be any time, any time at all, but almost certainly within the next forty-eight hours. All you have to do is let us know straight away, and ask her to come in around five fifty-five in the evening.'

'But, if it is in the next forty-eight hours, the Great Court closes at six p.m. from Sunday to Wednesday.'

'Like I said, we only expect it to take a couple of minutes and it will be easier if the museum is almost empty.'

Delahaye walked down the steps feeling something like remotely in control of the situation once again. 'Remotely' being the operative word if, thank God, no longer as remotely as it had been. Squaring Mansfield had been the last little element. Once it had been established that the ridiculous artefact that was drawing his quarry as surely as a wasp to a honeypot was at the British Museum, it had not taken a minute to find out which of the institution's resident 'keepers' was most likely to be an acquaintance of Nazreem Hashrawi. Edward Mansfield was a regular attendee at conferences in Cairo.

And now Hashrawi was back on British soil and so – far more importantly for the security community and the potential career advancement of one S. Delahaye in particular – was the man who until now had been nothing more than a video nasty, the man who called himself 'Son of Saladin'. If everything went according to plan, his salad days were about to be well and truly over.

Rashid Hussein al-Samarri, as it said on the Saddam-era Iraqi identity card he had not used for years, had entered the United Kingdom at eleven forty-five using a high-quality forged identity card under the name Abdul Youssef Bezier, latterly of Marseille, currently of Lille, *département du Nord*, on a coach sightseeing-excursion to Canterbury, crossing the channel on the ten-thirty a.m. (French time) Eurotunnel shuttle departure from Calais to Folkestone. Amongst the other passengers on board the coach was a Ms Nazreem Pascale Hashrawi travelling on a French (non-resident) passport.

The nutty professor had come through Calais on the P&O ferry in a black Renault Espace, accompanied by two French nationals of Algerian descent. So they were keeping them apart. It made sense. It made sense primarily if Frey and Hashrawi were reluctant collaborators, which according to the 'Box' man they almost certainly were.

There were, to say the least, elements of the operation Delahaye had never been happy with and he still wasn't. For a start, he had not got his head around the significance of the 'archaeological thing'. The idea that people were risking their lives for what might or might not be some statue of the Virgin Mary was beyond his comprehension. This was the twenty-first century for Christ's sake. The only Virgin Mary Seb Delahaye had ever known had been one of his sister's friends who came round to play on Saturdays. And that name hadn't stuck long.

Mr so-called Saladin on the other hand was a prize he sorely coveted. There were innumerable intelligence reports positively linking him to the beheadings of hostages, first in the early days of the occupation of Iraq, and latterly in the Gaza Strip where he was believed to have been amongst the most insidious influences on the hardline anti-negotiating elements within Hamas. There was also more than enough reason to want to question him in connection with both the London and Madrid bombings, but in truth the only real evidence trail had led to one of his associates, the one whose body parts had ended up split between an Israeli border post and a Bavarian monastery.

The tangential Madrid connection had been one of the reasons Delahaye had been unwilling to involve Spanish security forces. The temptation to grab the man for themselves would almost certainly have been too much for them, and the last thing anyone wanted – in particular the Americans – was for a player like 'Saladin' to end up slipping through a wide net because of insufficient evidence to hold up in a court of law. The transatlantic 'cousins' idea of a future for Mr al-Samarri was at the very best an orange jumpsuit and a piece of paper that said 'take me to Cuba' or wherever they now substituted for Guantanamo Bay. For that reason, even here in Britain, it was important to get Mr Saladin to blot his copybook in public. One excuse, that was all Delahaye needed.

As he left the museum gates on Great Russell Street he stopped and looked up at the imposing portico of the great building. Where he was standing was a favourite spot for tourists to take pictures of Sir Robert Smirke's masterpiece of the Greek Revival movement. But Sebastian Delahaye was not admiring the architecture. He was looking at the roof.

He had gone fishing and hooked a shark. Now he had played him back into his own swimming pool. It was a case of eat or be eaten.

64

The sun was setting slowly over the Victorian rooftops of Bloomsbury as the black Mercedes pulled up at one of the few parking meters within walking distance of the British Museum. Nazreem had her heart in her mouth as they approached the great steps. She had phoned Ed Mansfield who said he would be delighted to see her, and yes, of course, her bag was still where she left it. She almost detected a slight nervousness to his voice, but realised it was probably down to the man's foolish and ill-disguised infatuation. He was just plucking up the courage to ask her out. She had read that in his face the last time she had seen him. Now she wished she could have hinted he had a whole lot more to worry about.

The man by her side, who had listened to every word she said over the phone was the same man who had tailed her from Heathrow she had realised when he and two burly thugs had collected her, al-Saladin and a third bodyguard who had travelled on the coach from France with them, at a car park on the outskirts of Canterbury and supplied them with firearms. Now he was telling her to make sure the meeting was somewhere public, somewhere open. Saladin was not stupid enough to walk into some tight corner like a blind man. But she need not have worried:

'How about a cup of coffee in the Great Court,' Mansfield was saying. 'Upstairs round the back of the old Reading Room. It's very pleasant and quite quiet in the early evening, when most of the tourists have gone.' Next to her, Barani smiled his agreement. Public and open, he signalled to the spiritual leader he stood in awe of, even when the man was dressed as now so untypically in a cheap French business suit.

But at the entrance to the museum itself, she was relieved at last to see Marcus emerge from the Renault Espace, even if in the company of the two men she had feared at the slightest provocation would have killed him. He smiled, and she was happy to note there was still a genuine warmth in it. Over the past twenty-four hours, since she had witnessed three brutal murders in the space of an hour, her mind had been in turmoil. The risks she had taken were too great. Not too great for her, but too great for him. He thought she had lied to him, while she had told herself she had been trying to protect him, but the outcome had been the same.

Saladin took her firmly, but forcefully, by the arm and walked up the steps to where Marcus and his minders waited. Then together, leaving Barani and his men outside on the steps, they walked into the echoing marble foyer. On either side people were pouring out of the galleries. The main part of the museum was closing. Even the Great Court would close at six p.m. to all but reserved diners in the restaurant. They walked through the great double doors that opened onto the most grandiose space in London.

Above their heads the great soaring tessellated glass roof with its myriad triangular panes let in the last rose-tinged vestiges of the dying daylight to cast a surreal shadow network across the majestic pale limestone walls. From one corner a giant elongated stone head from Easter Island looked at them with its blind almond eyes, from another the great stone lion from the Mausoleum of Halicarnassus. And at its heart was a circular structure into which the great glass roof folded, a building within a building that had at least as much historical import as any of the museum's exhibits. This was the former Reading Room of the British Library, the repository of freely available learning in which Karl Marx had dreamt up the roots of what was to become one of the most oppressive social systems on earth. Amidst the relics of so many religions, here too the totem of another, the militant atheism of communism.

To Marcus all of this was – as ever – a source of constant wonder. To Saladin, as they climbed the steps that led to the Court Coffee Shop elevated behind the Reading Room, all of it was an irrelevance: heresy, apostasy and idolatry. There was no God but God. All others deserved destruction.

Edward Mansfield sat alone, at a table by the balcony looking down onto the rapidly emptying courtyard below. But for one or two bored-looking staff the café was deserted. All around the court concealed lighting had come on, turning the multi-paned roof above their heads into a gleaming celestial net that held the darkening sky with its handful of evening stars. From the Great Court the gleaming pristine Portland stone of the vast neoclassical gateway led into the collections from Iran, Arabia and ancient Egypt. And yet, thought Marcus, could it be that the nondescript garish nylon bag that lay on the floor by Mansfield's table contained an object as important at least as any wonder they contained?

'My dear, Dr Hashrawi,' said Mansfield, standing up as they approached. 'How very, very nice to see you again. And are you going to introduce me to these gentlemen?'

65

Sebastian Delahaye flicked open the Comms Link and checked his dispositions.

'All clear out front.'

'Affirmative. Support discreetly positioned. Most civilians moving off from immediate vicinity. We've had museum staff clear outer courtyard early. Both vehicles still in position outside. Owners feeding meters.'

Delahaye smiled: 'Well, I suppose if the worst comes to the worst, we can always book them for that. Keep me posted.'

'Will do.'

He switched to his other link. 'How's things with the night owls?' The voice on the other end was cool and calm.

'Couldn't be better. Lovely evening. Perfect view.'

'That's what I like to hear.'

'Oh, and by the way the apron really suits you.'

'Ha ha. Just do your job.'

He clicked off the Comms Link and moved out into the serving area. Hashrawi was even prettier close up.

'Can I get you ladies and gentlemen anything? A glass of wine perhaps. We shall be closing shortly.'

Saladin dismissed with an angry hand gesture the infidel waiter who had dared to offer him alcohol. His two heavies moved forward to flank him and Nazreem was surprised not to see the waiter rapidly retreat.

'I'm sorry,' she said rapidly, pulling out a chair next to the worried-looking Mansfield. 'My friend doesn't drink alcohol. Please bring us four coffees. For you, Edward?' Marcus was amazed at her cool.

'Not for me, thank you,' said the middle-aged academic, 'I really must be off.' Marcus thought he looked decidedly as if he meant it. 'Just wanted to be sure you got your bag. Good luck with the sale.'

'Sale?'

'Of the books. I hope you get a good price.'

'Oh, yes. I'm sure …'

Mansfield went to get up, but one of the two bodyguards crossed and put a hand on his shoulder. Nazreem turned angrily towards Saladin and said to him, in Arabic: 'What does this mean. Let this man go. He is not involved.'

Marcus was reduced to reading body language. Edward Mansfield, however, as an Arabic scholar, was clearly not at all happy about what he was hearing. The waiter meanwhile, far from fetching their coffee, was hovering about ten metres away and another one had come into sight. Marcus doubted if either would be much use against the two Algerian thugs, especially if they were packing guns, and he could not imagine they were not. His two minders had been handed weapons at a service station on the M20 into London.

Mansfield was staring transfixed at the tall man with his recently trimmed beard and ill-fitting dark suit who spoke as if he expected only obedience. 'Fetch the bag,' he heard him say and watched the other man lift the nylon bag and move it towards his master.

'You have what you want,' said Nazreem. 'Now take it and go.'

'Perhaps we should open it first, just to be sure.'

'You wish to burn your eyes with the image of a pagan idol, or the Christian Madonna, whichever you prefer? Take it away if you must and destroy it at your leisure.'

Mansfield jerked forward in his seat as if he had been kicked up the backside: 'The Madonna? You mean all this time …? No. You can't let some fundamentalist destroy it.' And then, with unexpected boldness he turned on the still standing Son of Saladin and his henchmen and all but shouted, in fluent Arabic: 'You, you would destroy a priceless archaeological find, a piece of world history.'

As if noticing him for the first time Saladin said: 'You speak the language of the prophet (peace be upon him). Then you should understand why it is necessary to rid the world of a blasphemy, a corruption of sanctity, a crime against God.'

For a moment Marcus thought Nazreem had taken leave of her senses. She threw back her head and laughed in the man's face.

'You're the one who doesn't know what he is talking about. Are you afraid of a Christian idol? Afraid that the Christian world will push Islam from their "holy land" because they have found the original image of the mother of their God? Are you that poor a Muslim?'

Marcus saw the man raise his hand as if to slap her face and wished he knew what the hell she was saying to him. Whatever it was, there was no stopping her:

'Because even if you are, there was never anything here to fear. Don't you understand? It's proof that for years these so-called Christians have had a joke played on them by their own priests. The statue that all their black Madonnas, their Holy Virgins are based on is not Mary, not the Maryam of the Qu'ran, but the ancient earth goddess of the Phrygians, the Magna Mater adopted by Rome, the figure that was fetched from its Asian home to protect their "Eternal City" when it was under threat from Hannibal. It is the graven image to end all graven images, proof of the foolishness of their idolatry.'

The man's hand had come down, but the fiery glint burning deep in his eyes suggested to Marcus, listening in helpless ignorance, that he was about to erupt in rage. Instead, he looked at Nazreem as if his eyes could burn through her and said: 'You are more – and perhaps less – of a fool than I expected. Do you not know what material your graven image is made of?'

For a second she was totally taken aback: 'Stone,' she said.

'But what sort of stone?'

This wasn't making sense: 'Black stone. Basalt, maybe, I don't know. I'm not a geologist.'

He almost smiled. 'No. Not that a study of earthly material would help when dealing with that which comes from the heavens. Have you so neglected your duty to your faith that you have never performed the Hajj?'

'The Hajj …? No, I … But what has that to do with …?' She was annoyed with him for throwing her religion – no, not her religion, her culture – in her face. What did the pilgrimage to Mecca have to do with anything. It had always annoyed her anyhow, the vast crowds, the whole ritual, the ridiculous superstitions, the throwing of stones at rocks, the endless circling of the … No, not that. It wasn't possible. A blinding light had appeared in front of her and she hid her eyes from it.

'You don't mean that! How could that be?' She stared at him aghast. Against all expectations, he had taken the wind from her.

He was nodding now, like a teacher whose pupil has finally seen the light, just too late:

'Yes. The Hajr-e-Aswad itself, the Black Stone of God, given to

Ishmael by the angel Gabriel, and the cornerstone of the Ka'aba itself, the first holy shrine built by Ibrahim. I trust you know the history: that when Ibrahim died the people reverted to their pagan ways and the Ka'aba once again became the home of idols.

'This thing, to which you have given sanctuary, is one such idol, the greatest offender of all, the ultimate blasphemy: a graven image carved from the holiest rock on earth. A rock not of this earth, but fallen from heaven. Go ahead, open it and touch the defiled heart of the universe. See the abomination at last for what it truly is. The ultimate blasphemy.'

For a moment it seemed as if Nazreem had lost the will to live. Her face was blank, her eyelids drooped as if she was still imagining the image in her mind's eye rather than opening the bag at her feet to see it in this new, alien light. Could it be? The holy stone of Islam carved into a graven image of a Christian icon. And yet it wasn't, was it? Not a Christian image. That was the point.

Al-Saladin was smiling as if he were a good shepherd watching one of his flock turn back from the edge of the cliff and return to the fold.

'Now you see why we want it,' he said, his eyes gleaming.

'To destroy it,' said Nazreem, her voice coming as if from underwater.

'Yes, of course,' there was triumphalism in the cleric's voice. 'But only after we have shown it for what it is. Shown the children of Islam how the Christians defiled the holy of holies. How should we be surprised that these infidels make cartoons of the prophet as if he were Mickey Mouse, when they can take the sacred black rock, the stone fallen from heaven, and carve it into a pagan totem pole.

'We will put your graven image on display, have no fear. We shall hold it aloft to show the world what Christianity thinks of Islam. We shall unite Shi'ite and Sunni in the pure hatred of the infidel pagan crusader. The armies of Islam need no graven images to win their battles for them, but we shall hold this one in our hearts, the ultimate symbol of sacrilege against the invisible God. We shall invoke the wrath of Allah, to spur us to victory. Once and for all.'

Marcus, who had understood next to nothing of an exchange conducted wholly in Arabic, watched the expression on Nazreem's face change from defiance to what appeared to be dumbstruck shock and then, just as quickly to anger as, apparently following orders she produced a key, knelt down, opened the padlock and tugged at the zip on the bag.

And then suddenly she was on her feet, lightning quick, a long, thin, razor-sharp stilletto in her hand, fished from the bag and now held against the mullah's throat. Marcus fell back against his chair, tumbled to the floor, lay there in shocked awe at the tableau before his eyes.

'So that was your excuse,' Nazreem, spitting in the eyes of her tormentor, shouted at him. 'You who defile the name of a great Muslim warrior, a man of virtue and honour, rather than a fanatic and a warmonger. A superstition about a piece of stone. That is your reason for stealing from your own people, for violating a trust, for' – screaming now – 'for violating ME!'

Yet for all of it she could see no fear in his eyes, only scorn and disbelief, maybe even admiration.

'You poor deluded bitch,' he said at last, his eyes studiously avoiding the blade at his throat. 'The man who raped you paid for his pleasure. I thought you knew that. He had ceased to be one of us. He had chosen to cease even to be a man. I granted his desire. We didn't just cut his heart out. We cut his balls off, and his prick. We took your revenge for you. Ask the nun,' he all but sneered in her face, 'though I doubt you will ever see her again.'

'What the …'

And then she was gone, spun round and fallen to the floor.

'No!' Marcus screamed. 'No.' But there was a gun pointing at his head. And another smoking from the barrel that had floored Nazreem. And a knife, more like a scimitar, a great curved blade good only for cutting the throats of halal cattle, or helpless humans, in the hands of the so-called Son of Saladin. Nazreem was not dead yet, but in an instant she would be.

And then, in a succession so swift it was almost simultaneous, her would-be slaughterer fell to the floor, a zing like an angry hornet pierced the air. In the distance glass shattered. And the Great Court exploded in a wash of light from above. And the waiter, of all people, was shouting, 'STOP or you're all dead!'

Gone were the soft seductive concealed lights that turned the night sky into a string bag full of stars, and in their place were halogen floodlights that poured luminescence of almost unbearable intensity into the Great Court. Dimly, like silhouettes in a magic lantern, Marcus could make out the shapes of men with long-barrelled weapons zeroing in on them from the other side of the glass roof. In one corner, a shattered pane in the tessellated weave indicated the direction of the high velocity bullet that had found its mark in Saladin's skull.

His erstwhile bodyguards had their hands held high. The waiter was holding his ear and talking urgently to his shirt cuff. And Nazreem was trying to sit up from the floor clutching her shoulder with blood oozing through her fingers. The nylon bag lay overturned on the floor, spilling its contents on the café floor: about a dozen heavy, dusty textbooks.

66

'Is that it?'

In spite of himself, Marcus could not help but feel disappointment. He did not know exactly what he had expected. Not some fabulous work of art to compare with the masterpieces of the Renaissance. But maybe something that at least caught the eye. Something if not on a par with the grave goods of ancient Egypt, something that at least spoke to the soul.

This said nothing to him. It was simplistic, primitive, devoid of any expression or artistic merit that he could discern. And yet, it was undeniably ancient – just how ancient they still had no idea, but older by far than the first century AD. And there was something about the stone itself; a matt black which somehow seemed to shine from within as if there were minerals unknown, like the ghosts of diamonds, waiting to be coaxed from its carved surface.

It was not where he had expected first to see the supposed image of the Mother of God, a drab self-storage warehouse in west London. Marcus and Nazreem had spent twenty-four hours as 'guests of Her Majesty', albeit in a comfortable house in Bloomsbury. They had told a succession of interrogators everything they wanted to know. But surprisingly the one thing they had wanted to know least about was the figure Nazreem was now holding, like a human child in her left arm, notwithstanding the heavy bandage on her right shoulder. She had been lucky, the nurse who came specially to the house had told her. She would mend. Given time.

And they would take time. Time to reassess. Old wounds and new. But before anything, he had to see, had to hold in his hands, what it had all been about. And now that he had done so, it was hard, laughably hard, to dismiss a sense of disappointment. They stood in the tiny cubicle, nine-feet square and eight feet high that Nazreem had rented, cash payment down, for a month, and wondered what it was about inanimate objects that could make human beings lay down their lives for them.

And then the answer came from behind him.

'I'll take that, please.'

Simultaneously they spun round to see a small, plumpish figure standing in the doorway. A dumpy woman, in a long coat.

'If you don't mind.'

Nazreem almost dropped the figure to the ground.

'Sister Galina! I don't believe it. We thought you were …'

'Dead. Yes. I know. Although as a matter of fact if it weren't for me you are the ones who would most likely be dead.'

The expression on Marcus's face wasn't exactly a smile but it almost passed for one. 'Do you know, I almost suspected as much. It just seemed too fantastic.' He turned to Nazreem: 'Your fairy godmother!'

'It was you, on the train?' she said, her voice fading away.

'And in Avila,' Marcus said. 'And in the monastery, tucking into the pasta in the far corner.'

'And now, please, may I have the Mother of God? You did promise, you know, to let me spend some time with her. And that was before I saved your life.'

There was confusion all over Nazreem's face. 'I don't understand. I mean, why, how?'

But it was Marcus who asked the question that she was just coming round to formulating: 'For a start what led you here?'

'This, it fell from your handbag in the train.'

It took Marcus a couple of seconds to recognise that what she was holding was a blue London Transport Oyster card.

'But how did that …?'

'They're very efficient, nowadays, you know, these British, much more so than their reputation. And very security conscious. You just need to touch this on a reader at any Underground station and it tells you every journey it has made. Like the one Nazreem here made, from Waterloo to Acton, on the afternoon she arrived in London.

'There aren't many reasons to come to Acton. But if you've got something to hide, then the presence of a secure storage facility only a short walk from the Underground is not a bad one. The only question was: which box? For the past two days, I've been waiting for you. Touching, isn't it?'

'That still doesn't explain how you got in here. This is supposed to be a secure facility. There's a security guard out there. They're only allowed to let in customers.'

For a microsecond the little woman's eyes closed. 'Oh, for God's sake, that's enough of this,' she said. And then there was a gun in her hand. 'Let's just say he won't be bothering us.'

Suddenly, too late, the last vestiges of a veil of illusion fell from Nazreem's eyes: 'Your devotion, to the Madonna, it seemed so real, so moving, but you're not a sister. You never were.'

'No,' interrupted Marcus. 'In fact, you're not even really a woman. You didn't do it yourself, did you?'

In a split second movement that belied her dumpiness the Glock pistol she held in her hand was pressed against Marcus's temple.

'You think you can make jokes? For centuries we have endured the scorn of people like you. I'm a sister, all right. A sister of an order that goes back longer than any Christian cult. And now I've come to reclaim what is ours. The sisters of Kybele have the right to their inheritance. The return of the Magna Mater is a sign.'

'Galina – the Gallae. The cult the Texan was going on about. It wasn't all lunacy. No wonder you could pass yourself off so easily as a man. You used to be one.'

Her grip on the trigger tightened. Marcus was pushing her too far. All of a sudden Nazreem felt it was all too much. Give the woman the figurine, let her go, let her take it away and worship it. Whatever. Just leave them in peace. Before the demented creature did something foolish.

Marcus flinched as he felt the saliva splatter against his cheek. The little creature snarling up at him had spat in his face. 'Men! You think the phallus is the key to the world. The male sexual organs strangle your brains. Sever yourself from them and you sever yourself from their obscene domination.'

The words jarred in Nazreem's brain. What was it Saladin had said, seconds before the bullets struck – 'we cut off his balls' – 'took your revenge' – 'ask the nun'.

'Like what they did to the thief. The one who ...'

'The one who went too far. Had his wicked way with you, did he? Well, I'm sorry – it wasn't in his instructions – but then you are a pretty little thing, aren't you? And it was his last fling, before he became one of us for real.'

'One of ... It was you. Who stole.. You who ...' Nazreem could scarcely control the violence of her emotion.

'Of course, it was, what did you expect, that we'd let you – them

– take the Holy Mother and make her a sterile museum piece! Or worse, give her to the cursed Christians to be their bitch Mary, the symbol of two thousand years of repression?! The thief was working for us, but he was a man, wasn't he? All he could think of was the money we promised, and then letting his cock out to play. He told that pious fool Saladin everything. Why do you think they sent me such a clear message as his cock and balls in a plastic bag?'

'That'll do. Put it down, sister. Or should I say, sir. Believe me, it makes no difference to me. I follow an equal opportunities rule.'

Marcus jerked to attention, not least because the voice from the doorway was uncannily familiar. Galina thought so too, but she wasn't taking any chances. She wheeled and fired, the shot narrowly missing the figure that flattened itself against the wall, then dropped to the floor. Galina screamed, flung herself forward, then fell prone, spreadeagled and motionless, a trickle of dark blood dripping from a hole behind her ear.

In a flash, the figure in the doorway was crouched over her, and turned over the limp body to reveal a neat, round entry hole below the right eye.

'I guess that pays for Joe,' he said, and turned towards where Marcus and Nazreem crouched in the corner, the bandage on his ear clearly visible.

'Freddie!'

'Si señor.'

'But you're …'

'Take it easy, Dr Frey.' The accent was suddenly impeccably English. 'I'm sorry about the treatment in Madrid, but it went with the territory.'

'I don't get it. You're …'

'Friendly. I guess you could say I'm on the side of the angels. Well, most of the time anyhow.'

'You … you …' Marcus was speechless.

'We're not completely the Americans' poodles that people sometimes think we are. For a couple of years now there have been people over here who've worried about the influence of the extreme Christian fundamentalists on the neocons in the last US administration.'

'You mean you're …'

'A spook? Yes, if you like. But it's not all glamour, as you can see.' He indicated his mutilated ear.

'But how did you …'

'Come out here? The boys across the river. "Five". Never mind. You don't need to know. I was told you were coming out today to retrieve the little lady there.' He pointed to the stone figure. 'I wanted to take a look, considering I'd suffered in her service, as it were. Also I thought I'd say hello. And goodbye. Lucky I did. Saw the guy in reception with a bullet in his brain, and thought I maybe ought to watch out. Can't say I'm sorry. She had it coming. I'd sort of got attached to old José, after spending two months working alongside him on a stinking cattle ranch on the Rio Grande. Gave me a real empathy for the Mexicanos.'

'What about … her?' Marcus gestured towards the prone body on the floor.

Freddie – Alfredo – whatever his name was, and it certainly wasn't either of those, was already pulling a phone from his pocket and tapping in a number.

'Don't you worry. I'm calling in the cleaning ladies. They should be here within the hour. If I were you, I'd make yourselves scarce. Easier that way.'

Together, Marcus and Nazreem nodded. She picked up the stone figure and began to put it back in her bag.

'Here, let me take a quick look,' the man with the phone to his ear said. She held it out to him. He examined it for a few seconds, then shook his head and shrugged.

'Mind how you go,' he said. 'Have a nice life.'

'We will,' she said, and slung the rucksack on her back to follow Marcus towards the open door and the rainy London skies beyond.

Epilogue

It was still raining two days later. A grey, slanting persistent rain that was more than a drizzle but not quite a downpour, a dull, depressing rain that drenched the streets and showed up the English summer for a lie. Marcus and Nazreem stood huddled under a cheap umbrella on the corner of Poultry and St Stephen Walbrook, streets whose very names reached back into the vanished mediaeval cityscape, surveying dismally the weathered Portland stone, grey concrete and improbable postmodernist pink marble. Taxis swished past, washing the kerbs with sprays of dirty water from their wheels. The rucksack on Nazreem's back – even now she refused to let Marcus carry it – was suddenly unaccountably heavy.

'Maybe he won't come,' she said and wondered if it was more in hope than expectation. And yet, deep down, she was weary of her burden.

It had been a difficult decision at first, but then as soon as it was made, suddenly not so difficult after all. The 'black Madonna' had gone. Stolen and never recovered. The world had forgotten about it. And in the end that was for the best. There was no way she could now consider unleashing anew the storm of controversy that she knew would surround its rediscovery. To ignite a new bonfire amid the already smouldering 'conflict of civilisations' between Christian and Muslim, to turn a spotlight on an ancient artefact that was an affront to the two main faiths on the planet. No. Better by far to entrust it to one who promised, and for some reason she believed him, to treasure it for what it was – part of mankind's history – and keep it safe until the day, should it ever come, when the world had grown up. It would, to be sure, mean that she had relinquished her hopes of overnight archaeological celebrity, to Gaza's claim to fame. But she would have other opportunities. And Gaza had trouble enough as it was. Besides, just right now she was not sure when – or if – she was going back.

Marcus clutched her hand. 'He'll come,' he said, and realised as he said it he was not sure if it sounded like a promise or a threat.

It was an unprepossessing site for a meeting: a bleak spot in the sterile jungle of the City of London's financial district. Yet the old abbot had been quite specific. But it was hard to imagine anything of eternal value in this warren of unlovely architecture where the only god was greed. The focal point, No 1 Poultry, was a great pink marble shop-and-offices complex that Marcus could vaguely remember Prince Charles or someone similar calling a 'coconut ice steamship'. Opposite it was a slab of a 1950s office block, a soulless monolith in the process of being demolished. The entrance to an underground garage yawned like a giant maw before it, and there were construction hoardings next to what looked like somebody's idea of a rock garden in which the plants had all died, behind a rusty railing.

A taxi stopped near the entrance to the shopping arcade at No 1 Poultry and Marcus craned his neck to see if the figure emerging was familiar but rather than a grey-haired elderly ecclesiastic it was two long-haired blonde women in pinstripe trouser suits who emerged, both talking separately into mobile phones. Marcus glanced at his watch. Already the man was fifteen minutes late, but that was nothing in Spanish terms and given the notorious unreliability of London's transport still nowhere near time to declare a 'no-show'. Out of idle curiosity he pulled up the collar of his jacket and strolled over to the bus stop. He thought it was unlikely that the abbot would arrive by bus, but you never knew.

The array of route numbers – 11, 26, 56, N76, N21 – meant nothing to him. A twenty-four-hour service theoretically operated via here to Foot's Cray wherever that was. He imagined bleary-eyed late-night revellers heading for home somewhere in the suburban fast-nesses of Kent peering out into the dark wondering why on earth their bus was stopping at … whatever this stop was called. And then he saw it. The reason they were here. Four little words in black on white, the name of the bus stop written above the route numbers: 'The Temple of Mithras'.

He turned to where Nazreem was still standing, looking increasingly miserable with her backpack and the dripping umbrella, and called her over. He almost didn't notice the little figure in a dark raincoat and Homburg hat scuttling across the road towards them. And then he was there, beside them, leaning over the little railing to look at the fragmen-tary ruins. Marcus leant beside him and examined the concrete-set rubble that he had at first taken for a neglected rock garden.

'That's why we're here?'

The old man nodded.

'The cult of Mithras went hand in hand with worship of Kybele. It was a soldier's religion and there was a tradition of bull sacrifice, but it did not only reach as far as Spain. Here you have the proof, at least what little they have left of it. The early Christians stole Mithras – just as they stole Kybele – and buried all memory of his cult. In fact they did their best to confuse it with devil worship, the legend of the Antichrist.'

'What do you mean? In what way?'

'In almost every way. Mithras was born at the midwinter solstice, on or around the 25th of December – roughly the same date that ancient Britons celebrated the turn of the year at Stonehenge. He was born of a virgin mother, a miracle witnessed by shepherds on a rocky mountainside. After his slaying of a bull – 'the horned beast' – he died, was entombed in a cave and rose again to his disciples. A central feature of the initiation into his mysteries involved bull's blood, as Christian communion involves the blood of Christ.'

'You're trying to say the whole Jesus story …'

'… borrowed what was useful, to persuade Mithraists to come over to a new, semi-homegrown version of their religion. Mithra-ism had its home in Persia, beyond the Roman Empire's borders, and therefore was no longer considered suitable. Christianity with its strict doctrines and hierarchies echoed the power structure of the empire itself. The irony was that as the emperors' power waned, that of the bishops and their overlord, the bishop of Rome, filled the vacuum. It was a takeover of the empire from within, and it brooked no opposition.

'Those who followed the old gods, the old beliefs in freedom of thought, were either exterminated, or found an accommodation. The Christians were fanatical and if they couldn't eliminate an old belief, they adapted it. But in so doing, they provided a lifeline for some followers of the old religions who found a convenient way of turning the tables back again from within, of becoming double agents, so to speak, using the memory of saints, often some of the most fanatical Christians, to mask the worship of old familiar faces.'

'A pagan conspiracy, at the heart of the Church for two thousand years?'

'Tch. Hardly a conspiracy. More accommodation, and not always an easy one. The zealots of Protestantism with their blind faith and fascist Puritanism were – and are – the most dangerous. Along with their bedmates from the fanatical side of Islam.'

'Are you a member of this sect … the Giuliani … is that what you call yourselves?'

'We don't call ourselves, such as we are, anything, except perhaps students, philosophers. But it is a name that has been used.'

'But nothing to do with Sister Galina, the Gallae?'

'Nothing at all. We were aware of their existence, of course. That is why I was in contact with Sister Galina, but we have always favoured less extreme behaviour. We were not aware that the sisterhood had paid to have the statue stolen.'

'Why? Where does it come from?'

'What do you know of the Emperor Julian?'

'Julius Caesar? As much as the next man. More than most.'

'Not Julius. I said Julian.'

'Julian? I don't think …' then not for the last time, Marcus's mental squirrel retrieved a piece of information he had thought discarded for ever, something from his first-year university history course's compulsory reading of Gibbon's *Decline and Fall of the Roman Empire*. 'A late emperor,' he said hesitantly. 'Fourth century or thereabouts. The one they called Julian the Apostate?'

The old abbot smiled, more appreciatively this time. 'The very same,' he said. 'Except that they did not call him that at the time. They would not have dared. Nor indeed for many years later. The name is an invention of those who worked scrupulously to darken the name of a man who was a friend of learning and an opponent of dogma.'

'You've lost me.'

'It's not surprising: history lost him. Julian was the nephew of the Emperor Constantius, great-nephew of Constantine, last of the imperial line. He only ever wanted to be a philosopher. But fate ruled otherwise. He turned out to be a brilliant general and on the death of his uncle was acclaimed emperor by his troops.

'Julian was an initiate into the mysteries of Mithras. He saw his elevation to the purple as an opportunity to abolish the faddish new religion he believed was strangling the minds of his contemporaries. He abolished all of Christianity's privileges. The Catholic Church today insists he tried to ban it, but in reality he simply stopped the Christians banning all others. It was they who were intolerant. And they got their revenge.'

'What do you mean, got their revenge?'

'Had Julian lived, the world might have been a different place. Christianity would never have become dominant. Islam might never have got off the ground. The whole dominance of the Judaeo-Christian-Islamic monotheistic religious edifice would never have taken off, crushing the more tolerant pluralist beliefs of the old Hellenic world.'

'But?'

'Julian died young. He died in battle, a futile war against the Persians. The manner of his death remains suspicious. A wound from the rear. Julian was not a man to run.'

'Friendly fire?'

'Or deliberate assassination. After his death the empire was run by a serious of weak dolts, the Christians gained the upper hand again, suppressed all the other cults and gradually took over the power structures from within. The rest is history. Literally.'

'And this is why people like you have lived like a secret society within the Catholic Church, trying to take it over from within?'

'Good God, no, if you will excuse the expression. We are not, as you might think, trying to take over anything from within. On the contrary, as I said, we like to think of ourselves as Julian did, as philosophers. No religion is wrong until it attempts to proscribe all others and claim for itself the sole right to truth, yet sadly that is what so many try to do.'

Nazreem nodded, as if suddenly she was indeed convinced that handing over her trophy to this man was the right thing to do.

'And this,' she said, handing him the rucksack, 'my "black Madonna" is really the Magna Mater, Kybele?'

'Almost certainly. The church where you found it was, I believe, supposedly dedicated to ...'

'Saint Julian.'

'Indeed. Not a saint at all, you see, but a covenant, a clue to future generations, a way to save the legacy of an emperor who believed in an alternative to autocracy – in heaven and on earth. I believe it must have been some of his Greek philosopher friends who brought it there from Rome, after his death. It's the sort of intellectual joke that would have appealed to them: sweet and sour all at once.'

'And yet in Rome they believed this lump of stone had magic powers, believed it saved the city.'

'In Rome,' the old priest smiled, 'there were people who would believe anything. There always have been, and still are. Yet maybe it did. Because they believed it. Maybe those who believe in miracles experience them. Maybe. The important thing is to have an open mind.'

'Open enough to believe this is also a chunk of the Hajr-e-Aswad, stolen from the Ka'aba itself.'

Marcus could hear the cynicism in her voice, but there was none in the Spaniard's reply.

'Many Muslims believe that the Black Stone fell from heaven in the time of Adam, who they too believe to have been the first man. Some scientists believe life on earth may have been brought here by chance, on a meteorite from another world.'

'You're not saying there's a connection?'

'I'm not saying anything except that in the end everything is connected. Myths, legends – religions if you like – intermingle, and anything is of importance if it reminds us of our real significance in the universe.'

'Infinitesimally small. Meaningless.'

'No, not at all. In size we may be infinitesimal but we are also infinite: each one of us as a manifestation of "the One" that is the Universe itself – which is what Plato suggested and Julian believed – we are all, after all, each of us our own universe, but only make sense of any sort in communion with others. It is not dissimilar, I think, to what quantum physics and string theory suggest. Science and belief are not necessarily so estranged as many people would believe. But what do I know? It is time for me to go.'

He took up his burden and hoisted it onto his back, not a cross but a small statue, little more than a lump of rock in a backpack, but a symbol nonetheless, and with a small bow towards Nazreem, turned and walked slowly away from them.

Marcus watched him, a small, slight figure, with the weight of the world on his shoulders, watched him walk away until he was lost in the crowd. Then he put his arm around Nazreem, and hugged her tight. As if the universe itself depended on it.

As maybe it did.

The End

Author's Note

The worship of Kybele goes back to the oldest days of human civilisation and is historically documented at great length. The goddess's name has taken many forms including Cybele, Kubhih and Kubaba.

She was linked to the Egyptian goddess Isis, the Greek Rhea and the earth goddess Gaia, and an idol in her shape made from a sacred black stone was indeed brought into Rome in 204 BC and credited with saving the city from invasion.

There has always been a transgender aspect to her worship, and her Roman followers did indeed practise voluntary self-castration.

There are many academic tomes about the study of Mithras, notably German scholar Manfred Clauss's *The Roman Cult of Mithras*, translated into English by Richard Gordon. The similarities between the story of the deity's life and that of Jesus Christ, including the date of birth, resurrection and virgin mother are remarkable to say the least. The nineteenth-century French philosopher, Ernest Renan, wrote: 'If the growth of Christianity had been arrested by some mortal malady, the world would have been Mithraic.'

The temple of Mithras in the City of London is real, though it has been relocated several times due to building work. At the time of writing it is still to be found in Queen Victoria Street and it really is a bus stop (see website below).

The Roman Emperor Julian ('the Apostate') is one of history's most intriguing figures. Quixotic and controversial, there is no doubt the world would have been a different place had he lived longer. There is an arresting and highly readable novelesque biography by Gore Vidal, entitled simply *Julian*.

The Black Stone set into the wall of the Ka'aba in Mecca dates back, according to Islamic tradition, to the time of Adam and Eve, when it was sent to earth by God to show Adam where to build a temple.

Most deities considered 'pagan' by mainstream religions have worshippers today. A Kybele-worshipping group in the US town of Catskill is fighting for religious recognition. I stress that my 'Gallae' belong firmly in the realm of fiction and have no reference to any modern adherents, other than drawing on the same historical religious background.

I apologise to anyone whose religious sensibilities might be in any way offended by the fictional content of this book. It is a piece of imaginative fun with no intended message, other than perhaps a plea for mutual toleration of our fellow humans. As for the views expressed by some of my fundamentalist characters, I stress they are theirs alone, not mine and I have no wish to promote them: believe me, there are enough nutters out there already.

There are myriad links on the internet to all the topics in this book. I offer only a couple of links to anyone interested in seeing some of the items mentioned in real life:

Useful information on the sites of the black Madonnas in Altötting and Guadalupe may be found at:

http://www.altoetting.de/cms/welcome_tour.phtml
http://www.paradores-spain.com/spain/pguadalupe.html
http://www.spanish-fiestas.com/extremadura/guadalupe.htm

The Temple of Mithras and its bus stop can be found at:

http://www.tfl.gov.uk/assets/downloads/central_bus_map.pdf

ALL GONE TO LOOK FOR AMERICA

Riding the Iron Horse Across a Continent (and Back)

PETER MILLAR

'Witty yet observant' *Time Out*

As the Bush era comes to a close there is unprecedented interest in an America on the cusp of change.

At the age of 52, with a shoestring budget, a backpack and an open mind, Peter Millar set about rediscovering the US, by following the last traces of the technological wonder that created the country in the first place: the railroad. On a rail network ravaged and reduced he managed to cross the continent two and a half times, talking to people, taking in their stories and their concerns, shaking stereotypes and challenging preconceptions, while watching the vast American landscape that most visitors fly over unfold in slow motion. In the tradition of Bill Bryson and Paul Theroux, wry, witty, intelligent and always observant, this 'inland empire' should appeal to modern Britons keen to get beneath the skin of the country that more than any other influence their lives, and to intelligent Americans open to an oblique look at their own country. And, of course, railway lovers everywhere.

'Witty yet observant ... this book smells of train travel and will appeal to wanderlusts as well as armchair train buffs' *Time Out*

'Succeeds in capturing the wonder of America that the iron horse made accessible to the world' *The Times*

'Fills a hole for those who love trains, microbrewery beer and the promise of big skies and wide open spaces' *Daily Telegraph*

Paperback
£8.99
9781906413637

1989 THE BERLIN WALL

My Part in Its Downfall

PETER MILLAR

'Irreverent and engaging' *Economist*

It was an event that changed history, bringing the Cold War to a sudden, unexpected end and seeing the collapse not just of Communism but of the Soviet Union itself. Stereotypes disappeared overnight, and the maps of a continent had to be redrawn. Peter Millar was in the middle of it, literally: caught in Checkpoint Charlie between bemused East German border guards and drunk western revellers prematurely celebrating the end of an era.

For over a decade Millar had been living not just in East Berlin but also Warsaw and Moscow. In this engaging, garrulous, bibulous memoir we follow him on a journey into the heart of Cold War Europe. From the hitchhiking trip that helped him discover a secret path into a career in journalism, through the carousing bars of Fleet Street in the seventies, to the East Berlin corner pub with its eclectic cast of customers who taught him the truth about living on the wrong side of the Wall. We relive the night it all disintegrated, gain insight into the domino effect that swept through Eastern Europe in its aftermath and find out how the author felt as he opened his Stasi files and discovered which of his friends had – or hadn't – been spying on him.

'The most entertaining read is *The Berlin Wall: My Part in Its Downfall*, a witty, wry, elegiac account of Millar's time as a Reuters and *Sunday Times* correspondent in Berlin throughout most of the 1980s' *Spectator*

'The best is [this] irreverent and engaging account. Fastidious readers who expect reporters to be a mere lens on events will be shocked at the amount of personal detail, including sexual antics and drinking habits of his colleagues in what now seems a Juvenalian age of dissolute British journalism. The author has a knack for befriending interesting people and tracking down important ones. He weaves their words with his clear-eyed reporting of events into a compelling narrative about the end of the cruel but bungling East German regime' *Economist*

'Part autobiography, part history primer and part Fleet Street gossip column, Millar cast aside the old chestnuts and set about reporting on the reality of life under communism ... Energetic and passionate' *Sunday Times*

Paperback
£11.99
9781906413477